SPECTRUM IV

Kingsley Amis and Robert Conquest, the editors of the SPECTRUM anthologies of science fiction, are both authorities on the field and writers themselves of s-f stories.

All four volumes of their SPECTRUM series have been most enthusiastically received by readers and critics alike.

"A galaxy of science fiction stories by some top science fiction writers."

—*Newsday*

"An eminent cast of contributors here . . . are an assurance of diverse speculations and literate entertainment."

—*Virginia Kirkus' Service, Inc.*

ALSO AVAILABLE

IN BERKLEY MEDALLION EDITIONS:

SPECTRUM	F733 50¢
SPECTRUM II	F950 50¢
SPECTRUM 3	X1108 60¢

SPECTRUM 4

EDITED BY

Kingsley Amis AND Robert Conquest

A BERKLEY MEDALLION BOOK

published by

BERKLEY PUBLISHING CORPORATION

ACKNOWLEDGMENTS
These stories are copyrighted by their authors and
The Marching Morons, which first appeared in *Galaxy,* 1951,
   by World Editions, Inc.
Gadget vs. Trend, which first appeared in *Analog,* 1962, by
   Condé Nast Publications Inc., and Scott Meredith Literary
   Agency Inc.
Such Stuff, which first appeared in *The Magazine of Fantasy
   and Science Fiction,* 1962, by Mercury Press Inc., and
   Scott Meredith Literary Agency Inc.
The Sellers of the Dream, which first appeared in *Galaxy,*
   1963, by Galaxy Publishing Corporation, and Scott
   Meredith Literary Agency Inc.
The Large Ant, which first appeared in *Fantastic Universe,*
   1960, by Great American Publications Inc.
Barrier, which first appeared in *Astounding Science Fiction,*
   1942, by Street and Smith Publications, Inc.
Compassion Circuit, which first appeared in the *Sunday
   Chronicle,* 1954, by Kemsley Newspapers Ltd., and Scott
   Meredith Literary Agency Inc.
A Planet Named Shayol, which first appeared in *Galaxy,* 1961,
   by Galaxy Publishing Corporation.
Into the Shop, which first appeared in *The Magazine of Fan-
   tasy and Science Fiction,* 1964, by Mercury Press Inc.
The Secret Songs, which first appeared in *The Magazine of
   Fantasy and Science Fiction,* 1962, by Mercury Press Inc.
Stranger Station, which first appeared in *The Magazine of
   Fantasy and Science, Fiction* 1956, by Fantasy House Inc.
The Great Nebraska Sea, which first appeared in *Galaxy,* 1963,
   by Galaxy Publishing Corporation.
Hot Planet, which first appeared in *Galaxy,* 1963, by Galaxy
   Publishing Corporation.
The Choice, which first appeared in *Punch,* 1952, by the
   Proprietors of *Punch.*
Unreal Estates first appeared in *SF Horizon,* 1964.

Published by arrangement with Harcourt, Brace & World, Inc.
BERKLEY MEDALLION EDITION, AUGUST, 1966
2nd Printing, November, 1969

SBN 425-01272-7

*BERKLEY MEDALLION BOOKS are published by
Berkley Publishing Corporation
200 Madison Avenue
New York, N.Y. 10016*

BERKLEY MEDALLION BOOKS ® TM 757,375

Printed in the United States of America

CONTENTS

Preface   vii

Unreal Estates *by C. S. Lewis, Brian W. Aldiss, Kingsley Amis*   9

The Marching Morons *by C. M. Kornbluth*   19

Gadget vs. Trend *by Christopher Anvil*   47

Such Stuff *by John Brunner*   61

The Sellers of the Dream *by John Jakes*   76

The Large Ant *by Howard Fast*   110

Barrier *by Anthony Boucher*   119

The Great Nebraska Sea *by Allan Danzig*   169

Compassion Circuit *by John Wyndham*   179

A Planet Named Shayol *by Cordwainer Smith*   188

Into The Shop *by Ron Goulart*   223

The Secret Songs *by Fritz Leiber*   232

Stranger Station *by Damon Knight*   242

Hot Planet *by Hal Clement*   265

The Choice *by Wayland Young*   286

These cardboard spacemen aren't enough,
Nor alien monsters, sketched in rough.
Character's the essential stuff.

The truest fiction of our age
Spreads subtler psyches on the page:
Half-witted pimp, blind coprophage.

PREFACE

This year we have decided to break with our custom of including an introductory discourse on current trends in and around science fiction. Advances in the field continue, but along largely expected lines; enormities of misunderstanding and prejudice still issue from its critics, but they are the same old enormities as those of five and ten years ago, and the thought of setting out to shoot them down all over again is uninviting.

We have placed a more formidable finger on the trigger by reprinting here the text of a taped discussion which one of us, in the company of Brian W. Aldiss, conducted with the late C. S. Lewis a few months before his death. The main part of Lewis's achievement, as teacher and writer, lies outside our present concern, but not much of his work—or of anybody else's—is more attractive and memorable than those novels of his which fuse science fiction with the theological romance. Few men have created other worlds as strange and as beautiful as his, or visualised their creations as clearly.

As always, our task of compilation has been much eased by the generous help of Messrs. Leslie Flood and Bruce Montgomery.

K.A.
R.C.

UNREAL ESTATES

ALDISS : One thing that the three of us have in common is that we have all had stories published in the *Magazine of Fantasy and Science Fiction*, some of them pretty far-flung stories. I take it we would all agree that one of the attractions of SF is that it takes us to unknown places.

AMIS : Swift, if he were writing today, would have to take us out to the planets, wouldn't he? Now that most of our terra incognita is—er, real estate.

ALDISS : That is so; there's a lot of the eighteenth-century equivalent of SF which is placed in Australia or similar unreal estates.

LEWIS : Exactly. Peter Wilkins and all that. By the way, is anyone ever going to do a translation of Kepler's *Somnium*?

AMIS : Groff Conklin told me he had read the book; I think it must exist in translation. But may we talk about the worlds you created? You chose the science fiction medium because you wanted to go to strange places? I remember with respectful and amused admiration your account of the space drive in *Out of the Silent Planet*. When Ransome and his friend get into the spaceship he says "How does this ship work?" and the man says "It operates by using some of the lesser known properties of—" what was it?

LEWIS : Solar radiation. Ransome was reporting words without a meaning to him, which is what a layman gets when he asks for a scientific explanation. Obviously it was vague, because I'm no scientist and not interested in the purely technical side of it.

ALDISS : It's almost a quarter of a century since you wrote that first novel of the trilogy.

LEWIS : Have I been a prophet?

ALDISS : You have to a certain extent; at least, the idea of vessels propelled by solar radiation is back in favour again. Cordwainer Smith used it poetically, Blish tried to use it technically in *The Star Dwellers*.

LEWIS : In my case it was pure mumbo-jumbo, and perhaps meant primarily to convince me.

AMIS : Obviously when one deals with isolated planets or isolated islands one does this for a certain purpose: a setting in contemporary London or a London of the future couldn't provide one with the same isolation and the heightening of consciousness it engenders.

LEWIS : The starting point of the second novel, *Perelandra*, was my mental picture of the floating islands. The whole of the rest of my labours in a sense consisted of building up a world in which floating islands could exist. And then of course the story about an averted fall developed. This is because, as you know, having got your people to this exciting country, something must happen.

AMIS : That frequently taxes people very much.

ALDISS : But I am surprised that you put it this way round. I would have thought that you constructed *Perelandra* for the didactic purpose.

LEWIS : Yes, everyone thinks that. They are quite wrong.

AMIS : If I may say a word on Professor Lewis's side, there was a didactic purpose of course, a lot of very interesting profound things were said, but—correct me if I'm wrong—I'd have thought a simple sense of wonder, extraordinary things going on, were the motive forces behind the creation.

LEWIS : Quite, but something has got to happen. The story of this averted fall came in very conveniently. Of course it wouldn't have been that particular story if I wasn't interested in those particular ideas on other grounds. But that isn't what I started from. I've never started from a message or a moral, have you?

AMIS : No, never. You get interested in the situation.

LEWIS : The story itself should force its moral upon you. You find out what the moral is by writing the story.

AMIS : Exactly. I think that sort of thing is true of all kinds of fiction.

ALDISS : I think it is; but a lot of science fiction has been written from the other point of view: these dreary sociological dramas that appear from time to time, they started with a didactic purpose—to make a preconceived point—and they've got no further.

LEWIS : I suppose *Gulliver* started from a straight point of view? Or did it really start because he wanted to write about a lot of big and little men?

AMIS : Possibly both, as Fielding's parody of Richardson

turned into *Joseph Andrews*. A lot of science fiction loses much of the impact it could have by saying, "Well, here we are on Mars, we all know where we are, and we're living in these pressure domes or whatever it is, and life is really very much like it is on earth, except there is a certain climatic difference . . ." They accept other men's inventions rather than forge their own.

LEWIS : It's only the first journey to a new planet that is of any interest to imaginative people.

AMIS : In your reading of science fiction have you ever come across a writer who's done this properly?

LEWIS : Well, the one you probably disapprove of because he's so very unscientific is David Lindsay, in *Voyage to Arcturus*. It's a remarkable thing, because scientifically it's nonsense, the style is appalling, and yet this ghastly vision comes through.

ALDISS : It didn't come through to me.

AMIS : Nor me. Still . . . Victor Gollancz told me a very interesting remark of Lindsay's about *Arcturus*; he said "I shall never appeal to a large public at all, but I think that as long as our civilisation lasts one person a year will read me." I respect that attitude.

LEWIS : Quite so. Modest and becoming. I also agree with something you said in a preface, I believe it was, that some science fiction really does deal with issues far more serious than those realistic fiction deals with; real problems about human destiny and so on. Do you remember that story about the man who meets a female monster landed from another planet with all its cubs hanging around it? It's obviously starving, and he offers them thing after thing to eat; they immediately vomit it up, until one of the young fastens on him, begins sucking his blood, and immediately begins to revive. This female creature is utterly unhuman, horrible in form; there's a long moment when it looks at the man—they're in a lonely place—and then very sadly it packs up its young, and goes back into its spaceship and goes away. Well now, you could not have a more serious theme than that; what is a footling story about some pair of human lovers compared with that?

AMIS : On the debit side, you often have these marvellous large themes tackled by people who haven't got the mental or moral or stylistic equipment to tackle them. A reading of more recent SF shows that writers are getting more capable of tackling them. Have you read Walter Miller's *Canticle for Leibowitz*? Have you any comments on that?

11

LEWIS : I thought it was pretty good. I only read it once; mind you, a book's no good to me until I've read it two or three times—I'm going to read it again. It was a major work, certainly.

AMIS : What did you think about its religious feeling?

LEWIS : It came across very well. There were bits of the actual writing which one could quarrel with, but on the whole it was well imagined and well executed.

AMIS : Have you seen James Blish's novel *A Case of Conscience*? Would you agree that to write a religious novel that isn't concerned with details of ecclesiastical practice and the numbing minutiae of history and so on, science fiction would be the natural outlet for this?

LEWIS : If you have a religion it must be cosmic; therefore it seems to me odd that this genre was late in arriving.

ALDISS : It's been around without attracting critical attention for a long time; the magazines themselves have been going since 1926, although in the beginning they appealed mainly to the technical side. As Kingsley says, people have come along who can write, as well as think up engineering ideas.

LEWIS : We ought to have said earlier that that's quite a different species of science fiction, about which I say nothing at all; those who were really interested in the technical side of it—it's obviously perfectly legitimate if it's well done . . .

AMIS : The purely technical and the purely imaginative overlap, don't they?

ALDISS : There are certainly the two streams, and they often overlap, for instance in Arthur Clarke's writings. It can be a rich mixture. Then there's the type of story that's not theological, but it makes a moral point. An instance—it sounds like a Sheckley story—is the one about Earth being blasted by radioactivity. The survivors of the human race have gone away to another planet for about a thousand years; and they come back to reclaim Earth and find it full of all sorts of gaudy armour-plated creatures, vegetation, etc. One of the party is saying "We'll clear this lot out, make it habitable for man again"; but in the end the decision is "Well, we made a mess of the place when it was ours, let's get out and leave it to them." Now this story was written about '49, when most people hadn't started thinking round the subject at all.

LEWIS : Yes. Most of the earlier stories start from the opposite assumption that we, the human race, are in the right, and everything else is ogres; I may have done a little towards

12

altering that, but the new point of view has come very much in. We've lost our confidence, so to speak.

AMIS : It's all terribly self-critical and self-contemplatory nowadays.

LEWIS : This is surely an enormous gain—a humane gain, that people should be thinking that way.

AMIS : The prejudice of supposedly educated persons towards this type of fiction is fantastic. If you pick up a good science fiction magazine, the range of interests appealed to and I.Q.s employed is pretty amazing. It's time more people caught on. We've been telling them about it for some while.

LEWIS : Quite true. The world of serious fiction is very narrow.

AMIS : Too narrow if you want to deal with a broad theme. For instance, Philip Wylie in *The Disappearance* wants to deal with the difference between men and women in a general way, in twentieth-century society, unencumbered by local and temporary considerations; his point, as I understand it, is that men and women, shorn of their social roles, are really very much the same. Science fiction, which can presuppose a major change in our environment, is the natural medium for discussing a subject of that kind. Look at the job of dissecting human nastiness carried out in Golding's *Lord of the Flies*.

LEWIS : That can't be science fiction.

AMIS : I would attack you on this. It starts off with a characteristic bit of SF situation, that World War III has begun, bombs dropped and all that . . .

LEWIS : Ah, well, you're now taking the German view that any romance about the future is science fiction. I'm not sure that this is a useful classification.

AMIS : Science fiction is such a hopelessly vague label.

LEWIS : And of course a great deal of it isn't *science* fiction. Really it's only a negative criterion: anything which is not naturalistic, which is not about what we call the real world.

ALDISS : I think we oughtn't to try to define it, because it's a self-defining thing in a way. We know where we are. You're right, though, about *Lord of the Flies*. The atmosphere is a science fiction atmosphere.

LEWIS : It was a very terrestrial island; the best island, almost, in fiction. Its actual sensuous effect on you is terrific.

ALDISS : Indeed. But it's a laboratory case.

AMIS : This business of isolating certain human characteristics, to see how they would work out . . .

LEWIS : The only trouble is that Golding writes so well. In one of his other novels, *The Inheritors,* the detail of every sensuous impression, the light on the leaves and so on, was so good that you couldn't find out what was happening. I'd say it was almost too well done. All these little details you only notice in real life if you've got a high temperature. You couldn't see the wood for the leaves.

ALDISS : You had this in *Pincher Martin*; every feeling in the rocks, when he's washed ashore, is done with an hallucinatory vividness.

AMIS : It is, that's exactly the phrase. I think thirty years ago if you wanted to discuss a general theme you would go to the historical novel; now you would go to what I might describe in a prejudiced way as science fiction. In science fiction you can isolate the factors you want to examine. If you wanted to deal with the theme of colonialism, for instance, as Poul Anderson has done, you don't do it by writing a novel about Ghana or Pakistan . . .

LEWIS : Which involves you in such a mass of detail that you don't want to go into . . .

AMIS : You set up worlds in space which incorporate the characteristics you need.

LEWIS : Would you describe Abbot's *Flatland* as science fiction? There's so little effort to bring it into any sensuous—well, you couldn't do it, and it remains an intellectual theorem . . . But probably the great work in science fiction is still to come. Futile books about the next world came before Dante, Fanny Burney came before Jane Austen, Marlowe came before Shakespeare.

AMIS : We're getting the prolegomena.

LEWIS : If only the modern highbrow critics could be induced to take it seriously . . .

AMIS : Do you think they ever can?

LEWIS : No, the whole present dynasty has got to die and rot before anything can be done at all.

ALDISS : Splendid!

AMIS : What's holding them up, do you think?

LEWIS : Matthew Arnold made the horrible prophecy that literature would increasingly replace religion. It has, and it's taken on all the features of bitter persecution, great intolerance, and traffic in relics. All literature becomes a sacred text. A sacred text is always exposed to the most monstrous exegesis; hence we have the spectacle of some wretched scholar taking a pure divertissement written in the seventeenth century and getting the most profound ambiguities and social criticisms out of it, which of course aren't there at all . . . It's the discovery of the mare's nest by the pursuit of the red herring. (Laughter.) This is going to go on long after my lifetime; you may be able to see the end of it, I shan't.

AMIS : You think this is so integral a part of the Establishment that people can't overcome—

LEWIS : It's an industry, you see. What would all the people be writing D.Phil. theses on if this prop were removed?

AMIS : An instance of this mentality the other day: somebody referred to "Mr. Amis's I suspect rather affected enthusiasm for science fiction . . ."

LEWIS : Isn't that maddening!

AMIS : You can't really like it.

LEWIS : You must be pretending to be a plain man or something . . . I've met the attitude again and again. You've probably reached the stage too of having theses written on yourself. I received a letter from an American examiner asking "Is it true that you meant this and this and this?" A writer of a thesis was attributing to me views which I have explicitly contradicted in the plainest possible English. They'd be much wiser to write about the dead, who can't answer.

ALDISS : In America, I think science fiction is accepted on a more responsible level.

AMIS : I'm not so sure about that, you know, Brian, because when *Spectrum I* came out in the States we had less friendly and less understanding treatment from "serious" reviewers than we did over here.

LEWIS : I'm surprised at that, because in general all American reviewing is more friendly and generous than in England.

AMIS : People were patting themselves on the back in the States for not understanding what we meant.

LEWIS : This extraordinary pride in being exempt from temptation that you have not yet risen to the level of! Eunuchs boasting of their chastity! (Laughter.)

AMIS : One of my pet theories is that serious writers as yet unborn or still at school will soon regard science fiction as a natural way of writing.

LEWIS : By the way, has any science fiction writer yet succeeded in inventing a third sex? Apart from the third sex we all know.

AMIS : Clifford Simak invented a set-up where there were seven sexes.

LEWIS : How rare happy marriages must have been then!

15

ALDISS : Rather worth striving for perhaps.

LEWIS : Obviously when achieved they'd be wonderful. (Laughter.)

ALDISS : I find I would much rather write science fiction than anything else. The dead weight is so much less there than in the field of the ordinary novel. There's a sense in which you're conquering a fresh country.

AMIS : Speaking as a supposedly realistic novelist, I've written little bits of science fiction and this is such a tremendous liberation.

LEWIS : Well, you're a very ill-used man; you wrote a farce and everyone thought it a damning indictment of Redbrick. I've always had great sympathy for you. They will not understand that a joke is a joke. Everything must be serious.

AMIS (quoting) : "A fever chart of society".

LEWIS : One thing in science fiction that weighs against us very heavily is the horrible shadow of the comics.

ALDIS : I don't know about that. Titbits Romantic Library doesn't really weigh against the serious writer.

LEWIS : That's a very fair analogy. All the novelettes didn't kill the ordinary legitimate novel of courtship and love.

ALDISS : There might have been a time when SF and comics were weighed together and found wanting, but that at least we've got past.

AMIS : I see the comic books that my sons read, and you have there a terribly vulgar reworking of the themes that science fiction goes in for.

LEWIS : Quite harmless, mind you. This chatter about the moral danger of the comics is absolute nonsense. The real objection is against the appalling draughtsmanship. Yet you'll find the same boy who reads them also reads Shakespeare or Spenser. Children are so terribly catholic. That's my experience with my step-children.

ALDISS : This is an English habit, to categorise: that if you read Shakespeare you can't read comics, that if you read science fiction you can't be serious.

AMIS : That's the thing that annoys me.

LEWIS : Oughtn't the word "serious" to have an embargo slapped on it? "Serious" ought to mean simply the opposite of comic, whereas now it means "good" or "Literature with a capital L".

ALDISS : You can be serious without being earnest.

LEWIS : Leavis demands moral earnestness; I prefer morality.

AMIS : I'm with you every time on that one.

LEWIS : I mean I'd sooner live among people who don't cheat at cards than among people who are earnest about not cheating at cards. (Laughter.) Look, you want to borrow Abbot's *Flatland*, don't you? I must go to dinner, I'm afraid. (Hands over *Flatland*.) The original manuscript of the *Iliad* could not be more precious. It's only the ungodly who borroweth and payeth not again.

AMIS (reading) : By A. Square.

LEWIS : But of course the word "square" hadn't the same sense then.

ALDISS : It's like the poem by Francis Thompson that ends "She gave me tokens three, a look, a word of her winsome mouth, and a sweet wild raspberry"; there again the meaning has changed. It really was a wild raspberry in Thompson's day. (Laughter.)

LEWIS : Or the lovely one about the Bishop of Exeter, who was giving the prizes at a girls' school. They did a performance of *A Midsummer Night's Dream*, and the poor man stood up afterwards and made a speech and said (piping voice) "I was very interested in your delightful performance, and among other things I was very interested in seeing for the first time in my life a female Bottom."

Magdalene College,
Cambridge.

THE MARCHING MORONS

by *C. M. Kornbluth*

Some things had not changed. A potter's wheel was still a potter's wheel and clay was still clay. Efim Hawkins had built his shop near Goose Lake, which had a narrow band of good fat clay and a narrow beach of white sand. He fired three bottle-nosed kilns with willow charcoal from the wood lot. The wood lot was also useful for long walks while the kilns were cooling; if he let himself stay within sight of them, he would open them prematurely, impatient to see how some new shape or glaze had come through the fire, and—*ping!*—the new shape or glaze would be good for nothing but the shard pile back of his slip tanks.

A business conference was in full swing in his shop, a modest cube of brick, tile-roofed, as the Chicago-Los Angeles "rocket" thundered overhead—very noisy, very sweptback, very fiery jets, shaped as sleekly swift-looking as an airborne barracuda.

The buyer from Marshall Field was turning over a black-glazed one-litre carafe, nodding approval with his massive, handsome head. "This is real pretty," he told Hawkins and his own secretary, Gomez-Laplace. "This has got lots of what ya call real est'etic principles. Yeah, it is real pretty."

"How much?" the secretary asked the potter.

"Seven-fifty in dozen lots," said Hawkins. "I ran up fifteen dozen last month."

"They are real est'etic," repeated the buyer from Field's. "I will take them all."

"I don't think we can do that, doctor," said the secretary. "They'd cost us $1,350. That would leave only $532 in our quarter's budget. And we still have to run down to East Liverpool to pick up some cheap dinner sets."

"Dinner sets?" asked the buyer, his big face full of wonder.

"Dinner sets. The department's been out of them for two months now. Mr. Garvy-Seabright got pretty nasty about it yesterday. Remember?"

"Garvy-Seabright, that meat-headed bluenose," the buyer

said contemptuously. "He don't know nothin' about est'etics. Why for don't he lemme run my own department?" His eye fell on a stray copy of *Whambozambo Comix* and he sat down with it. An occasional deep chuckle or grunt of surprise escaped him as he turned the pages.

Uninterrupted, the potter and the buyer's secretary quickly closed a deal for two dozen of the litre carafes. "I wish we could take more," said the secretary, "but you heard who I told him. We've had to turn away customers for ordinary dinnerware because he shot the last quarter's budget on some Mexican piggy banks some equally enthusiastic importer stuck him with. The fifth floor is packed solid with them."

"I'll bet they look mighty est'etic."

"They're painted with purple cacti."

The potter shuddered and caressed the glaze of the sample carafe.

The buyer looked up and rumbled, "Ain't you dummies through yakkin' yet? What good's a seckertary for if'n he don't take the burden of *de*-tail off'n my back, harh?"

"We're all through, doctor. Are you ready to go?"

The buyer grunted peevishly, dropped *Whambozambo Comix* on the floor and led the way out of the building and down the log corduroy road to the highway. His car was waiting on the concrete. It was, like all contemporary cars, too low-slung to get over the logs. He climbed down into the car and started the motor with a tremendous sparkle and roar.

"Gomez-Laplace," called out the potter under cover of the noise, "did anything come of the radiation programme they were working on the last time I was on duty at the Pole?"

"The same old fallacy," said the secretary gloomily. "It stopped us on mutation, it stopped us on culling, it stopped us on segregation, and now it's stopped us on hypnosis."

"Well, I'm scheduled back to the grind in nine days. Time for another firing right now. I've got a new lustre to try . . ."

"I'll miss you. I shall be 'vacationing'—running the drafting room of the New Century Engineering Corporation in Denver. They're going to put up a two hundred storey office building, and naturally somebody's got to be on hand."

"Naturally," said Hawkins with a sour smile.

There was an ear-piercingly sweet blast as the buyer leaned on the horn button. Also, a yard-tall jet of what looked like flame spurted up from the car's radiator cap; the car's power plant was a gas turbine, and had no radiator.

"I'm coming, doctor," said the secretary dispiritedly. He

climbed down into the car and it whooshed off with much flame and noise.

The potter, depressed, wandered back up the corduroy road and contemplated his cooling kilns. The rustling wind in the boughs was obscuring the creak and mutter of the shrinking refractory brick. Hawkins wondered about the number-two kiln —a reduction fire on a load of lustreware mugs. Had the clay chinking excluded the air? Had it been a properly smoky blaze? Would it do any harm if he just took one close—?

Common sense took Hawkins by the scruff of the neck and yanked him over to the tool shed. He got out his pick and resolutely set off on a prospecting jaunt to a hummocky field that might yield some oxides. He was especially low on coppers.

The long walk left him sweating hard, with his lust for a peek into the kiln quiet in his breast. He swung his pick almost at random into one of the hummocks; it clanged on a stone which he excavated. A largely obliterated inscription said:

ERSITY OF CHIC
OGICAL LABO
ELOVED MEMORY OF
KILLED IN ACT

The potter swore mildly. He had hoped the field would turn out to be a cemetery, preferably a once-fashionable cemetery full of once-massive bronze caskets mouldered into oxides of tin and copper.

Well, hell, maybe there was some around anyway.

He headed lackadaisically for the second largest hillock and sliced into it with his pick. There was a stone to undercut and topple into a trench, and then the potter was very glad he'd stuck at it. His nostrils were filled with the bitter smell and the dirt was tinged with the exciting blue of copper salts. The pick went *clang*!

Hawkins, puffing, pried up a stainless steel plate that was quite badly stained and was also marked with incised letters. It seemed to have pulled loose from rotting bronze; there were rivets on the back that brought up flakes of green patina. The potter wiped off the surface dirt with his sleeve, turned it to catch the sunlight obliquely and read:

HONEST JOHN BARLOW

"Honest John," famed in university annals, represents a

challenge which medical science has not yet answered: revival of a human being accidentally thrown into a state of suspended animation.

In 1988 Mr. Barlow, a leading Evanston real estate dealer, visited his dentist for treatment of an impacted wisdom tooth. His dentist requested and received permission to use the experimental anaesthetic Cycloparadimethanol-B-7, developed at the University.

After administration of the anaesthetic, the dentist resorted to his drill. By freakish mischance, a short circuit in his machine delivered 220 volts of 60-cycle current into the patient. (In a damage suit instituted by Mrs. Barlow against the dentist, the University and the makers of the drill, a jury found for the defendants.) Mr. Barlow never got up from the dentist's chair and was assumed to have died of poisoning, electrocution or both.

Morticians preparing him for embalming discovered, however, that their subject was—though certainly not living—just as certainly not dead. The University was notified and a series of exhaustive tests was begun, including attempts to duplicate the trance state on volunteers. After a bad run of seven cases which ended fatally, the attempts were abandoned.

Honest John was long an exhibit at the University museum, and livened many a football game as mascot of the University's Blue Crushers. The bounds of taste were overstepped, however, when a pledge to Sigma Delta Chi was ordered in '03 to "kidnap" Honest John from his loosely guarded glass museum case and introduce him into the Rachel Swanson Memorial Girls' Gymnasium shower room.

On May 22, 2003, the University Board of Regents issued the following order: "By unanimous vote, it is directed that the remains of Honest John Barlow be removed from the University museum and conveyed to the University's Lieutenant James Scott III Memorial Biological Laboratories and there be securely locked in a specially prepared vault. It is further directed that all possible measures for the preservation of these remains be taken by the Laboratory administration and that access to these remains be denied to all persons except qualified scholars authorised in writing by the Board. The Board reluctantly takes this action in view of recent notices and photographs in the nation's press which, to say the least, reflect but small credit upon the University."

It was far from his field, but Hawkins understood what had

22

happened—an early and accidental blundering on to the bare bones of the Levantman shock anaesthesia, which had since been replaced by other methods. To bring subjects out of Levantman shock, you let them have a squirt of simple saline in the trigeminal nerve. Interesting. And now about that bronze . . .

He heaved the pick into the rotting green salts, expecting no resistance, and almost fractured his wrist. *Something* down there was *solid*. He began to flake off the oxides.

A half hour of work brought him down to phosphor bronze, a huge casting of the almost incorruptible metal. It had weakened structurally over the centuries; he could fit the point of his pick under a corroded boss and pry off great creaking and grumbling striae of the stuff.

Hawkins wished he had an archaeologist with him, but didn't dream of returning to his shop and calling one to take over the find. He was an all-around man: by choice and in his free time, an artist in clay and glaze; by necessity, an automotive, electronics and atomic engineer who could also swing a project in traffic control, individual and group psychology, architecture or tool design. He didn't yell for a specialist every time something out of his line came up; there were so few with so much to do . . .

He trenched around his find, discovering that it was a great brick-shaped bronze mass with an excitingly hollow sound. A long strip of mouldering metal from one of the long vertical faces pulled away, exposing red rust that went *whoosh* and was sucked into the interior of the mass.

It had been de-aired, thought Hawkins, and there must have been an inner jacket of glass which had crystallised through the centuries and quietly crumbled at the first clang of his pick. He didn't know what a vacuum would do to a subject of Levantman shock, but he had hopes, nor did he quite understand what a real estate dealer was, but it might have something to do with pottery. And *anything* might have a bearing on Topic Number One.

He flung his pick out of the trench, climbed out and set off at a dog-trot for his shop. A little rummaging turned up a hypo and there was a plasticontainer of salt in the kitchen.

Back at his dig, he chipped for another half hour to expose the juncture of lid and body. The hinges were hopeless; he smashed them off.

Hawkins extended the telescopic handle of the pick for the best leverage, fitted its point into a deep pit, set its built-in

23

fulcrum, and heaved. Five more heaves and he could see, inside the vault, what looked like a dusty marble statue. Ten more and he could see that it was the naked body of Honest John Barlow, Evanston real estate dealer, uncorrupted by time.

The potter found the apex of the trigeminal nerve with his needle's point and gave him 60 cc.

In an hour Barlow's chest began to pump.

In another hour, he rasped, "Did it work?"

"*Did* it!" muttered Hawkins.

Barlow opened his eyes and stirred, looked down, turned his hands before his eyes—

"I'll sue!" he screamed. "My clothes! My fingernails!" A horrid suspicion came over his face and he clapped his hands to his hairless scalp. "My hair!" he wailed. "I'll sue you for every penny you've got! That release won't mean a damned thing in court—I didn't sign away my hair and clothes and fingernails!"

"They'll grow back," said Hawkins casually. "Also your epidermis. Those parts of you weren't alive, you know, so they weren't preserved like the rest of you. I'm afraid the clothes are gone, though."

"What is this—the University hospital?" demanded Barlow. "I want a phone. No, you phone. Tell my wife I'm all right and tell Sam Immerman—he's my lawyer—to get over here right away. Greenleaf 7-4022. Ow!" He had tried to sit up, and a portion of his pink skin rubbed against the inner surface of the casket, which was powdered by the ancient crystallised glass. "What the hell did you guys do, boil me alive? Oh, you're going to pay for this!"

"You're all right," said Hawkins, wishing now he had a reference book to clear up several obscure terms. "Your epidermis will start growing immediately. You're not in the hospital. Look here."

He handed Barlow the stainless steel plate that had labelled the casket. After a suspicious glance, the man started to read. Finishing, he laid the plate carefully on the edge of the vault and was silent for a spell.

"Poor Verna," he said at last. "It doesn't say whether she was stuck with the court costs. Do you happen to know—"

"No," said the potter. "All I know is what was on the plate, and how to revive you. The dentist accidentally gave you a dose of what we call Levantman shock anaesthesia. We haven't used it for centuries; it was powerful, but too dangerous."

"Centuries . . ." brooded the man. "Centuries . . . I'll bet Sam

24

swindled her out of her eyeteeth. Poor Verna. How long ago was it? What year is this?"

Hawkins shrugged. "We call it 7-B-936. That's no help to you. It takes a long time for these metals to oxidise."

"Like that movie," Barlow muttered. "Who would have thought it? Poor Verna!" He blubbered and sniffled, reminding Hawkins powerfully of the fact that he had been found under a flat rock.

Almost angrily, the potter demanded, "How many children did you have?"

"None yet," sniffed Barlow. "My wife didn't want them. But Verna wants one—wanted one—but we're going to wait until—we *were* going to wait until—"

"Of course," said the potter, feeling a savage desire to tell him off, blast him to hell and gone for his work. But he choked it down. There was the Problem to think of; there was always the Problem to think of, and this poor blubberer might unexpectedly supply a clue. Hawkins would have to pass him on.

"Come along," Hawkins said. "My time is short."

Barlow looked up, outraged. "How can you be so unfeeling! I'm a human being like—"

The Los Angeles-Chicago "rocket" thundered overhead and Barlow broke off in mid-complaint. "Beautiful!" he breathed, following it with his eyes. "Beautiful!"

He climbed out of the vault, too interested to be pained by its roughness against his infantile skin. "After all," he said briskly, "this should have its sunny side. I never was much for reading, but this is just like one of those stories. And I ought to make some money out of it, shouldn't I?" He gave Hawkins a shrewd glance.

"You want money?" asked the potter. "Here." He handed over a fistful of change and bills. "You'd better put my shoes on. It'll be about a quarter-mile. Oh, and you're—uh, modest?—yes, that was the word. Here." Hawkins gave him his pants, but Barlow was excitedly counting the money.

"Eighty-five, eighty-six—and it's dollars, too! I thought it'd be credits or whatever they call them. 'E Pluribus Unum' and 'Liberty'—just different faces. Say, is there a catch to this? Are these real, genuine, honest twenty-two-cent dollars like we had or just wallpaper?"

"They're quite all right, I assure you," said the potter. "I wish you'd come along. I'm in a hurry."

25

The man babbled as they stumped towards the shop. "Where are we going—The Council of Scientists, the World Co-ordinator or something like that?"

"Who? Oh, no. We call them 'President' and 'Congress'. No, that wouldn't do any good at all. I'm just taking you to see some people."

"I ought to make plenty out of this. *Plenty!* I could write books. Get some smart young fellow to put it into words for me and I'll bet I could turn out a best-seller. What's the set-up on things like that?"

"It's about like that. Smart young fellows. But there aren't any best-sellers any more. People don't read much nowadays. We'll find something equally profitable for you to do."

Back in the shop, Hawkins gave Barlow a suit of clothes, deposited him in the waiting room and called Central in Chicago. "Take him away," he pleaded. "I have time for one more firing and he blathers and blathers. I haven't told him anything. Perhaps we should just turn him loose and let him find his own level, but there's a chance—"

"The Problem," agreed Central. "Yes, there's a chance."

The potter delighted Barlow by making him a cup of coffee with a cube that not only dissolved in cold water but heated the water to boiling point. Killing time, Hawkins chatted about the "rocket" Barlow had admired, and had to haul himself up short; he had almost told the real estate man what its top speed really was—almost, indeed, revealed that it was not a rocket.

He regretted, too, that he had so casually handed Barlow a couple of hundred dollars. The man seemed obsessed with fear that they were worthless since Hawkins refused to take a note or I.O.U. or even a definite promise of repayment. But Hawkins couldn't go into details, and was very glad when a stranger arrived from Central.

"Tinny-Peete, from Algeciras," the stranger told him swiftly as the two of them met at the door. "Psychist for Poprob. Polasigned special overtake Barlow."

"Thank Heaven," said Hawkins. "Barlow," he told the man from the past, "this is Tinny-Peete. He's going to take care of you and help you make lots of money."

The psychist stayed for a cup of the coffee whose preparation had delighted Barlow, and then conducted the real estate man down the corduroy road to his car, leaving the potter to speculate on whether he could at last crack his kilns.

Hawkins, abruptly dismissing Barlow and the Problem, happily picked the chinking from around the door of the number-two kiln, prying it open a trifle. A blast of heat and the heady, smoky scent of the reduction fire delighted him. He peered and saw a corner of a shelf glowing cherry-red, becoming obscured by wavering black areas as it lost heat through the opened door. He slipped a charred wood paddle under a mug on the shelf and pulled it out as a sample, the hairs on the back of his hand curling and scorching. The mug crackled and pinged and Hawkins sighed happily.

The bismuth resinate lustre had fired to perfection, a haunting film of silvery-black metal with strange bluish lights in it as it turned before the eyes, and the Problem of Population seemed very far away to Hawkins then.

Barlow and Tinny-Peete arrived at the concrete highway where the psychist's car was parked in a safety bay.

"What—a—*boat*!" gasped the man from the past.

"Boat? No, that's my car."

Barlow surveyed it with awe. Swept-back lines, deep-drawn compound curves, kilogrammes of chrome. He ran his hands futilely over the door—or was it the door?—in a futile search for a handle, and asked respectfully, "How fast does it go?"

The psychist gave him a keen look and said slowly, "Two hundred and fifty. You can tell by the speedometer."

"Wow! My old Chevvy could hit a hundred on a straightaway, but you're out of my class, mister!"

Tinny-Peete somehow got a huge, low door open and Barlow descended three steps into immense cushions, floundering over to the right. He was too fascinated to pay serious attention to his flayed dermis. The dashboard was a lovely wilderness of dials, plugs, indicators, lights, scales and switches.

The psychist climbed down into the driver's seat and did something with his feet. The motor started like lighting a blowtorch as big as a silo. Wallowing around in the cushions, Barlow saw through a rear-view mirror a tremendous exhaust filled with brilliant white sparkles.

"Do you like it?" yelled the psychist.

"It's terrific!" Barlow yelled back. "It's—"

He shut up as the car pulled out from the bay into the road with a great *voo-oo-ooom!* A gale roared past Barlow's head, though the windows seemed to be closed; the impression of speed was terrific. He located the speedometer on the dashboard and saw it climb past 90, 100, 150, 200.

"Fast enough for me," yelled the psychist, noting that Barlow's face fell in response. "Radio?"

He passed over a surprisingly light object like a football

helmet, with no trailing wires, and pointed to a row of buttons. Barlow put on the helmet, glad to have the roar of air stilled, and pushed a push-button. It lit up satisfyingly and Barlow settled back ever farther for a sample of the brave new world's super-modern taste in ingenious entertainment.

"TAKE IT AND STICK IT!" a voice roared in his ears.

He snatched off the helmet and gave the psychist an injured look. Tinny-Peete grinned and turned a dial associated with the push-button layout. The man from the past donned the helmet again and found the voice had lowered to normal.

"The show of shows! The supershow! The super-duper show! The quiz of quizzes! *Take it and stick it!*"

There were shrieks of laughter in the background.

"Here we got the contes-tants all ready to go. You know how we work it. I hand a contes-tant a triangle-shaped cutout and like that down the line. Now we got these here boards, they got cut-out places the same shape as the triangles and things, only they're all different shapes, and the first contes-tant that sticks the cutouts into the board, he wins.

"Now I'm gonna innaview the first contes-tant. Right here, honey. What's your name?"

"Name? Uh—"

"Hoddaya like that, folks? She don't remember her name! Hah? *Would you buy that for a quarter?*" The question was spoken with arch significance, and the audience shrieked, howled and whistled its appreciation.

It was dull listening when you didn't know the punch lines and catch lines. Barlow pushed another button, with his free hand ready at the volume control.

"—latest from Washington. It's about Senator Hull-Mendoza. He is still attacking the Bureau of Fisheries. The North California Syndicalist says he got affidavits that John Kingsley-Schultz is a bluenose from way back. He didn't publistat the affidavits, but he says they say that Kingsley-Schultz was saw at bluenose meetings in Oregon State College and later at Florida University. Kingsley-Schultz says he gotta confess he did major in fly-casting at Oregon and got his Ph.D. in game-fish at Florida.

"And here is a quote from Kingsley-Schultz: 'Hull-Mendoza don't know what he's talking about. He should drop dead.' Unquote. Hull-Mendoza says he won't publistat the affidavits to pertect his sources. He says they was sworn by three former employees of the Bureau which was fired for in-competence and in-com-pat-ibility by Kingsley-Schultz.

"Elsewhere they was the usual run of traffic accidents. A three-way pile-up of cars on Route 66 going outta Chicago took twelve lives. The Chicago-Los Angeles morning rocket crashed and exploded in the Mo-have—Mo-javvy—whatever-you-call-it Desert. All the 94 people aboard got killed. A Civil Aeronautics Authority investigator on the scene says that the pilot was buzzing herds of sheep and didn't pull out in time.

"Hey! Here's a hot one from New York! A Diesel tug run wild in the harbour while the crew was below and shoved in the port bow of the luck-shury liner S.S. *Placentia*. It says the ship filled and sank taking the lives of an es-ti-mated 180 passengers and 50 crew members. Six divers was sent down to study the wreckage, but they died too, when their suits turned out to be fulla little holes.

"And here is a bulletin I just got from Denver. It seems . . ."

Barlow took off the headset uncomprehendingly. "He seemed so callous," he yelled at the driver. "I was listening to a newscast . . ."

Tinny-Peete shook his head and pointed at his ears. The roar of air was deafening. Barlow frowned baffledly and stared out of the window.

A glowing sign said:

MOOGS!
WOULD YOU BUY IT
FOR A QUARTER?

He didn't know what Moogs was or were; the illustration showed an incredibly proportioned girl, 99.9 per cent naked, writhing passionately in animated full colour.

The roadside jingle was still with him, but with a new feature. Radar or something spotted the car and alerted the lines of the jingle. Each in turn sped along a roadside track, even with the car, so it could be read before the next line was alerted.

IF THERE'S A GIRL
YOU WANT TO GET
DEFLOCCULISE
UNROMANTIC SWEAT.
"A*R*M*P*I*T*T*O"

Another animated job, in two panels, the familiar "Before and After". The first said, "Just Any Cigar?" and was illustrated with a two-person domestic tragedy of a wife holding her nose
29

while her coarse and red-faced husband puffed a slimy-looking rope. The second panel glowed, "Or a VUELTA ABAJO?" and was illustrated with . . .

Barlow blushed and looked at his feet until they had passed the sign.

"Coming into Chicago!" bawled Tinny-Peete.

Other cars were showing up, all of them dreamboats.

Watching them, Barlow began to wonder if he knew what a kilometer was, exactly. They seemed to be travelling so slowly, if you ignored the roaring air past your ears and didn't let the speedy lines of the dreamboats fool you. He would have sworn they were really crawling along at twenty-five, with occasional spurts up to thirty. How much was a kilometer, anyway?

The city loomed ahead, and it was just what it ought to be: towering skyscrapers, overhead ramps, landing platforms for helicopters . . .

He clutched at the cushions. Those two 'copters. They were going to—they were going to—they . . .

He didn't see what happened because their apparent collision courses took them behind a giant building.

Screamingly sweet blasts of sound surrounded them as they stopped for a red light. "What the hell is going on here?" said Barlow in a shrill, frightened voice, because the braking time was just about zero, and he wasn't hurled against the dashboard. "Who's kidding who?"

"Why, what's the matter?" demanded the driver.

The light changed to green and he started the pick-up. Barlow stiffened as he realised that the rush of air past his ears began just a brief, unreal split-second before the car was actually moving. He grabbed for the door handle on his side.

The city grew on them slowly: scattered buildings, denser buildings, taller buildings, and a red light ahead. The car rolled to a stop in zero braking time, the rush of air cut off an instant after it stopped, and Barlow was out of the car and running frenziedly down a sidewalk one instant after that.

They'll track me down, he thought, panting. *It's a secret police thing. They'll get you—mind-reading machines, television eyes everywhere, afraid you'll tell their slaves about freedom and stuff. They don't let anybody cross them, like that story I once read.*

Winded, he slowed to a walk and congratulated himself that he had guts enough not to turn around. That was what they always watched for. Walking, he was just another business-suited back among hundreds. He would be safe, he would be safe—

A hand gripped his shoulder and words tumbled from a large coarse, handsome face thrust close to his: "Wassamatta bumpinninna people likeya owna sidewalk gotta miner slamya inna mushya bassar!" It was neither the mad potter nor the mad driver.

"Excuse me," said Barlow. "What did you say?"

"Oh, yeah?" yelled the stranger dangerously, and waited for an answer.

Barlow, with the feeling that he had somehow been suckered into the short end of an intricate land-title deal heard himself reply belligerently, "Yeah!"

The stranger let go of his shoulder and snarled, "Oh, yeah?"

"Yeah!" said Barlow, yanking his jacket back into shape.

"Aaah!" snarled the stranger, with more contempt and disgust than ferocity. He added an obscenity current in Barlow's time, a standard but physiologically impossible directive, and strutted off hulking his shoulders and balling his fists.

Barlow walked on, trembling. Evidently he had handled it well enough. He stopped at a red light while the long, low dreamboats roared before him, and pedestrians in the sidewalk flow with him threaded their ways through the stream of cars. Brakes screamed, fenders clanged and dented, hoarse cries flew back and forth between drivers and walkers. He leaped backwards frantically as one car swerved over an arc of sidewalk to miss another.

The signal changed to green, the cars kept on coming for about thirty seconds and then dwindled to an occasional light-runner. Barlow crossed warily and leaned against a vending machine, blowing big breaths.

Look natural, he told himself. *Do something normal. Buy something from the machine.*

He fumbled out some change, got a newspaper for a dime, a handkerchief for a quarter and a candy bar for another quarter.

The faint chocolate smell made him ravenous suddenly. He clawed at the glassy wrapper printed *"CRIGGLIES"* quite futilely for a few seconds, and then it divided neatly by itself. The bar made three good bites, and he bought two more and gobbled them down.

Thirsty, he drew a carbonated orange drink in another one of the glassy wrappers from the machine for another dime. When he fumbled with it, it divided neatly and spilled all over his knees. Barlow decided he had been there long enough and walked on.

The shop windows were—shop windows. People still wore and bought clothes, still smoked and bought tobacco, still ate and bought food. And they still went to the movies, he saw with pleased surprise as he passed and then returned to a glittering place whose sign said it was THE BIJOU.

The place seemed to be showing a quintuple feature, *Babies Are Terrible, Don't Have Children,* and *The Canali Kid.*

It was irresistible; he paid a dollar and went in.

He caught the tail-end of *The Canali Kid* in three-dimensional, full-colour, full-scent production. It appeared to be an interplanetary saga winding up with a chase scene and a reconciliation between estranged hero and heroine. *Babies Are Terrible* and *Don't Have Children* were fantastic arguments against parenthood—the grotesquely exaggerated dangers of painfully graphic childbirth, vicious children, old parents beaten and starved by their sadistic offspring. The audience, Barlow astoundedly noted, was placidly champing sweets and showing no particular signs of revulsion.

The *Coming Attractions* drove him into the lobby. The fanfares were shattering, the blazing colours blinding, and the added scents stomach-heaving.

When his eyes again became accustomed to the moderate lighting of the lobby, he groped his way to a bench and opened the newspaper he had bought. It turned out to be *The Racing Sheet,* which afflicted him with a crushing sense of loss. The familiar boxed index in the lower left hand corner of the front page showed almost unbearably that Churchill Downs and Empire City were still in business—

Blinking back tears, he turned to the Past Performances at Churchill. They weren't using abbreviations any more, and the pages because of that were single-column instead of double. But it was all the same—or was it?

He squinted at the first race, a three-quarter-mile maiden claimer for thirteen hundred dollars. Incredibly, the track record was two minutes, ten and three-fifths seconds. Any beetle in his time could have knocked off the three-quarter in one-fifteen. It was the same for the other distances, much worse for route events.

What the hell had happened to everything?

He studied the form of a five-year-old brown mare in the second and couldn't make head or tail of it. She'd won and lost and placed and showed and lost and placed without rhyme or reason. She looked like a front-runner for a couple of races and then she looked like a no-good pig and then she looked like a mudder but the next time it rained she wasn't and then she was a stayer and then she was a pig again. In a good five thousand dollar allowances event, too!

Barlow looked at the other entries and it slowly dawned on him that they were all like the five-year-old brown mare. Not a single damned horse running had the slightest trace of class.

Somebody sat down beside him and said, "That's the story."

Barlow whirled to his feet and saw it was Tinny-Peete, his driver.

"I was in doubts about telling you," said the psychist, "but I see you have some growing suspicions of the truth. Please don't get excited. It's all right, I tell you."

"So you've got me," said Barlow.

"*Got* you?"

"Don't pretend. I can put two and two together. You're the secret police. You and the rest of the aristocrats live in luxury on the sweat of these oppressed slaves. You're afraid of me because you have to keep them ignorant."

There was a bellow of bright laughter from the psychist that got them blank looks from other patrons of the lobby. The laughter didn't sound at all sinister.

"Let's get out of here," said Tinny-Peete, still chuckling. "You couldn't possibly have it more wrong." He engaged Barlow's arm and led him to the street. "The actual truth is that the millions of workers live in luxury on the sweat of the handful of aristocrats. I shall probably die before my time of overwork unless—" He gave Barlow a speculative look. "You may be able to help us."

"I know that gag," sneered Barlow. "I made money in my time and to make money you have to get people on your side. Go ahead and shoot me if you want, but you're not going to make a fool out of me."

"You nasty little ingrate!" snapped the psychist, with a kaleidoscopic change of mood. "This damned mess is all your fault and the fault of people like you! Now come along and no more of your nonsense."

He yanked Barlow into an office building lobby and an elevator that, disconcertingly, went *whoosh* loudly as it rose. The real estate man's knees were wobbly as the psychist pushed him from the elevator, down a corridor and into an office.

A hawk-faced man rose from a plain chair as the door closed

behind them. After an angry look at Barlow, he asked the psychist, "Was I called from the Pole to inspect this—this—?"

"Unget updandered. I've dee-probed etfind quasichance exhim Poprobattackline," said the psychist soothingly.

"Doubt," grunted the hawk-faced man.

"Try," suggested Tinny-Peete.

"Very well. Mr. Barlow, I understand you and your lamented had no children."

"What of it?"

"This of it. You were a blind, selfish stupid ass to tolerate economic and social conditions which penalised child-bearing by the prudent and foresighted. You made us what we are today, and I want you to know that we are far from satisfied. Damn-fool rockets! Damn-fool automobiles! Damn-fool cities with overhead ramps!"

"As far as I can see," said Barlow, "you're running down the best features of your time. Are you crazy?"

"The rockets aren't rockets. They're turbo-jets—good turbo-jets, but the fancy shell around them makes for a bad drag. The automobiles have a top speed of one hundred kilometers per hour—a kilometer is, if I recall my paleolinguistics, three-fifths of a mile—and the speedometers are all rigged accordingly so the drivers will think they're going two hundred and fifty. The cities are ridiculous, expensive, unsanitary, wasteful conglomerations of people who'd be better off and more productive if they were spread over the countryside.

"We need the rockets and trick speedometers and cities because, while you and your kind were being prudent and foresighted and not having children, the migrant workers, slum dwellers and tenant farmers were shiftlessly and short-sightedly having children—breeding, breeding. My God, how they bred!"

"Wait a minute," objected Barlow. "There were lots of people in our crowd who had two or three children."

"The attrition of accidents, illness, wars and such took care of that. Your intelligence was bred out. It is gone. Children that should have been born never were. The just-average, they'll-get-along majority took over the population. The average IQ now is 45."

"But that's far in the future—"

"So are you," grunted the hawk-faced man sourly.

"But who are *you* people?"

"Just people—real people. Some generations ago, the geneticists realised at last that nobody was going to pay any attention to what they said, so they abandoned words for deeds.

Specifically, they formed and recruited for a closed corporation intended to maintain and improve the breed. We are their descendants, about three million of us. There are five billion of the others, so we are their slaves.

"During the past couple of years I've designed a skyscraper, kept Billings Memorial Hospital here in Chicago running, headed off war with Mexico and directed traffic at LaGuardia Field in New York."

"I don't understand! Why don't you let them go to hell in their own way?"

The man grimaced. "We tried it once for three months. We holed up at the South Pole and waited. They didn't notice it. Some drafting-room people were missing, some chief nurses didn't show up, minor government people on the non-policy level couldn't be located. It didn't seem to matter.

"In a week there was hunger. In two weeks there were famine and plague, in three weeks war and anarchy. We called off the experiment; it took us most of the next generation to get things squared away again."

"But why *didn't* you let them kill each other off?"

"Five billion corpses mean about five hundred million tons of rotting flesh."

Barlow had another idea. "Why don't you sterilise them?"

"Two-and-one-half billion operations is a lot of operations. Because they breed continuously, the job would never be done."

"I see. Like the marching Chinese!"

"Who the devil are they?"

"It was a—uh—paradox of my time. Somebody figured out that if all the Chinese in the world were to line up four abreast, I think it was, and start marching past a given point, they'd never stop because of the babies that would be born and grow up before they passed the point."

"That's right. Only instead of 'a given point', make it 'the largest conceivable number of operating rooms that we could build and staff'. There could never be enough."

"Say!" said Barlow. "Those movies about babies—was that your propaganda?"

"It was. It doesn't seem to mean a thing to them. We have abandoned the idea of attempting propaganda contrary to a biological drive."

"So if you work *with* a biological drive—?"

"I know of none which is consistent with inhibition of fertility."

Barlow's face went poker-blank, the result of years of careful discipline. "You don't, huh? You're the great brains and you can't think of any?"

"Why, no," said the psychist innocently. "Can you?"

"That depends. I sold ten thousand acres of Siberian tundra—through a dummy firm, of course—after the partition of Russia. The buyers thought they were getting improved building lots on the outskirts of Kiev. I'd say that was a lot tougher than this job."

"How so?" asked the hawk-faced man.

"Those were normal, suspicious customers and these are morons, born suckers. You just figure out a con they'll fall for; they won't know enough to do any smart checking."

The psychist and the hawk-faced man had also had training; they kept themselves from looking with sudden hope at each other.

"You seem to have something in mind," said the psychist.

Barlow's poker face went blanker still. "Maybe I have. I haven't heard any offer yet."

"There's the satisfaction of knowing that you've prevented Earth's resources from being so plundered," the hawk-faced man pointed out, "that the race will soon become extinct."

"I don't know that," Barlow said bluntly. "All I have is your word."

"If you really have a method, I don't think any price would be too great," the psychist offered.

"Money," said Barlow.

"All you want."

"More than you want," the hawk-faced man corrected.

"Prestige," added Barlow. "Plenty of publicity. My picture and my name in the papers and over TV every day, statues to me, parks and cities and streets and other things named after me. A whole chapter in the history books."

The psychist made a facial sign to the hawk-faced man that meant, "Oh, brother!"

The hawk-faced man signalled back, "Steady, boy!"

"It's not too much to ask," the psychist agreed.

Barlow, sensing a seller's market, said, "Power!"

"Power?" the hawk-faced man repeated puzzledly. "Your own hydro station or nuclear pile?"

"I mean a world dictatorship with me as dictator!"

"Well, now—" said the psychist, but the hawk-faced man interrupted, "It would take a special emergency act of Congress but the situation warrants it. I think that can be guaranteed."

"Could you give us some indication of your plan?" the psychist asked.

"Ever hear of lemmings?"

"No."

"They are—were, I guess, since you haven't heard of them—little animals in Norway, and every few years they'd swarm to the coast and swim out to sea until they drowned. I figure on putting some lemming urge into the population."

"How?"

"I'll save that till I get the right signatures on the deal."

The hawk-faced man said, "I'd like to work with you on it, Barlow. My name's Ryan-Ngana." He put out his hand.

Barlow looked closely at the hand, then at the man's face. "Ryan what?"

"Ngana."

"That sounds like an African name."

"It is. My mother's father was a Watusi."

Barlow didn't take the hand. "I thought you looked pretty dark. I don't want to hurt your feelings, but I don't think I'd be at my best working with you. There must be somebody else just as well qualified, I'm sure."

The psychist made a facial sign to Ryan-Ngana that meant, "Steady *yourself,* boy!"

"Very well," Ryan-Ngana told Barlow. "We'll see what arrangement can be made."

"It's not that I'm prejudiced, you understand. Some of my best friends—"

"Mr. Barlow, don't give it another thought. Anybody who could pick on the lemming analogy is going to be useful to us."

And so he would, thought Ryan-Ngana, alone in the office after Tinny-Peete had taken Barlow up to the helicopter stage. So he would. Poprob had exhausted every rational attempt and the new Poprobattacklines would have to be irrational or subrational. This creature from the past with his lemming legends and his improved building lots would be a fountain of precious vicious self-interest.

Ryan-Ngana sighed and stretched. He had to go and run the San Francisco subway. Summoned early from the Pole to study Barlow, he'd left unfinished a nice little theorem. Between interruptions, he was slowly constructing an n-dimensional geometry whose foundations and superstructure owed no debt whatsoever to intuition.

Upstairs, waiting for a helicopter, Barlow was explaining to

37

Tinny-Peete that he had nothing against Negroes, and Tinny-Peete wished he had some of Ryan-Ngana's imperturbability and humour for the ordeal.

The helicopter took them to International Airport where, Tinny-Peete explained, Barlow would leave for the Pole.

The man from the past wasn't sure he'd like a dreary waste of ice and cold.

"It's all right," said the psychist. "A civilised layout. Warm, pleasant. You'll be able to work more efficiently there. All the facts at your fingertips, a good secretary—"

"I'll need a pretty big staff," said Barlow, who had learned from thousands of deals never to take the first offer.

"I meant a private, confidential one," said Tinny-Peete readily, "but you can have as many as you want. You'll naturally have top-primary-top priority if you really have a workable plan."

"Let's not forget this dictatorship angle," said Barlow.

He didn't know that the psychist would just as readily have promised him deification to get him happily on the "rocket" for the Pole. Tinny-Peete had no wish to be torn limb from limb; he knew very well that it would end that way if the population learned from this anachronism that there was a small elite which considered itself head, shoulders, trunk and groin above the rest. The fact that this assumption was perfectly true and the fact that the elite was condemned by its superiority to a life of the most grinding toil would not be considered; the difference would.

The psychist finally put Barlow aboard the "rocket" with some thirty people—real people—headed for the Pole.

Barlow was airsick all the way because of a post-hypnotic suggestion Tinny-Peete had planted in him. One idea was to make him as averse as possible to a return trip, and another idea was to spare the other passengers from his aggressive, talkative company.

Barlow during the first day at the Pole was reminded of his first day in the Army. It was the same now-where-the-hell-are-we-going-to-put-*you*? business until he took a firm line with them. Then instead of acting like supply sergeants they acted like hotel clerks.

It was a wonderful, wonderfully calculated build-up, and one that he failed to suspect. After all, in his time a visitor from the past would have been lionised.

At day's end he reclined in a snug underground billet with the

38

sixty-mile-an-hour gales roaring yards overhead, and tried to put two and two together.

It was like old times, he thought—like a coup in real estate where you had the competition by the throat, like a 50 per cent rent boost when you knew damned well there was no place for the tenants to move, like smiling when you read over the breakfast orange juice that the city council had decided to build a school on the ground you had acquired by a deal with the city council. And it was simple. He would just sell tundra building lots to eagerly suicidal lemmings, and that was absolutely all there was to solving the Problem that had these double-domes spinning.

They'd have to work out most of the details, naturally, but what the hell, that was what subordinates were for. He'd need specialists in advertising, engineering, communications—did they know anything about hypnotism? That might be helpful. If not, there'd have to be a lot of bribery done, but he'd make sure—damned sure—there were unlimited funds.

Just selling building lots to lemmings . . .

He wished, as he fell asleep, that poor Verna could have been in on this. It was his biggest, most stupendous deal. Verna—that sharp shyster, Sam Immerman, must have swindled her . . .

It began the next day with people coming to visit him. He knew the approach. They merely wanted to be helpful to their illustrious visitor from the past and would he help fill them in about his era, which unfortunately was somewhat obscure historically, and what did he think could be done about the Problem? He told them he was too old to be roped any more, and they wouldn't get any information out of him until he got a letter of intent from at least the Polar President, and a session of the Polar Congress empowered to make him dictator.

He got the letter and the session. He presented his programme, was asked whether his conscience didn't revolt at its callousness, explained succinctly that a deal was a deal and anybody who wasn't smart enough to protect himself didn't deserve protection—"Caveat emptor", he threw in for scholarship, and had to translate it to "Let the buyer beware." He didn't, he stated, give a damn about either the morons or their intelligent slaves; he'd told them his price and that was all he was interested in.

Would they meet it or wouldn't they?

The Polar President offered to resign in his favour, with

39

certain temporary emergency powers that the Polar Congress would vote him if he thought them necessary. Barlow demanded the title of World Dictator, complete control of world finances, salary to be decided by himself, and the publicity campaign and historical write-up to begin at once.

"As for the emergency powers," he added, "they are neither to be temporary nor limited."

Somebody wanted the floor to discuss the matter, with the declared hope that perhaps Barlow would modify his demands.

"You've got the proposition," Barlow said. "I'm not knocking off even 10 per cent."

"But what if the Congress refuses, sir?" the President asked.

"Then you can stay up here at the Pole and try to work it out yourselves. I'll get what I want from the morons. A shrewd operator like me doesn't have to compromise; I haven't got a single competitor in this whole cockeyed moronic era."

Congress waived debate and voted by show of hands. Barlow won unanimously.

"You don't know how close you came to losing me," he said in his first official address to the joint Houses. "I'm not the boy to haggle; either I get what I ask, or I go elsewhere. The first thing I want is to see designs for a new palace for me—nothing *un*ostentatious, either—and your best painters and sculptors to start working on my portraits and statues. Meanwhile, I'll get my staff together."

He dismissed the Polar President and the Polar Congress, telling them that he'd let them know when the next meeting would be.

A week later, the programme started with North America the first target.

Mrs. Garvy was resting after dinner before the ordeal of turning on the dishwasher. The TV, of course, was on and it said: "Oooh!"—long, shuddery and ecstatic, the cue for the *Parfum Assault Criminale* spot commercial. "Girls," said the announcer hoarsely, "do you want your man? It's easy to get him—easy as a trip to Venus."

"Huh?" said Mrs. Garvy.

"Wassamatter?" snorted her husband, starting out of a doze. "Ja hear that?"

"Wha'?"

"He said 'easy like a trip to Venus'."

"So?"

"Well, I thought ya couldn't get to Venus. I thought they just had that one rocket thing that crashed on the Moon."

"Aah, women don't keep up with the news," said Garvy righteously, subsiding again.

"Oh," said his wife uncertainly.

And the next day, on *Henry's Other Mistress*, there was a new character who had just breezed in: Buzz Rentshaw, Master Rocket Pilot of the Venus run. On *Henry's Other Mistress*, "the broadcast drama about you and your neighbours, *folksy* people, *ordinary* people, *real* people!" Mrs. Garvy listened with amazement over a cooling cup of coffee as Buzz made hay of her hazy convictions.

MONA : Darling, it's so good to see you again!

BUZZ : You don't know how I've missed you on that dreary Venus run.

SOUND : *Venetian blind run down, key turned in door lock.*

MONA : Was it *very* dull, dearest?

BUZZ : Let's not talk about my humdrum job, darling. Let's talk about us.

SOUND : *Creaking bed.*

Well, the programme was back to normal at last. That evening Mrs. Garvy tried to ask again whether her husband was sure about those rockets, but he was dozing right through *Take It and Stick It*, so she watched the screen and forgot the puzzle.

She was still rocking with laughter at the gag line, "Would you buy it for a quarter?" when the commercial went on for the detergent powder she always faithfully loaded her dishwasher with on the first of every month.

The announcer displayed mountains of suds from a tiny piece of the stuff and coyly added: "Of course, Cleano don't lay around for you to pick up like the soap root on Venus, but it's pretty cheap and it's almost pretty near just as good. So for us plain folks who ain't lucky enough to live up there on Venus, Cleano is the real cleaning stuff!"

Then the chorus went into their "Cleano-is-the-stuff" jingle, but Mrs. Garvy didn't hear it. She was a stubborn woman, but it occurred to her that she was very sick indeed. She didn't want to worry her husband. The next day she quietly made an appointment with her family freud.

In the waiting room she picked up a fresh new copy of *Readers Pablum* and put it down with a faint palpitation. The lead article, according to the table of contents on the cover, was titled, "The Most Memorable Venusian I Ever Met".

"The freud will see you now," said the nurse, and Mrs. Garvy tottered into his office.

41

His traditional glasses and whiskers were reassuring. She choked out the ritual: "Freud, forgive me, for I have neuroses."

He chanted the antiphonal: "Tut, my dear girl, what seems to be the trouble?"

"I got like a hole in the head," she quavered. "I seem to forget all kinds of things. Things like everybody seems to know and I don't."

"Well, that happens to everybody occasionally, my dear. I suggest a vacation on Venus."

The freud stared, open-mouthed, at the empty chair. His nurse came in and demanded, "Hey, you see how she scrammed? What was the matter with *her*?"

He took off his glasses and whiskers meditatively. "You can search me. I told her she should maybe try a vacation on Venus." A momentary bafflement came into his face and he dug through his desk drawers until he found a copy of the four-colour, profusely illustrated journal of his profession. It had come that morning and he had lip-read it, though looking mostly at the pictures. He leafed to the article *Advantages of the Planet Venus in Rest Cures*.

"It's right there," he said.

The nurse looked. "It sure is," she agreed. "Why shouldn't it be?"

"The trouble with these here neurotics," decided the freud, "is that they all the time got to fight reality. Show in the next twitch."

He put on his glasses and whiskers again and forgot Mrs. Garvy and her strange behaviour.

"Freud, forgive me, for I have neuroses."

"Tut, my dear girl, what seems to be the trouble?"

Like many cures of mental disorders, Mrs. Garvy's was achieved largely by self-treatment. She disciplined herself sternly out of the crazy notion that there had been only one rocket ship and that one a failure. She could join without wincing, eventually, in any conversation on the desirability of Venus as a place to retire, on its fabulous floral profusion. Finally she went to Venus.

All her friends were trying to book passages with the Evening Star Travel and Real Estate Corporation, but naturally the demand was crushing. She considered herself lucky to get a seat at last for the two-week summer cruise. The spaceship took off from a place called Los Alamos, New Mexico. It looked just like all the spaceships on television and in the picture magazines, but was more comfortable than you would expect.

Mrs. Garvy was delighted with the fifty or so fellow-passengers assembled before take-off. They were from all over the country and she had a distinct impression that they were on the brainy side. The captain, a tall, hawk-faced, impressive fellow named Ryan-Something or other, welcomed them aboard and trusted that their trip would be a memorable one. He regretted that there would be nothing to see because, "due to the meteorite season", the ports would be dogged down. It was disappointing, yet reassuring that the line was taking no chances.

There was the expected momentary discomfort at take-off and then two monotonous days of droning travel through space to be whiled away in the lounge at cards or craps. The landing was a routine bump and the voyagers were issued tablets to swallow to immunise them against any minor ailments.

When the tablets took effect, the lock was opened, and Venus was theirs.

It looked much like a tropical island on Earth, except for a blanket of cloud overhead. But it had a heady, other-worldly quality that was intoxicating and glamorous.

The ten days of the vacation were suffused with a hazy magic. The soap root, as advertised, was free and sudsy. The fruits, mostly tropical varieties transplanted from Earth, were delightful. The simple shelters provided by the travel company were more than adequate for the balmy days and nights.

It was with sincere regret that the voyagers filed again into the ship, and swallowed more tablets doled out to counteract and sterilise any Venus illnesses they might unwittingly communicate to Earth.

Vacationing was one thing. Power politics was another.

At the Pole, a small man was in a soundproof room, his face deathly pale and his body limp in a straight chair.

In the American Senate Chamber, Senator Hull-Mendoza (Synd. N. Cal.) was saying: "Mr. President and gentlemen, I would be remiss in my duty as a legislature if'n I didn't bring to the attention of the au-gust body I see here a perilous situation which is fraught with peril. As is well known to members of this au-gust body, the perfection of space flight has brought with it a situation I can only describe as fraught with peril. Mr. President and gentlemen, now that swift American rockets now traverse the trackless void of space between this planet and our nearest planetarial neighbour in space—and, gentlemen, I refer to Venus, the star of dawn, the brightest jewel in fair Vulcan's diadome—now, I say, I want to inquire what steps are being taken to colonise Venus with a vanguard of patriotic citizens like those minutemen of yore.

"Mr. President and gentlemen! There are in this world nations, envious nations—I do not name Mexico—who by fair means or foul may seek to wrest from Columbia's grasp the torch of freedom of space; nations whose low living standards and innate depravity give them an unfair advantage over the citizens of our fair republic.

"This is my programme: I suggest that a city of more than 100,000 population be selected by lot. The citizens of the fortunate city are to be awarded choice lands on Venus free and clear, to have and to hold and convey to their descendants. And the national government shall provide free transportation to Venus for these citizens. And this programme shall continue, city by city, until there has been deposited on Venus a sufficient vanguard of citizens to protect our manifest rights in that planet.

"Objections will be raised, for carping critics we have always with us. They will say there isn't enough steel. They will call it a cheap giveaway. I say there *is* enough steel for *one* city's population to be transferred to Venus, and that is all that is needed. For when the time comes for the second city to be transferred, the first, emptied city can be wrecked for the needed steel! And is it a giveaway? Yes! It is the most glorious giveaway in the history of mankind! Mr. President and gentlemen, there is no time to waste—Venus must be American!"

Black-Kupperman, at the Pole, opened his eyes and said feebly, "The style was a little uneven. Do you think anybody'll notice?"

"You did fine, boy; just fine," Barlow reassured him.

Hull-Mendoza's bill became law.

Drafting machines at the South Pole were busy around the clock and the Pittsburgh steel mills spewed millions of plates into the Los Alamos spaceport of the Evening Star Travel and Real Estate Corporation. It was going to be Los Angeles, for logistic reasons, and the three most accomplished psycho-kineticists went to Washington and mingled in the crowd at the drawing to make certain that the Los Angeles capsule slithered into the fingers of the blindfolded Senator.

Los Angeles loved the idea and a forest of spaceships began to blossom in the desert. They weren't very good spaceships, but they didn't have to be.

A team at the Pole worked at Barlow's direction on a mail

44

set-up. There would have to be letters to and from Venus to keep the slightest taint of suspicion from arising. Luckily Barlow remembered that the problem had been solved once before—by Hitler. Relatives of persons incinerated in the furnaces of Lublin or Majdanek continued to get cheery postal cards.

The Los Angeles flight went off on schedule, under tremendous press, newsreel and television coverage. The world cheered the gallant Angelenos who were setting off on their patriotic voyage to the land of milk and honey. The forest of spaceships thundered up, and up, and out of sight without untoward incident. Billions envied the Angelenos, cramped and on short rations though they were.

Wreckers from San Francisco, whose capsule came up second, moved immediately into the city of the angels for the scrap steel their own flight would require. Senator Hull-Mendoza's constituents could do no less.

The president of Mexico, hypnotically alarmed at this extension of *yanqui imperialismo* beyond the stratosphere, launched his own Venus-colony programme.

Across the water it was England versus Ireland, France versus Germany, China versus Russia, India versus Indonesia. Ancient hatreds grew into the flames that were rocket ships assailing the air by hundreds daily.

Dear Ed, how are you? Sam and I are fine and hope you are fine. Is it nice up there like they say with food and close grone on trees? I drove by Springfield yesterday and it sure looked funny all the buildings down but of coarse it is worth it we have to keep the greasers in their place. Do you have any truble with them on Venus? Drop me a line some time. Your loving sister, Alma.

Dear Alma, I am fine and hope you are fine. It is a fine place here fine climate and easy living. The doctor told me today that I seem to be ten years younger. He thinks there is something in the air here keeps people young. We do not have much trouble with the greasers here they keep to theirselves it is just a question of us outnumbering them and staking out the best places for the Americans. In South Bay I know a nice little island that I have been saving for you and Sam with lots of blanket trees and ham bushes. Hoping to see you and Sam soon, your loving brother, Ed.

Sam and Alma were on their way shortly.

Poprob got a dividend in every nation after the emigration had passed the halfway mark. The lonesome stay-at-homes were unable to bear the melancholy of a low-population density; their conditioning had been to swarms of their kin. After that point it was possible to foist off the crudest stripped-down accommodations on would-be emigrants; they didn't care.

Black-Kupperman did a final job on President Hull-Mendoza, the last job that genius of hypnotics would ever do on any moron, important or otherwise.

Hull-Mendoza, panic-stricken by his presidency over an emptying nation, joined his constituents. The *Independence*, aboard which travelled the national government of America, was the most elaborate of all the spaceships—bigger, more comfortable, with a lounge that was handsome, though cramped, and cloakrooms for Senators and Representatives. It went, however, to the same place as the others and Black-Kupperman killed himself, leaving a note that stated he "couldn't live with my conscience".

The day after the American President departed, Barlow flew into a rage. Across his specially built desk were supposed to flow all Poprob high-level documents and this thing—this outrageous thing—called Poprob*term* apparently had got into the executive stage before he had even had a glimpse of it!

He buzzed for Rogge-Smith, his statistician. Rogge-Smith seemed to be at the bottom of it. Poprobterm seemed to be about first and second and third derivatives, whatever they were. Barlow had a deep distrust of anything more complex than what he called an "average".

While Rogge-Smith was still at the door, Barlow snapped, "What's the meaning of this? Why haven't I been consulted? How far have you people got and why have you been working on something I haven't authorised?"

"Didn't want to bother you, Chief," said Rogge-Smith. "It was really a technical matter, kind of a final clean-up. Want to come and see the work?"

Mollified, Barlow followed his statistician down the corridor.

"You still shouldn't have gone ahead without my okay," he grumbled. "Where the hell would you people have been without me?"

"That's right, Chief. We couldn't have swung it ourselves; our minds just don't work that way. And all that stuff you knew

46

from Hitler—it wouldn't have occurred to us. Like poor Black-Kupperman."

They were in a fair-sized machine shop at the end of a slight upward incline. It was cold. Rogge-Smith pushed a button that started a motor, and a flood of arctic light poured in as the roof parted slowly. It showed a small spaceship with the door open.

Barlow gaped as Rogge-Smith took him by the elbow and his other boys appeared: Swenson-Swenson, the engineer; Tsutsugimushi-Duncan, his propellants man; Kalb-French, advertising.

"In you go, Chief," said Tsutsugimushi-Duncan. "This is Poprobterm."

"But I'm the World Dictator!"

"You bet, Chief. You'll be in history, all right—but this is necessary, I'm afraid."

The door was closed. Acceleration slammed Barlow cruelly to the metal floor. Something broke and warm, wet stuff, salty-tasting, ran from his mouth to his chin. Arctic sunlight through a port suddenly became a fierce lancet stabbing at his eyes; he was out of the atmosphere.

Lying twisted and broken under the acceleration, Barlow realised that some things had not changed, that Jack Ketch was never asked to dinner however many shillings you paid him to do your dirty work, that murder will out, that crime pays only temporarily.

The last thing he learned was that death is the end of pain.

GADGET vs. TREND

by *Christopher Anvil*

Boston, Sept. 2, 1976. Dr. R. Milton Schummer, Professor of Sociology at Wellsford College, spoke out against "creeping conformism" to an audience of twelve hundred in Swarton Hall last night.

Professor Schummer charged that America, once the land of the free, is now "the abode of the stereotyped mass-man, shaped from infancy by the moron-moulding influences of television, mass-circulation newspapers and magazines, and the pervasive influence of advertising manifest in all these media. The result is the mass-production American with interchangeable parts and built-in taped programme."

What this country needs, said Dr. Schummer, is "freedom to differ, freedom to be eccentric". But, he concluded, "the momentum is too great. The trend, like the tide, cannot be reversed by human efforts. In two hundred years, this nation has gone from individualism to conformism, from independence to interdependence, from federalism to fusionism, and the end is not yet. One shrinks at the thought of what the next one hundred years may bring."

Rutland, Vt., March 16, 1977. Dr. J. Paul Hughes, grandson of the late inventor, Everett Hughes, revealed today a device which his grandfather kept under wraps because of its "supposedly dangerous side-effects". Dubbed by Dr. Hughes a "privacy shield", the device works by the "exclusion of quasi-electrons". In the words of Dr. Hughes:

"My grandfather was an eccentric experimenter. Surprisingly often, though, his wild stabs would strike some form of pay dirt, in a commercial sense. In this present instance, we have a device unexplainable by any sound scientific theory, but which may be commercially quite useful. When properly set up, and connected to a suitable electrical outlet, the device effectively soundproofs material surfaces, such as walls, doors, floors, and the like, and thus may be quite helpful in present-day crowded living conditions."

Dr. Hughes explained that the device was supposed to operate by "the exclusion of 'quasi-electrons', which my grandfather thought governed the transmission of sound through solid bodies, and performed various other esoteric functions. But we needn't take this too seriously."

New York, May 12, 1977. Formation of Hughes QuietWall Corporation was announced here today.

President of the new firm is J. Paul Hughes, grandson of the late inventor, Everett Hughes.

New York, Sept. 18, 1977. One of the hottest stocks on the market today is Hughes QuietWall. With demand booming, and the original president of the firm kicked upstairs to make room for the crack management expert, Myron L. Sams, the corporation has tapped a gold mine.

Said a company spokesman: "The biggest need in this country today is privacy. We live practically in each other's pockets, and if we can't do anything else, at least QuietWall can soundproof the pockets."

The QuietWall units, which retail for $289.95 for the basic room unit, are said to offer dealer, distributor, and manufacturer a generous profit. And no one can say that $289.95 is not a reasonable price to pay to keep out the noise of other people's TV, record players, quarrels and squalling babies.

Detroit, December 23, 1977. Santa left an early present for the auto industry here today.

A test driver trying out a car equipped with a Hughes Quiet-Wall unit went into a skid on the icy test track, rolled over three times, and got out shaken but unhurt. The car itself, a light supercompact, was found to be almost totally undamaged.

Tests with sledgehammers revealed the astonishing fact that with the unit turned on, the car would not dent, and the glass could not be broken. The charge filler cap could not be unscrewed. The hood could not be raised. And neither windows nor doors could be opened till the unit was snapped off. With the unit off, the car was perfectly ordinary.

This is the first known trial of QuietWall unit in a motor vehicle.

Standard house and apartment installations use a specially designed basic unit to soundproof floor and walls, and small additional units to soundproof doors and windows. This installation tested today apparently lacked such refinements.

December 26, 1977. J. Paul Hughes, chairman of the board of directors of the QuietWall Corp., stated to reporters today that his firm has no intention to market the Hughes QuietWall unit for use in motor cars.

Hughes denied the Detroit report of a QuietWall-equipped test car that rolled without damage, calling it "impossible".

Hartford, January 8, 1978. Regardless of denials from the QuietWall Corporation, nationwide experiments are being conducted into the use of the corporation's sound-deadening units as a safety device in cars. Numerous letters, telegrams, and phone calls are being received at the head offices of some of the nation's leading insurance companies here.

Hartford, January 9, 1978. Tests carried out by executives of the New Standard Insurance Group indicate that the original Detroit reports were perfectly accurate.

Cars equipped with the QuietWall units cannot be dented, shattered, scratched, or injured in any way by ordinary tools.

Austin J. Ramm, Executive Secretary of New Standard Group, stated to reporters:

"It's the damndest thing I ever saw.

"We've had so many communications, from people all over the country who claim to have connected QuietWall units to their cars, that we decided to try it out ourselves.

"We tried rocks, hammers, and so forth, on the test vehicle. When these didn't have any effect, I tried a quarter-inch electric drill and Steve Willoughby—he's our president—took a crack at the centre of the windshield with a railroad pickaxe. The pickaxe bounced. My drill just slid around over the surface and wouldn't bite in.

"We have quite a few other things we want to try.

"But we've seen enough to know there definitely is truth in these reports."

New York, January 10, 1978. Myron L. Sams, president of the Hughes QuietWall Corporation, announced today that a special automotive attachment is being put on sale throughout the country. Mr. Sams warns that improper installation may, among other things, seize up all or part of the operating machinery of the car. He urges that company representatives be allowed to carry out the installation.

Dallas, January 12, 1978. In a chase lasting an hour, a gang of bank robbers got away this afternoon with $869,000 in cash and negotiable securities.

Despite a hail of bullets, the escape car was not damaged. An attempt to halt it at a roadblock failed, as the car crashed through without injury.

There is speculation here that the car was equipped with one of the Hughes QuietWall units that went on sale a few days ago.

Las Vegas, January 19, 1978. A gang of eight to ten criminals held up the Silver Dollar Club tonight, escaping with over a quarter of a million dollars.

It was one of the most bizarre robberies in the city's history.

The criminals entered the club in golf carts fitted with light aluminum- and transparent-plastic covers, and opened a gun battle with club employees. A short fight disclosed that it was impossible to even dent the light shielding on the golf carts. Using the club's patrons and employees as hostages, the gunmen received the cash they demanded, rolled across the sidewalk and up a ramp into the rear of a waiting truck, which drove out of town, smashing through a hastily erected roadblock.

As police gave chase, the truck proved impossible to damage. In a violent exchange of gunfire, no one was injured, as the police cars were equipped with newly installed QuietWall units, and it was evident that the truck was also so equipped.

Well outside of town, the truck reached a second roadblock. The robbers attempted to smash through the seemingly flimsy barrier, but were brought to a sudden stop when the roadblock, fitted with a QuietWall unit, failed to give way.

The truck, and the golf carts within, were found to be undamaged. The bandits are now undergoing treatment for concussion and severe whiplash injuries.

The $250,000.00 has been returned to the Silver Dollar Club, and Las Vegas is comparatively quiet once more.

New York, January 23, 1978. In a hastily called news conference, J. Paul Hughes, chairman of the board of Hughes QuietWall Corporation, announced that he is calling upon the Federal Government to step in and suspend the activities of the corporation.

Pointing out that he has tried without success to suspend the company's operations on his own authority, Dr. Hughes stated that as a scientist he must warn the public against a dangerous technological development, "the menacing potentialities of which I have only recently come to appreciate".

No response has as yet been received from Washington.

New York, January 24, 1978. President Myron L. Sams today acknowledged the truth of reports that a bitter internal struggle is being waged for control of the Hughes QuietWall Corporation.

Spring Corners, Iowa, January 26, 1978. Oscar B. Nelde, a farmer on the outskirts of town, has erected a barricade that has backed up traffic on the new Cross-State Highway for twenty miles in both directions.

Mr. Nelde recently lost a suit for additional damages when the highway cut his farm into two unequal parts, the smaller
51

one containing his house and farm buildings, the larger part containing his fields.

The barricade is made of oil drums, saw horses, and barbed wire. The oil drums and saw horses cannot be moved, and act as if welded to the frozen earth. The barbed wire is weirdly stiff and immovable. The barricade is set up in a double row of these immovable obstacles, spaced to form a twenty-foot-wide lane connecting the two separated parts of Mr. Nelde's farm.

Mr. Nelde's manure spreader was seen crossing the road early today.

Heavy road machinery has failed to budge the obstacles. The experts are stumped. However, the local QuietWall dealer recalls selling Mr. Nelde a quantity of small units recently and adds, "but no more than a lot of other farmers have been buying lately".

It may be worth mentioning that Mr. Nelde's claim is one of many that have been advanced locally.

New York, January 27, 1978. The Hughes QuietWall Corporation was today reorganised as QuietWall, Incorporated, with Myron L. Sams holding the positions of president and chairman of the board of directors. J. Paul Hughes, grandson of Everett Hughes, continues as a director.

Spring Corners, Iowa, January 28, 1978. Traffic is flowing once again on the Cross-State Highway.

This morning a U.S. Army truck-mounted earth auger moved up the highway and drilled a number of holes six feet in diameter, enabling large chunks of earth to be carefully loosened and both sections of the barricade to be lifted out as units. The wire, oil drums, saw horses, and big chunks of earth, which remained rigid when lifted out, are being removed to the U.S. Army Research and Development Laboratories for study. No QuietWall units have been found, and it is assumed that they are imbedded, along with their power source, inside the masses of earth.

The sheriff, the police chief of Spring Corners, and state and federal law enforcement agents are attempting to arrest Oscar B. Nelde, owner of the farm adjacent to the highway.

This has proved impossible, as Mr. Nelde's house and buildings are equipped with a number of QuietWall units controlled from within.

Boston, February 1, 1978. Dr. R. Milton Schummer,

Professor of Sociology at Wellsford College, and a severe critic of "creeping conformism", said tonight, when questioned by reporters, that some of the effects of the QuietWall units constitute a hopeful sign in the long struggle of the individual against the State and against the forces of conformity. However, Dr. Schummer does not believe that "a mere technological gadget can affect these great movements of sociological trends".

Spring Corners, Iowa, February 2, 1978. A barbed-wire fence four feet high, fastened to crisscrossed railroad rails, now blocks the Cross-State Highway near the farm home of Leroy Weaver, a farmer whose property was cut in half by the highway, and who has often stated that he has received inadequate compensation.

It has proved impossible for highway equipment on the scene to budge either wire or rails.

Mr. Weaver cannot be reached for comment, as his house and buildings are equipped with QuietWall units, and neither the sheriff nor federal officials have been able to effect entry on to the premises.

Washington, D.C., February 3, 1978. The Bureau of Standards reports that tests on QuietWall units show them to be essentially "stasis devices". That is to say, they prevent change in whatever material surface they are applied to. Thus, sound does not pass, because the protected material is practically noncompressible, and is not affected by the alternate waves of compression and rarefaction in the adjacent medium.

Many potential applications are suggested by Bureau of Standards spokesmen who report, for instance, that thin slices of apples and pears placed directly inside the surface field of the QuietWall device were found totally unchanged when the field was switched off, after test periods of more than three weeks.

New York, February 3, 1978. Myron L. Sams, president of QuietWall, Incorporated, reports record sales, rising day by day to new peaks. QuietWall, Inc., is now operating factories in seven states, Great Britain, the Netherlands, and West Germany.

Spring Corners, Iowa, February 4, 1978. A U.S. Army truck-mounted earth auger has again removed a fence across the

Cross-State Highway here. But the giant auger itself has now been immobilised, apparently by one or more concealed stasis (QuietWall) devices.

As the earth auger weighs upwards of thirty tons, and all the wheels of truck and trailer appear to be locked, moving it presents no small problem.

Los Angeles, February 5, 1978. Police here report the capture of a den of dope fiends and unsavoury characters of all descriptions, after a forty-hour struggle.

The hideout, known as the "Smoky Needle Club", was equipped with sixteen stasis devices manufactured by Quiet-Wall, Inc., and had an auxiliary electrical supply line run in through a drain pipe from the building next door. Only when the electrical current to the entire neighbourhood was cut off were the police able to force their way in.

New York, February 5, 1978. Myron L. Sams, president of QuietWall, Inc., announced today a general price cut, due to improved design and volume production economies, on all QuietWall products.

In future, basic QuietWall room units will sell for $229.95 instead of $289.95. Special small stasis units, suitable for firming fence posts, reinforcing walls, and providing barred-door household security, will retail for as low as $19.95. It is rumoured that this price, with improved production methods, still provides an ample profit for all concerned, so that prices may be cut in some areas during special sales events.

Spring Corners, Iowa, February 6, 1978. A flying crane today lifted the immobilised earth auger from the eastbound lanes of Cross-State Highway.

A total of fourteen small stasis units have thus far been removed from the auger, its truck and trailer, following its removal from the highway by air. Difficulties were compounded by the fact that each stasis unit apparently "freezes" the preceding units applied within its range. The de-stasis experts must not only locate the units. They must remove them in the right order, and some are very cleverly hidden.

Seaton Bridge, Iowa, February 9, 1978. The Cross-State Highway has again been blocked, this time by a wall of cow manure eighty-three feet long, four feet wide at the base, and two and a half feet high, apparently stabilised by imbedded stasis units and as hard as cement. National Guard units are now patrolling the Seaton Bridge section of road to either side of the block.

New York, February 10, 1978. Representatives of Quiet-Wall, Inc., report that study of stasis devices removed from the auger at Spring Centre, Iowa, reveals that they are "not devices of QW manufacture, but crude, cheap bootleg imitations. Nevertheless, they work."

Spring Centre, Iowa, February 12, 1978. The Cross-State Highway, already cut at Seaton Bridge, is now blocked in three places by walls of snow piled up during last night's storm by farmers' bulldozers, and stabilised by stasis devices. Newsmen who visited the scene report that the huge mounds look like snow, but feel like concrete. Picks and shovels do not dent them, and flame throwers fail to melt them.

New York, February 15, 1978. Dr. J. Paul Hughes, a director of QuietWall, Inc., tonight reiterated his plea for a government ban on stasis devices. He recalled the warning of his inventor grandfather Everett Hughes, and stated that he intends to spend the rest of his life "trying to undo the damage the device has caused".

New York, February 16, 1978. Myron L. Sams, president of QuietWall, Inc., announced today that a fruit fly had been kept in stasis for twenty-one days without suffering visible harm. QW's research scientists, he said, are now working with the problem of keeping small animals in stasis. If successful, Sams said, the experiments may open the door to "one-way time-travel", and enable persons suffering from serious diseases to wait, free from pain, until such time as a satisfactory cure has been found.

Bonn, February 17, 1978. Savage East German accusations against the West today buttressed the rumours that "stasis-unit enclaves" are springing up like toadstools throughout East Germany.
Similar reports are coming in from Hungary, while Poland reports a number of "stasis-frozen" Soviet tanks.

Havana, February 18, 1978. In a frenzied harangue tonight, "Che" Garcia, First Secretary of the Cuban Communist Party, announced that the government is erecting "stasis walls" all around the island, and that "stasis blockhouses" now being built will resist "even the Yankees' worst hydrogen weapons". In a torrent of vitriolic abuse, however, Mr. Garcia threatened that "any further roadblocks and centres of degenerate individualism that spring up will be eradicated from the face of the soil of the motherland by blood, iron, sweat, and the forces of monolithic socialism".

There have been rumours for some time of dissatisfaction with the present regime.

Mr. Garcia charged that the C.I.A. had flagrantly invaded Cuban air space by dropping "millions of little vicious stasis units, complete with battery packs of fantastic power", all over the island, from planes which could not be shot down because they were protected by "still more of these filthy sabotage devices".

Des Moines, February 21, 1978. The Iowa state government following the unsuccessful siege of four farm homes near the Cross-State Highway today announced that it is opening new hearings on landowners' compensation for land taken for highway-construction purposes.

The governor appealed to owners of property adjoining the highway to be patient, bring their complaints to the capital, and meanwhile open the highway to traffic.

Staunton, Vt., February 23, 1978. Hiram Smith, a retired high school science teacher whose family has lived on the same farm since before the time of the Revolution, was ordered last fall to leave his family home.

A dam is to be built nearby, and Mr. Smith's home will be among those inundated.

At the time of the order, Mr. Smith, who lives on the farm with his fourteen-year-old grandson, stated that he would not leave "until carried out dead or helpless".

This morning, the sheriff tried to carry out the eviction order, and was stopped by a warning shot fired from the Smith house. The warning shot was followed by the flight of a small, battery-powered model plane, apparently radio-controlled, which alighted about two thousand yards from the Smith home, near an old apple orchard.

Mr. Smith called to the sheriff to get out of his car and lie down, if the car was not stasis-equipped, and in any case to look away from the apple orchard.

There was a brilliant flash, a shock, and a roar which the sheriff likened to the explosion of "a hundred tons of TNT". When he looked at the orchard, it was obscured by a pink glow and boiling clouds, apparently of steam from vaporised snow.

Mr. Smith called out to the sheriff to get off the property, or the next "wink bomb" would be aimed at him.

No one has been out to the Smith property since the sheriff's departure.

New York, February 25, 1978. Mr. Myron L. Sams, president of QuietWall, Inc., announced today that "there is definitely no connection between the Staunton explosion and the QW Corp. stasis unit. The stasis unit is a strictly defensive device and cannot be used for offensive purposes".

New York, February 25, 1978. Dr. J. Paul Hughes tonight asserted that the "wink bomb" exploded at Staunton yesterday, and now known to have left a radioactive crater, "probably incorporated a stasis unit". The unit was probably "connected to a light metallic container holding a small quantity of radioactive material. It need not necessarily be the radioactive material we are accustomed to think of as suitable for fission bombs. It need not be the usual amount of such material. When the stasis unit was activated by a radio signal or timing device, high-energy particles thrown off by the radioactive material would be unable to pass out through the container, now in stasis, and equivalent to a very hard, dense, impenetrable, nearly ideal boundary surface. The high-energy particles would bounce back into the interior, bombarding the radioactive material. As the population of high-energy particles within the enclosing stasis field builds up, the radioactive material, regardless of its quantity, reaches the critical point. Precisely what will happen depends on the radioactive material used, the size of the sample, and the length of the 'wink'—that is, the length of time the stasis field is left on."

Dr. Hughes added that "this is a definite, new, destructive use of the stasis field, which Mr. Myron Sams assures us is perfectly harmless".

Montpelier, Vt., February 26, 1978. The governor today announced temporary suspension of the Staunton Dam Project, while an investigation is carried out into numerous landowners' complaints.

Moscow, February 28, 1978. A "certain number" of "isolated cells" of "stasis-controlled character" are admitted to have sprung up within the Soviet Union. Those that are out of the way are said to be left alone, on the theory that the people have to come out sometime. Those in important localities are being reduced by the Red Army, using tear gas, sick gas, toothache gas, flashing searchlights, "war of nerves" tactics, and, in some cases, digging out the "cell" and carrying it off wholesale. It is widely accepted that there is nowhere near the amount of trouble here as in the satellite countries, where the problem is mounting to huge proportions.

Spring Corners, Iowa, May 16, 1978. The extensive Cross-State Highway claims having been settled all around, traffic is once again flowing along the highway. A new and surprising feature is the sight of farm machinery disappearing into tunnels constructed under the road to allow the farmers to pass from one side to the other.

Staunton, Vt., July 4, 1978. There was a big celebration here today as the governor and a committee of legislators announced that the big Staunton Dam Project has been abandoned, and a number of smaller dams will be built according to an alternative plan put forth earlier.

Bonn, August 16, 1978. Reports reaching officials here indicate that the East German government, the Hungarian government, and also to a considerable extent the Polish government, are having increasing difficulties as more and more of the "stasis-unit enclaves" join up, leaving the governments on the outside looking in. Where this will end is hard to guess.

Washington, September 30, 1978. The Treasury Department sent out a special "task force" of about one hundred and eighty men this morning. Their job is to crack open the mushrooming Anti-Tax League, whose membership is now said to number about one million enthusiastic businessmen. League members often give Treasury agents an exceedingly rough time, using record books and files frozen shut with stasis units, office buildings stasis-locked against summons-servers, stasis-equipped cars which come out of stasis-equipped garages connected with stasis-locked office buildings, to drive to stasis-equipped homes where it is physically impossible for summons-servers to enter the grounds.

Princeton, N.J., October 5, 1978. A conference of leading scientists, which gathered here today to exchange views on the nature of the stasis unit, is reported in violent disagreement. One cause of the disagreement is the reported "selective action" of the stasis unit, which permits ordinary light to pass through transparent bodies, but blocks the passage of certain other electromagnetic radiations.

Wild disorders broke out this afternoon during a lecture by Dr. J. Paul Hughes, on the "Quasi-Electron Theory of Wave Propagation". The lecture was accompanied by demonstration of the original Everett Hughes device, powered by an old-fashioned generator driven by the inventor's original steam engine. As the engine gathered speed, Dr. Hughes was able to demonstrate the presence of a nine-inch sphere of completely reflective material in the supposedly empty focus of the apparatus. This sphere, Dr. Hughes asserted, was the surface of a space totally evacuated of quasi-electrons, which he identified as "units of time".

It was at this point that the disturbance broke out.

Despite the disorder, Dr. Hughes went on to explain the limiting value of the velocity of light in terms of the quasi-electron theory, but was interrupted when the vibration of the steam engine began to shake down the ceiling.

There is a rumour here that the conference may recess at once without issuing a report.

Washington, D.C., August 16, 1979. Usually reliable sources report that the United States has developed a "missile screen" capable of destroying enemy missiles in flight, and theoretically capable of creating a wall around the nation through which no enemy projectile of any type could pass. This device is said to be based on the original Everett Hughes stasis unit, which creates a perfectly rigid barrier of variable size and shape, which can be projected very rapidly by turning on an electric current.

Other military uses for stasis devices include protection of missile sites, storage of food and munitions, impenetrising of armour plate, portable "turtle-shields" for infantry, and quick-conversion units designed to turn any ordinary house or shed into a bombardment-proof strongpoint.

Veteran observers of the military scene say that the stasis unit completely reverses the advantage until recently held by offensive, as opposed to defensive, weapons. This traditionally alternating advantage, supposed to have passed permanently with the development of nuclear explosives, has now made one more pendulum swing. Now, in place of the "absolute weapon", we have the "absolute defence". Properly set up, hydrogen explosions do not dent it.

But if the nation is not to disintegrate within as it becomes impregnable without, officials say we must find some effective way to deal with stasis-protected cults, gangsters, anti-tax enthusiasts, seceding rural districts, space-grabbers, and proprietors of dens. Latest problem is the travelling roadblock, set up by chisellers who select a busy highway, collect "toll" from motorists who must pay or end up in a traffic jam, then move on quickly before police have time to react, and stop again in some new location to do the same thing all over. There must be an answer to all these things, but the answer has yet to be found.

Boston, September 2, 1979. Dr. R. Milton Schummer, Professor of Sociology at Wellsford College, spoke out against "galloping individualism" to an audience of six hundred in Swarton Hall last night.

Professor Schummer charged that America, once the land of co-operative endeavour, is now "a seething hotbed of rampant individualists, protesters, quick-rich artists, and minute-men of all kinds, each over-reacting violently from a former condition which may have seemed like excessive conformism at the time, but now in the perspective of events appears as a desirable cohesiveness and unity of direction. The result today is the fractionating American with synthetic rough edges and built-in bellicose sectionalism."

What this country needs, said Dr. Schummer, is "co-ordination of aims, unity of purpose, and restraint of difference". But, he concluded, "the reaction is too violent. The trend, like the tide, cannot be reversed by human efforts. In three years, this nation has gone from cohesion to fractionation, from interdependence to chaos, from federalism to splinterism, and the end is not yet. One shrinks at the thought of what the next hundred years may bring."

SUCH STUFF

by *John Brunner*

With the leads of the electroencephalograph stringing out from his skull like webs spun by a drunken spider, the soft adhesive pads laid on his eyes like pennies, Starling resembled a corpse which time had festooned with its musty garlands. But a vampire-corpse, plump and rosy in its state of not-quite-death. The room was as still as any mausoleum, but it smelt of floor-polish, not dust; his coffin was a hospital bed and his shroud a fluffless cotton blanket.

Except for the little yellow pilot lights in the electronic equipment beside the bed, which could just be seen through the ventilation holes in the casing, the room was in darkness. But when Wills opened the door from the corridor the shaft of light which came over his shouder enabled him to see Starling clearly.

He would rather not have seen him at all—laid out thus, lacking candles only because he was not dead. That could be remedied, given the proper tools: a sharpened stake, a silver bullet, crossroads at which to conduct the burial—

Wills checked himself, his face prickly with new sweat. It had hit him again! The insane idea kept recurring, like reflex, like pupils expanding under belladonna, for all he could do to drive it down. Starling lay like a corpse because he had grown used to not pulling loose the leads taped to his head—*that's all! That's all! That's all!*

He used the words like a club to beat his mind into submission. Starling had slept like this for months. He lay on one side, in a typical sleeper's attitude, but because of the leads he barely moved enough in the course of a night to disturb the bedclothes. He breathed naturally. Everything was normal.

Except that he had done it for months, which was incredible and impossible and not in the least natural.

61

Shaking from head to foot, Wills began to step back through the doors. As he did so, it happened again—now it was happening dozens of times a night. A dream began.

The electroencephalograph recorded a change in brain activity. The pads on Starling's eyes sensed eye movements and signalled them. A relay closed. A faint but shrill buzzer sounded.

Starling grunted, stirred, moved economically as though to disturb a fly that had settled on him. The buzzer stopped. Starling had been woken; the thread of his dream was snapped.

And he was asleep again.

Wills visualised him waking fully and realising he was not alone in the room. Cat-silent, he crept back into the corridor and closed the door, his heart thundering as though he had had a narrow escape from disaster.

Why? In daytime he could talk normally with Starling, run tests on him as impersonally as on anyone else. Yet at night . . .

He slapped down visions of Starling by day, Starling corpselike in his bed at night, and moved down the long corridor with his teeth set to save them from chattering. He paused at other doors, pressing his ear to them or glancing inside for a moment. Some of those doors led to private infernos which ought to have jarred on his own normality with shocking violence, as they always used to. But none affected him like Starling's passiveness—not even the moaning prayers of the woman in Room 11, who was being hounded to death by imaginary demons.

Conclusion: his normality had gone.

That thought also recurred in spite of attempts to blank it out. In the long corridor which framed his aching mind like a microwave guide tube, Wills faced it. And found no grounds for rejecting it. They were in the wards; he in the corridor. So what? Starling was in a ward, and he was not a patient. He was sane, free to leave whenever he wished. In remaining here he was simply being co-operative.

And telling him to go away would solve nothing at all.

His rounds were over. He went back towards the office like a man resolutely marching towards inevitable doom. Lambert —the duty nurse—was snoring on the couch in the corner; it was against regulations for the duty nurse to sleep, but Wills had had more than he could bear of the man's conversation about drink and women and what he was missing tonight on television and had told him to lie down.

He prodded Lambert to make him close his mouth and sat down at the desk, drawing the night report towards him. On the printed lines of the form his hand crawled with its shadow limping behind, leaving a trail of words contorted like the path of a crazy snail.

5 a.m. All quiet except Room 11. Patient there normal.

Then he saw what he had written. Angrily he slashed a line through the last word, another and another till it was illegible, and substituted "much as usual". Normal!

I am in the asylum of myself.

He tilted the lamp on the desk so it shone on his face and turned to look at himself in the wall-mirror provided for the use of female duty nurses. He was a little haggard after the night without sleep, but nothing else was visibly wrong with him. Much as usual, like the patient in Room 11.

And yet Starling was sleeping the night away without dreams, undead.

Wills started, fancying that something black and thread-like had brushed his shoulder. A picture came to him of Starling reaching out from his bed with the tentacle leads of the e.e.g., as if he were emitting them from spinnerets, and weaving the hospital together into a net of his own, trapping Wills in the middle like a fly.

He pictured himself being drained of his juices, like a fly.

Suddenly Lambert was sitting up on the couch, his eyes flicking open like the shutters of a house being aired for a new day. He said, "What's the matter, doc? You're as white as a flaming sheet!"

There was no black thread-like thing on his shoulder. Wills said with an effort, "Nothing. Just tired, I think."

He thought of sleeping, and wondered what he would dream.

The day was bright and warm. He was never good at sleeping in the daytime; when he woke for the fourth or fifth time, unrested, he gave up. It was Daventry's day for coming here, he remembered. Maybe he should go and talk to him.

He dressed and went out of doors, his eyes dark-ringed. In the garden a number of the less ill patients were working listlessly. Daventry and the matron moved among them, complimenting them on their flowers, their thorough weeding, the lack of aphis and blackfly. Daventry had no interest in gardening except in so far as it was useful for therapy. The patients, no matter how twisted their minds were, recognised this, but Daventry apparently didn't know they knew. Wills might have laughed, but he felt laughter was receding from him. Unused faculties, like unused limbs, atrophy.

Daventry saw him approach. The bird-eyes behind his glasses flicked poultry-wise over him, and a word passed from the thin-lipped mouth to the matron, who nodded and moved away. The sharp face was lit by a smile; brisk legs began to carry him over the tiny lawn, which was not mown by the patients because mowers were too dangerous.

"Ah, Harry!" in Daventry's optimistic voice. "I want a word with you. Shall we go to the office?" He took Wills's arm as he turned, companionably; Wills, who found the habit intolerable, broke the grip before it closed.

He said, "As it happens, I want a word with you too."

The edginess of his tone sawed into Daventry's composure. The bird-eyes scanned his face, the head tipped a little on one side. The list of Daventry's mannerisms was a long one, but he knew the reasons for all of them and often explained them.

"Hah!" he said. "I can guess what this will be about!"

They passed into the building and walked side by side with their footsteps beating irregularly like two palpitating hearts. In the passageway Daventry spoke again.

"I presume there's been no change in Starling, or you'd have left a note for me—you were on night duty last night, weren't you? I didn't see him today, unfortunately; I was at a conference and didn't get here till lunchtime."

Wills looked straight ahead, to the looming door of Daventry's office. He said, "No—no change. But that's what I wanted to talk about. I don't think we should go on."

"Ah!" said Daventry. It was automatic. It meant something altogether different, like "I'm astonished"—but professionally Daventry disavowed astonishment. The office accepted them, and they sat down to the idiot noise of a bluebottle hammering its head on the window.

"Why not?" Daventry said abruptly.

Wills had not yet composed his answer. He could hardly speak of the undead Starling with pads on his eyes like pennies, of the black tentacles reaching out through the hospital night, of the formulated but suppressed notion that he must be treated with sharp stakes and silver bullets, and soon. He was forced to throw up improvisation like an emergency earthwork, knowing it could be breached at a dozen points.

"Well—all our other cases suggest that serious mental disturbance results from interference with the dreaming process. Even the most resistant of our other volunteers broke down after less than two weeks. We've prevented Starling from dreaming every night for five months now, and even if there are no signs of harm yet it's probable that we *are* harming him."

Daventry had lit a cigarette while Wills talked. Now he waved it in front of him, as though to ward off Wills's arguments with an adequate barrier—a wisp of smoke.

"Good gracious Harry!" he said affably. "What damage are we doing? Did you detect any signs of it last time you ran Starling through the tests?"

"No—that was last week and he's due for another run tomorrow—no, what I'm saying is that everything points to dreaming being essential. We may not have a test in the battery which shows the effect of depriving Starling of his dreams, but the effect must be there."

Daventry gave a neutral nod. He said, "Have you asked Starling's own opinion on this?"

Again, concede defeat from honesty: "Yes. He said he's perfectly happy to go on. He said he feels fine."

"Where is he at the moment?"

"Today's Tuesday. He goes to see his sister in the town on Tuesday afternoons. I could check if you like, but—"

Daventry shrugged. "Don't bother. I have good news for you, you see. In my view, six months is quite long enough to establish Starling's tolerance of dream-deprivation. What's next of interest is the nature of his dreams when he's allowed to resume. So in three weeks from now I propose to end the experiment and find out."

"He'll probably wake himself up reflexively," Wills said.

Daventry was prepared to take the words with utmost seriousness. He said, "What makes you think that?"

Wills had meant it as a bitter joke; when he re-considered, he found reason after all. He said, "The way he's stood the treatment when no one else could. Like everyone else we tested, his dreaming frequency went up in the first few days; then it peaked at about thirty-four times a night, and dropped back to its current level of about twenty-six, which has remained constant for about four months now. Why? His mind seems to be malleable, and I can't believe that. People need dreams; a man who can manage without them is as unlikely as one who can do without food or water."

"So we thought," Daventry said briskly. Wills could see the conference papers being compiled in his mind, the reports for the *Journal of Psychology* and the four pages in *Scientific*

American, with photographs. And so on. "So we thought. Until we happened across Starling, and he just proved we were wrong."

"I—" began Wills. Daventry took no notice and went on.

"Dement's work at Mount Sinai wasn't utterly definitive, you know. Clinging to first findings is a false attitude. We're now compelled to drop the idea that dreaming is indispensable, because Starling has gone without dreams for months and so far as we can tell—oh, I grant that: so far and no further—he hasn't suffered under the experience."

He knocked ash into a bowl on his desk. "Well, that was my news for you, Harry: that we finish the Starling series at the six-month mark. Then we'll see if he goes back to normal dreaming. There was nothing unusual about his dreaming before he volunteered; it will be most interesting . . ."

It was cold comfort, but it did give him a sort of deadline to work to. It also rid him of part of the horror he had suffered from having to face the presence in his mind of the vampire-corpse like a threat looming down the whole length of his future life-path. It actually heartened him till the time came to re-test Starling.

He sat waiting in his office for half an hour beforehand, because everything was otherwise quiet and because before he came up for psychological examination Starling always underwent a physical examination by another member of the staff. Not that physicals ever turned anything up. But the psychologicals hadn't either. It was all in Wills's mind. Or in Starling's. But if it was in Starling's he himself didn't know.

He knew the Starling file almost by heart now—thick, much thumbed, annotated by himself and by Daventry. None the less he turned back to the beginning of it, to the time five months and a week ago when Starling was just one volunteer among six men and six women engaged in a follow-up to check on Dement's findings of 1960 with superior equipment.

There were transcripts of dreams with Freudian commentary, in their limited way extraordinarily revealing, but not giving a hint of the most astonishing secret—that Starling could get by without them.

I am in a railway station. People are going to work and coming home at the same time. A tall man approaches and asks for my ticket. I try to explain that I haven't bought one yet. He grows angry and calls a policeman, but the policeman is my grandfather. I cannot understand what he says.

I am talking to one of my schoolteachers, Mr. Bullen. I am very rich and I have come to visit my old school. I am very happy. I invite Mr. Bullen to ride in my car which is big and new. When he gets in the door handle comes off in his hand. The door won't lock. I cannot start the engine. The car is old and covered with rust. Mr. Bullen is very angry but I do not care very much.

I am in a restaurant. The menu is in French and I order something I don't know. When it comes I can't eat it. I call the manager to make a complaint and he arrives in a sailor's uniform. The restaurant is on a boat and rocks so that I feel ill. The manager says he will put me in irons. People in the restaurant laugh at me. I break the plates on which the food is served, but they make no noise and no one notices. So I eat the food after all.

That last one was exactly what you would expect from Starling, Wills thought. He ate the food after all, and liked it.

These were records extracted from the control period—the week during which his dreams and those of the other volunteers were being noted for comparison with later ones, after the experiment had terminated. In all the other eleven cases that was from three days to thirteen days later. But in Starling's—!

The dreams fitted Starling admirably. Miserable, small-minded, he had gone through life being frustrated, and hence the dreams went wrong for him, sometimes through the intervention of figures of authority from childhood, such as his hated grandfather and the schoolteacher. It seemed that he never fought back; he—ate the food after all.

No wonder he was content to go on co-operating in Daventry's experiment, Wills thought bleakly. With free board and lodging, no outside problems involved, he was probably in paradise.

Or a kind of gratifying hell.

He turned up the dreams of the other volunteers—the ones who had been driven to quit after a few nights. The records of their control week showed without exception indications of sexual tension, dramatised resolutions of problems, positive attacks on personal difficulties. Only Starling provided continual evidence of total surrender.

Not that he was outwardly inadequate. Considering the frustration he had endured first from his parents, then from his tyrannical grandfather and his teachers, he had adjusted well. He was mild-mannered and rather shy, and he lived with his sister and her husband, but he held down a fairly good job, and he had a small, constant circle of acquaintances mainly met through his sister's husband, on whom he made no great impression but who all "quite liked" him.

Quite was a word central to Starling's life. Hardly any absolutes. Yet—his dreams to the contrary—he could never have surrendered altogether. He'd made the best of things.

The volunteers were a mixed bag: seven students, a teacher on sabbatical leave, an out-of-work actor, a struggling writer, a beatnik who didn't care, and Starling. They were subjected to the process developed by Dement at New York's Mount Sinai Hospital, as improved and automatised by Daventry—the process still being applied to Starling even now, which woke him with a buzzer whenever the signs indicating dreaming occurred. In the eleven other cases, the effect found was the same as what Dement established: interrupting the subject's dreaming made them nervous, irritable, victims of uncontrolled nervous tension. The toughest quit after thirteen days.

Except for Starling, that was to say.

It wasn't having their sleep disturbed that upset them; that could be proved by waking them between, instead of during, dreams. It was not being *allowed* to dream that caused trouble.

In general, people seemed to spend about an hour a night dreaming, in four or five "instalments". That indicated that dreaming served a purpose: what? Dissipation of antisocial tensions? A grooming of the ego as repressed desires were satisfied? That was too glib to answer. But without Starling to cock a snook in their faces, the experimenters would have accepted a similar generalisation and left the matter there till the distant day when the science of mind was better equipped to weigh and measure the impalpable stuff of dreams.

Only Starling *had* cropped up. At first he reacted predictably. The frequency of his dreaming shot up from five times a night to twenty, thirty and beyond, as the buzzer aborted each embryo dream, whirling into nothing his abominable grandfather, his tyrannical teachers—

Was there a clue there? Wills had wondered that before. Was it possible that, whereas other people *needed* to dream, Starling hated it? Were his dreams so miserable that to go without them was a liberation to him?

The idea was attractive, because straightforward, but it didn't hold water. In the light of previous experiments, it was about equivalent to saying that a man could be liberated from the need to excrete by denying him food and water.

But there was no detectable effect on Starling! He had not lost weight, nor grown more irritable; he talked lucidly, he

68

responded within predictable limits to IQ tests and Rorschach tests and every other test Wills could find. It was purely unnatural.

Wills checked himself. Facing his own reaction squarely, he saw it for what it must be—an instinctive but irrational fear like the fear of the stranger who comes over the hill with a different accent and different table-manners. Starling was human; ergo, his reactions were natural; ergo, either the other experiments had agreed by coincidence and dreaming wasn't indispensable, or Starling's reactions were the same as everyone's and were just being held down until they blew like a boiler straining past its tested pressure.

There were only three more weeks to go, of course.

The habitual shy knock came to the door. Wills grunted for Starling to come in, and wondered as he looked at him how the sight of him passive in bed could inspire him to thoughts of garlic, sharpened stakes and burial at crossroads.

The fault must be in his own mind, not in Starling's.

The tests were exactly as usual. That wrecked Wills's tentative idea about Starling welcoming the absence of his dreams. If indeed he was liberated from a burden, that should show up in a trend towards a stronger, more assured personality. The microscopic trend he actually detected could be assigned to the fact that for several months Starling had been in this totally undemanding and restful environment. No help there.

He shoved aside the pile of test papers. "Mr. Starling," he said, "what made you volunteer for these experiments in the first place? I must have asked you before, but I've forgotten. It was all on the file, but he wanted to check.

"Why, I don't really know, doctor," Starling's mild voice said. Starling's cow-like eyes rested on his face. "I think my sister knew someone who had volunteered, and my brother-in-law is a blood donor and kept saying that everyone should do something to benefit society, and while I didn't like the idea of being bled because I've never liked injections and things like that this idea seemed all right, so I said I'd do it. Then of course when Dr. Daventry said I was unusual and would I go on with it I said I hadn't suffered by it and I didn't see why I shouldn't if it was in the cause of science—"

The voice droned on, adding nothing new. Starling was very little interested in new things. He had never asked Wills the purpose of any test he submitted to; probably he had never asked his own doctor what was on a prescription form filled out for him, being content to regard the medical abbreviations as a kind of talisman. Perhaps he was so used to being snubbed or choked off if he showed too much interest that he felt he was incapable of understanding the pattern of which Wills and the hospital formed part.

He *was* malleable. It was the galling voice of his brother-in-law, sounding off about his uselessness, which pushed him into this. Watching him, Wills realised that the decision to offer himself for the experiment was probably the biggest he had ever taken, comparable in the life of anyone else with a decision to marry, or to go into a monastery. And yet that was wrong, too. Starling didn't take decisions on such a level. Things like that would merely happen to him.

Impulsively Wills said, "And how about when the experiment is over, Mr. Starling? I suppose it can't go on for ever."

Placid, the voice shaped inevitable words. "Well, you know, doctor, I hadn't given that very much thought."

No, it wasn't a liberation to him to be freed of his dreaming. It was nothing to him. Nothing was anything to him. Starling was undead. Starling was neuter in a human scale of values. Starling was the malleable thing that filled the hole available for it, the thing without will of its own which made the best of what there was and did nothing more.

Wills wished he could punish the mind that gave him such thoughts, and asked their source to go from him. But though his physical presence went, his non-existent existence stayed, and burned and loomed and was impassive and cocked snooks in every hole and corner of Willis's chaotic brain.

Those last three weeks were the worst of all. The silver bullet and the sharpened stake, the crossroads for the burial—Wills chained the images down in his mind, but he ached from the strain of hanging on to the chains. *Horror, horror, horror,* sang an eldritch voice somewhere deep and dark within him. *Not natural,* said another in a professionally judicious tone. He fought the voices and thought of other things.

Daventry said—and was correct according to the principles of the experiment, of course—that so as to have a true control for comparison they must simply disconnect the buzzer attached to the e.e.g. when the time came, and not tell Starling what they had done, and see what happened. He would be free to finish his dreams again. Perhaps they would be more vivid, and he would remember more clearly after such a long interruption. He would—

But Wills listened with only half an ear. They hadn't predicted Starling's reaction when they deprived him of dreams; why should they be able to predict what would happen when he received them back? A chill premonition iced solid in his mind, but he did not mention it to Daventry. What it amounted to was this: whatever Starling's response was, it would be the wrong one.

He told Daventry of his partial breaking of the news that the experiment was to end, and his chief frowned.

"That's a pity, Harry," he said. "Even Starling might put two and two together when he realises six months have gone by. Never mind. We'll let it run for another few days, shall we? Let him think that he was wrong about the deadline."

He looked at the calendar. "Give him three extra days," he said. "Cut it on the fourth. How's that?"

By coincidence—or not?—Wills's turn for night duty came up again on that day; it came up once in eight days, and the last few times had been absolutely unbearable. He wondered if Daventry had selected the date deliberately. Maybe. What difference did it make?

He said, "Will you be there to see what happens?"

Daventry's face set in a reflex mask of regret. "Unfortunately no—I'm attending a congress in Italy that week. But I have absolute confidence in you, Harry, you know that. By the way, I'm doing up a paper on Starling for *Journ. Psych.*"—mannerisms as always: he made it into the single word "jurnsike"—"and I think you should appear as co-author."

Cerberus duly sopped, Daventry went on his way.

That night the duty nurse was Green, a small clever man who knew judo. In a way that was a relief; Wills usually didn't mind Green's company, and had even learned some judo holds from him, useful for restraining but not harming violent patients. Tonight, though . . .

They spoke desultorily together for the first half-hour of the shift, but Wills sometimes lost track of the conversation because his mind's eye was distracted by a picture of what was going on in that room along the corridor where Starling held embalmed court among shadows and pilot lights. No one breached his privacy now as he went to bed; he did everything for himself, attached the leads, planted the penny-pads on his eyes, switched

71

on the equipment. There was some risk of him discovering that the buzzer was disconnected, but it had always been set to sound only after thirty minutes or more of typical simple sleep-readings.

Starling, though he never did anything to tire himself out, always went to sleep quickly. Another proof of his malleable mind, Wills thought sourly. To get into bed suggested going to sleep, and he slept.

Usually it was three-quarters-of-an-hour before the first attempted dream would burgeon in his round skull. For six months and a couple of days the buzzer had smashed the first and all that followed; the sleeper had adjusted his position without much disturbing the bedding, and—

But not tonight.

After forty minutes Wills got up, dry-lipped. "I'll be in Starling's room if you want me," he said. "We've turned off his buzzer, and he's due to start dreaming again—normally." The word sounded unconvincing.

Green nodded, picking up a magazine from the table. "On to something pretty unusual there, aren't we, doc?" he said.

"God only knows," Wills said, and went out.

His heart was pumping so loudly he felt it might waken the sleepers around him; his footsteps sounded like colossal hammer-blows and his blood roared in his ears. He had to fight a dizzy, tumbling sensation which made the still lines of the corridor—floor-with-wall a pair of lines, wall-with-ceiling another pair—twist like a four-strand plait, like the bit of a hand-drill or a stick of candy turned mysteriously and topologically outside-in. Swaying as though drunk he came to Starling's door and watched his hand go to the handle.

I refuse the responsibility. I'll refuse to co-author the paper on him. It's Daventry's fault.

None the less he acquiesced in opening the door, as he had acquiesced all along in the experiment.

He was intellectually aware that he entered soundlessly, but he imagined himself going like an elephant on broken glass. Everything was as usual, except of course the buzzer.

He drew a rubber-shod chair to a position from which he could watch the paper tapes being paid out by the e.e.g., and sat down. As yet there were only typical early-sleep rhythms— Starling had not yet started his first dream of the night. If he waited till that dream arrived, and saw that all was going well, perhaps it would lay the phantoms in his mind.

He put his hand in the pocket of his jacket and closed it around a clove of garlic.

Startled, he drew the garlic out and stared at it. He had no memory of putting it there. But last time he was on night duty and haunted by the undead appearance of Starling as he slept, he had spent most of the silent hours drawing batwing figures, stabbing their hearts with the point of his pencil, sketching crossroads around them, throwing the paper away with the hole pierced in the centre of the sheet. Oh, God! It was going to be such a relief to be free of this obsession!

But at least providing himself with a clove of garlic was a harmless symptom. He dropped it back in his pocket. He noticed two things at the same time directly afterwards. The first was the alteration in the line on the e.e.g. tapes which indicated the beginning of a dream. The second was that he had a very sharp pencil in his pocket, as well as the clove of garlic—

No, not a pencil. He took it out and saw that it was a piece of rough wood, about eight inches long, pointed at one end. That was all he needed. That, and something to drive it home with. He fumbled in all his pockets. He was carrying a rubber hammer for testing reflexes. Of course, that wouldn't do, but anyway . . .

Chance had opened a gap in Starling's pyjama jacket. He poised the stake carefully over his heart and swung the hammer.

As though the flesh were soft as cheese, the stake sank home. Blood welled up around it like a spring in mud, trickled over Starling's chest, began to stain the bed. Starling himself did not awaken, but simply went more limp—naturally, for he was undead and not asleep. Sweating, Wills let the rubber hammer fall and wondered at what he had done. Relief filled him as the unceasing stream of blood filled the bed.

The door behind him was ajar. Through it he heard the cat-light footfalls of Green, and his voice saying urgently, "It's Room 11, doc! I think she's—"

And then Green saw what had been done to Starling.

His eyes wide with amazement, he turned to stare at Wills. His mouth worked, but for a while his expression conveyed more than the unshaped words he uttered.

"*Doc!*" Green said finally, and that was all.

Wills ignored him. He looked down at the undead, seeing the blood as though it were luminous paint in the dim-lit room—on his hands, his coat, the floor, the bed, flooding out now in a river, pouring from the pens that waggled the traces of a dream

73

on the paper tapes, making his feet squelch stickily in his wet shoes.

"You've wrecked the experiment," Daventry said coldly as he came in. "After I'd been generous enough to offer you co-authorship of my paper in *Journ. Psych.*, too! How could you?"

Hot shame flooded into Wills's mind. He would never be able to face Daventry again.

"We must call a policeman," Daventry said with authority. "Fortunately he always said he thought he ought to be a blood donor."

He took up from the floor a gigantic syringe, like a hypodermic for a titan, and after dipping the needle into the river of blood hauled on the plunger. The red level rose inside the glass.

And *click*.

Through a crack in Wills's benighted skull a fact dropped. Daventry was in Italy. Therefore he couldn't be here. Therefore he wasn't. Therefore—

Wills felt his eyes creak open like old heavy doors on hinges stiff with rust, and found that he was looking down at Starling in the bed. The pens tracing the activity of his brain had reverted to a typical sleep-rhythm. There was no stake. There was no blood. Weak with relief, Wills shuddered at remembered horror. He leaned back in his chair, struggling to understand.

He had told himself that whatever Starling's reaction to being given back his dreams might be, it would be the wrong one. Well, here it was. He couldn't have predicted it. But he could explain it now—more or less. Though the mechanics of it would have to wait a while.

If he was right about Starling, a lifetime of frustration and making the best of things had sapped his power of action to the point at which he never even considered tackling an obstacle. He would just meekly try and find a way around it. If there wasn't one—well, there wasn't, and he left it at that.

Having his dreams stopped was an obstacle. The eleven other volunteers, more aggressive, had developed symptoms which expressed their resentment in manifold ways: irritability, rage, insulting behaviour. But not Starling. To Starling it was unthinkable to express resentment.

Patiently, accustomed to disappointment because that was the constant feature of his life, he had sought a way around the obstacle. And he had found it. He had learned how to dream with someone else's mind instead of his own.

Of course, until tonight the buzzer had broken off every

74

dream he attempted, and he had endured that like everything else. But tonight there was no buzzer, and he had dreamed *in* and *with* Wills. The driving of the stake, the blood, the intrusion of Green, the appearance of Daventry, were part of a dream to which Wills contributed some images and Starling contributed the rest, such as the policeman who didn't have time to arrive, and the giant hypodermic. He feared injections.

Wills made up his mind. Daventry wouldn't believe him—not unless he experienced the phenomenon himself—but that was a problem for tomorrow. Right now he had had enough, and more than enough. He was going to reconnect the buzzer and get to hell out of here.

He tried to lift his arm towards the boxes of equipment on the bedside table, and was puzzled to find it heavy and sluggish. Invisible weights seemed to hang on his wrist. Even when, sweating, he managed to force his hand towards the buzzer his fingers felt like sausages and would not grip the delicate wire he had to attach to the terminal.

He had fought for what seemed like an eternity, and was crying with frustration, when he finally understood.

The typical pattern of all Starling's dreams centred on failure to achieve what he attempted; he expected his greatest efforts to be disappointed. Hence Wills, his mind somehow linked to Starling's and his consciousness seeming to Starling to be a dream, would never be able to re-connect that buzzer.

Wills let his hands fall limp on his dangling arms. He looked at Starling, naked fear rising in his throat. How much dreaming could a man do in a single night when he had been deprived for six mortal months?

In his pocket was a sharp wooden stake and a hammer. He was going to put an end to Starling's dreaming once and for all.

He was still in the chair, weeping without tears, tied by invisible chains, when Starling awoke puzzled in the morning and found him.

THE SELLERS OF THE DREAM

by *John Jakes*

I

His gaudy wristwatch showed thirty minutes past nine, sixth July. It was time. From here on it was do the job right or be ruined. If not physically, then professionally.

Finian Smith dug for tools in the pouches of his imitation stomach. The left eye of the watch's moon face gave a ludicrous wink to complete the time signal. Finian hated the watch. He'd got used to the confines of the camouflaged polymer leech clinging to the keel of the hydrofoiler. He'd got used to performing necessary bodily functions in intimate contact with the leech's servomechanisms for thirty-six hours. But the watch—never.

It was effete, like his clothes. Effeteness was big this year. Next year it would be hand-loomed woollens. But he wasn't being paid to inherit the soul of the man he was impersonating, after all. He applied the first of his meson torches to the thick hull. His long, pleasantly ugly face began to bead with perspiration.

He had precisely four minutes to cut through.

His face was half shadowed by the hull as he worked, half washed in flickering sunlight through anemone and brain coral. He defused a large U-shaped section and replaced the torch with a pistol unit fitted with a round cup at the muzzle. This cup he applied to the hull. A blue whine of power—he forced the hull inward far enough to accommodate entry to the fuel baffle chamber.

He set a small black box to blow the polymer leech off the hull in fifty seconds, glad that he'd spent a full twenty nights under the hypnolearner. The penetration plan was drummed so deeply into his skull he could operate like an automaton.

With a last tool he re-sealed the hull, touched a stud and watched the tool collapse to gritty pumice. Right now the leech should be quietly disintegrating, without so much as a murmur to disturb the TTIC spy radar. It took a lot of money to arrange this penetration, Finian thought. Knowing how much made him nervous.

Finian hurried up a lonely companionway. Before stepping to the yacht's deck he dusted his pleatless puce satin pantaloons and also made sure the precision camera, a combined effort of G/S dental technicians and optics men, was in place where his right front incisor had once been. The blade shutter's release was a knob on the tooth's inner surface, triggered by tongue pressure. Fake enamel would fly aside a micro-instant and TTIC secrets would be recorded for posterity, not to mention G/S market analysts.

On deck, Finian adjusted his identification badge.

Beneath his picture it said *Woodrow Howslip, Missoula, Mont., Upper North American Distributorship*. Finian hoped Woodrow Howslip was still lost in the Mojave Desert. If so, the only thing Finian had to worry over was his old enemy.

Every few yards along the deck armed TTIC security men stood at attention: TTIC seemed to have innumerable armed guards. So did G/S for that matter. Finian often wondered why. No one got angry any more, why have armed guards?

"Hi, there, I'm Woody Howslip."

"Morning, sir." The guard stared into the Pacific's cobalt swell.

"Say, fella. Last year when I came to see the new models in-nerduced, I ran into a hell of a swell person—Spool or Stool. Sure like to buy him a drink. Is he on board?"

"I don't believe so, sir."

"Oh, too bad. Maybe he'll show up. They always have the top dogs at these distributor shows. I hear Stool's a top dog. Chief of company spies or something."

The guard concealed irritation.

"*Sprool*, sir. Chief of industrial investigation."

Finian gigged the man's ribs. "Keeps those Goods/Services jerks hopping, huh? Well, sorry Sprool isn't around. Maybe later. See you in the videofunnies—"

Overdoing it, Finian thought as he hurried along. Still, it was reassuring to know the intelligence was correct: Sprool was in Bombay. Finian had run up against him most recently when TTIC tried to steal G/S designs for the mid-year hair-do changes during the 2004-5 season.

Finian joined a crowd of distributors hurrying into an auditorium beneath a banner reading:

WELCOME
Things to Come Incorporated
World Distributors
*"Last Year's Woman Is This
Year's Consumer"*

As he took a seat in the shadowy hall he listened to voices all around:

"It's rumoured she's of the Grecian mode," said the European Common Market distributor.

"What? Copy the tripe G/S peddled two years ago?" That was the White/Blue Nile man.

The Chinese distributor protested: "Last year, too severe. Humble per cent of market drop severely. Five thousand years in fields, China women do not desire box haircut, woollen socks."

"Hope it's a real smasher this time," said the British Empire distributor, a seedy fellow wearing Cologne. One rundown warehouse in Jamaica comprised the Empire any more. TTIC or G/S could buy or sell the Empire a thousand times. Or any other country. Finian was sweating. No wonder the stakes were so high.

On an austere platform up front sat three men. One was a florid old gentleman with dewlaps and blue, vaguely crossed eyes. Another—a spindly type with a flower at each cuff—rose and was introduced by a loudspeaker as Corporate Director of Sales, Northcote Hastings.

"Thank you, thank you. I won't waste time, gentlemen. You've travelled thousands of miles in secrecy and we appreciate it. We trust you also appreciate why we must maintain the mobility of our personality design centre. One never knows when the—ah—competition might infiltrate a permanent site. They can't match our sales in new personalities, so they try to outfight us with punches below the belt."

He fingered his, of ermine, to illustrate. Finian joined the laughter, but meant his.

"After luncheon, gentlemen, you're scheduled for individual sessions with our designers, psychiatrists, plastic surgeons and sociability co-ordinators, not to mention apparel teams and accessory experts."

Hastings glanced at the old gentleman with the vaguely crossed eyes.

"Before we proceed, however, I should like to introduce

TTIC's beloved chairman of the board, Mr. Alvah Loudermilk. Stand up, Mr. Loudermilk." The sales manager was plainly annoyed by having to make the introduction. The old dodderer took a step towards the podium. Hastings let a tolerant smile be seen by the distributors but did not relinquish the mike.

"You can talk with Mr. Loudermilk personally later, gentlemen."

The florid old gentleman sat down again, as though no one appreciated him. Smoothly Hastings continued, "Let me get on by bringing forward the great design chief of Things to Come Incorporated—" He flung out a hand. "Dr. Gerhard Krumm."

The famed Krumm, an obese toad with the inevitable disarrayed look of the corporate intellectual, walked to the podium. His apricot slippers, pantaloons and bolero jacket seemed to have come from a dustbin. Behind Krumm stage blowers whirred. They were readying curtains and screen.

Finian slid his tongue near his tooth.

"Gentlemen," Krumm said, "first the bad news."

At the unhappy grumble he held up his hand. "Next year—I promise!—TTIC will absolutely and without qualification be ready to introduce the concept of the obsolescent male personality, exactly as we did in the female market ten years ago. I can only emphasise again the tremendous physical problems confronting us, and point to the lag in male fashion obsolescence that was not finally overcome until the late twentieth century, by the sheer weight of promotion. Men, unlike women, accept new decorative concepts slowly. TTIC has a lucrative share of the semi-annual male changeover, but we are years behind the female personality market. Next year we catch up."

"May we see what you have for the girls, old chap?" someone asked. "Then we'll decide whether we're happy."

"Very well." Krumm began to read from a promotion script: "This year we steal a leaf from yesterday's—uh—scented album." The lights dimmed artfully. Perfume sprayed the chamber from hidden ducts. A stereo orchestra swelled. The curtains parted. Finian's upper lip was rolled back as far as possible.

A nostalgic solido view of New York when it was once populated by people flashed on the screen. Violins throbbed thrillingly.

"Remember the sweet, charming girl of yesteryear? We capture her for you—warm, uncomplicated, revelling in—uh, let's see—sunlight and outdoor sports."

A series of solido slides, illustrating Krumm's points with shots of nuclear ski lifts or the Seine, merged one into another.

"Gone is the exaggerated IQ of this year, gone the modish clothing. A return of softness. A simple mind, clinging, sweet. The stuff of everyman's dreams. Gentlemen, I give you—"

Hidden kettledrums swelled. The name flashed on the screen: DREAM DESIRE.

"Dream Desire! New Woman of the 2007-08 market year!"

Over enthusiastic applause Krumm continued: "At our thirty thousand personality alteration centres over the world, every woman will be able to change her body and mind, by means of surgical and psychological techniques of which TTIC is the acknowledged master, to become Dream Desire. Backed by the most intensive promotion programme in history, we promise that more women will become Dream Desire than have ever become one of our previous models. Because, gentlemen, no woman could possibly resist becoming—this."

Sitting forward with tooth ready to shoot, Finian was unprepared for the shock that awaited him.

On the screen slid the naked figure of a girl. Only her back was exposed. Nothing could be seen of her face. Her hair was yellow, that was all. The flesh itself was tanned, in sharp contrast to the pale library look currently being merchandised. The proportions of the girl's buttocks had been surgically worked out to be almost the apex of voluptuousness. But what shook Finian to the soles of his mink slippers was a star-shaped raspberry mark on the new model's left rear.

That isn't Dream Desire, he thought wildly. *That's—that's—*

"We begin with the, uh, rear elevation," said Krumm. "In that colourful mark you see TTIC marketing genius. That mark will stamp the woman who buys this new personality as a genuine Dream Desire, not a shoddy G/S counterfeit. To be frank, adoption of this unique—ah—signature, was not planned. When we sought a girl for our prototype, we discovered the girl we chose was blessed with such a mark. It inspired serendipity. But this is just the beginning. See what we have done with the face."

Only just in time did Finian remember to trigger his tooth and take a shot of the rear elevation before the front view flashed on. The girl, naked and coy on a divan, had pink cheeks, red lips, china blue doll eyes. Pretty, in a cuddlesome, vapid way.

Quickly he exposed two more frames. He was falling apart,

80

muffing the job. Krumm's voice became a drone detailing the surgical and analytical procedures necessary for a woman to buy the appearance and personality of Dream Desire. Finian didn't hear a thing about price schedules or what lower-priced models were contemplated. He photographed each slide mechanically, thinking of the raspberry mark.

It's not Dream Desire, he said to himself. *My God—it's Dolly Novotny.*

Not the face, not the breasts. But *there,* far down in the eyes. They weren't even brown any more. But coloured contacts could change eyes so easily.

Never had he been more profoundly shocked. His own sweet lost Dolly!

A heavy hand seized his shoulder.

"Here he is!"

Finian was dragged from his seat. A searing light flashed in his face.

"Well, well. Finian Smith. When you took hold of that rail coming into the hall, you should have recalled we have sweat prints for all you G/S boys. Give me the camera and come along quietly," finished Sprool.

II

"I thought you were in Bombay," said Finian. "I got bum information."

Sprool smiled somewhere in the depths of his almost colourless eyes. His pale, saturnine face, however, was devoid of humour.

"Never trust Lyman Pushkyn for information, Fin. Since when is an advertising man qualified to supervise an industrial investigation programme?"

"You're right. I tried to get them to give me the post once."

"Did you? I didn't realise that. When?"

"Right after I was cashiered by the DOCs and finished my first case for G/S." He couldn't repress a smile. "The time I stole your men's changeover layouts by disguising myself as part of the lavatory wall. When you still had the design centre on land, out in California."

Sprool chuckled flatly. "We've been friendly enemies quite a while, haven't we, Fin?"

"You never put one over on me like this, though."

"Shame you forgot sweat prints."

81

"My own damned fault." Finian thrust out his jaw. "I'll take what's coming. I was counting on this play to cut through all that stupid bureaucracy at the top of G/S and maybe net me the chief investigator's post." Finian scowled out of the office porthole to the heaving blue Pacific. Sprool smoothed thinning hair.

"Might as well give me the camera."

Finian made a show of dipping into his artificial paunch. He came up with a palm-sized micro 35mm. and snapped open the case release. He pulled the leader on the cassette all the way out, exposing the film. Chuckling, Sprool picked up the cylinder.

"Very nice, Finian. May I now have the real camera?"

"Ah, you slick bastard," grumbled Finian. This time he took a piece of equipment from beneath his singlet. Sprool dropped it down a hissing disposal tube.

"You look positively vengeful, Fin."

"I could smash a few heads right now. That damn G/S Comptroller Central makes investigators do their own penetration work-ups. They're nickel-nursers besides. I *thought* of sweat prints. They said the corrective was too expensive. I wasn't positive you had the index on file, so—"

"Fin, please don't bristle. Remember we have telephotos on you at this very moment. In that bust of Loewy, for instance. His collar button is watching you. Don't fight me and you won't get hurt. TTIC is a business operation just like G/S. Firm but paternalistic. When we dispose of an irritant, we do it with flexibility and permanence, but no physical pain."

"That's nice to know, considering you'll probably ruin my career."

"Were you ever really cut out for business, Fin?"

"If I wasn't *what* the hell was I cut out for? Not the DOCs."

Sprool raised a chiding finger. "See? That burst of temper is all too typical of you. People simply don't rock the boat these days, Fin. Why, if either G/S or TTIC went for more than a 50 per cent share of the renewal personality market—plus or minus the 2 per cent gain or loss as a result of spying, design leaks and so forth—the U.N. would have its economic cycle theorists down on us instantly."

"God, Sprool, I try and try. I guess I just wasn't meant to be a twenty-first century man. I never had the proper education, like those reading primers written by the market boys from—where was it?—BBDO? I went to private school. On my Pop's knee."

"Then your attitudes are understandable. How can you expect to be anything but yourself when your father was a

Galbraither? Perhaps the last of that persuasion allowed to teach economics in public universities? Your father was dead set against the kind of obsolescence practised by the corporations we both represent. The two largest corporations in the world!"

"Pop wanted consumer money spent on libraries, schools, highways, pretty green roadside picnic parks."

"None of which contributes very much to keeping the world plant running at top output. None of which provides the millions of jobs needed to give black and yellow and white alike ample opportunity for the good life. If you'd only understand yourself, how you fit the scheme of things."

"I don't. That's the trouble. What the hell am I supposed to do, join the prisoners in New York? I keep quiet about what I think. I call it well enough to be an operative for the Department of Obsolescence Control. I was doing all right until—"

Memory clouded his brow. He wriggled deep down in the foam of his chair. He wished he were free of this hellish interview, free to think on the problem of Dream Desire who was not Dream Desire at all but Dolly.

"Until what? I never really knew."

"Until I rocked the boat, God damn it! I was chief of the Indiana bureau. I tried to stop a car-smash rally a week before the new models came out. The district supervisor was there, making a speech. I thought I saw a kid inside one of the levacars the crowd was pushing into the Wabash River. I went to see, hold back the crowd. The district supervisor told me to stop. I hit him. *I hit him.* You know what happens when you hit an executive."

Finian pinched the bridge of his nose to shut out the ugly memory. At length he added, "In case you never heard the rest of the story either, a wreck crew examined the levacar afterwards. There was no kid inside. Only a big mechanical doll somebody had forgotten to take out before the smash."

"Very touching," said Sprool emptily.

"Come on, Sprool. Let's get this over."

"Of course. But let me make one more point. Do you know why I'm here, not in Bombay?"

"The mental riot at the TTIC nylon plant was a fake."

"Not at all. The rioters were manning the controls of the motorised strike gangs day and night, from their homes. The moment TTIC cabled agreement to their demand for two extra holidays, before and after Nehru's birthday, they gave up all their other requests—for free anti-cigarette immunisation and the like. People are soft, Fin. They co-operate. It must be so, or the plant would stop functioning. How many billions do G/S and TTIC employ? Put those people out of work—disaster! Hunger, pestilence, *real* rioting. The people also have another role to fill, as consumers. If they're unhappy, they respond less adequately to advertising. The plant slows down. Why, until TTIC conceived the idea of introducing new female personalities every year, not just new clothes but complete new mental patterns, the world was headed for ruin. We ran out of new gadgets long ago."

"Don't kid me," Finian said cynically. "Personality obsolescence was thought up by Old Man Pharoh of G/S. His granddad told him a story about the Kennedy lady's mushroom hair changing the style overnight and it started him thinking."

"He had considerable help from Alvah Loudermilk."

"Who cares? All I say is, it's a hell of a shame the Triple Play War didn't end in something besides a stalemate. We wouldn't have had everybody palsy-walsy, black and white and yellow. And this damned population problem—the first rockets rusting on the moon and nobody interested in following them in person. Everybody's a consumer and a worker and—and damn it, soft as jello. And it's a miserable mess from top to bottom."

Sprool was genuinely shocked.

"Fin, are you seriously advocating periodic wars?"

Finian shielded his eyes from the sun falling through the port.

"Oh, no. I can't think of anything else, that's all. Fatness or fighting, fighting or fatness. In my book they're both lousy. I wish there were a third way. I can't think of one. Maybe if I were smart like you—" Finian stopped, bitterly.

Sprool dialled a magenta visorphone. "Really, Fin, this is becoming pointless temperament." Into the phone he said, "We're ready, Doctor." To Finian again: "Please don't try to reform our delicately balanced world, my friend. At least not until we scrub your mind clean of what you saw in the auditorium."

A shiver crawled on Finian's spine.

"Scrub—?"

Too late. Pneumatic doors slid aside. Two unsavoury specimens in white smocks bordered with lace wheeled a rubber-tyred mechanism into the room. Before Finian could move they adjusted several wing nuts and lowered a bowl device over his head. He tried to stand up, cursing. He was quickly but painlessly pinioned by sleek tubular metal arms clasping him from the back of the chair.

"The worst damage you did was on film," Sprool said, striding back and forth, dry-washing his hands. "I naturally assume that in your heightened nervous state, what you saw with your eyes didn't make much of an impression. But we'll be sure. Give him a mild jolt to start, boys."

Several sinister cathode tubes began to hiss at various points on the machine. Finian felt a tingle on his scalp, similar to a healthful massage. He closed his eyes and tried to remember the rear elevation of Dream Desire.

He panicked.

Almost as though there were a mental vacuum cleaner in his head, certain synapses were blocked, certain memory receptors temporarily sucked dry. The technique was a portion of that employed in changing the female consumer's intelligence quotient from year to year to conform to the new personality design she purchased. It made Finian fume to think of them tampering with his skull. He was no rotten Metropolis wife merchandised into adopting the latest fashion trend. He writhed ferociously. Sprool looked on with disapproval.

Try as he might, Finian could not remember what—*good lord!* He'd forgotten the name!

What did she look like? *What?*

He had a blurry recollection of colours on a screen, little else. The laboratory cretins unhooded him. The chair relaxed. Sprool assisted him to his feet.

"Feeling better? Free of unpleasant memories?"

"You've no business tampering—"

Dolly Novotny had a raspberry mark.

So did Dream Desire.

"Yeah, Yeah. I'm okay."

It took all Finian's strength to keep from revealing that the mental dyke had just burst.

He wasn't really surprised. Dolly Novotny had once meant far more to him than assignment could. She would again, when he learned how and why she—

He laughed inwardly. Poor Sprool. He'd stolen a march. Two. Finian still had the tooth camera. And how could Sprool know Finian wanted to—*must*—remember Dolly Novotny, because she was the only creature he ever really loved?

Dolly was the girl to whom he'd been engaged, before her

parents broke it off after he was cashiered from the DOCs. An ex-DOC who became an industrial investigator was little more than a low-life spy in their estimations. Finian had been away so much, on assignment. Dolly had tried to resist her parents, but they held the cash-box for a modelling career. She tried; she loved him. But one day when he came back to Bala Cynwyd she was gone. The whole family had moved.

Finian received one final letter. He thought from the words, or rather what was between them, really, that she still loved him. The words were obviously parentally ghosted.

Blinking at Sprool now, scratching his scalp to relieve the prickle, Finian realised anew the rather disheartening truth. He was a maverick. Pop had made him so, against his mother's shrill protests. So be it. Especially since someone—the system, maybe, he didn't know, cared less because a man couldn't really fight a system, not an ordinary man anyway—had corrupted the flesh he loved so well.

Finian was vaguely aware of Sprool, bland, pointing.

"Up that stairway, Fin. Directly to the vertijet take-off stage. Spare you the embarrassment of going on deck." He extended his hand. "Luck, Fin. I hope the sacking isn't too bad."

Finian slipped the hand aside. He grinned. If you had to be a loony, why not enjoy it?

"Thanks for nothing, pal."

He marched defiantly up the stairs into sunlight.

Who had Sprool been kidding about paternalism? Three hours later the vertijet hovered six inches from Lyman Pushkyn's green front door, the lawn of Panpublix on the outskirts of the Eastern metropolis. Finian was rudely pushed out. The vertijet climbed a white column of vapour into the sky.

Finian picked fresh-cut grass from his pantaloons. Oh, that kind, gentle Sprool. On his instructions the vertijet pilot had beamed an anonymous message on the Panpublix band, announcing that Finian Smith was being returned to continental U.S. by a TTIC skycraft. Still, Finian had one ace to stave off financial disaster.

Five minutes later he lost it.

A squad of G/S industrial guards boiled on to the lawn and hustled Finian to a cold tile room in the personnel wing. There, he discovered two astonishing things. One, the corporation was not quite so paternalistic as it masked itself to appear. The policemen roughed him as they stripped him. Two, the vast G/S industrial police force was not the harmless, aimless body it looked to be from outside. Apparently the guards were paid so well because they had to move savagely if a bubble boiled up the bland surface of the world stew.

In fact, their professionalism with the see-rays in the personnel lab relieved him, howling and kicking and pummelling, of the precious tooth-camera, just before he was hustled to Pushkyn's floor.

III

Panpublix was the wholly owned internal advertising agency for G/S. The building loomed forty storeys. Within its curtain-walls quite a few thousand communicators devoted themselves to the task of planning and executing campaigns to move the bodies, as the expression went. The fortieth, or solarium, floor belonged to the agency's executive officer, Pushkyn, into whose presence Finian was unceremoniously thrust.

"You miserable creep," Lyman said, as he shooed away his masseuse and beetled his thick Ukranian brows. "You bumbler, you! We heard all about your incredible performance from Sprool's agents. You're fired. Blackballed. Eradicated. *Kapoosht.*"

Finian had a hard light in his eyes. He sat down, tilted his feet to the chaise footrest and dialled the arm for a B-complex cocktail. "Lyman, those goonies of yours messed me up. I never knew they were more than window dressing. I didn't know they were supposed to fight."

Pudgy Pushkyn snapped the elastic of his old rose knickerbockers. His stomach, lumpy and white as the rest of him, hung out unglamorously.

"Rock the boat some more, creepnik. You'll find out how they can fight."

"Oh shut up. I delivered your pictures. Even if your men did take them by force."

Pushkyn turned his back. "Peddle it another place, jerk. You're through."

"You can't talk to me that way. If you hadn't chintzed about a lousy sweat-print job—"

Pushkyn squinted around. "So *that's* how. That Sprool, he's a regular fiend."

"Damn it, Lyman—"

Extending a trembling sausage finger Pushkyn breathed, "*You* we ought to have psyched, deep and permanent. What a fool I was to string along with you for years! A stumblebum private cop dignifying himself by calling himself an industrial investigator. Come in here storming, cursing—no wonder the DOCs kicked you out!"

Momentarily bewildered, Finian countered, "Lyman, your own guards—"

"Quiet! We'll get a nice fat rap in the public image when the investigator trade journals pick up the story of how G/S flopped."

Glowering, Finian stalked him. "Regardless of that, I delivered. I want my fee."

"I'll be damned if I—"

Conflict was temporarily forestalled by the arrival of a thin assistant art director, carrying a square item masked in grey silk. Finian stared moodily at the G/S model announcement layouts in the wall display racks. The trade-name of the new G/S woman and her figure were greeked; but from the woodcut and steel-engraving technique of the gatefold and bleed comps, Finian suspected G/S was going to market a bit of nostalgia even older than the kind chosen by TTIC. Bustless, mandolins and stereopticons by gaslight? Finian had a prepossessing urge to throw up.

"Want to see this, chief?" said the assistant art director.

He whipped off the silk, revealing an oil painting in a platinum frame.

"What the rinkydink hell is that?" Pushkyn cried.

The art director blanched. "Why, chief it's R. R. Pharoh III!"

"Of course, of course, jerkola. You think I don't know? I haven't seen the old smeller in three years maybe, but think I don't know the chairman of my own bread and butter? Why the fancy-fancy oil treatment? You do it?"

"Spare time, only, chief," trembled the art director. "Got a memo. Salinghams—you know, the audiotonal effects veep —memoised Pharoh. Wanted a personal portrait of his leader. Pharoh memoised me, okaying having his picture done. I patched together this little work from the descriptive PR biog. There aren't any good portraits extant."

"Why bring it to me?"

"But chief! You memoised me when I memoised you that—"

"I did? Oh, yeah. Well, I'm busy. Take it to Salinghams."

The art director veiled his creation and disappeared down the tube. Puskyn was about to speak to Finian when he noted the grey sweat patina on Finian's face. He demanded to know whether Finian was ill.

"Nothing, nothing's wrong," said Finian, shivering, wildly curious.

The image in the portrait burned into Finian's skull. It was that of a florid old gentleman with dewlaps and blue, vaguely crossed eyes.

Tightening his nerves, Finian said, "Pushkyn, let me lay it out. I got to have the fee. I need it to find the prototype of the TTIC girl. I used to know her."

A visorphone glowed. Pushkyn slapped the command button. A pale man danced up and down on the screen.

"Chief, chief, it's a breakthrough, a breakthrough! We turned up the TTIC pilot plant just an hour ago. Molecular triangulation. My God, sir, it's a miracle of deception. Manhattan! The prison! An old rundown distillery company building in the worst stews of—" He consulted a paper. "Parkave, that's the place."

Listening transfixed, Pushkyn started, slid his gaze to Finian and snarled at the screen, "Oh, boy, is *your* fat in the fire. Call me back." He shut off and squinted at Finian, whose mind churned. "You were talking?"

Finian swallowed hard. "Pushkyn, I must find out what's happened to the girl they made into the TTIC prototype. If they've changed her they've done wrong. She was sweet and desirable. They've made her all soft and disgusting. Like marshmallow."

"The new TTIC broad? You were hot for her once, that it?"

"That's it. I was only holding back the camera so you'd pay me. Give me a chance!"

"Think we run a snivelling charity?" Pushkyn's sweeping gesture encompassed the heavens and the pulsing, over-populated smog blanks beneath. "We gotta keep the plant running! Create demand every minute! Off with the old woman! On with the new! The old woman, she smells, she's out of date! We got a crusade here at Panpublix! We got a holy mission! You want the plant wheels to stop like they put sand in them? While we take care of your *personal* problems? Don't be a jerkola. Like to argue about the fee? I'll call up the guards again."

Something akin to a cool rush of air swept Finian's brain.

"Then I'll find her without the fee, Lyman."

"Hah-hah, sure. Big independent operator, big millionaire. Go get psyched and lose those hostile tendencies. Don't rock the world, she don't rock so good. Everybody's happy, you be happy. Go grub and be happy."

"I'm not happy. All of a sudden I'm not happy, if people like you make the only girl I ever fell in love with obsolete."

"Get out, chummo. I don't like you any more. You're dangerous."

Finian Smith nodded crisply. "I could very well be." And left.

As Finian left the Panpublix building he heard a menacing hiss. He tried to dodge the rainbow spray. Too late.

His clothing was soon soaked with a noxious admixture of water, special nitrites and phosphorous compounds shot into the air by the underground sprinkler system.

At the levacar station he finally controlled his anger. How petty they could be, to order the lawns sprinkled just then.

Waiting passengers moved away and made rude remarks about his smell. Finian found himself sole occupant of the front car on the ride down the Philadelphia spur.

The enforced loneliness gave him a chance to organise his muddled thoughts and decide what course of action he had to pursue concerning Dolly Novotny.

Two facts he possessed. What they meant, he didn't know.

A likely place to find her was the TTIC pilot plant on Manhattan, the prison island. Still, he was certain to have a rough time getting on to the island and into the plant after that. With few resources at his disposal it might be better to pursue the other thread a bit.

Its significance left him even more muddled. Alvah Loudermilk, TTIC chairman, had appeared at the dealer presentation, somewhat to the annoyance of his inferiors. And R. R. Pharoh, top G/S executive, hadn't been acting quite sensibly either when he permitted an oil portrait of himself to be painted. Finian had never seen a public photo of either man. Both executives were practically legendary.

Then why in the name of Galbraith did they look so much like each other?

When Finian thought on it, one cold, unpleasant word gnawed his head. *Conspiracy*.

A moment later his professional memory dredged up a source of proving or disproving his odd theory. What he intended to do with evidence, if any existed, he couldn't say. But he had a vague desire to be armed with a little more certainty before he sought Dolly.

An achingly musical name. *Dolly, Dolly*—

He remembered her so well, from summer evenings on the back porch before Bala Cynwyd, like the other suburbs, was swallowed in the fester of the metropolis.

Her dark hair. Her gentle eyes. Her animated mouth. And the raspberry mark, one night during an electrical storm.

She'd tentatively shared Finian's inherited ideas about their constantly obsolete world, ideas long suppressed in him and now flooding back under the double stimulus of Sprool's lecture and Pushkyn's vindictive parsimony. Dolly hadn't exactly been sympathetic. The philosophy of enduring worth was too daring even then. (Today it was sheer lunacy.) But neither had she been as adamant as most citizens. As her parents, for example. They replaced their furniture monthly with the latest G/S fibreboard laminate imitation Finnish modern modes. Good consumers, both. Then came his dismissal from the DOCs, the enforced break-up—

The levacar slowed for Bala Cynwyd. In the abstract, remodelling a woman's mind to make her the pattern to which nearly all other women in the world could conform was acceptable to Finian. When it came to the specific of changing Dolly to the marshmallow-trumpery creature looming on the screen behind Krumm, that was too much.

As he stepped off at Bala Cynwyd, it began to rain. He hurried along beneath warped building fronts of chartreuse and electric blue extruded plastic. From a doorway a hapless bum in last year's pseudo-cotton sport clothes begged for three dollars for a tube of model cement to sniff. Finian shuddered and walked faster. He stopped at Abe Kane's Autosuiter, the last shop left open on the block, selected a few new clothes from the plastic catalogue sheets fastened to the walls, and fed his universal credit card into the slot after punching out his measurements.

A red lucite sign blinked on: *Credit N. G.*

Finian frowned, hit the cancel lever and tried again. The third time he tried his card was not returned.

Pushkyn! Damn the vindictive bastard.

He trudged on through the rain, never having felt so alone in his life. It was a queer sensation, the total absence of credit. Once, he remembered dimly, Pop had brought home a suit of clothes purchased with cash. It had caused a near-riot among Bala Cynwyd burghers.

Reaching his shabby apartment, Finian changed from the effete suit, scrubbed up as best he could, packed his few belongings into a satchel and walked back into the rain. He passed a crowd of workers from the local G/S visorphone plant. It specialised in treating receiver parts with reagents that would crack the plastic precisely eight months after installation.

A little smog had mixed with the rain, turning the street ghostly. At a corner booth Finian used his last few coins to make a toll call to the House of Sinatra in Los Angeles.

A sound truck rolled past, repeating over and over, *"Gee-ess, Gee-ess, don't guess, it's bess—Take free shuttle at Exit 5-6 to the G/S Plaza—Gee-ess, don't—"*

A dapper young man appeared on the screen, snapping his fingers. "Hiyah. What can this gasser of a full-service bank do for you, Clyde?"

Finian showed his bank identification card.

"I'd like to withdraw my balance."

The banker came back into view a moment later. "Get lost. Your balance is nonesville. Garnisheed at noon. Unperformance and non-fulfilling of verbal contract, with waiver of co-operation. You signed it, Charlie."

"Damn it, I performed—" Finian began.

The screen had already blacked.

He staggered into the drifting smog. So Pushkyn had gone that far. Just for the sake of meanness. Well, Finian Smith would show the whole rotten bunch. They had angered him now. He wasn't quite witless, not yet.

Gee-ess, Gee-ess, it's bess came a lonely bellow. The polluted smog made Finian cough. His eyes smarted as he turned his pockets inside out.

A dollar left. Enough for a cup of coffee. No transportation. Just a single walking man in a cloud of industrial fumes and a long, empty night for thinking of Dolly.

Resolutely Finian hefted his satchel and started out to walk to Missouri.

IV

Thirty-six days later Finian staggered into the National Record Office in Rolla. Thirty-six frightening, alarming, eye-opening, solitary, transfiguring days they had been, too.

Days of dodging robot levacars whose spot-beams hunted him in the shadows beneath the elevated turnpikes, seeking to arrest him for pedestrianship.

Days of remembering his Pop. And nights too. Especially nights, thinking as he lay under a berry bush half-starved and chilly, how Pop had enjoyed prize-fights, anti-social, uncooperative prize-fights. How young Finian had been dragged to lonely boxcars or dim garages where furtive men watched the sport before it was finally stamped out in the name of bland humanity.

The world too was one bland custard, blandly happy. Except not really, as Finian, horrified, discovered.

No plant could function at total efficiency, at complete peak year after year. A low percentage of chronic unemployment had never been whipped by the cyclic theorists. Strange wild caravans of men and wives and children, human wolves almost passed Finian occasionally on red-leafed back-roads in Pennsylvania and Ohio. He almost fell into the hands of one such band. Thereupon he decided he must possess a weapon of self-defence at all costs. His belly he could protect by shovelling in wild berries and an occasional stolen chunk of honeycomb. But his life, against such a seething pack of wild creatures as he had fled from on that lonely road, needed more dependable protection.

Difficult problem. Under law, weapons were prohibited except upon special occasions. What necessity for weapons when all was pleasant co-operation.

Yet the G/S guards carried weapons. So did the TTIC internal force. Finian was beginning to believe he knew why that might be so. Too early to tell, however. And the other problem pressed him to concentration upon it.

Weapon-devotees were even more suspect than pedestrians in the lonely country between metropolises. Occasionally Finian glimpsed a wire compound, acres and acres, against the sunburnt horizon. Manhattan Prison was too far for local DOCs to send recalcitrant Hoosier or Buckeye anti-obsols, so they were thrown into smaller country compounds, together with those few madmen who settled disputes with fists. Such compound inmates were described as juves, Finian remembered, passing one such wire enclosure on a white moonlit night and shuddering. He didn't recognise the term juve, but it obviously meant the middle-aged or geriatric specimens huddled within the cages, a few defiantly wearing ancient gaudy jackets with mottoes stitched on them, forgotten anarchist slogans like Pfluger's Idle Hour Pin Barons.

On the outskirts of South Bend, Finian luckily came upon an obsolescence carnival.

Several thousand people swarmed across a treeless terrain in a housing project smash. Motorised workgangs stood at the development's fringe, waiting to set up new prefab Moorish Manors to replace obsolete Five-Bedroom Geneva Chateaux.

Finian infiltrated the wild carnival crowd, ripping draperies and smashing furniture with feigned laughter ringing from his lips. When the carnival wore itself out near dawn and the workgangs rolled in through clouds of soy-fuel smoke, Finian filched a shiny flick-blade knife from a Boy Scout chopping up a last slab of plastic plaster and lath.

The Scout shrieked for the DOCs on duty. Finian was away and running through a hydro-ponic cornfield before he could be caught.

Now, dressed in his only presentable suit, last year's G/S Nubby Oppenheimer, he flashed his personal identification card before the computer grid in the empty green marble rotunda of the National Record Office. Personal identity was one quantity Pushkyn couldn't revoke.

Finian felt his fingers tingle as the grid scanned the card.

"Investigator Smith, Bond Number PA-5006, you are recognised."

"Permission to examine ownership statements for corporations over one billion, please."

"What year?" buzzed the mechanical voice.

"Not certain," Finian replied. "Could be as far back as 1980 or even 1970."

"Second tier from lowest level. Tube nine, your left."

It gave Finian a weird sensation, plummeting in the airtube and realising he was dropping eighty storeys into the depths of the nation's largest insane asylum. But legal transactions had proliferated so in the past decades, as had neurotic behaviour, that only a combined institution and record office was feasible for saving space and offering a less-than-fatal end for hopeless maniacs.

The reading room below ground smelled of mould. Grey block walls heightened the unpleasant mood. Finian sat at the call-out console. He manipulated the controls and spoke into the unit:

"Let me have the volume covering Goods/Service corporation for—ah—1974, please."

Several minutes passed. A door slid aside. A white male, perhaps seventy, with yellow-rimmed lack-lustre eyes and a lantern jaw, shuffled in and waited with docile manner. The creature wore a seedy twill uniform, anciently cut.

"What do you have on any asset transfers for Goods/-Services, please?" Finian asked.

The elderly gentleman did not so much as blink. He hesitated only a moment as the index system in his sick skull, instilled by hypnolearning, turned over record after invisible record. Finally he said vacantly, "No asset transfers."

"Nothing in the way of stock, even?"

"No asset transfers, no asset transfers."

"Thank you, that's all."

But the man had already departed, needing no thanks. Finian turned to the console again wondering whether he could endure as many days as it might take:

"Let me have the volume covering Goods/Services corporation for 1975."

A total of eighteen hours went by, relieved only by three short naps above ground, Finian sleeping in a magnolia bush on Rolla's outskirts, before he found what he wanted.

He'd worked through Goods/Services from its 1969 inception to 1997, interviewing assorted madmen and women who shuffled in, reeled off figures and names or lack of them, then shuffled back out. Asset transfers exhausted itself as a lead. He tried register of directorship as well as deposition of tangible real-estate sale. Useless, useless. Only then did it slip back.

In some dim time in the past—Pushkyn had mentioned it once—public stock of G/S had been called off the market.

Once more he began with a different set of volumes, working his way down the years. In 1992 he located it: All certificates de-deemed.

The scent overpowered the must of the underground box like the smell of blood. He called out the volume covering Things to Come Incorporated for the same year. It was a naturalised Japanese weighing close to three hundred pounds.

One month after the G/S redemption came a callback by the board of TTIC. Finian almost wished the poor Japanese could appreciate tea. He'd have bought him a bucket, had he the money.

Tensely his fingers flew to the console.

"Two volumes, please. For 1992 and 1993. Covering Flotations without tangible assets."

When 1992 arrived (a mulatto with his face fixed in a perpetual grin) Finian was disappointed. Nothing. The volume for 1993 (a strikingly voluptuous red-haired girl who had eyes that made him think hauntingly of Dolly) was another case entirely. Finian trembled:

"Give me what you have on holding companies, please."

The third was it, the redhead staring through him:

"Holders Limited. Ten thousand shares privately issued."

Finian was on his feet, sweating, his empty belly a-churn. "Officers, please."

"Chairman of the board, Alvah Pharoh."

"There must be some mistake. Uh—re-check, please. What is the name?"

"Full legal name Alvah Robert Loudermilk Pharoh."

A florid old gentleman with dewlaps and blue, vaguely crossed—by heaven!

Finian almost forgot to return the volume to its detention cell after he got the names of the other registered corporate executives, which meant nothing to him. But Alvah Robert Loudermilk Pharoh most certainly did.

Finian wondered, as he left the National Record building and turned his face east again, what had possessed the old man to think it safe to occasionally appear as head of both companies. Not that he appeared often, mind you. The painting *must* have been a slip. So too the appearance on the hydrofoiler, displeasing his underlings. Senility? Senility and a strength that had refused to completely drain away, as the dewlaps lengthened?

Hungry and tattered though he was, Finian felt renewed as he threw himself into the weary tramp back to Manhattan. The flick-blade knife armed him. So did the knowledge that even the most mighty, even those who kept the plant running at all costs, including the cost of sloth, could occasionally slip.

And they still had Dolly.

V

Ahead in the gloomy purple twilight, giant rats were squealing after blood.

Quickening his step, Finian unshipped the flick-knife. Making headway was hard. This particular section of the Hudson Bluffs National Dump was a miniature mountain range of discarded but eminently serviceable—except for the usual engineered-to-fail tubes and cracked cabinets—solido sets. To the east behind the rubble the towers of Manhattan Prison thrust into the darkening sky.

Finian walked rapidly away from the squee-squee of the rats.

He'd glimpsed a pack of them earlier, down by the Tunnel at the far end of the hundred-thousand-acre junk tract. They were nearly three feet long from drinking the waste spewed out by the pharmaceutical factories upriver. Hoping to avoid a meeting with needly fangs, Finian was suddenly arrested by a fresh sound.

A human voice, in fright.

He doubled back in his tracks, cold sweat all over him. The vitaminised beasts were attacking a real person!

Finian rounded a solido heap. A little wisp-haired balloon of a man in a ragged grey smock was backed against a trash peak, trying vainly to swing at three of the rats, armed only with a plastic leg broken from a solido console. The man's left trouser leg was shredded, black-shining with blood. The blood maddened the rats. They danced and snapped and squee-squeed and made the little man even more pale.

Finian snatched up a solido cabinet and heaved. One of the rats yipped, turned and scuttled at Finian like a small furry tank. Shaking, Finian stood his ground. He tried to dodge the creature's leap but was not agile enough. Hellish teeth sank into his arm.

Finian jammed his flick-knife into the smelly hair at the base of the rat's brain. Squirting blood like a fountain, the rat flipped over in the air and gave a death-squee. Its comrades received solid whacks between the eyes from the other man. They turned tail and vanished.

"Let me see that arm," said the man, a filthy spectre with moist, disappointed eyes. "Oh, not good at all. Come along. I'm a doctor. Humphrey Cove."

Finian gaped as he was lead along the bluff. "A doctor? In the National Dump?"

"I live here. Never mind, I'll explain later. I have a shack. Hurry, we don't want those rat toxins to run through you. I think I have immunisation. Oh, I was really done for until you came along."

The small doctor giggled as he hustled Finian along. Finian was not too sure he approved of his would-be saviour. In spite of Dr. Cove's rather pitiful mien, there was a certain unsteadiness in his wet eyes. He clucked and talked to himself as he led the way to a ramshackle structure nearly the size of a small private dwelling, constructed solely of panels from solido consoles jerryrigged together with wire and other scrap materials.

"No one comes here. No humans. Only the littersweep

convoys from up and down the coast, all mech-driven. The only people I ever talk with are the poor juves in the prison. What's your name? What are you doing here?"

At the hovel entrance Cove suddenly halted, stared at Finian and turned pale.

"Did you come to arrest—?"

Finian shook his head. "I came to get into Manhattan."

"Via the Dumps?" Cove blinked suspiciously. "There's the Tunnel."

"To use the Tunnel, you have to be a priest going in for last rites. Or a coroner or a psychiatry student. Or have a DOC pass. I watched the Tunnel three hours." Suddenly Finian had an impulse to trust this odd little person: "I have no pass. I'll be entering the prison illegally."

"Well, then! Come inside, do come inside!"

Names were exchanged again, Cove having forgotten he'd given his. From behind a triple stack of ancient medical texts Cove said he'd rescued from dump piles, the doctor produced a frowsy leather-plas diagnostic kit. He clamped the analyser to Finian's upper arm and switched on the battery. A whir. A moment later the proper medication had been pressure-sprayed through Finian's epidermal cells.

Cove watched with proud glowing eyes, saying as he unstrapped the unit:

"A miracle I found this kit, I'll tell you. Three years ago. The only persons who use it are the poor juves. No regular medical help for them, I'm afraid. So I've a skiff. Actually an old levacar inverted. I paddle across once a month after dark." He giggled. "The DOCs at the Tunnel post would psych me if I got caught. But I feel I'm doing my bit to keep the anti-obsols content in their unhappiness."

Through a rift in the wall Cove's moist eyes sought the darkening towers. His voice was quickly vengeful.

"I'd like to see those buildings fall to ash. Margarita, ah poor Margarita." He whipped his head around, eyes almost as vicious as those of the rats. "Who are you? If this is all a clever trap to smoke me out—"

"No trap," Finian assured him. "I'll tell you about it. But do you have any food?"

Cove nodded and fetched a brown gallon pharmaceutical bottle, instructing Finian to drink.

"Protein and vitamins. Distill it myself from the drug sludge in the river. After you drink I may or may not give you one of the soy bars I get from the juves. When their wives bear children, it's the only way they can pay, you know. They're very proud, always pay."

Cove squatted with difficulty, an oddly savage little man in the fading light.

"Whether I let you have a soy bar depends on your story. If you're an enemy, I can run away and leave you to wander the Dumps at night. You won't last long with the rats, being a stranger."

"There's a woman over on that island I have to find," said Finian and launched out.

As he recounted his tale, careful not to become too emotional about it, he noticed a growing excitement in Cove's damp eyes. Finally, when he had concluded, Cove leaped up.

"Capital, Smith, that's capital. Let me help. Let me ferry you across."

Finian smiled grudgingly. "Okay. I was prepared to swim it."

"The sludge would poison you before you got halfway."

"What's your stake in this, Cove? I mean, this food pays me back for the rats."

Cove's little eyes were miserable.

"Margarita. My wife. She died over there."

Painfully the story came out, dredged from an unhappy past: Cove had been a plastic surgeon by speciality, in the employ of TTIC at its Bangor Personality Salon. But a quirk in his nature made him rebel against the work, permitted him to fall prey to dangerous Galbraither notions. His wife had informed on him.

Cove discovered it before the TTIC police could arrest him. He fled to the outskirts of Bangor, hiding there in the woods while a few reluctant friends supplied him with food. TTIC industrial police combed the woods with talk-horns, threatening to psych his wife into anti-obsol attitudes if he didn't surrender.

"The filth!" Cove rocked on his haunches. "I thought it was a trick, a lever. I ran away. Margarita, poor thing, was on their side. She couldn't help what she did. She came of a respected family. TTIC middle management. But a year later I found out. They did it anyway. Oh, they smile and smile and treat the mob kindly. But underneath, when they're opposed—I learned Margarita had been sentenced to Manhattan. It took me another nine months to get here and find means of crossing. By that time she'd died of pneumonia. No antibiotics allowed the juves, you see. Juves are worthless. She died." Cove rocked and rocked, wild-eyed. "Died, died."

"Doctor Cove, will you help me get across?"

"Of course, of course. But to hunt that pilot plant, a knife won't be much good. The moment you're discovered they'll set on you like wild dogs."

"Then I'll need something else."

Finian's brain ran rapidly with his career with G/S. He recalled Leveranz, an unfortunate operative charged with a dangerous penetration of the TTIC Marketing Office in Beirut.

"I knew a man once who was bombed. Is there anything here—?" Finian's gesture swept the shack and dump beyond. "Do you remember enough, even if we could find an explosive source, to bomb me?"

The moist eyes of Cove widened with malicious delight. "Blow them up?"

Now Finian himself felt hard and cold.

"I just might, if they've hurt her."

"Possibly we could use the charger pack from an old solido." Cove was warming to the challenge. "Yes, we very well might. Extremely miniaturised. I'd have to check the formula but I think I have a chem text in that pile. And a military medicine volume, too." He began to tear through the books. "No anaesthesia, or precious little. Perhaps I could knock you out."

"What for a trigger?" Finian questioned. He showed his mouth. "I have this empty socket where I carried a camera once."

Chortling, Cove scuffled among his belongings and produced a cardboard carton full of ivory chips of all sizes.

"Why, that ought to work, Smith. The miserable juves aren't fluoridated either. I do quite a few extractions. Imagine a plastic surgeon doing extractions! Let's see, give me a minute to find the chem text . . ."

Dr. Humphrey Cove unearthed the text in two minutes. The rest took four days.

Finian suffered excruciatingly, especially during the operation. Cove kept smacking him on the head with a solido leg when the pain grew too hideous. Finian dug his nails into his palms and thought of murmurous summer evenings on the back porch in Bala Cynwyd, and vowed in his pain-streaked mind the hurt was worth it if only he had a means to strike at them if they'd hurt Dolly, his own Dolly.

When he was ready to enter the prison, his left foot flesh carried a small capsule that would detonate an explosive force when the yellowing tooth in his dead socket was turned a proper one-half turn in its clumsily hand-chiselled housing.

An old trick, bombing. A relic of the Triple Play War. But it gave Finian a little more courage to go hunting death.

In an unpleasant mist-clammy midnight, Dr. Cove paddled the improvised skiff through the sticky penicillin waste forming a crust on the Hudson, to the dilapidated pier that once belonged to the Cunard division of G/S. Off down black, ruined streets distant reddish lights pulsed. Cove shook his hand fervently. "I hope you kill them. I hope you don't co-operate and kill them all."

Then the skiff slithered away into the smelly broth. Finian shivered and walked.

Three blocks from the pier a ragged band of thirty-odd men and women, with a couple of malnourished youngsters hanging at the fringes, slipped out of an alley and closed around him.

They hissed and backed a terrified Finian against a polybrick wall. The leader of the juve pack, an oldster of eighty in tapered blue denim trousers and an antiquarian jacket spangled with fake platinum stars and buckles swaggered up and down, thumbs hooked in a six-inch belt.

"Sending DOCs into the streets these days, are they, sonny?"

"I'm no DOC." Finian searched the hostile eyes for succour. There was none.

"We eat DOCs alive in the prison. They step off the guard post, we swallow 'em up and chew 'em to pieces, sonnyboy."

"A DOC stew tonight! Oh, wunnerful!" piped a seven-year-old.

"Scream a little for us, will you please?" said the ageing juve with a smile, shuffling forward.

Finian thought of the flick-knife and whipped it out. Another sibilant hiss ran from mouth to mouth as the blade caught the distant red glow.

"Look, don't kill me. See this? It's a knife, a real knife. You people can recognise a genuine useful antique twentieth-century artifact, can't you? Non-obsolescent. Non-obsolescent, see? Still works?"

A touched stud and the blade retracted. Another touch and it sprang out.

"Would I be a DOC and carry this?"

The juve leader had an almost religious expression on his face. His hand shook as he extended it.

101

"Uh—could you—leave me see?"

Finian thrust it into his hand.

"Yours. Listen, take it." A dark, malicious streak forced out the next words. "Could you make more? Why don't you try? Now you have a pattern. Then you wouldn't have to wait for the DOCs to leave the guard post. Then a lot of you could pay them a visit."

Whispering over their icon, the juves melted into the night.

VI

Keeping to back streets, Finian crossed Bway several blocks above a strange complex of glittering red lights. Cove had told him it was the prison recreation area, a kind of open plaza known, unpronounceably, as Timesq. Hurrying on, he reached Parkave.

Several blocks south he saw a white chain working its way across the ruined thoroughfare. Approaching in the cover of shadows, he gazed up at a glistening glass structure with windows painted over. Then he looked down to the street again.

The white chain came apart into individual females, double-timing along between a cordon of TTIC industrial guards. One chain rushed west, another east, vanishing into the building. Finian skulked, grinning mirthlessly, estimating the time to be somewhere in the neighbourhood of eleven at night. Protected, the pilot plant nursing staff was changing shift. Cove had told Finian about the nurses, and also what might be done. He hurried back towards Bway.

The recreation area was curiously deserted of juves at this hour. Finian wondered whether the flick-knife was really that much of a talisman. It must be, since he'd seen no juves after the first encounter. Cove said there were several hundred thousand on the island. Perhaps they'd gone underground to the ruined transportation tubes.

Timesq featured open shops subsidised out of national taxes as a sop to the theory of rehabilitaton . . . antiques, genuine meatburgers, bizarre novelty stores where articles were actually displayed on open counters instead of behind automated windows. But the shops were actually intended to pander to the vices of the juves. Else why would Finian have been able to slip so easily into a deserted costumer's?

Half starved, his shanks frozen by wind whistling under the

102

ancient white uniform and the musty grey wig prickling his ears, Finian dozed the daylight hours away in an alley, blearily on the alert for juves. He saw one large pack passing a block away, several hundred on the run. They didn't see him. Otherwise he was undisturbed until night fell again.

Midway between the hotel which apparently served as nurses' quarters and the ruined liquor building, Finian ducked into one of the double-timing white chains as the eleven o'clock shift changed. He hoped his male shoes wouldn't be too noticeable. But the street was dark. The hundred or so nurses were on dangerous extra-pay duty from the way they rushed along between the guard cordons, not speaking, intent only on gaining the safety of the pilot plant.

As in all hospitals, lights burned low in the marble mausoleum of a lobby as the nurses fanned out to the various tube banks. Finian spied a rest room next to a boarded-up newsstand, slipped inside and waited half an hour out of sight.

Then he returned to the lobby. A late nurse was hurrying to the tubes. Outside, the TTIC guard cordons were no more. Finian ran up behind the nurse, thinking smugly that it had been easy so far. He'd remembered to touch no doors, in case there was a sweat-print check.

The nurse gave a frightened *kkk* sound as Finian looped his elbow around her neck.

"Where's the prototype kept, lady? Tell me or I'll crack you in half."

"Tw-twelve," came the panicky answer. "I can't breathe!"

"You won't ever again unless you take me up there."

"It's not my floor—"

"With lights out who'll know? There's the tube. Inside! Don't speak to anyone. Don't even raise an eyebrow, or I'll throttle you."

In the deserted tube the alarmed woman, elderly, eyed Finian's wig, all too obvious in the full illumination.

"What are you, some kind of degenerate?"

"Yes, but not the kind you think."

Finian laughed, feeling frightened and brave all at once.

On twelve, isolated pools of radiance interspersed vast islands of aseptic black. Three nurses clustered at a floor desk to the right. Finian's terrified victim led him to the left.

Double doors loomed at the far corridor end. Why was it so easy? Finian felt vague alarm as he shoved the old lady through the doors. The isolation, that must be it, he reasoned. The improbable isolation here on Manhattan where no investigator would dream of looking for a pilot plant.

Still, Pushkyn's people had discovered it by molecular-triangulation sonics. Were they penetrating even now?

In the chamber a white blur stretched naked in the warm, purified air. Finian held tight to the old nurse's arm and approached the dreaming girl. The raspberry mark stood out black in the faint gleam from the half-open door of an attached dispensary. There encephalographs and other equipment winked, chromed and cold.

"Dolly?" Finian's lips felt like shreds of paper, crinkled dry. "Dolly, hear me?"

A vacuous mewing sound came from the girl. She twisted deeper in silk coverlets. "Wake her," Finian ordered.

"You're a madman! I don't know how. I'm on six, neurosearch."

He shoved her rudely. "There must be a chart in the dispensary."

Finian had to threaten to cuff her several times before she tremblingly translated the medical Latin in the last twelve thick casebooks on the dispensary shelf. From the section marked *Emergency Antidotal Procedures* she read out the correct mix of ampoules from the wall-wide freezer.

Finian was acutely conscious of the silence of the great dark room, the whisper of Dolly's breathing from the bed, the rush of controlled air in and out of blowers. Time was moving inexorably. What he would do when and if he wakened Dolly he was not precisely sure. All he could tell was that he must talk to her. Talking to her once was what he had worked and tramped and almost died for.

The pressuredermic barrel gleamed in the light. Finian snatched it from the nurse.

"If you've tricked me—I don't take to hurting women, but I will!"

"I swear to Loudermilk I didn't. Only please don't hurt me."

"In there," Finian instructed. He latched the dispensary door behind her. There was no visorphone inside. He would be safe a moment longer.

With shaking hands he pressed the instilling cup near the raspberry mark, and plunged.

Slowly, slowly, the naked girl rolled over, lids fluttering

drowsily. Finian crouched by the bed. His hand knotted up in the silken sheets. He'd turned up a rheostat to provide a gleam for judging her eyes. Doll-blue, they flew open—

Blank, unknowing.

"Why, hello there." The voice tormented him. It was so speaking, so silly. "Whatever are you doing in Dream's bedroo— Dream's bed—"

Like a broken mechanism the voice ran down. One of her voluptuous hands crept tentatively towards his. *"Finian?"*

"Oh, my God, my God, Dolly."

He buried his head on her shoulder, almost crying.

When he had controlled himself sufficiently to talk, he asked her what it was like.

"Not too terrible." Dolly's voice now, not her body but for the mark, only her voice trying painfully to re-form old associations. "When we moved . . . Well, it was luck and a little moral compromise that snared me a chance to be the prototype."

"Do you remember anything? I mean, when you're under?"

"A little. A very little. Far down in my head, like the bottom of a well. I won't in a week or two, so they say."

"It's wrong, Dolly! It's wrong for them to change you!"

She laughed tolerantly, not a little sadly.

"Those wild old ideas of yours again."

"I love you, Dolly. I want you the way you were."

"Impossible, Fin. My body's changed." One hand lifted the hem of the sheet. "It's part of the price for being the prototype. I nearly died when my parents made us move. I wasn't strong. I'm not much stronger now. This"—a gesture to the room —"when they're finished with me, in a week or two, I'll never be able to go back. The prototype can't. Other women can, the change isn't so deep when it's purchased. But in return I'll receive more money than most women ever see. I wish you hadn't come here, Fin. I'd nearly got over you."

"Take out the contacts, Dolly. Then tell me it's all over."

"Fin, I can't. They're permanent." She clutched his arm. "If you're caught here—"

Rapidly he told her of what he'd learned at the National Record Office. "Some kind of conspiracy, Dolly. Awful, awful. Hell, I'm not bright enough to fathom what it means. Maybe Pop could have. I'm just certain I want you out before this crazy doublecross blows right up."

Dolly hesitated. "I'm not sure. My mind's full of someone else—"

"Don't let him frighten you," said a voice. "He's done anyway."

Caught, heartbeat wild and racing, Finian turned as all the lights blazed up in the room. Dolly shrieked and burrowed under the sheet.

Outside the closing panel Finian glimpsed a phalanx of armed TTIC police. The three men inside moved swiftly towards him. Sprool and Pushkyn shoulder to shoulder, and shuffling behind, Alvah Robert Loudermilk Pharoh with his dewlaps jiggling and his blue, vaguely crossed eyes filled with fright.

"We should of killed the jerko," Pushkyn offered.

"Be quiet." Sprool breathed tightly, thinking hard.

"No one listens to me," Alvah Robert Loudermilk Pharoh whined. "No one listens any more even though I'm the chief executive of Holders."

"You simpleton!" Sprool spun on him, barely able to control his fury. "You incredible wreck! I wish Pushkyn and I had retired you to a senility farm long ago. If your addled brain could have understood it wasn't safe for you to go around making public appearances! Having your portrait painted!"

"Holders is my firm!"

"It *was*. Before your brains turned to mashed potatoes," said Pushkyn.

"You wouldn't have penetrated the pilot plant, would you, Pushkyn?" Finian was suddenly enraged, and beginning to understand. "Even though you knew where it was."

Pushkyn sneered. "Whaddya think, put sand in the wheels? Always the funny finko, huh? If it wasn't for me, Sprool and a few others on both sides, running the show while this old bone-bag sits on the Holders board—"

"He means to say," Sprool put in, somewhat sadly, "we have done our best to keep the plant running. You, Fin, have done your best to stop it."

"How did you find me?" Finian demanded.

Sprool shrugged. "See-ray."

"I never touched a doorknob anyplace!"

"There is a false socket in your head. Every person entering or leaving this plant is rayed for dental coding. Yours failed to check. It took a few minutes to collect Pushkyn. And the old man. I want him to see the fruits of his senility. We vertijetted."

106

"Ah, damn," said Finian, impotently.

"I very nearly admire you," Sprool told him. "In proper circumstances you might have filled a responsible position with Holders. Do you realise what a difficult and exciting enterprise it is to run this world, Fin?"

"I realise you sold everybody a bill of goods, kept them soft, sucked their guts out."

"Would you rather have howling millions out of work and rioting?"

"Yes! Yes. I mean, no. I don't want people to starve, but this way—I'd rather have some guts in life. Trouble and guts."

"Trouble we have, Finian," Sprool returned with a sigh. "Do you know what we saw as we came over the Tunnel in the vertijet? The DOC post in ruins. The juves are breaking out, Fin, actually breaking out. Most of them are dead, of course. But several hundred escaped. There's a pitched battle going on in Jersey this minute. The juves will die as soon as I give the mobilisation order. A few may get away and start in other cities, inciting riot, pulling down what we've built so carefully to insure everyone a decent life. Both TTIC and G/S are alerting industrial guards trained for trouble such as this. We'll also have to apply considerable pressure for the DOCs to move. But we'll win. We gave up war long ago, Fin. We won't permit another to start."

"The creeps had knives!" Pushkyn bellowed. "Real knives! You stupid, did you—?"

"I think so," Finian looked up. "I hope so."

Again Sprool sighed, almost sympathetically.

"Fin, Fin. You seem to think we're evil men. We're not. We're *businessmen*. We didn't begin the system. We only inherited it. But you've never understood, have you? Always, I think, you resented us as a result of what your father taught you." Sprool was white now, impassioned. "We had no choice! Either we maintained calm or—"

"You changed Dolly! I don't understand your theories beyond that!"

Sprool outshouted him: "The alternative to a rocked boat is *chaos*!"

"There's got to be another way."

"Go to the guard post! See the mangled bodies and then say that."

"I don't *care*, Sprool! I'm taking Dolly off the island."

"Creep, you won't set one foot from here."

107

Finian peeled his lips back.

"Look at the tooth, Lyman. You know what was there before." He waggled his left foot. "I'm bombed. The tooth will set it off. Either instantaneously or on timed delay. Stop me from walking out with Dolly and find out."

"Salinghams wanted my portrait—" the florid old gentleman began.

"Bluffer! Lousy, rotten bluffer!" Screaming, Pushkyn rushed forward.

Sprool's hand flew up.

"*Don't!* I believe him."

For the first time Finian Smith saw Sprool perspiring.

"He's the kind to do it, Pushkyn. I don't want slaughter here, too. So you keep quiet and remember who's senior troubleshooter."

Cold, shrewd lights glittered in Sprool's eyes. "Fin, what guarantee can you offer if we release this woman to you, allow her to go with you under duress?"

"No."

Heads swung, startled. Dolly went on slowly:

"I think—I want—"

A disgusted sigh came from Sprool's lips. He controlled himself. "Very well, Fin. If we permit you to leave, what guarantees do you offer that you'll cause no further trouble? We'll have our hands full quelling the disturbances the juves will start. It hasn't got too far out of hand yet. But if I don't give the mobilisation order, it could go nationwide. Even to other countries. I have to be around to stop it. It can be done, even though I don't much like removing the velvet glove."

"Guarantees?" said Finian. "My word. That's all."

Sprool walked quickly to the door and opened it. The threatening knot of industrial police still waited in the shadows. Finian bundled Dolly into the bedclothes and moved her towards the entrance as Sprool said, "Let him pass."

"I won't stand for it!" Pushkyn leaped forward and landed a solid one that rocked Finian on his heels. Then Sprool snapped his fingers. The TTIC police carried the foam-lipped Pushkyn into the dispensary.

Trembling, suddenly cold and trembling clear through, Finian made an effort to keep his face an inflexible mask as he guided Dolly through the aisle between the guards. He hoped she wouldn't question him, wouldn't relent until they were free. Sick fear engulfed him as he touched the tip of his tongue gingerly to the fake tooth while the tube shot down.

Dolly leaned on his shoulder, her hair warm. She made frightened mewing sounds. Finian shepherded her into the night, began the long, terrible walk to the Tunnel, hoping she wouldn't come to her senses until they reached the opposite shore. In time she'd be herself again. That much he could give her even if his search had been all for nothing.

The DOC post at the Tunnel entrance was afire. Juve corpses sprawled everywhere.

Midway along the empty tunnel Finian halted. A figure capered towards them.

"Capital, oh, marvellous!" Humphrey Cove trilled, stepping over a dead DOC's open-mouthed head. "Three hundred of them got out, running for their lives. I think it will spread this time. The local camps, the jobless—full-scale! There are so many really lovely pockets of resistance!"

"Shut up and walk." Finian pushed Cove back towards the Jersey side.

"What in heaven's name is wrong with you, Smith?"

"Armed." Finian whispered it so Dolly couldn't hear. "A guy hit me, I'm armed. Can't have more than half an hour before I blow. Cove, don't you say anything. When we're outside, you take care of this girl, understand? Watch out for her until she recovers. She's free of them, I bought her that much."

They passed a shrilling visorphone in a lighted kiosk at the far Tunnel mouth. A DOC alert was being scheduled for Philadelphia. Juve gangs were forming in the streets there, hand-made knives were appearing. The mask was off. Full mobilisation of combined TTIC and G/S industrial police was being ordered by Sprool. Cove clapped his hands.

Rain was falling as Finian led Dolly out of the Tunnel. Three DOC vertijets from the south were homing on Manhattan, agleam with emergency lights. Dolly murmured. Finian lifted her chin and stared into the doll-blue eyes a moment, conscious of the bomb working, working towards detonation in the flesh of his foot. He couldn't even feel the death seed. Wasn't that a joke?

"Cove'll take care of you," Finian said. He kissed her. Bewildered, Dolly called for him as he turned and walked rapidly away, not seeing the rain or the littered bodies.

He had gone but a dozen steps when something felled him and brought the dark.

Pain, incredible pain was his first sensation.

Then a warmth of flesh. Dolly bending over him. Through a

109

slatted section of solido panel he saw vertijets winking over Manhattan. Finian wriggled, then struggled up, screaming: "My leg . . . *what happened?*"

Crying, Dolly pressed him down.

"Cove did it. Cove operated. He hates them, Fin. He hates TTIC. Something about his wife. He said you ought to live, even with—I wish my mind would straighten out. I can't say things all right yet."

Finian fought the terror, the dull-fire agony. "Where is he?"

Dolly shuddered. "He packed it in a valise and ran for the Tunnel."

In a burst of fire the centre of Manhattan Prison blew up.

When the reverberations and Dolly's screams had stopped, the two of them clung together, listening to the hysterical automatic sirens at both ends of the island wailing as they hadn't wailed since the Triple Play War. Confused, hurting, glad of life, guilty and fearsomely glad and yet sickened by the suddenly swarming sky full of vertijets, their flaring emergency lights promising violence across the land, violence maybe everywhere, Finian clutched the girl to his shoulder and stared at the inferno of the prison island.

"My God, I think I started a war, Dolly. Sprool said—I didn't mean to start—"

The words tore out of him, almost animal: *"Is this the only way?"*

Dolly sobbed. There wasn't any other answer, except the sirens multiplying all around in the disrupted night.

THE LARGE ANT

by *Howard Fast*

There have been all kinds of notions and guesses as to how it would end. One held that sooner or later there would be too many people; another that we would do each other in, and the atom bomb made that a very good likelihood. All sorts of notions, except the simple fact that we were what we were. We could find a way to feed any number of people and perhaps even a way to avoid wiping each other out with the bomb; those things we are very good at, but we have never been any good at changing ourselves or the way we behave.

I know. I am not a bad man or a cruel man; quite to the contrary, I am an ordinary, humane person, and I love my wife and my children and I get along with my neighbours. I am like a great many other men, and I do the things they would do and just as thoughtlessly. There it is in a nutshell.

I am also a writer, and I told Lieberman, the curator, and Fitzgerald, the government man, that I would like to write down the story. They shrugged their shoulders. "Go ahead," they said, "because it won't make one bit of difference."

"You don't think it would alarm people?"

"How can it alarm anyone when nobody will believe it?"

"If I could have a photograph or two."

"Oh, no," they said then. "No photographs."

"What kind of sense does that make?" I asked them. "You are willing to let me write the story—why not the photographs so that people could believe me?"

"They still won't believe you. They will just say you faked the photographs, but no one will believe you. It will make for more confusion, and if we have a chance of getting out of this, confusion won't help."

"What will help?"

They weren't ready to say that, because they didn't know. So here is what happened to me, in a very straightforward and ordinary manner.

Every summer, sometime in August four good friends of mine and I go for a week's fishing on the St. Regis chain of lakes in the Adirondacks. We rent the same shack each summer; we drift around in canoes, and sometimes we catch a few bass. The fishing isn't very good, but we play cards well together, and we cook out and generally relax. This summer past, I had some things to do that couldn't be put off. I arrived three days late, and the weather was so warm and even and beguiling that I decided to stay on by myself for a day or two after the others left. There was a small flat lawn in front of the shack, and I made up my mind to spend at least three or four hours at short putts. That was how I happened to have the putting iron next to my bed.

The first day I was alone, I opened a can of beans and a can of beer for my supper. Then I lay down in my bed with *Life on the Mississippi*, a pack of cigarettes, and an eight-ounce chocolate bar. There was nothing I had to do, no telephone, no demands and no newspapers. At that moment, I was about as contented as any man can be in these nervous times.

It was still light outside, and enough light came in through the window above my head for me to read by. I was just reaching for a fresh cigarette, when I looked up and saw it on the foot of my bed. The edge of my hand was touching the golf club, and with a single motion I swept the club over and down, struck it a savage and accurate blow, and killed it. That was what I referred to before. Whatever kind of a man I am, I react as a man does. I think that any man, black, white or yellow, in China, Africa or Russia, would have done the same thing.

First I found that I was sweating all over, and then I knew I was going to be sick. I went outside to vomit, recalling that this hadn't happened to me since 1943, on my way to Europe on a tub of a Liberty Ship. Then I felt better and was able to go back into the shack and look at it. It was quite dead, but I had already made up my mind that I was not going to sleep alone in this shack.

I couldn't bear to touch it with my bare hands. With a piece of brown paper, I picked it up and dropped it into my fishing creel. That, I put into the trunk case of my car, along with what luggage I carried. Then I closed the door of the shack, got into my car and drove back to New York. I stopped once along the road, just before I reached the Thruway, to nap in the car for a little over an hour. It was almost dawn when I reached the city, and I had shaved, had a hot bath and changed my clothes before my wife awoke.

During breakfast, I explained that I was never much of a hand at the solitary business, and since she knew that, and since driving alone all night was by no means an extraordinary procedure for me, she didn't press me with any questions. I had two eggs, coffee and a cigarette. Then I went into my study, lit another cigarette, and contemplated my fishing creel, which sat upon my desk.

My wife looked in, saw the creel, remarked that it had too ripe a smell, and asked me to remove it to the basement.

"I'm going to dress," she said. The kids were still at camp. "I have a date with Ann for lunch—I had no idea you were coming back. Shall I break it?"

"No, please don't. I can find things to do that have to be done."

Then I sat and smoked some more, and finally I called the Museum, and asked who the curator of insects was. They told me his name was Bertram Lieberman, and I asked to talk to him. He had a pleasant voice. I told him that my name was Morgan, and that I was a writer, and he politely indicated that he had seen my name and read something that I had written. That is normal procedure when a writer introduces himself to a thoughtful person.

I asked Lieberman if I could see him, and he said that he had a busy morning ahead of him. Could it be tomorrow?

"I am afraid it has to be now," I said firmly.

"Oh? Some information you require."

"No. I have a specimen for you."

"Oh?" The "oh" was a cultivated, neutral interval. It asked and answered and said nothing. You have to develop that particular "oh".

"Yes. I think you will be interested."

"An insect?" he asked mildly.

"I think so."

"Oh? Large?"

"Quite large," I told him.

"Eleven o'clock? Can you be here then? On the main floor, to the right, as you enter."

"I'll be there," I said.

"One thing—dead?"

"Yes, it's dead."

"Oh?" again. "I'll be happy to see you at eleven o'clock, Mr. Morgan."

My wife was dressed now. She opened the door to my study and said firmly, "Do get rid of that fishing creel. It smells."

"Yes, darling. I'll get rid of it."

"I should think you'd want to take a nap after driving all night."

"Funny, but I'm not sleepy," I said. "I think I'll drop around to the museum."

My wife said that was what she liked about me, that I never tired of places like museums, police courts and third-rate night clubs.

Anyway, aside from a racetrack, a museum is the most interesting and unexpected place in the world. It was unexpected to have two other men waiting for me, along with Mr Lieberman, in his office. Lieberman was a skinny, sharp-faced man of about sixty. The government man, Fitzgerald, was small, dark-eyed, and wore gold-rimmed glasses. He was very alert, but he never told me what part of the government he represented. He just said "we", and it meant the government. Hopper, the third man, was comfortable-looking, pudgy, and genial. He was a United States senator with an interest in entomology, although before this morning I would have taken better than even money that such a thing not only wasn't, but could not be.

The room was large and square and plainly furnished, with shelves and cupboards on all walls.

We shook hands, and then Lieberman asked me, nodding at the creel, "Is that it?"

"That's it."

"May I?"

"Go ahead," I told him. "It's nothing that I want to stuff for the parlour. I'm making you a gift of it."

"Thank you, Mr. Morgan," he said, and then he opened the creel and looked inside. Then he straightened up, and the other two men looked at him inquiringly.

He nodded. "Yes."

The senator closed his eyes for a long moment. Fitzgerald took off his glasses and wiped them industriously. Lieberman spread a piece of plastic on his desk, and then lifted the thing out of my creel and laid it on the plastic. The two men didn't move. They just sat where they were and looked at it.

"What do you think it is, Mr. Morgan?" Lieberman asked me.

"I thought that was your department."

"Yes, of course. I only wanted your impression."

"An ant. That's my impression. It's the first time I saw an ant fourteen, fifteen inches long. I hope it's the last."

"An understandable wish," Lieberman nodded.

Fitzgerald said to me, "May I ask how you killed it, Mr. Morgan?"

"With an iron. A golf club, I mean. I was doing a little fishing with some friends up at St. Regis in the Adirondacks, and I brought the iron for my short shots. They're the worst part of my game, and when my friends left, I intended to stay on at our shack and do four or five hours of short putts. You see—"

"There's no need to explain," Hopper smiled, a trace of sadness on his face. "Some of our very best golfers have the same trouble."

"I was lying in bed, reading, and I saw it at the foot of my bed. I had the club—"

"I understand," Fitzgerald nodded.

"You avoid looking at it," Hopper said.

"It turns my stomach."

"Yes—yes, I suppose so."

114

Lieberman said, "Would you mind telling us why you killed it, Mr. Morgan."

"Why?"

"Yes—why?"

"I don't understand you," I said. "I don't know what you're driving at."

"Sit down, please, Mr. Morgan," Hopper nodded. "Try to relax. I'm sure this has been very trying."

"I still haven't slept. I want a chance to dream before I say how trying."

"We are not trying to upset you, Mr. Morgan," Lieberman said. "We do feel, however, that certain aspects of this are very important. That is why I am asking you why you killed it. You must have had a reason. Did it seem about to attack you?"

"No."

"Or make any sudden motion towards you?"

"No. It was just there."

"Then why?"

"This is to no purpose," Fitzgerald put in. "We know why he killed it."

"Do you?"

"The answer is very simple, Mr. Morgan. You killed it because you are a human being."

"Oh?"

"Yes. Do you understand?"

"No, I don't."

"Then why did you kill it?" Hopper put in.

"I was scared to death. I still am, to tell the truth."

Lieberman said, "You are an intelligent man, Mr. Morgan. Let me show you something." He then opened the doors of one of the wall cupboards, and there eight jars of formaldehyde and in each jar a specimen like mine—and in each case mutilated by the violence of its death. I said nothing. I just stared.

Lieberman closed the cupboard doors. "All in five days," he shrugged.

"A new race of ants," I whispered stupidly.

"No. They're not ants. Come here!" He motioned me to the desk and the other two joined me. Lieberman took a set of dissecting instruments out of his drawer, used one to turn the thing over and then pointed to the underpart of what would be the thorax in an insect.

"That looks like part of him, doesn't it, Mr. Morgan?"

"Yes, it does."

Using two of the tools, he found a fissure and pried the bottom apart. It came open like the belly of a bomber; it was a pocket, a pouch, a receptacle that the thing wore, and in it were four beautiful little tools or instruments or weapons, each about an inch and a half long. They were beautiful the way any object of functional purpose and loving creation is beautiful—the way the creature itself would have been beautiful, had it not been an insect and myself a man. Using tweezers, Lieberman took each instrument off the brackets that held it, offering each to me. And I took each one, felt it, examined it, and then put it down.

I had to look at the ant now, and I realised that I had not truly looked at it before. We don't look carefully at a thing that is horrible or repugnant to us. You can't look at anything through a screen of hatred. But now the hatred and the fear was dilute, and as I looked, I realised it was not an ant although like an ant. It was nothing that I had ever seen or dreamed of.

All three men were watching me, and suddenly I was on the defensive. "I didn't know! What do you expect when you see an insect that size?"

Lieberman nodded.

"What in the name of God is it?"

From his desk Lieberman produced a bottle and four small glasses. He poured and we drank it neat. I would not have expected him to keep good Scotch in his desk.

"We don't know," Hopper said. "We don't know what it is."

Lieberman pointed to the broken skull, from which a white substance oozed. "Brain material—a great deal of it."

"It could be a very intelligent creature," Hopper nodded.

Lieberman said, "It is an insect in developmental structure. We know very little about intelligence in our insects. It's not the same as what we call intelligence. It's a collective phenomenon—as if you were to think of the component parts of our bodies. Each part is alive, but the intelligence is a result of the whole. If that same pattern were to extend to creatures like this one—"

I broke the silence. They were content to stand there and stare at it.

"Suppose it were?"

"What?"

"The kind of collective intelligence you were talking about."

"Oh? Well, I couldn't say. It would be something beyond our wildest dreams. To us—well, what we are to an ordinary ant."

"I don't believe that," I said shortly, and Fitzgerald, the government man, told me quietly, "Neither do we. We guess."

116

"If it's that intelligent, why didn't it use one of those weapons on me?"

"Would that be a mark of intelligence?" Hopper asked mildly.

"Perhaps none of these are weapons," Lieberman said.

"Don't you know? Didn't the others carry instruments?"

"They did," Fitzgerald said shortly.

"Why? What were they?"

"We don't know," Lieberman said.

"But you can find out. We have scientists, engineers—good God, this is an age of fantastic instruments. Have them taken apart!"

"We have."

"Then what have you found out?"

"Nothing."

"Do you mean to tell me," I said, "that you can find out nothing about these instruments—what they are, how they work, what their purpose is?"

"Exactly," Hopper nodded. "Nothing, Mr. Morgan. They are meaningless to the finest engineers and technicians in the United States. You know the old story—suppose you gave a radio to Aristotle? What would he do with it? Where would he find power? And what would he receive with no one to send? It is not that these instruments are complex. They are actually very simple. We simply have no idea of what they can or should do."

"But there must be a weapon of some kind."

"Why?" Lieberman demanded. "Look at yourself, Mr. Morgan—a cultured and intelligent man, yet you cannot conceive of a mentality that does not include weapons as a prime necessity. Yet a weapon is an unusual thing, Mr. Morgan. An instrument of murder. We don't think that way, because the weapon has become the symbol of the world we inhabit. Is that civilised, Mr. Morgan? Or is the weapon and civilisation in the ultimate sense incompatible? Can you imagine a mentality to which the concept of murder is impossible—or let me say absent. We see everything through our own subjectivity. Why shouldn't some other—this creature, for example—see the process of mentation out of his subjectivity? So he approaches a creature of our world—and he is slain. Why? What explanation? Tell me, Mr. Morgan, what conceivable explanation could we offer a wholly rational creature for

117

this—" pointing to the thing on his desk. "I am asking you the question most seriously. What explanation?"

"An accident?" I muttered.

"And the eight jars in my cupboard? Eight accidents?"

"I think, Dr. Lieberman," Fitzgerald said, "that you can go a little too far in that direction."

"Yes, you would think so. It's a part of your own background. Mine is as a scientist. As a scientist, I try to be rational when I can. The creation of a structure of good and evil, or what we call morality and ethics, is a function of intelligence—and unquestionably the ultimate evil may be the destruction of conscious intelligence. That is why, so long ago, we at least recognised the injunction, 'thou shalt not kill!' even if we never gave more than lip service to it. But to a collective intelligence, such as this might be a part of, the concept of murder would be monstrous beyond the power of thought."

I sat down and lit a cigarette. My hands were trembling. Hopper apologised. "We have been rather rough with you, Mr. Morgan. But over the past days, eight other people have done just what you did. We are caught in the trap of being what we are."

"But tell me—where do these things come from?"

"It almost doesn't matter where they come from," Hopper said hopelessly. "Perhaps from another planet—perhaps from inside this one—or the moon or Mars. That doesn't matter. Fitzgerald thinks they come from a smaller planet, because their movements are apparently slow on earth. But Dr. Lieberman thinks that they move slowly because they have not discovered the need to move quickly. Meanwhile, they have the problem of murder and what to do with it. Heaven knows how many of them have died in other places—Africa, Asia, Europe."

"Then why don't you publicise this? Put a stop to it before it's too late!"

"We've thought of that," Fitzgerald nodded. "What then—panic, hysteria, charges that this is the result of the atom bomb? We can't change. We are what we are."

"They may go away," I said.

"Yes, they may," Lieberman nodded. "But if they are without the curse of murder, they may also be without the curse of fear. They may be social in the highest sense. What does society do with a murderer?"

"There are societies that put him to death—and there are other societies that recognise his sickness and lock him away,

118

where he can kill no more," Hopper said. "Of course, when a whole world is on trial, that's another matter. We have atom bombs now and other things, and we are reaching out to the stars—"

"I'm inclined to think that they'll run," Fitzgerald put in. "They may just have that curse of fear, Doctor."

"They may," Lieberman admitted. "I hope so."

But the more I think of it the more it seems to me that fear and hatred are the two sides of the same coin. I keep trying to think back, to recreate the moment when I saw it standing at the foot of my bed in the fishing shack. I keep trying to drag out of my memory a clear picture of what it looked like, whether behind that chitinous face and the two gently waving antennae there was any evidence of fear and anger. But the clearer the memory becomes, the more I seem to recall a certain wonderful dignity and repose. Not fear and not anger.

And more and more, as I go about my work, I get the feeling of what Hopper called "a world on trial". I have no sense of anger myself. Like a criminal who can no longer live with himself, I am content to be judged.

BARRIER

by *Anthony Boucher*

The first difficulty was with language.

That is only to be expected when you jump five hundred years; but it is none the less perplexing to have your first casual query of: "What city is this?" answered by the sentence: "Stappers will get you. Or be you Slanduch?"

It was significant that the first word John Brent heard in the State was "Stappers". But Brent could not know that then. It was only some hours later and fifty years earlier that he learned the details of the Stapper system. At the moment all that concerned him was food and plausibility.

His appearance was plausible enough. Following Derringer's advice he had travelled naked—"the one costume common to all ages," the scientist had boomed; "which would astonish you more, lad: a naked man, or an Elizabethan courtier in full

119

apparel?"—and commenced his life in the twenty-fifth century by burglary and the theft of a complete outfit of clothing. Iridescent woven plastics tailored in a half-clinging, half-flowing style that looked precious to Brent, but seemed both comfortable and functional.

No man alive in 2473 would have bestowed a second glance on the feloniously clad Brent, but in his speech, he realised at once, lay the danger. He pondered the alternatives presented by the stranger. The Stappers would get him, unless he was a Slanduch. Whatever the Stappers were, things that Get You sound menacing. "Slanduch," he replied.

The stranger nodded. "That bees O.K.," he said, and Brent wondered what he had committed himself to. "So what city is this?" he repeated.

"*Bees,*" the stranger chided. "Stappers be more severe now since Edict of 2470. Before they doed pardon some irregularities, but now none even from Slanduch."

"I be sorry," said Brent humbly, making a mental note that irregular verbs were for some reason perilous. "But for the third time—"

He had thought the wall beside them was solid. He realised now that part of it, at least, was only a deceptive glasslike curtain that parted to let forth a tall and vigorous man, followed by two shorter aides. All three of these wore robes similar to the iridescent garments of Brent and his companion, but of pure white.

The leader halted and barked out, "George Starvel?"

Brent saw a quiet sort of terror begin to grow on his companion's face. He nodded and held out his wrist.

The man in white glanced at what Brent decided must be an identification plaque. "Starvel," he announced, "you speaked against Barrier."

Starvel trembled. "Cosmos knows I doed not."

"Five mans know that you doed."

"Never. I only sayed—"

"You only! Enough!"

The rod appeared in the man's hand only for an instant. Brent saw no flame or discharge, but Starvel was stretched out on the ground and the two aides were picking him up as callously as though he were a log.

The man turned towards Brent, who was taking no chances. He flexed his legs and sprang into the air. His fingertips grasped the rim of the balcony above them, and his feet shot out into the white-robed man's face. His arm and shoulder muscles tensed to

120

their utmost. The smooth plastic surface was hell to keep a grip on. Beneath, he could see his adversary struggling blindly to his feet and groping for the rod. At last, desperately, Brent swung himself up and over the edge.

There was no time to contemplate the beauties of the orderly terrace garden. There was only time to note that there was but one door, and to make for it. It was open and led to a long corridor. Brent turned to the nearest door. Once you've damned yourself with Authority, any private citizen chosen at random is preferable to meeting your nemesis. He started at the door, and it opened before him. He hurried into an empty room.

He looked back at the door. It was shut now, and no one was near to have touched it. He peered into the two adjoining rooms, whose doors were equally obliging. Bathroom and bedroom. No kitchen. And no exit but the door he had come through.

He forced himself to sit down and think. Anything might happen before the Stapper caught up with him, for he had no doubt that was what the white-robed man must be. What had he learned about the twenty-fifth century in this brief encounter?

You must wear an identification plaque. (Memo. How to get one?) You must not use irregular verbs (or nouns; the Stapper had said "mans"). You must not speak against Barrier, whoever or whatever that meant. You must beware white-robed men who lurk behind false walls. You must watch out for rods that kill (query: or merely stun?). Doors open by selenium cells (query: how do they lock?). You must—

The door opened. But it was not the Stapper who stood there, but a tall and majestic woman of, at a guess, sixty. A noble figure—"Roman matron" were the words that flashed into Brent's mind.

The presence of a total stranger in her apartment seemed nowise disconcerting. She opened her arms in a broad gesture of welcome. "John Brent!" she exclaimed in delighted recognition. "It has beed so long!"

"I don't want a brilliant young scientific genius!" Derringer had roared when Brent answered his cryptically worded ad. "I've got 'em here in the laboratory. They've done grand work on the machine. I couldn't live without 'em, and there's not a one of 'em I'd trust out of this century. Not out of this decade. What I want is four things: A knowledge of history, for a background of analogy to understand what's being going on; linguistic ability, to adjust yourself as rapidly as possible to the

121

changes in language; physical strength and dexterity, to get yourself out of the scrapes that are bound to come up; and social adaptability. A chimpanzee of reasonably sub-human intelligence could operate the machine. What counts is what you'll be able to do and learn after you get there."

The knowledge of history and the physical qualities had been easy to demonstrate. The linguistic ability was a bit more complex; Derringer had contrived an intricate series of tests involving adjustment to phonetic changes and the capacity to assimilate the principles of a totally fictitious language invented for the occasion. The social adaptability was measured partly by an aptitude test, but largely, Brent guessed, by Derringer's own observation during the weeks of preparation after his probationary hiring.

He had passed all four requirements with flying colours. At least Derringer had grinned at him through the black beard and grunted the reluctant, "Good man!" that was his equivalent of rhapsodic praise. His physical agility had already stood him in good stead, and his linguistic mind was rapidly assimilating the new aspects of the language (there were phonetic alterations as well as the changes in vocabulary and inflection—he was particularly struck by the fact that the vowels *a* and *o* no longer possessed the diphthongal off-glide so characteristic of English, but were pure vowels like the Italian *e* and *o*) but his social adaptability was just now hitting a terrific snag.

What the hell do you do when a Roman matron whom you have never seen, born five hundred years after you, welcomes you by name and exclaims that it has beed a long time? (This regular past participle of *be,* Brent reflected, gives the speaker something of the quality of a Bostonian with a cold in the nose.)

For a moment he toyed with the rash notion that she might likewise be a time traveller, someone whom he had known in 1942. Derringer had been positive that this was the first such trip ever attempted; but someone leaving the twentieth century later might still be an earlier arrival in the twenty-fifth. He experimented with the idea hesitantly.

"I suppose," Brent ventured, "you could call five hundred years a long time, in its relative way."

The Roman matron frowned. "Do not jest, John. Fifty years be not five hundred. I will confess that first five years seemed at times like five centuries, but after fifty—one does not feel so sharply."

Does was of course pronounced *dooze.* All r's, even terminal, were lightly trilled. These facts Brent noted in the back of his mind, but the fore part was concerned with the immediate situation. If this woman chose to accept him as an acquaintance—it was nowise unlikely that his double should be wandering about in this century—it meant probable protection from the Stapper. His logical mind protested, "Could this double have your name?" but he shushed it.

"Did you," he began, and caught himself. "Doed you see anyone in the hall—a man in white?"

The Roman matron moaned. "Oh, John! Do Stappers seek you again? But of course. If you have comed to destroy Barrier, they must destroy you."

"Whoa there!" Brent had seen what happened to one person who had "speaked against Barrier." "I didn't . . . doedn't . . . say anything against Barrier. Not me."

The friendliness began to die from her clear blue eyes. "And I believed you," she said sorrowfully. "You telled us of this second Barrier and sweared to destroy it. We think you beed one of us. And now—"

No amount of social adaptability can resist a sympathetic and dignified woman on the verge of tears. Besides, this apartment was for the moment a valuable haven, and if she thought he was a traitor of some sort—

"Look," said Brent. "You see, I am—there isn't any use at this moment trying to be regular—I am not whoever you think I am. I never saw you before. I couldn't have conceivably. Because this is the first instant I've ever been in your time."

"If you wish to lie to me, John—"

"I'm not lying. And I'm not John—at least not the one you're thinking of. I'm John Brent, I'm twenty-eight years old, and I was born in 1914—a good five and a half centuries ago."

You'd think a remark like that would have some effect. It sounds like an impressive curtain line. There should at least be a tableau of stunned reaction. But the Roman matron simply stared at him sadly and murmured, "I know, John, I know. Then why do you deny me and all our plans? What will Stephen think?"

The amazement turned out to be Brent's. "You . . . you know that I'm a time traveller?"

"John, my dear, why be you so foolish? You be safe from Stappers here. Stephen has treated walls against listening. And you know that to admit to being time traveller is as dangerous as to admit your plans against Barrier. Trust me, John."

"For some unknown reason, madam, I do trust you. That's why I'm telling you everything. I'm asking you to be my ally. And you persist in—"

The door opened. The man who entered was as tall as the Stapper, but wore the civilian's iridescent robes. His long beard seemed to have caught a little of their rainbow influence; it was predominantly red, but brown and black and white glinted in it. The hair on his head was greying. He might have been anywhere from forty-five to a vigorous and well-preserved seventy.

"We have a guest, sister?" he asked politely.

The Roman matron made a despairing gesture. "You don't recognise him? And John—you don't know Stephen?"

Stephen slapped his thigh and barked—a sound that seemed to represent a laugh of pleasure. "Cosmos!" he cried. "John Brent! I told you, Martha. I knew he wouldn't fail us."

"Stephen!" she exclaimed in shocked tones.

"Hang the irregularities! Can't I greet John with the old words that comed—no, by Cosmos—came from the same past he came from? See, John—don't I talk the old language well? I even use article—pardon me, the article."

Brent's automatic mental notebook recorded the fact, which he had already suspected, that an article was as taboo as an irregular verb. But around this self-governing notation system swirled utter confusion. It might possibly have been just his luck to run into a madwoman. But two mad brains in succession with identical delusions were too much. And Stephen had known he was from the past, with no cue given him.

"I'm afraid," he said simply, "this is too much for me. Suppose we all sit down and have a drink of something and talk this over."

Stephen smiled. "You remember our bond, eh? And not many places in State you'll find it. Even fewer than before." He crossed to a cabinet and returned with three glasses of colourless liquid.

Brent seized his eagerly and downed it. A drink might help the swirling. It might— The drink had gone down smoothly and tastelessly. Now, however, some imp began dissecting atoms in his stomach and shooting off a bombardment stream of particles that zoomed up through his throat into his brain, where they set off a charge of explosive of hitherto unknown power. Brent let out a strangled yelp.

Stephen barked again. "Good bond, eh, John?"

124

Brent managed to focus his host through the blurring lens of his tears. "Sure," he nodded feebly. "Swell. And now let me try to explain—"

The woman looked sadly at her brother. "He denies us, Stephen. He sayes that he haves never seed me before. He forgets all that he ever sweared about Barrier."

A curious look of speculation came into Stephen's brown eyes. "Bees this true, John? You have never seed us before in your life?"

"But, Stephen, you know—"

"Hush, Martha. I say in *his* life. Bees it true, John?"

"It bees. God knows it bees. I have never seen . . . seed either of you in my life."

"But, Stephen—"

"I understand now, Martha. Remember when he telled us of Barrier and his resolve?"

"Can I forget?"

"How doed he know of Barrier? Tell me that."

"I don't know," Martha confessed. "I have wondered—"

"He knowed of Barrier then because he bees here now. He telled me then just what we must now tell him."

"Then for Heaven's sake," Brent groaned, "tell me."

"Your pardon, John. My sister bees not so quick to grasp source of these temporal confusions. More bond?" He had the bottle in his hand when he suddenly stopped, thrust it back in the cabinet, and murmured, "Go into bedroom."

Brent obeyed. This was no time for displaying initiative. And no sooner had the bedroom door closed behind him than he heard the voice of the Stapper. (The mental notebook recorded that apartment buildings must be large, if it had taken this long for the search to reach here.)

"No," Stephen was saying. "My sister and I have beed here for past half-hour. We seed no one."

"State thanks you," the Stapper muttered so casually that the phrase must have been an official formula. His steps sounded receding. Then they stopped, and there was the noise of loud sniffs.

"Dear God," thought Brent, "have they crossed the bulls with bloodhounds?"

"Bond," the Stapper announced.

"Dear me," came Martha's voice. "Who haves beed in here today, Stephen?"

"I'm a homeopath," said the Stapper. "Like cures like. A little bond might make me forget I smelled it."

125

There was a bark from Stephen and a clink of glasses. No noise from either of them as they downed the liquor. Those, sir, were men. (Memo: Find out why such unbelievable rotgut is called *bond,* of all things.)

"State thanks you," said the Stapper, and laughed. "You know George Starvel, don't you?"

A slightly hesitant "Yes" from Stephen.

"When you see him again, I think you'll find he haves changed his mind. About many things."

There was silence. Then Stephen opened the bedroom door and beckoned Brent back into the living room. He handed the time traveller a glass of bond and said, "I will try to be brief."

Brent, now forewarned, sipped gingerly at the liquor and found it cheerfully warming as he assimilated the new facts.

In the middle of the twenty-fourth century, he learned, civilisation had reached a high point of comfort, satisfaction, achievement—and stagnation. The combination of atomic power and De Bainville's revolutionary formulation of the principles of labour and finance had seemed to solve all economic problems. The astounding development of synthetics had destroyed the urgent need for raw materials and colonies and abolished the distinction between haves and have-nots among nations. Schwarzwalder's "Compendium" had achieved the dream of the early Encyclopaedists—the complete systematisation of human knowledge. Farthing had regularised the English language, an achievement paralleled by the work of Zinsmeister, Timofeov, and Tamayo y Sárate in their respective tongues. (These four languages now dominated the earth. French and Italian had become corrupt dialects of German, and the Oriental languages occupied in their own countries something the position of Greek and Latin in nineteenth-century Europe, and doomed soon to the complete oblivion which swallowed up those classic tongues in the twenty-first.)

There was nothing more to be achieved. All was known, all was accomplished. Nakamura's Law of Spacial Acceleration had proved interplanetary travel to be impossible for all time. Charnwood's Law of Temporal Metabolism had done the same for time travel. And the Schwarzwalder "Compendium," which everyone admired and no one had read, established such a satisfactory and flawless picture of knowledge that it was obviously impossible that anything remained to be discovered.

It was then that Dyce-Farnsworth proclaimed the Stasis of Cosmos. A member of the Anglo-Physical Church, product of the long contemplation by English physicists of the metaphysical aspects of science, he came as the prophet needed to pander to the self-satisfaction of the age.

He was cautiously aided by Farthing's laws of regularity. The article, direct or indirect, Farthing had proved to be completely unnecessary—had not languages as world-dominant as Latin in the first centuries and Russian in the twenty-first found no need for it?—and semantically misleading. "Article," he said in his final and comprehensive study "This Bees Speech", "bees prime corrupter of human thinking."

And thus the statement so beloved in the twentieth century by metaphysical-minded scientists and physical-minded divines, "God is the cosmos," became with Dyce-Farnsworth "God bees cosmos," and hence, easily and inevitably, "God bees Cosmos," so that the utter scientific impersonality became a personification of Science. Cosmos replaced Jehovah, Baal and Odin.

The love of Cosmos was not man nor his works, but Stasis. Man was tolerated by Cosmos that he might achieve Stasis. All the millenniums of human struggle had been aimed at this supreme moment when all was achieved, all was known, and all was perfect. Therefore this supernal Stasis must at all costs be maintained. Since Now was perfect, any alteration must be imperfect and taboo.

From this theory logically evolved the State, whose duty was to maintain the perfect Stasis of Cosmos. No totalitarian government had ever striven so strongly to iron out all doubt and dissension. No religious bigotry had ever found heresy so damnable and worthy of destruction. The Stasis must be maintained.

It was, ironically, the aged Dyce-Farnsworth himself who, in a moment of quasi-mystical intuition, discovered the flaw in Charnwood's Law of Temporal Metabolism. And it was clear to him what must be done.

Since the Stasis of Cosmos did not practice time travel, any earlier or later civilisation that did so must be imperfect. Its emissaries would cause imperfection. There must be a Barrier.

The mystic went no further than that dictum, but the scientists of the State put his demand into practical terms. "Do not ask how at this moment," Stephen added. "I be not man to explain that. But you will learn." The first Barrier was a failure. It destroyed itself and to no apparent result. But now, fifty years later, the fears of time travel had grown. The original idea of the imperfection of emissaries had been lost. Now time travel was

127

in itself imperfect and evil. Any action taken against it would be an offering of praise to Cosmos. And the new Barrier was being erected.

"But John knows all this," Martha protested from time to time, and Stephen would shake his head sadly and smile sympathetically at Brent.

"I don't believe a word of it," Brent said at last. "Oh, the historical outline's all right. I trust you on that. And it works out so sweetly by analogy. Take the religious fanaticism of the sixteenth century, the smug scientific self-satisfaction of the nineteenth, the power domination of the twentieth—fuse them and you've got your State. But the Barrier's impossible. There's no principle on which it could work, and nuts to it."

"Charnwood claimed there beed no principle on which time travel canned work. And here you be."

"That's different," said Brent vaguely. "But all this talk of destroying the Barrier is nonsense. There's no need to."

"Indeed there bees need, John. For two reasons: one, that we may benefit by wisdom of travellers from other ages; and two, that positive act of destroying this Barrier, which bees worshipped now with something like fetishism, bees strongest weapon with which can strike against State. For there be these few of us who hope to save mankind from this fanatical complacency that race have fallen into. George Starvel beed one," Stephen added sadly.

"I saw Starvel— But that isn't what I mean. There's no need because the Barrier won't work."

"But you told us that it haved to be destroyed," Martha protested. "That it doed work, and that we—"

"Hush," said Stephen gently. "John, will you trust us far enough to show us your machine? I think I can make matters clearer to Martha then."

"If you'll keep me out of the way of Stappers."

"That we can never guarantee—yet. But day will come when mankind cans forget Stappers and State, that I swear." There was stern and noble courage in Stephen's face and bearing as he drained his glass of bond to that pledge.

"I had a break when I landed here," John Brent explained on the way. "Derringer equipped the machine only for temporal motion. He explained that it meant running a risk; I might find that the coast line had sunk and I'd arrive under water, or God knows what. But he hadn't worked out the synchronised adjustment for temporo-spacial motion yet, and he wanted to

128

get started. I took the chance, and luck was good. Where the Derringer lab used to be is now apparently a deserted warehouse. Everything's dusty and not a sign of human occupation."

Stephen's eyes lit up as they approached the long low building of translucent bricks. "Remember, Martha?"

Martha frowned and nodded.

Faint light filtered through the walls to reveal the skeletal outlines of the machine. Brent switched on a light on the panel which gave a dim glow.

"There's not much to see even in a good light," he explained. "Just these two seats—Derringer was planning on teams when he built it, but decided later that one man with sole responsibility to himself would do better—and this panel. These instruments are automatic—they adjust to the presence of another machine ahead of you in the time line. The only control the operator bothers with is this." He indicated the double dial set at 2473.

"Why doed you choose this year?"

"At random. Derringer set the outer circle at 2400—half a millennium seemed a plausible choice. Then I spun the inner dial blindfold. When this switch here is turned, you create a certain amount of temporal potential, positive or negative—which is as loose as applying those terms to magnetic poles, but likewise just as convenient. For instance if I turn it to here"—he spun the outer dial to 2900—"you'll have five hundred years of positive potential which'll shoot you ahead to 2973. Or set it like this, and you'll have five centuries of negative, which'll pull you back practically to where I started from."

Stephen frowned. "*Ahead* and *back* be of course nonsense words in this connection. But they may be helpful to Martha in visualising it. Will you please show Martha the back of your dial?"

"Why?" There was no answer. Brent shrugged and climbed into the seat. The Roman matron moved around the machine and entered the other seat as he loosed the catch on the dial and opened it, as one did for oiling the adjusting gears.

Stephen said, "Look well, my dear. What be the large wheels maked of?"

"Aceroid, of course. Don't you remember how Alex—"

"Don't remember, Martha. Look. What *be* they?"

Martha gasped. "Why, they . . . they be pure aluminium."

"Very well. Now don't you understand—*Ssh!*" He broke off

and moved towards the doorway. He listened there a moment, then slipped out of sight.

"What does he have?" Brent demanded as he closed the dial. "The ears of an elk-hound?"

"Stephen have hyperacute sense of hearing. He bees proud of it, and it haves saved us more than once from Stappers. When people be engaged in motive work against State—"

A man's figure appeared again in the doorway. But its robes were white. "Good God!" Brent exclaimed. "Jiggers, the Staps!"

Martha let out a little squeal. A rod appeared in the Stapper's hand. Brent's eyes were so fixed on the adversary that he did not see the matron's hand move towards the switch until she had turned it. Then he shut his eyes and groaned.

Brent had somehow instinctively shut his eyes during his first time transit. *During,* he reflected, is not the right word. *At the time of?* Hardly. How can you describe an event of time movement without suggesting another time measure perpendicular to the time line? At any rate, he had shut them in a laboratory in 1942 and opened them an instant later in a warehouse in 2473.

Now he kept them shut. He had to think for a moment. He had been playing with the dial—where was it set when Martha jerked the switch? 1973, as best he remembered. And he had now burst into that world in plastic garments of the twenty-fifth century, accompanied by a Roman matron who had in some time known him for fifty years.

He did not relish the prospect. And besides he was bothered by that strange jerking, tearing sensation that had twisted his body when he closed his eyes. He had felt nothing whatsoever on the previous trip. Had something gone wrong this time? Had—

"It doesn't work!" said Martha indignantly.

Brent opened his eyes. He and Martha sat in the machine in a dim warehouse of translucent brick.

"We be still here," she protested vigorously.

"Sure we're still here." Brent frowned. "But what you mean is, we're still *now*."

"You talk like Stephen. What do you mean?"

"Or are we?" His frowned deepened. "If we're still now, where is that Stapper? He didn't vanish just because you pulled a switch. How old is this warehouse?"

"I don't know. I think about sixty years. It beed fairly new when I beed a child. Stephen and I used to play near here."

130

"Then we could have gone back a few decades and still be here. Yes, and look—those cases over there. I'd swear they weren't here before. After. Whatever. Then, when we saw the Stapper." He looked at the dial. It was set to 1973. And the warehouse was new some time around 2420.

Brent sat and stared at the panel.

"What bees matter?" Martha demanded. "Where be we?"

"Here, same like always. But what bothers me is just *when* we are. Come on; want to explore?"

Martha shook her head. "I want to stay here. And I be afraid for Stephen. Doed Stappers get him? Let's go back."

"I've got to check on things. Something's gone wrong, and Derringer'll never forgive me if I don't find out what and why. You stay here if you want."

"Alone?"

Brent suppressed several remarks concerning women, in the abstract and the particular. "Stay or go, I don't care. I'm going."

Martha sighed. "You have changed so, John—"

In front of the warehouse was an open field. There had been buildings there when Brent last saw it. And in the field three young people were picnicking. The sight reminded Brent that it was a long time since he'd eaten. How you could measure gaps between meals when you shoot about among centuries, he didn't know; but he was hungry.

He made towards the trio. There were two men and a girl. One man was blond, the other and the girl were brilliantly red-headed. The girl had much more than even that hair to recommend her. She— Brent's eyes returned to the red-headed man. There was no mistaking those deep brown eyes, that sharp and noble nose. The beard was scant, but still there was no denying—

Brent sprang forward with an eager cry of "Stephen!"

The young man looked at him blankly. "Yes," he said politely. "What do you want?"

Brent mentally kicked himself. He had met Stephen in advanced age. What would the Stephen of twenty know of him? And suddenly he began to understand a great deal. The whole confusion of that first meeting started to fade away.

"If I tell you," he said rapidly, "that I know that you be Stephen, that you have sister Martha, that you drink bond despite Stappers, and that you doubt wisdom of Barrier, will you accept me as a man you can trust?"

131

"Cosmos aeons!" the blond young man drawled. "Stranger knows plenty, Stephen. If he bees Stapper, you'll have your mind changed."

The scantily bearded youth looked a long while into Brent's eyes. Then he felt in his robe, produced a flask, and handed it over. Brent drank and returned it. Their hands met in a firm clasp.

Stephen grinned at the others. "My childs, I think stranger brings us adventure. I feel like someone out of novel by Varnichek." He turned back to Brent. "Do you know these others, too?"

Brent shook his head.

"Krasna and Alex. And your name?"

"John Brent."

"And what can we do for you, John?"

"First tell me year."

Alex laughed, and the girl smiled. "And how long have you beed on a bonder?" Alex asked.

A bonder, Brent guessed, would be a bond bender. "This bees my first drink," he said, "since 1942. Or perhaps 2473, according as how you reckon."

Brent was not disappointed in the audience reaction this time.

It's easy to see what must have happened, Brent wrote that night in the first entry of the journal Derringer had asked him to keep. He wrote longhand, an action that he loathed. The typewriter which Stephen had kindly offered him was equipped with a huge keyboard bearing the forty-odd characters of the Farthing phonetic alphabet, and Brent declined the loan.

We're at the first Barrier—the one that failed. It was dedicated to Cosmos and launched this afternoon. My friends were among the few inhabitants not ecstatically present at the ceremony. Since then they've collected reports for me. The damned contrivance had to be so terrifically overloaded that it blew up. Dyce-Farnsworth was killed and will be a holy martyr to Cosmos for ever.

But in an infinitesimal fraction of a second between the launching and the explosion, the Barrier existed. That was enough. It is gone now. It is of no use to protect the people of this smug and sacred Stasis from raids from a more human future. But it existed at that one point in time, existed effectively enough to stop me dead.

Which makes keeping this journal, my dear Dr. Derringer, a magnificently silly act. In all likelihood neither you nor anyone else before 2423 will ever see it. (Will ever have seen it?) But you see, sir, I obey instructions. Nice of me, isn't it?

And I've been finding out all I can. Stephen is good on history, but lousy on science. The blond young Alex reverses the combination. From him I've learned, or tried to learn, the theory back of the Barrier.

The Barrier established, in that fractional second, a powerful magnetic field in the temporal dimension. As a result, any object moving along the time line is cutting the magnetic field. Hysteresis sets up strong eddy currents which bring the object, in this case me, to an abrupt halt. Cf. that feeling of twisting shock that I had when my eyes were closed.

I pointed out to Alex that I must somehow have crossed this devilish Barrier in going from 1942 to 2473. He accounts for that apparent inconsistency by saying that I was then travelling with the time stream, though at a greater rate; the blockage lines of force were end-on and didn't stop me.

Brent paused and read the last two paragraphs aloud to the young scientist who was tinkering with the travelling machine. "How's that, Alex? Clear enough?"

"It will do." Alex frowned. "Of course we need whole new vocabulary for temporal concepts. We fumble so helplessly in analogies—" He rose. "There bees nothing more I can do for this now. Tomorrow I'll bring out some tools from shop, and see if I can find some aceroid gears to fit control."

"Good man. I may not be able to go back in time from here; but one thing I can do is go forward. Forward to just before they launch that second Barrier. I've got a job to do."

Alex gazed admiringly at the machine. "Wonderful piece of work. Your Dr. Derringer bees great man."

"Only he didn't allow for the effects of temporo-magnetic hysteresis on his mechanism. Thank God for you, Alex."

"Willn't you come back to house?"

Brent shook his head. "I'm taking no chances on curious Stappers. I'm sticking here with Baby. See that the old lady's comfortable, will you?"

"Of course. But tell me: who bees she? She willn't talk at all."

"Nobody. Just a temporal hitch-hiker."

Martha's first sight of the young Stephen had been a terrible shock. She had stared at him speechlessly for long minutes, and then gone into a sort of inarticulate hysteria. Any attempt at explanation of her status, Brent felt, would only make matters

133

worse. There was nothing to do but leave her to the care—which seemed both tender and efficient—of the girl Krasna, and let her life ride until she could resume it normally in her own time.

He resumed his journal:

Philological notes: Stapper, as I should have guessed, is a corruption of Gestapo. Slanduch, *which poor Starvel suggested I might be, had me going for a bit. Asking about that, learned that there is more than one State. This, the smuggest and most fanatical of them all, embraces North America, Australia, and parts of Eastern Asia. Its official language is, of course, Farthingised English. Small nuclear groups of English-speaking people exist in the other States, and have preserved the older and irregular forms of speech. (Cf. American mountaineers, and Spanish Jews in Turkey.) A Slanduch is a member of one of these groups.*

It took me some time to realise the origin of this word, but it's obvious enough: Auslandsdeutsche, *the Germans who existed similarly cut off from the main body of their culture. With these two common loan words suggesting a marked domination at some time of the German language, I asked Alex—and I must confess almost fearfully—"Then did Germany win the war?"*

He not unnaturally countered with, "Which war?"

"The Second World War. Started in 1939."

"Second—Cosmis æons, John, you can't expect me to remember numbers of all those twentieth-century World Wars, can you?"

I am almost afraid to ask the more historically accurate Stephen.

Brent paused, and wished for Stephen's ears to determine the nature of that small noise outside. Or was it pure imagination? He went on:

These three—Stephen, Alex and Krasna—have proved to be the ideal hosts for a traveller of my nature. Any devout believer in Cosmos, any loyal upholder of the Stasis would have turned me over to the Stappers for my first slip in speech or ideas.

They seem to be part of what corresponds to the Underground Movements of my own century. They try to accomplish a sort of boring from within, a subtle sowing of doubts as to the Stasis. Eventually they hope for more positive action; so far it is purely mental sabotage.

Their motives are various. Some are crackpots, pure and simple. Some are artists who rebel against the limitations imposed by the State. Some are scientists who remain

134

unconvinced that Schwarzwalder solved everything. Stephen says simply that he is a Christian—which most of the others consider an almost comic anachronism—and that Cosmos is a false god; but I think the Christian love of mankind is a stronger motive force in him than any doctrinal matter of the rivalry of names for godhead. Alex is a Seepy—a word the meaning of which I haven't yet been able to gather. Krasna—

It *was* a noise. Brent set down his stylus and moved along the wall as quietly as possible to the door. He held his breath while the door slid gently inward. Then, as the figure entered, he pounced.

Stappers have close-cropped hair and flat manly chests. Brent released the girl abruptly and muttered a confused apology.

"It bees only me," she said shyly. "Krasna. Doed I startle you?"

"A bit," he confessed. "Alex and Stephen warned me what might happen if a Stapper stumbled on my machine here."

"I be sorry, John."

"It's all right. But you shouldn't be wandering around alone at night like this. In fact, you shouldn't be mixed up in this at all. Leave it to Stephen and Alex and me."

"Mans!" she pouted. "Don't you think womans have any right to fun?"

"I don't know that fun's exactly the word. But since you're here, milady, let me extend the hospitality of the camp. Alex left me some bond. That poison grows on you. And tell me why's it called that?"

"Stephen told me once, but I can't— Oh, yes. When they prohibited all drinking because drinking makes you think world bees better than it really bees and of course if you make yourself different world that bees against Stasis and so they prohibited it but they keeped on using it for medical purposes and that beed in warehouses and pretty soon no one knowed any other kind of liquor so it bees called bond. Only I don't see why."

"I don't suppose," Brent remarked, "that anybody in this century has ever heard of one Gracie Allen, but her spirit is immortal. The liquor in the warehouses was probably kept under government bond."

"Oh—" she said meekly. "I'll remember. You know everything, don't you?"

Brent looked at her suspiciously, but there was no irony in the remark. "How's the old lady getting on?"

"Fine. She bees sleeping now at last. Alex gave her some dormitin. She bees nice, John."

135

"And yet your voice sounds worried. What's the matter?"

"She bees so much like my mother only, of course, I don't remember my mother much because I beed so little when Stappers taked my father and then my mother doedn't live very long but I do remember her some and your old lady bees so much like her. I wish I haved knowed my mother goodlier, John. She beed dear. She—" She lowered her voice in the tone of one imparting a great secret. "She cooked!"

Brent remembered their tasteless supper of extracts, concentrates, and synthetics, and shuddered. "I wish you had known her, Krasna."

"You know what cooking means? You go out and you dig up roots and you pick leaves off plants and some people they even used to take animals, and then you apply heat and—"

"I know. I used to be a fair-to-middling cook myself, some five hundred years ago. If you could lead me to a bed of coals, a clove of garlic, and a two-inch steak, milady, I'd guarantee to make your eyes pop."

"Garlic? Steak?" Her eyes were wide with wonder. "What be those?"

Brent explained. For ten minutes he talked of the joys of food, of the sheer ecstatic satisfaction of good eating that passes the love of woman, the raptures of art, or the wonders of science. Then her questions began to pour forth.

"Stephen learns things out of books and Alex learns things in lab but I can't do that so goodly and they both make fun of me only you be real and I can learn things from you, John, and it bees wonderful. Tell me—"

And Krasna, with a greedy ear, devoured up his discourse.

"—and men were free," he ended. "Free to damn and ruin themselves if they choose, but free also to live nobly, enriching the world and themselves by their striving. For all perfection comes from within and the 'perfection' that is imposed from without is as frivolous and stupid as the trimmings on ginger-cake. The free man may be bad, but only the free man can be good. And all the kingdom and the power and the glory—call it of God, call it of Cosmos—must arise from the free will of man."

He stopped, somewhat surprised at his own eloquence. The tyrannical smugness of this age was working upon him powerfully.

Krasna was kneeling at his feet. He could feel the warmth of her body against his. "Go on," she whispered. Her large eyes glowed up at him.

"That's all. And damned if I know how I talked that long."
His hands rested on the soft mass of her flowing red hair.

"You be wonderful," she murmured.

Brent coughed and said, "Nuts!" His hand stroked her head
gently.

The rest of that evening was not recorded in the Derringer
journal.

The machine was not repaired the next day, or the next. Alex
kept making plausible, if not quite intelligible, technical
excuses. Martha kept to her room and fretted; but Brent rather
welcomed the delay. There was no hurry; leaving this time
several days later had no effect on when they reached 2473. But
he had some difficulty making that point clear to the matron.

This delay gave him an opportunity to see something of the
State in action, and any information acquired was apt to be
useful when the time came. With various members of Stephen's
informal and illicit group he covered the city. He visited a
church of Cosmos and heard the official doctrine on the failure
of the Barrier—the Stasis of Cosmos did not permit time travel,
so that even an attempt to prohibit it, by recognising its
existence affronted the Stasis. He visited libraries and found
only those works which had established or upheld the Stasis, all
bound in the same uniform format which the Cosmic
Bibliographical Committee of 2407 had ordained as ideal and
static. He visited scientific laboratories, and found brilliant
young dullards plodding away endlessly at what had already
been established; imaginative research was manifestly perilous.

He heard arid stretches of intolerable music composed according to the strict Farinelli system, which forbade, among
other things, any alteration of key or time for the duration of a
composition. He went to a solly, which turned out to be a
deceptively solid three-dimensional motion picture. It was a flat
and undramatic exposition of the glories of Stasis; but Brent
suspected the author of being an Undergrounder. The villain,
even though triumphantly bested by the Stappers in the end,
had all the most plausible and best-written speeches, some of
them ingenious and strong enough to sow doubts in the
audience.

If, Brent thought disgustedly, anything could sow doubts in
this smug herd of cattle. For the people of the State seemed to
take the deepest and most loving pride in everything pertaining
to the State and to the Stasis of Cosmos. The churches, the
libraries, the laboratories, the music, the sollies, all represented
137

humanity at its highest peak. We have attained perfection, have we not? Then all this bees perfect, and we love it.

"What we need," he expostulated to Alex and Stephen one night, "is more of me. Lots more. Scads of us pouring in from all ages to light firecrackers under these dopes. Every art and every science has degenerated far worse than anything did in the Dark Ages. The surface attainment is still there; but everything's gone from under it. Man cannot be man without striving; and all striving is abolished. God, I think if I lived in this age and believed in the Stasis, I'd become a Stapper. Better their arrogant cruelty than the inhuman indifference of everybody else."

"I have brother who bees Stapper," said Stephen. "I do not recommend it. To descend to level of cows and oxes bees one thing. To become wolves and jackals bees another."

"I've gathered that those rods paralyse the nerve centres, right? But what happens to you after that in Stappers' hands?"

"It bees not good. First you be treated according to expert psychoanalytic and psychometric methods so as to alter your concepts and adjust you to Stasis. If that fails, you can be carefully reduced to harmless idiocy. Sometimes they find mind that bees too strong for treatment. He bees killed, and Stappers be allowed to play with him first."

Brent shuddered. "Not nice."

"It'll never happen to me," Alex said earnestly. "I be prepared. You see this?" He indicated a minute plastic box suspended around his neck. "It contains tiny amount of radioactive matter sensitised to wave length of Stappers' rods. They will never change my mind."

"It explodes?"

Alex grinned. "Stay away from me if rods start waving."

"It seems," Brent mused, "as though cruelty were the only human vice left. Games are lost, drinking is prohibited—and that most splendid of vices, imaginative speculation, is unheard of. I tell you, you need lots of me."

Stephen frowned. "Before failure of Barrier, we often wondered why we never seed time travellers. We doubted Charnwood's Law and yet— We decided there beed only two explanations. Either time travel bees impossible, or time travellers cannot be seed or intervene in time they visit. Now, of course, we can see that Barrier stopped all from future, and perhaps you be only one from past. And still—"

"Exactly," said Alex. "And still. If other travellers came from future, why beed they not also stopped by Barrier? One of our friends haves haved opportunity to search Stapper records since breakdown of Barrier. No report on strange and unidentified travellers anywhere."

"That cans mean only one thing." Stephen looked worried. "Second Barrier, Barrier you telled us of, John, must be successful."

"The hell it will be. Come on, Alex. I'm getting restless. When can I start?"

Alex smiled. "Tomorrow. I be ready at last."

"Good man. Among us, we are going to blow this damned Stasis back into the bliss of manly and uncertain striving. And in fifty years we'll watch it together."

Krasna was waiting outside the room when Brent left. "I knowed you willed be talking about things I doedn't understand."

"You can understand this, milady. Alex has got everything fixed, and we leave tomorrow."

Krasna put her soft hand gently in his and wordlessly walked back to the warehouse with him.

"Now," said Brent to Stephen after what was euphemistically termed breakfast, "I've got to see the old lady and find out just what the date is for the proposed launching of the second Barrier."

Stephen beamed. "It bees such pleasure to hear old speech, articles and all."

Alex had a more practical thought. "How can you set it to one day? I thinked your dial readed only in years."

"There's a vernier attachment that's accurate—or should be, it's never been tested yet—to within two days. I'm allowing a week's margin. I don't want to be around too long and run chances with Stappers."

"Krasna will miss you."

"Krasna's a funny name. You others have names that were in use back in my day."

"Oh, it bees not name. It bees only what everyone calls red-headed girls. I think it goes back to century of Russian domination."

"Yes," Alex added. "Stephen's sister's real name bees Martha, but we never call her that."

John Brent gaped. "I . . . I've got to go see the old lady," he stammered. "The old lady—the red-head—Martha—Krasna Stephen's sister—"

Small wonder she was shocked when he didn't know her!

From the window of the grey-haired Martha-Krasna he could see the red-headed Krasna-Martha outside. He held on to a solid and reassuring chair and said, "Well, madam, I have news. We're going back today."

"Oh thank Cosmos!"

"But I've got to find out something from you. What was the date set for the launching of the second Barrier?"

"Let me see— I know it beed holiday. Yes, it beed May 1st."

"My, my! May Day a holiday now? Workers of the World Unite, or simply Gathering Nuts in May?"

"I don't understand you. It bees Dyce-Farnsworth's birthday, of course."

"Oh. Well, be out at the warehouse in half an hour, and we'll be off."

The young Krasna-Martha was alone in the warehouse when Brent got there. He looked at her carefully, trying to see in her youthful features the worn ones of the woman he had just left. It made sense.

"I comed first," she said, "because I wanted to say goodbye without others."

"Goodbye, milady," Brent murmured into her fine red hair. "In a way I'm not leaving you because I'm taking you with me and still I'll never see you again. And you don't understand that, and I'm not sure you've ever understood anything I've said, but you've been very sweet."

"And you will destroy Barrier? For me?"

"For you, milady. And a few billion others. And here come our friends."

Alex carried a small box which he tucked under one of the seats. "Dial and mechanism beed repaired days ago," he grinned. "I've beed working on this for you, in lab while I should have been re-proving Tsvetov's hypothesis. Temporal demagnetiser—guaranteed. Bring this near Barrier and field will be breaked. Your problem bees to get near Barrier."

Martha, the matron, climbed into the machine. Martha, the girl, turned away to hide watering eyes. Brent set the dial to 2473 and adjusted the vernier to April 24th, which gave him a week's grace. "Well, friends," he faltered. "My best gratitude—and I'll be seeing you in fifty years."

Stephen started to speak, and then suddenly stopped to listen. "Quick, Krasna, Alex. Behind those cases. Turn switch quickly, John."

Brent turned the switch, and nothing happened. Stephen and Krasna were still there, moving towards the cases. Alex darted to the machine. "Cosmos blast me; I maked disconnection to prevent anyone's tampering by accident. And now—"

"Hurry, Alex," Stephen called in a whisper.

"Moment—" Alex opened the panel and made a rapid adjustment. "There, John. Goodbye."

In the instant before Brent turned the switch, he saw Stephen and Krasna reach a safe hiding place. He saw a Stapper appear in the doorway. He saw the flicker of a rod. The last thing he saw in 2423 was the explosion that lifted Alex's head off his shoulders.

The spattered blood was still warm in 2473.

Stephen, the seventy-year-old Stephen with the long and parti-coloured beard, was waiting for them. Martha dived from the machine into his arms and burst into dry sobbing.

"She met herself," Brent explained. "I think she found it pretty confusing."

Stephen barked: "I can imagine. It bees only now that I have realised who that woman beed who comed with you and so much resembled our mother. But you be so late. I have beed waiting here ever since I evaded Stappers."

"Alex—" Brent began.

"I know. Alex haves gived you magnetic disruptor and losed his life, poor devil. But that bees fifty-year-old sorrow, and we have no time for it. Why have you beed so long?"

"I didn't want to get here too long before May Day—might get into trouble. So I allowed a week, but I'll admit I might be a day or so off. What date is it?"

"This bees May 1st, and Barrier will be launched within hour. We must hurry."

"My God—" Brent glared at the dial. "It can't be that far off. But come on. Get your sister home and we'll plunge on to do our damnedest."

Martha roused herself. "I be coming with you."

"No, dear," said Stephen. "We can do better alone."

Her lips set stubbornly. "I be coming. I don't understand anything that happens, but you be Stephen and you be John, and I belong with you."

The streets were brightly decorated with banners bearing the double loop of infinity, the sacred symbol of Cosmos that had replaced crescent, swastika, and cross. But there was hardly a soul in sight. What few people they saw were all hurrying in the same direction.

"Everyone will be at dedication," Stephen explained.

141

"Tribute to Cosmos. Those who stay at home must beware Stappers."

"And if there's hundreds of thousands thronging the dedication, how do we get close to Barrier to disrupt it?"

"It bees all arranged. Our group bees far more powerful than when you knowed it fifty years ago. Slowly we be honeycombing system of State. With bribery and force when necessary, with persuasion when possible, we can do much. And we have arranged this."

"How?"

"You be delegate from European Slanduch. You speak German?"

"Well enough."

"Remember that haves beed regularised, too. But I doubt if you need to speak any. Making you Slanduch will account for irregular slips in English. You come from powerful Slanduch group. You will be gladly welcomed here. You will occupy post of honour. I have even accounted for box you carry. It bees tribute you have bringed to Cosmos. Here be your papers and identity plaque."

"Thanks." Brent's shorter legs managed to keep up with the long strides of Stephen, who doubled the rate of the moving sidewalk by his own motion. Martha panted along resolutely. "But can you account for why I'm so late? I set my indicator for April 24th, and here we are rushing to make a date on May 1st."

Stephen strode along in thought, then suddenly slapped his leg and barked. "How many months in 1942?"

"Twelve, of course."

"Ha! Yes, it beed only two hundred years ago that thirteen-month calendar beed adopted. Even months of twenty-eight days, plus Year Day, which belongs to no month. Order, you see. Now invaluable part of Stasis—" He concentrated frowningly on mental arithmetic. "Yes, your indicator worked exactly. May 1st of our calendar bees April 24th of yours."

Chalk up one slip against Derringer—an unthinking confidence in the durability of the calendar. And chalk up one, for Brent's money, against the logic of the Stasis; back in the twentieth century, he had been an advocate of calendar reform, but a staunch upholder of the four-quarter theory against the awkward and indivisible thirteen months.

They were nearing now the vast amphitheatre where the machinery of the Barrier had been erected. Stappers were stopping the few other travellers and forcing them off the moving sidewalk into the densely packed crowds, faces aglow with the smug ecstasy of the Stasis, but Brent's Slanduch credentials passed the three through every guard station, with short but infuriating delays.

"We'll make it." Stephen's eyes were afire. "Remember what you sayed to Alex and me? How State needs hundreds of you, to put explosive beneath it and blow it into awareness? If we——" He broke off speaking as they neared another Stapper.

This one looked at the credentials and grinned. *"Also! Sie wesen Slandsdeutsch and zwar aus Deutschland!"* he burst out in Zinsmeisterised German. *"Seit jahre habe ich kein Wort deutsch gehört. Mein eltere wesen von deutsch kerkunft."*

Brent's curious mind recorded the necessary notes on this perverted language, but there was no time to waste. He tried to avoid irregular slips as he replied, *"Freut mich sehr. Aber jetst habe ich kein zeit. Ich müsse eilen. Später vielleicht könne ich——"*

But the Stapper was, for a Stapper, amazingly friendly—a pleasing phenomenon at any other time, but hardly now. He rattled on in this correct speech until Brent glanced around to see that Stephen had precipitated action by dragging Martha on ahead. *"Ach!"* Brent cried. *"Mein freunde wesen schon gegeht. Verzeihen sie!"* And he sped after them.

The representative of the German Slanduch pushed his way into the crowd of eminent dignitaries just as Dyce-Farnsworth's grandson pressed the button. The magnificent mass of tubes and wires shuddered and glowed as the current pulsed through it. Then the glow became weird and arctic. There was a shaking, a groaning, and then, within the space of a second, a cataclysmic roar and a blinding glare. Something heavy and metallic pressed Brent to the ground.

The roar blended into the excited terror of human voices. The splendid Barrier was a mass of twisted wreckage. It was more wreckage that weighted Brent down, but this was different. It looked strangely like a variant of his own machine. And staring down at him from a warped seat was the enormous and huge-eyed head of a naked man.

A woman in a metallic costume equally strange to this age and to Brent's own straddled the body of Dyce-Farnsworth's grandson, who had met his ancestor's martyrdom. And wherever Brent's eyes moved he saw another strange and outlandish—no, out-time-ish—figure.

He heard Martha's voice. "It bees clear that Time Barrier haves beed erected and destroyed by outside force. But it haves

143

existed and created impenetrable instant of time. These be travellers from all future."

Brent gasped. Even the sudden appearance of these astounding figures was topped by Martha's speaking perfect logical sense.

Brent wrote in his journal: *This Stasis is at least an admirably functional organism. All hell broke loose there for a minute, but almost automatically the Stappers went into action with their rods—odd how that bit of crook's cant has become perfectly literal truth—and in no time had the situation well in hand.*

They had their difficulties. Several of the time intruders were armed, and managed to account for a handful of Stappers before the nerve rays paralysed them. One machine was a sort of time-travelling tank and contrived to withstand siege until a suicide squad, Stephen said, blew it up with detonite; we shall never know from what sort of a future the inhabitants of that tank came to spatter their shredded flesh about the amphitheatre.

But these events were mere delaying action, token resistance. Ten minutes after the Barrier had exploded, the travellers present were all in the hands of the Stappers, and cruising Stapper bands were efficiently combing all surrounding territory.

(The interesting suggestion comes amazingly from Martha that all time machines capable of physical movement were irresistibly attracted to the amphitheatre by the temporomagnetic field. Only such pioneer and experimental machines as my Derringer, which can move only temporally, would be arrested in other locations. Whether or not this theory is correct, it seems justified by the facts. Only a few isolated reports have come in of sudden appearances elsewhere at the instant of the Barrier's explosion; the focus of arrivals of the time travellers was the amphitheatre.)

The Chief of Stappers mounted the dais where an infinity-bedecked banner now covered the martyred corpse of young Dyce-Farnsworth, and announced the official ruling of the Head of State: That these intruders and disrupters of the Stasis were to be detained—tested and examined and studied until it became apparent what the desire of Cosmos might be.

(The Head of State, Stephen explained, is a meaningless figurehead, part high priest and—I paraphrase—part Alexander Throttlebottom. The Stasis is supposedly so perfect and so self-sustaining that his powers are as nominal as those of

the pilot of a ship in drydock, and all actual power is exercised by such subordinates as the Editor of State and the Chief of Stappers.)

Thanks to Stephen's ingenuity, this rule for the treatment of time travellers does not touch me. I am simply a Slanduch envoy. (I must remember to polish myself in that highly obnoxious Zinsmeisteriert German.) Some Stappers search party has certainly by now found the Derringer machine in the warehouse, which I no longer dare approach.

With two Barriers now between me and 1942, it is obvious that I am keeping this journal only for myself. I am stuck here—and so are all the other travellers, for this field, far stronger than the first, has wrecked their machines beyond the repairing efforts of a far greater talent than poor Alex. We are all here for good.

And it must be for good.

I still firmly believe what I said to Stephen and Alex: that this age needs hundreds of me to jolt it back into humanity. We now have, if not hundreds, at least dozens; and I, so far as we yet know, am the only one not in the hands of the Stappers. It is my clearest duty to deliver those others, and with their aid to beat some sense into this Age of Smugness.

"But how?" Brent groaned rhetorically. "How am I going to break into the Stappers' concentration camp and set free all these fellow travellers to aid me?"

Martha wrinkled her brows. "I think I know. Let me work on problem while longer; I believe I see how we can at littlest make start."

Brent stared at her. "What's happened to you, madam? Always before you've shrunk away from every discussion Stephen and I have had. You've said we talk of things you know nothing about. And now, all of a sudden—boom!—you're right in the middle of things and doing very nicely thank you. What's got into you?"

"I think," said Martha, smiling, "you have hitted on right phrase, John."

Brent's puzzled expostulation was broken off by Stephen's entrance. "And where have you been?" he demanded. "I've been trying to work out plans, and I've got a weird feeling Martha's going to beat me to it. What have you been up to?"

Stephen looked curiously at his sister. "I've been out galping. Interesting results, too."

"Galping?"

"You know. Going among people, taking samples of opinion,

using scientific method to reduce carefully choosed samples to general trends."

"Oh." (Mr. Gallup, thought Brent, had joined Captain Boycott and M. Guillotin as a verb.) "And what did you learn?"

"People be confused by arrival of time travellers. If Stasis bees perfect, they argue, why be such arrivals allowed? Seeds of doubt be sowed, and we be carefully watering them. Head of State has problem on his hands. I doubt if he cans find any solution to satisfy people."

"If only," Brent sighed, "there were some way of getting directly at the people. If we could see these travellers and learn what they know and want, then somehow establish contact between them and the people, the whole thing ought to be a pushover. But we're up against that 'if only—' "

It was Martha who answered. "It bees very simple, John. You be linguist."

"Yes. And how does that—"

"Stappers will need interpreters. You will be one. From there on you must develop your own plans, but that will at littlest put you in touch with travellers."

"But the State must have its own trained linguists who—"

Stephen barked with pleasure and took up the explanation. Since Farthing's regularisation of English, the perfect immutability of language had become part of the Stasis. A linguist now was a man who knew Farthing's works by heart, and that was all. Oh, he might also be well acquainted with Zinsmeister German, or Tamayo y Sárate Spanish; but he knew nothing of general linguistic principles, which are apt to run completely counter to the fine theories of these great synthesists, and he had never had occasion to learn adaptability to a new language. Faced by the probably strange and incomprehensible tongues of the remote future, the State linguist would be lost and helpless.

It was common knowledge that only the Slanduch had any true linguistic aptitude. Brought up to speak three languages —Farthing-ised English, their own archaic dialect, and the language of the country in which they resided—their tongues were deft and adjustable. In ordinary times, this aptitude was looked on with suspicion; ingenuity and cleverness in any field were obviously heretical threats to the Stasis. But now there would doubtless be a heavy demand for Slanduch interpreters, and there was no doubt that a little cautious wire pulling could land Brent the job.

"And after that," said Stephen, "as Martha rightly observes, you be on your own."

146

"Lead me to it," grinned John Brent.

"Isn't that Starvel?" Brent demanded.

Stephen paused and looked at the man on the other mobile walk. "So it bees indeed."

"The Stappers must have released him. Shall we—"

The man had noticed them and now crossed over. "George!" Stephen cried. "Cosmos! but it rejoices my heart to see you again."

George Starvel held himself aloof and glanced suspiciously at Brent. "I wished to speak to you, Stephen, only to tell you that I will not see you again."

"George!"

"Stasis bees perfect, Stephen. Your ideas for some little time deluded me, but now I know. Cosmos bees all-perfect and his perfection lies in his Stasis. If ever again you try to persuade me of lies to contrary, I will have to advise Stappers. Goodbye." And he had left them.

Brent looked after him in amazement. "He meant that. He was perfectly sincere."

"I know. He haves haved his mind changed. He believes what haves been forced upon him, but he believes it honestly. It bees sad. He beed most vigorous and active Seepy I have knowed since Alex."

Stephen frowned. "It bees hard to explain. But most of rebels against Stasis come from old families holding old beliefs. Many, like me, be Christians, and some be Seepies. I do not know myself all their beliefs, but they belong to schism of Mark."

Brent contemplated this statement for a moment, and then burst into a loud guffaw. "By Hobson and Jobson, this is sweet! Schism of Mark, Mark schism, Marxism. Seepy, C.P., Communist Party. And right in there fighting shoulder to shoulder with the Christians!" His face became graver. "And let's remember one thing, Stephen. They can change the mind of an individual. But when it comes to thousands, and tens of thousands—it may be their own minds that'll change."

"Amen," said Stephen. It was the only time Brent ever heard him utter a characteristically Christian phrase.

The rabbity little State linguist received Brent effusively. "Ah, thank Cosmos!" he gasped. "Travellers be driving me mad! Such gibberish you have never heared! Such irregularities! Frightful! It bees shocking! You be Slanduch?"

"I be. I have speaked several languages all my life. I can even speak pre-Zinsmeister German." And he began to recite *Die*

Lorelei. *"Die Luft ist kühl und es dunkelt, und ruhig fliesst der Rhein—"*

"Terrible! *Ist!* Such vile irregularity! And articles! But come, young man. We'll see what you can do with these temporal barbarians!"

There were three travellers in the room Brent entered, with the shocked linguist and two rodded Stappers in attendance. One of the three was the woman he had noticed in that first cataclysmic instant of arrival, a strapping Amazonic blonde who looked as though she could break any two unarmed Stappers with her bare fingers. Another was a neat little man with a curly and minute forked beard and restless hands. The third—

The third was hell to describe. They were all dressed now in the conventional robes of the Stasis, but even in these familiar garments he was clearly not quite human. If man is a featherless biped, then this was a man; but men do not usually have greenish skin with vestigal scales and a trace of a gill-opening behind each ear.

"Ask each of them three things," the linguist instructed Brent. "When he comes from, what his name bees, and what be his intentions."

Brent picked Tiny Beard as the easiest-looking start. "O.K. You!" He pointed, and the man stepped forward. "What part of time do you come from?"

"A pox o' three, sirrah, and the goodyears take thee! An thou wouldst but hearken to me, thou might'st learn all."

The State linguist moaned. "You hear, young man? How can one interpret such jargon?"

Brent smiled. "It bees O.K. This bees simply English as it beed speaked thousand years ago. This man must have beed aiming at earlier time and prepared himself. . . . Thy pardon, sir. These kerns deem all speech barbaric save that which their own conceit hath evolved. Bear with me, and all will be well."

"Spoken like a true knight!" the traveller explained. "Forgive my rash words, sir. Surely my good daemon hath led thee hither. Thou wouldst know—"

"Whence comest thou?"

"From many years hence. Thousands upon thousands of summers have yet to run their course ere I—"

"Forgive me, sir; but of that much we are aware. Let us be precise."

"When then, marry, sir, 'tis from the fifth century."

Brent frowned. But to attempt to understand the gentleman's system of dating would take too much time at the moment. "And thy name, sir?"

"Kruj, sir. Or an thou would'st be formal and courtly, Kruj Krujil Krujilar. But let Kruj suffice thee."

"And what most concerneth these gentlemen here is the matter of thine intentions. What are thy projects in this our earlier world?"

"My projects?" Kruj coughed. "Sir, in thee I behold a man of feeling, of sensibility, a man to whom one may speak one's mind. Many projects have I in good sooth, most carefully projected for me by the Zhurmandril. Much must I study in these realms of the great Elizabeth—though 'sblood! I know not how they seem so different from my conceits. But one thing above all else do I covet. I would to the Mermaid Tavern."

Brent grinned. "I fear me, sir, that we must talk at greater length. Much hast thou mistaken and much must I make clear to thee. But first I must talk with these others."

Kruj retired, frowning and plucking at his shred of beard. Brent beckoned forward the woman. She strode forth so vigorously that both Stappers bared their rods.

"Madam," Brent ventured tentatively, "what part of time do you come from?"

"Evybuy taws so fuy," she growled. "Bu I unnasta. Wy cachoo unnasta *me*?"

Brent laughed. "Is that all that's the trouble? You don't mind if I go on talking like this, do you?"

"Naw. You taw howeh you wanna, slonsoo donna like I dih taw stray."

Fascinating, Brent thought. All final consonants lost, and many others. Vowels corrupted along lines indicated in twentieth-century colloquial speech. Consonants sometimes restored in liaison as in French. "What time do you come from, then?"

"Twenny-ni twenny-fie. N were am I now?"

"Twenty-four seventy-three. And your name, madam?"

"Mimi."

Brent had an incongruous vision of this giantess dying operatically in a Paris garret. "So. And your intentions here?"

"Ai gonno intenchuns. Juh wanna see wha go."

"You will, madam, I assure you. And now—" He beckoned to the green-skinned biped, who advanced with a lurching motion like a deep-sea diver.

"And you, sir. When do you come from?"

"Ya studier langue earthly. Vyerit todo langue isos. Ou comprendo wie govorit people."

Brent was on the ropes and groggy. The familiarity of some of the words made the entire speech even more incomprehensible. "Says which?" he gasped.

The green man exploded. "Ou existier nada but dolts, cochons, duraki v this terre? Nikovo parla langue earthly? Potztausend Sapperment en la leche de tu madre and I do mean you!"

Brent reeled. But even reeling he saw the disapproving frown of the State linguist and the itching fingers of the Stappers. He faced the green man calmly and said with utmost courtesy, " 'Twas brillig and the slithy toves did gyre and gimble over the rivering waters of the hitherandthithering waters of pigeons on the grass alas. Thank you, sir." He turned to the linguist. "He says he won't talk."

Brent wrote in the never-to-be-read journal: *It was Martha again who solved my green man for me. She pointed out that he was patently extraterrestrial. (Apparently Nakamura's Law of Spacial Acceleration is as false as Charnwood's Law of Temporal Metabolism.) The vestigial scales and gills might well indicate Venus as his origin. He must come from some far distant future when the earth is overrun by inhabitants of other planets and terrestrial culture is all but lost. He had prepared himself for time travel by studying the speech of earth—langue earthly—reconstructed from some larger equivalent of the Rosetta Stone, but made the mistake of thinking that there was only one earthly speech, just as we tend imaginatively to think of Martian or Venusian as a single language. As a result, he's talking all earthly tongues at once. Martha sees a marked advantage in this, even more than in Mimi's corrupt dialect—*

"Thou, sir," said Brent to Kruj on his next visit, "art a linguist. Thou knowest speech and his nature. To wit, I would wager that thou couldst with little labour understand this woman here. One who hath so mastered our language in his greatest glory—"

The little man smirked. "I thank thee, sir. In sooth since thou didst speak with her yestereven I have already made some attempts at converse with her."

Mimi joined in. "He says fuy, bu skina cue."

"Very well then. I want you both, and thee in particular,

150

Kruj, to hearken to this green-skinned varlet here. Study his speech, sir, and learn what thou may'st."

"Wy?" Mimi demanded belligerently.

"The wench speaks sooth. Wherefore should we so?"

"You'll find out. Now let me at him."

It was slow, hard work, especially with the linguist and the Stappers ever on guard. It meant rapid analysis of the possible origin of every word used by the Venusian, and a laborious painstaking attempt to find at random words that he would understand. But in the course of a week both Brent and the astonishingly adaptable Kruj had learned enough of this polygot *langue earthly* to hold an intelligible conversation. Mimi was hopelessly lost, but Kruj occasionally explained matters to her in her own corrupt speech, which he had mastered by now as completely as Elizabethan.

It had been Stephen's idea that any project for the liberation of the time travellers must wait until more was learned of their nature. "You be man of good will, John. We trust you. You and mans like you can save us. But imagine that some travellers come from worlds far badder even than ours. Suppose that they come seeking only power for themselves? Suppose that they come from civilisation of cruelty and terror and be even more evil than Stappers?"

It was a wise point, and it was Martha who saw the solution in the Venusian's amazing tongue. In that mélange of languages, Brent could talk in front of the linguist and the Stappers with complete safety. Kruj and the Venusian, who must have astonishing linguistic ability to master the speech of another planet even so perversely, could discuss matters with the other travellers, and could tell him anything he needed to know before all the listening guards of the State.

All this conversation was, of course, theoretically guided by the linguist. He gave questions to Brent and received plausible answers, never dreaming that his questions had not been asked.

As far as his own three went, Brent was satisfied as to the value of their liberation. Mimi was not bright, but she seemed to mean well and claimed to have been a notable warrior in her own matriarchal society. It was her feats in battle and exploration that had caused her to be chosen for time travel. She would be in some respects a useful ally.

Kruj was indifferent to the sorry state of the world until Brent mentioned the tasteless and servile condition of the arts. Then he was all afire to overthrow the Stasis and bring about a new renaissance. (Kruj, Brent learned, had been heading for the past

151

to collect material for an historical epic on Elizabethan England, a fragment of pre-historic civilisation that had always fascinated him.)

Of the three, Nikobat, the Venusian, seemed the soundest and most promising. To him, terrestrial civilisation was a closed book, but a beautiful one. In the life and struggles of man he found something deep and moving. The aim of Nikobat in his own world had been to raise his transplanted Venusian civilisation to the levels, spiritual and scientific, that had once been attained by earthly man, and it was to find the seed of inspiration to accomplish this that he had travelled back. Man degenerate, man self-complacent, man smug, shocked him bitterly, and he swore to exert his best efforts in the rousing.

Brent was feeling not unpleased with himself as he left his group after a highly successful session. Kruj was accomplishing much among the other travellers and would have a nearly full report for him tomorrow. And once that report had been made, they could attempt Martha's extraordinary scheme of rescue. He would not have believed it ordinarily possible; but both he and Stephen were coming to put more and more trust in the suggestions of the once scatter-brained Martha. Stephen's own reports were more than favourable. The Underground was boring beautifully from within. The people of the State were becoming more and more restless and doubting. Slowly these cattle were resuming the forms of men.

Brent was whistling happily as he entered the apartment and called out a cheery "Hi!" to his friends. But they were not there. There was no one in the room but a white-clad Stapper, who smiled wolfishly as he rose from a chair and asked politely, "You be time traveller, be you not?"

This was the most impressive Stapper that Brent had yet seen—impressive even aside from the startling nature of his introductory remark. The others, even the one he had kicked in the face, or the one who killed Alex, Brent had thought of simply as so many Stappers. This one was clearly an individual. His skin was exceptionally dark and smooth and hairless, and two eyes so black that they seemed all pupil glowed out of his face and dominated the room.

Brent tried to seem casual. "Nonsense. I be Slanduch envoy from Germany, staying here with friends and doing linguistic service for State. Here bees my identification."

The Stapper hardly glanced at it. "I know all about your

152

'linguistic services', John Brent. And I know about machine finded in deserted warehouse. It beed only machine not breaked by Barrier. Therefore it comed not from Future, but from Past."

"So? We have travellers from both directions? Poor devil will never be able to get back to own time then." He wondered if this Stapper were corruptible; he could do with a drink of bond.

"Yes, he bees losed here in this time like others. And he foolishly works with them to overthrow Stasis."

"Sad story. But how does it concern me? My papers be in order. Surely you can see that I be what I claim?"

The Stapper's eyes fixed him sharply. "You be clever, John Brent. You doubtless travelled naked and clothed yourself as citizen of now to escape suspicion. That bees smartest way. How you getted papers I do not know. But communication with German Slanduch cans disprove your story. You be losed, Brent, unless you be sensible."

"Sensible? What the hell do you mean by that?"

The Stapper smiled slowly. "Article," he drawled.

"I be sorry. But that proves nothing. You know how difficult it bees for us Slanduch to keep our speech entirely regular."

"I know." Suddenly a broad grin spread across the Stapper's face and humanised it. "I have finded this Farthing speech hellishly difficult myself."

"You mean you, too, be Slanduch?"

The Stapper shook his head. "I, too, Brent, be traveller."

Brent was not falling for any such trap. "Ridiculous! How canned traveller be Stapper?"

"How canned traveller be Slanduch envoy? I, too, travelled naked, and man whose clothes and identification I stealed beed Stapper. I have finded his identity most useful."

"I don't believe you."

"You be stubborn, Brent. How to prove—" He gestured at his face. "Look at my skin. In my century facial hair haves disappeared; we have breeded away from it. Where in this time could you find skin like that?"

"A sport. Freak of chromosomes."

The black eyes grew even larger and more glowing. "Brent, you must believe me. This bees no trap for you. I need you. You and I, we can do great things. But how to convince you"—he snapped his fingers. "I know!" He was still for a moment. The vast eyes remained opened but somehow veiled, as though secret calculations were going on behind them. His body

153

shivered. For a moment of strange delusion Brent thought he could see the chair through the Stapper's body. Then it was real and solid again.

The Stapper's eyes resumed their light, and he looked about the room expectantly for a moment. "Delay," he muttered disappointedly. "But no matter. In a moment—"

"What bees this—"

"My name," said the Stapper, with the patience of a professor addressing a retarded class, "bees Bokor. I come from tenth century after consummation of terrestrial unity, which bees, I believe, forty-third reckoning from date of birth of Christian god. I have travelled, not with machine, but solely by use of Vunmurd formula, and, therefore, I alone of all travellers stranded here can still move. Hysteresis of Barrier arrests me, but can not destroy my formula as it shatters machines."

"Pretty story."

"I have sended myself back to Barrier again by formula, but trip from Barrier to now seems longer for me this time. I—" He broke off as the door opened. "Ah," he said. "Here I be!"

The Stapper in the doorway fixed Brent with his glowing black eyes and said, "Now do you believe that I be traveller?"

Brent gawped from one identical man to the other. The one in the doorway went on. "I need you."

"It isn't possible. It's a gag. You're twin Stappers, and you're trying to—"

Boker in the chair said, "Do I have to do it again?"

Bokor-Sub-One in the doorway said, "I have hitted Barrier twice. Therefore I exist twice in that one point of time. Therefore each of those two continues into present."

Brent said, "You may both be Stappers. You may turn out to be a whole damned regiment of identical multiple births. I don't give a damn; I want some bond. How about you boys?"

The two Bokors downed their drinks and frowned. "Weak," they said.

Brent shook his head feebly. "All right. We'll skip that. Now what the sweet hell do you need me for?"

Boker closed his eyes and seemed to doze. Bokor-Sub-One said, "You have plans to liberate travellers and overthrow Stasis. As Stapper I have learned much. I worked on changing mind of one of your Underground friends."

"And you want to throw your weight in with us? Good, we can use a Stapper. Or two. But won't the Chief of Stappers be bothered when he finds he has two copies of one man?"

"He will never need to see more than one. Yes, I want to help you—up to a point. We will free travellers. But you be innocent, Brent. We will not overthrow Stasis. We will maintain it—as ours."

Brent frowned. "I'm not sure I get you. And I don't think I like it if I do."

"Do not be fool, Brent. We have opportunity never before gived to man, we travellers. We come into world where already exists complete and absolute State control, but used stupidly and to no end. Among us all we have great knowledge and power. We be seed sowed upon fallow ground. We can spring up and engulf all about us." The eyes glowed with black intensity. "We take this Stasis and mould it to our own wishes. These dolts who now be slaves of Cosmos will be slaves of us. Stapper, whose identity I have, bees third in succession to Chief of Stappers. Chief and other two will be killed accidentally in revolt of travellers. With power of all Stappers behind me, I make you Head of State. Between us we control this State absolutely."

"Nuts," Brent snorted. "The State's got too damned much control already. What this world needs is a return to human freedom and striving."

"Innocent," Boker-Sub-One repeated scornfully. "Who gives damn what world needs? Only needs which concern man be his own, and his strongest need bees always for power. Here it bees gived us. Other States be stupid and self-complacent like this. We know secrets of many weapons, we travellers. We turn our useless scholastic laboratories over to their production. Then we attack other States and subject them to us as vassals. And then the world itself bees ours, and all its riches. Alexander, Caesar, Napoleon, Hitler, Gospodinov, Tirazhul—never in its past or future haves world knowed nor will it know conquerors like us."

"You can go to hell," said Brent lightly but firmly. "All two of you."

"Do not be too clever, my friend. Remember that I be Stapper and can—"

"You be two Stappers, which may turn out to be a little awkward. But you could be a regiment of Stappers, and I still wouldn't play ball. Your plan stinks, Bokor, and you know what you can do with it."

Bokor-Sub-One took the idiom literally. "Indeed I do know, Brent. It willed have beed easier with your aid, but even without you it will succeed." He drew out his rod and contemplated it

155

reflectively. "No," he murmured, "there bees no point to taking you in and changing your mind. You be harmless to me, and your liberation of travellers will be useful."

The original Bokor opened his eyes. "We will meet again, Brent. And you will see what one man with daring mind can accomplish in this world." Bokor and Bokor-Sub-One walked to the door and turned. "And for bond," they spoke in unison, in parody of the conventional Stapper's phrase, "State thanks you."

Brent stood alone in the room, but the black-eyed domination of the two Bokors lingered about him. The plan was so damned plausible, so likely to succeed if put into operation. Man has always dreamed of power. But damn it, man has always dreamed of love, too, and of the rights of his fellow man. The only power worthy of man is the power of all mankind struggling together towards a goal of unobtainable perfection.

And what could Bokor do against Kruj and Mimi and Nikobat and the dozens of others that Kruj reported sympathetic?

Nevertheless there had been a certainty in those vast glowing eyes that the duple Bokor knew just what he could do.

The release of the travellers was a fabulous episode. Stephen had frowned and Brent had laughed when Martha said simply, "Only person who haves power to release them bees Head of State by will of Cosmos. Very well. We will persuade him to do so." But she insisted, and she had been so uncannily right ever since the explosion of the second Barrier that at last, when Kruj had made his final report, Brent accompanied her on what he was certain was the damnedest fool errand he'd got himself into yet.

Kruj's report was encouraging. There were two, perhaps three among the travellers who had Bokorian ideas of taking over the State for their own purposes. But these were far outweighed by the dozens who saw the tremendous possibilities of a reawakening mankind. The liberation was proved a desirable thing; but why should the Head of State so readily loose these disrupters upon his Stasis?

Getting to see the Head of State took the best part of a day. There were countless minor officials to be interviewed, all of them guarded by Stappers who looked upon the supposed Slanduch envoy with highly suspicious eyes. But one by one, with miraculous consistency, these officials beamed upon Brent's errand and sent him on with the blessing of Cosmos.

"You wouldn't like to pinch me?" he murmured to Martha after the fifth such success. "This works too easy. It can't be true."

Martha looked at him blankly and said, "I don't understand it. But what be we doing here? What be we going to say?"

Brent jumped. "Hey! Look, madam. This was all your idea to start with. You were going to talk the Head of State into—And now you say, 'What be we going to say?' If you don't—"

But a Stapper was already approaching to conduct them to the next office, and Brent fell silent.

It was in the anteroom of the Head of State that they met Bokor. Just one of him this time. He smiled confidentially at Brent and said, "Shocking accident today. Stapper beed killed in fight with prisoner who beed to have his mind changed. Odd thing—Stapper beed second in succession to Chief of Stappers."

"You're doing all right," said Brent.

"I be curious to see what you plan here. How do you hope to achieve this liberation? I talked with Head of State yesterday and he bees strongly opposed."

"Brother," said Brent sincerely, "I wish to Cosmos I knew."

In a moment Bokor ushered them into the sanctorum of the Head of State. This great dignitary was at first glance a fine figure of a man, tall and well built and noble. It was only on second glance that you noticed the weak lips and the horribly empty eyes. The stern and hawk-nosed Chief of Stappers stood beside him.

"Well!" the latter snapped. "Speak your piece!"

Brent faltered and glanced at Martha. She looked as vacant and helpless as ever she had before the Barrier. He could only fumble on and pray that her unrevealed scheme would materialise.

"As you know, sir," he bagan, "I, as interpreter, have beed in very close contact with travellers. Having in my mind good of Cosmos and wishing to see it as rich and fully developed as possible, it seems to me that much may be accomplished by releasing travellers so that they may communicate with people." He gulped and swore at himself for venturing such an idiotic request.

The empty eyes of the Head of State lit up for a moment. "Excellent idea," he boomed in a dulcet voice. "You have permission of State and Cosmos. Chief, I give orders that all travellers be released."

Brent heard Bokor's incredulous gasp behind him. The Chief of Stappers murmured "Cosmos!" fervently. The Head of State

157

looked around him for approval and then reverted to formal vacancy.

"I thank State," Brent managed to say, "for this courageous move."

"What bees courageous?" the Head demanded. His eyes shifted about nervously. "What have I doed? What have I sayed?"

The Chief of Stappers bowed. "You have proclaimed freedom of travellers. May I, too, congratulate you on wisdom of action?" He turned to Bokor. "Go and give necessary orders."

Brent saw the dazed faces of Bokor and Martha and wondered if his own looked quite so ridiculously incredulous. That the Head of State and the Chief of Stappers should sanction a policy that any dolt could see must inevitably be fatal to the Stasis of Cosmos— It was mad. It was a dream. But it was certainly a damned agreeable one.

Martha did not say a word till they were outside on the moving sidewalk again. Then she asked, "What happened? Why in Cosmos' name doed he consent?"

"Madam, you have me there. But you should know. It was all your idea."

Understanding came back to her face. "Of course. It bees time now that you know all about me. But wait till we be back in apartment. Stephen haves right to know this, too. And Martha," she added.

That oral postscript was too much for Brent. When you begin talking of yourself as a third party—

"Come on home, madam," he said. "You'll feel better."

They had left Bokor behind them in the sanctum, and they met Bokor outside the building. That did not worry Brent, but he was admittedly perturbed when he passed a small group of people just off the sidewalk and noticed that its core was a third Bokor. He pulled Martha off the moving path and drew near the group.

Bokor was not a Stapper this time. He was in ordinary iridescent robes. "I tell you I know," he was insisting vigorously. "I am . . . I be Slanduch from State of South America, and I can tell you deviltry they be practising there. Armament factories twice size of laboratories of Cosmos. Bees this for nothing? They plan to destroy us; I know."

A Stapper shoved his way past Brent. "Here now!" he growled. "What bees going on here?"

Bokor hesitated. "Nothing, sir. I was only—"

"*Was*, huh?"

"Pardon, sir. *Beed*. I be Slanduch, you see, and—"

One of the men in the crowd interrupted. "He beed telling us what all State needs to know—plans of State of South America to invade and destroy us."

"Hm-m-m!" the Stapper ejaculated. "You be right, man. That sounds like something we all need to know. Go on, you."

Bokor resumed his rumour-mongering, and the Stapper lent it official endorsement by his listening silence. Brent moved to get a glimpse of the Stapper's face. His guess was right. It was another Bokor.

This significant byplay had delayed them enough so that Brent's three travellers had reached the apartment before them. When they arrived, Stephen was deep in a philosophical discussion with the Venusian of the tragic nobility of human nature, while Kruj and Mimi were experimenting with bond. Their respective civilisations could not have been markedly alcoholic; Kruj had reached the stage of sweeping and impassioned gestures, while Mimi beamed at him and interposed an occasional irrelevant giggle.

All three had discarded the standardised robes of the Stasis and resumed, in this friendly privacy, the clothes in which they had arrived—Kruj, a curiously simplified and perverted version of the ruffled court costume of the Elizabethan era he had hoped to reach, Mimi, the startling armour of an unfamiliar metal which was her uniform as Amazon warrior, and Nikobat a simple bronze-coloured loincloth against which his green skin assumed a certain strange beauty.

Brent introduced Martha's guests to their hostess and went on. "Now for a staff meeting of G.H.Q. We've got to lay our plans carefully, because I warn you we're up against some stiff opposition. There's one other traveller who—"

"One moment," said Martha's voice. "Shouldn't you introduce me, too?"

"I beg your pardon, madam. I just finished that task of courtesy. And now—"

"I be sorry," her voice went on. "You still do not understand. You introduced Martha, yes; but not me."

Stephen turned to the travellers. "I must apologise for my sister. She haves goed through queer experiences of late. She travelled with our friend John and meeted herself in her earlier life. I fear that shock has temporarily—and temporally—unbalanced her."

159

"Can none of you understand so simple thing?" the woman's voice pleaded. "I be simply using Martha's voice as instrument of communication. I can just as easily—"

" 'Steeth!" Kruj exclaimed. " 'Tis eke as easy and mayhap more pleasant to borrow this traveller's voice from mine explications."

"Or," Mimi added, "I cou taw li thih, but I do' like ih vey muh."

Stephen's eyes popped. "You mean that you be traveller without body?"

"Got it in one," Brent heard his own voice saying. "I can wander about any way I damned please. I picked the woman first because her nearly empty mind was easy to occupy, and I think I'll go on using her. Brent here's a little hard to keep under control."

Stephen nodded. "Then all good advice Martha haves beed giving us—"

"Bees mine, of course." The bodiless traveller was back in Martha now.

Brent gasped. "And now I see how you wangled the release of the travellers. You got us in by usurping the mind and speech of each of the minor officials we tackled; and then ousted the Head of State and Chief of Stappers to make them give their consent.

Martha nodded. "Exactly."

"This is going to be damned useful. And where do you come from, sir? Or is it madam?"

"I come from future so far distant that even our Venusian friend here cannot conceive of it. And distinction between *sir* and *madam* bees then meaningless."

The dapper Kruj glanced at the hulking Amazon beside him.

" 'Twere pity," he murmured.

"And your intentions here, to go on with the State linguist's questionnaire?"

"My intentions? Listen, all of you. We cannot shape ends. Great patterns be shaped outside of us and beyond us. I beed historian in my time. I know patterns of mankind even down to minute details. And I know that Stephen here bees to lead people of this Age of Smugness out of their stupidity and back to humanity."

Stephen coughed, embarrassed. "I have no wish to lead. But for such cause man must do what he may."

"That bees ultimate end of this section of pattern. That bees fixed. All that we travellers can do bees to aid him as wisely as

160

we can and to make the details of the pattern as pleasingly beautiful as may be. And that we will do."

Stephen must have been so absorbed in this speech that his hearing was dulled. The door opened without warning, and Bokor entered.

" 'Swounds!" Kruj cried out. "A Stapper!"

Stephen smiled. "Why fear Stappers? You be legally liberated."

"Stapper, hell!" Brent snorted. "Well, Bokor? You still want to declare yourself in with your racket?"

Bokor's deep eyes swept the room. He smiled faintly. "I merely wished to show you something, Brent. So that you know what you be up against. I have finded two young scientists dissatisfied with scholastic routine of research for Cosmos. Now they work under my instructions, and they have maked for me—this." He held a bare rod in his hand.

"So it's a rod. So what next?"

"But it bees different rod, Brent. It does not paralyse. It destroys." The point of the rod wavered and covered in turn each individual in the room. "I want you to see what I can accomplish."

"You suvvabih!" Mimi yelled and started to rise. Kruj restrained her.

"State thanks you, madam, for making up my mind. I will demonstrate on you. Watch this, Brent, and realise what chance you have against me." He pointed the rod firmly at Mimi.

"Do something!" Martha screamed.

It all happened at once, but Brent seemed to see it in slow motion even as he moved. Mimi lunged forward furiously and recklessly. Kruj dived for her feet and brought her to the floor out of the line of fire. At the same time Brent threw himself forward just as Bokor moved, so that the rod now pointed directly at Brent. He couldn't arrest his momentum. He was headed straight at Bokor's new instrument of death. And then the rod moved to Bokor's own head.

There was no noise, no flash. But Bokor's body was lying on the floor, and the head was nowhere.

"That beed hard," said Martha's voice. "I haved to stay in his mind long enough to actuate rod, but get out before death. Matter of fractions of seconds."

"Nice work, sir-madam," Brent grunted. He looked down at the headless corpse. "But that was only one of them."

Brent quoted in his journal: *Love, but a day, and the world has changed! A week, to be more exact, but the change is none the less sudden and impressive.*

Our nameless visitant from the future—they seem to need titles as little as sexes in that time—whom I have for convenience labelled Sirdam, has organised our plans about the central idea of interfering as little as possible—forcing the inhabitants of the Stasis to work out their own salvation. The travellers do not appear openly in this great change. We work through Stephen's associates.

The best single example to show the results we obtain is the episode of Professor Harrington, whose special department of so-called learning is the preservation of the Nakamura Law of Spacial Acceleration, which had so conclusively proved to the founders of the Stasis the impossibility of interplanetary travel.

This fell obviously within Nikobat's field. A young scientist affiliated with the Underground—a nephew, I have since learned, of Alex's—expounded the Nakamura doctrine as he had learned and re-proved it. It took the Venusian less than five minutes to put his finger on the basic flaw in the statement—the absolute omission, in all calculations, of any consideration of galactic drift. Once this correction was applied to the Nakamura formulas, they stood revealed as the pure nonsense which, indeed, Nikobat's very presence proved them.

It was not Nikobat but the young man who placed this evidence before Professor Harrington. The scene must have been classic. "I saw," the young man later told us—they are all trying desperately to unlearn Farthing-ised English—"his mouth fall open and gap spread across his face as wide as gap he suddenly finded in universe—the universe."

For the professor was not stupid. He was simply so conditioned from childhood to the acceptance of the Stasis of Cosmos that he had never questioned it. Besides, he had doubtless had friends whose minds were changed when they speculated too far.

Harrington's eyes lit up after the first shock. He grabbed pencil and paper and furiously checked through the revised equations again and again. He then called in a half-dozen of his best students and set them to what was apparently a routine exercise—interpolating variations for galactic drift in the Nakamura formulas.

They ended as astonished as their instructor. The first one done stared incredulously at his results and gasped, "Nakamura beed wrong!"

One of them, horrified, destroyed his calculations, saying, "This bees against Stasis."

The professor smiled. "Not against, my boy. It bees beyond Cosmos."

That was typical. The sheep are ready to be roused, each in his individual way. Kruj has been training men to associate with the writers of the Stasis. The man's knowledge of literature of all periods, and especially of his beloved Elizabethan Age, is phenomenal and his memory something superhuman. And four writers out of five who hear his disciples discourse on the joys of creative language and quote from the Elizabethan dramatists and the King James Bible will never be content again to write Stasis propaganda for the sollies or the identically bound books of the State libraries.

I have myself been contributing a fair amount to the seduction of the world by teaching cooks. I was never in my own time acknowledged as better than a fair-to-middling non-professional, but here I might be Escoffier or Brillat-Savarin. We steal plants and animals from the scientific laboratories, and in our hands they become vegetables and meat; and many a man in the street, who doesn't give a damn if his science is false and his arts synthetic, has suddenly realised that he owes the State a grudge for feeding him on concentrates.

The focus of everything is Stephen. It's hard to analyse why. Each of us travellers has found among the Undergrounders someone far more able in his own special field, yet all of us, travellers and Undergrounders alike, unquestioningly acknowledge Stephen as our leader. It may be the sheer quiet kindliness and goodness of his nature. It may be that he and Alex, in their organisation of this undercover group of instinctive rebels, were the first openly to admit that the Stasis was inhuman and to do something about it. But from whatever cause, we all come to depend more and more on the calm reliability of Stephen.

Nikobat says—

Bret broke off as Kruj Krujil Krujilar staggered into the room. The little man was no longer dapper. His robes were tattered, and their iridescence was overlaid with solid red of blood.

He panted his first words in his own tongue, then recovered himself. "We must act apace, John. Where is Stephen?"

"At Underground quarters, I think. But what's happened?"

"I was nearing the building where they do house us travellers when I beheld hundreds of people coming along the street.

Some wore our robes, some wore Stappers'. And they all—" He shuddered. "They all had the same face—a brown hairless face with black eyes."

Brent was on his feet. "Bokor!" The man had multiplied himself into a regiment. One man who was hundreds—why not thousands? millions?—could indeed be such a conqueror as the world had never known. "What happened?"

"They entered the building. I knew that I could do nothing there, and came to find you and Stephen and the bodiless one. But as I came along the street, lo! on every corner there was yet another of that face, and always urging the people to maintain the Stasis and destroy the travellers. I was recognised. By good hap those who set upon me had no rods, but 'sbody! 'Twas a close thing that I escaped with my life."

Brent thought quickly. "Martha is with Stephen, so Sirdam is probably there, too. Go to him at once and warn him. I'm going to the travellers' building and see what's happened. Meet you at the headquarters as soon as I can."

Kruj hesitated. "Mimi—"

"I'll bring her with me if I can. Get going."

The streets were mad. Wild throngs jammed the moving roadways. Somewhere in the distance mountainous flames leaped up and their furious glitter gleamed back from the eyes of the mob.

And those were not the deeply glowing black eyes of multitudinous Bokors. These were the ordinary citizens of the Stasis, no longer cattle, or rather cattle stampeded and raging.

A voice blared seemingly out of the heavens. Brent recognised the public address system used for vital State messages. "Revolt of travellers have spreaded to amphitheatre of Cosmos. Flames lighted by travellers now attack sacred spot. People of Cosmos. Destroy travellers!"

"The Reichstag fire!" Brent muttered. "Technique doesn't change much—" If only he could avoid running into a Bokor. There was nothing to mark him superficially as a traveller. He pushed along with the mob, shouting as rabidly as any other. He could make no headway. He was borne along on these foaming human waves.

Then in front of him he saw three Bokors pushing against the mob. If they spied him— His hands groped along the wall. Just as a Bokor looked his way, he found what he was seeking—one of the spying niches of the Stappers. He slipped into the false wall in safety.

He peered out cautiously for a moment to escape. From the next door he saw a man emerge whom he knew by sight—a leading dramatist of the sollies, who had promised to be an eventual convert of Kruj's disciples. Three citizens of the mob hailed him as he stepped forth.

"What bees your name?"

"Where be you going?"

"When do you come from?"

"Answer every man directly."

The solly writer hesitated. "I be going to amphitheatre. Speaker have sayed—"

"When do you come from?"

"Why, from now."

"What bees your name?"

"John—"

"Ha!" the first citizen yelled. "Stappers have telled us to find this John. Tear him to pieces; he bees traveller."

"No, truly. I be no traveller; I be writer of sollies. I be of now."

One of the citizens chortled cruelly. "Tear him for his bad sollies!"

There was one long scream—

The smugness of the Stasis had been inhuman. Stephen and the travellers had sought to make the citizens human again in the noblest traditions of man's striving. But there was another manner of being human, and Bokor had found and roused it.

Fire breeds fire, literally as well as metaphorically. The dwelling of the travellers was ablaze when Brent reached it. A joyous mob cheered and gloated before it.

Brent started to push his way through, but a hand touched his arm and a familiar voice whispered, "Achtung! Ou vkhodit."

He interpreted the warning and let the Venusian draw him aside. Nikobat rapidly explained in Brent's own speech.

"The Stappers came and subdued the whole crowd with paralysing rods. They took them away—God knows what they'll do with them. There's no one in there now; the fire's just a gesture." The red flames glittered on the green skin.

"But you—How did you—"

"My nerve centres don't react the same. I lay doggo and got away. Mimi escaped, too; her armour has deflecting power. I think she's gone to warn the Underground."

"Then come on."

"Don't stay too close to me," Nikobat warned. "They'll recognise me as a traveller; stay out of range of rods aimed at

165

me. And here. I took these from a Stapper I strangled. This one is a paralysing rod; the other's an annihilator."

The next half-hour was a nightmare—a montage of flames and blood and sweating bodies of hate. The Stasis of Stupidity was becoming a Stasis of Cruelty. For a moment Brent wondered if he could find where the Stappers had taken his machine. That Derringer model was the only machine unshattered—the only one that, though still helpless against the Barrier, could at least take him forward to what might be a better world—Kruj's aesthetic paradise or even Mimi's matriarchy. But he thought of Stephen and Martha, and he pushed on towards the Underground headquarters.

Twice groups of citizens stopped him. They were unarmed; Bokor wisely kept weapons to himself, knowing that the fangs and claws of an enraged mob are enough. The first group Brent left paralysed. The second time he confused his weapons. He had not meant to kill, but he could not regret it.

He did not confuse his weapons when he bagged a brace of Bokors. But what did the destruction of two matter? He fought his way on, finally catching up with Nikobat at their goal. As they met, the voice boomed once more from the air. "Important! New Chief of Stappers announces that offices of Chief of Stappers and Head of State be henceforth maked one. Under new control, travellers will be wiped out and Stasis preserved. Then on to South America for glory of Cosmos!"

Brent shuddered. "And we started out so beautifully on our renaissance!"

Nikobat shook his head. "But the bodiless traveller said that Stephen was to destroy the Stasis. This multiple villain cannot change what has happened."

"Can't he? We're taking no chances."

The headquarters of the Underground was inappositely in a loft. The situation helped. The trap entrance was unnoticeable from below and had gone unheeded by the mobs. Brent delivered the proper raps, and the trap slid open and dropped a ladder. Quickly he and the Venusian mounted.

The loft was a sick bay. A half-dozen wounded members of Stephen's group lay groaning on the floor. With them was Kruj. Somewhere the little man had evaded the direct line of an annihilator, but lost his hand. Blood was seeping out of his bandages, and Mimi, surprisingly feminine and un-Amazonic, held his unconscious head in her lap.

"You don't seem to need warning," Brent observed tersely.

166

Stephen shook his head sadly. "We be trapped here. Here we be safe for at littlest small while. If we go out—"

Brent handed him his rods. "You're the man we've got to save, Stephen. You know what Sirdam's said—it all depends on you. Use these to protect yourself, and we'll make a dash for it. If we can lose ourselves in the mob as ordinary citizens there's a chance of getting away with it. Or"—he turned to Martha-Sirdam—"have you any ideas?"

"Yes. But only as latest resort."

Nikobat was peering out of the window. "It's the last resort now," he said. "There's a good fifty of those identical Stappers outside, and they're headed here. They act as though they know what this is."

Brent was looking at Stephen, and he saw a strange thing. Stephen's face was expressionless, but somewhere behind his eyes Brent seemed to sense a struggle. Stephen's body trembled with an effort of will, and then his eyes were clear again. "No," he said distinctly. "You do not need to control me. I understand. You be right. I will do as you say." And he lifted the annihilator rod.

Brent started forward, but his muscles did not respond to his commands. Force his will though he might, he stood still. It was the bodiless traveller who held him, he realised, held him motionless to watch Stephen place the rod to his temple.

"This bees goodest thing that I can do for mans," said Stephen simply. Then his headless corpse thumped on the floor.

Brent was released. He dashed forward, but vainly. There was nothing men could do for Stephen now. Brent let out a choking gasp of pain and sorrow.

Then the astonished cries of the Undergrounders recalled him from his friend's body. He looked about him. Where was Nikobat? Where were Kruj and Mimi?

A small inkling of the truth began to reach him. He hurried to the window and looked out.

There were no Bokors before the house. Only a few citizens staring dazedly at a wide space of emptiness.

At that moment the loud-speaker sounded. "Announcement," a shocked voice trembled. "Chief of Stappers has just disappeared." And in a moment it added, "Guards report all travellers have vanished."

The citizens before the house were rubbing their eyes like men coming out of a nightmare.

"But don't you see, madam— No? Well, let me try again." Brent was not finding it easy to explain her brother's heroic death to an untenanted Martha. "Remember what your inhabitant told us? The Stasis was overthrown by Stephen."

"But Stephen bees dead."

"Exactly. So listen: All these travellers came from a future wherein Stephen had overthrown the Stasis. So that when Stephen destroyed himself, as Sirdam realised, he likewise destroyed that future. A world in which Stephen died unsuccessful is a world that cannot be entered by anyone from the other future. Their worlds vanished and they with them. It was the only way of abolishing the menace of the incredibly multiplied Bokor."

"Stephen bees dead. He cans not overthrow Stasis now."

"My dear madam— Hell, skip it. But the Stasis is damned none the less in this new world created by Stephen's death. I've been doing a little galping on my own. The people are convinced now that the many exemplars of Bokor were some kind of evil invader. They rebound easy, the hordes; they dread the memory of those men and they dread also the ideas of cruelty and conquest to which the Bokors had so nearly converted them.

"But one thing they can't rebound from is the doubts and the new awarenesses that we planted in their minds. And there's what's left of your movement to go on with. No, the Stasis is damned, even if they are going to erect yet another Barrier."

"Oh," Martha shuddered. "You willn't let them do that, will you?"

Brent grinned. "Madam, there's damned little letting I can do. They're going to, and that's that. Because, you see, all the travellers vanished."

"But why—"

Brent shrugged and gave up. "Join me in some bond?" It was clear enough. The point of time which the second Barrier blocked existed both in the past of the worlds of Nikobat and Sirdam, and in the past of this future they were now entering. But no travellers had come from this future. Therefore there must be a Barrier yet ahead of them.

Would the Stasis by then be dissolved into a normal human society? Would man have cast aside his purse-proud garment of smugness and become his struggling, striving, failing, ridiculous, noble self? And the travellers from this coming future—would they be Sirdams to counsel and guide man, or Bokors to corrupt and debase him?

Brent lifted his glass of bond. "To the moment after the next Barrier!" he said.

THE GREAT NEBRASKA SEA

by *Allan Danzig*

Everyone—all the geologists, at any rate—had known about the Kiowa Fault for years. That was before there was anything very interesting to know about it. The first survey of Colorado traced its course north and south in the narrow valley of Kiowa Creek about twenty miles east of Denver; it extended south to the Arkansas River. And that was about all even the professionals were interested in knowing. There was never so much as a landslide to bring the Fault to the attention of the general public.

It was still a matter of academic interest when in the late 'forties geologists speculated on the relationship between the Kiowa Fault and the Conchas Fault farther south, in New Mexico, which followed the Pecos as far south as Texas.

Nor was there much in the papers a few years later when it was suggested that the Niobrara Fault (just inside and roughly parallel to the eastern border of Wyoming) was a northerly extension of the Kiowa. By the mid 'sixties it was definitely established that the three Faults were in fact a single line of fissure in the essential rock, stretching almost from the Canadian border well south of the New Mexico-Texas line.

It is not really surprising that it took so long to figure out the connection. The population of the states affected was in places as low as five people per square mile! The land was so dry it seemed impossible that it could ever be used except for sheep-farming.

It strikes us today as ironic that from the late 'fifties there was grave concern about the level of the watertable throughout the entire area.

The even more ironic solution to the problem began in the summer of 1973. It had been a particularly hot and dry August, and the Forestry Service was keeping an anxious eye out for the fires it knew it could expect. Dense smoke was reported rising above a virtually uninhabited area along Black Squirrel Creek, and a plane was sent out for a report.

The report was—no fire at all. The rising cloud was not smoke, but dust. Thousands of cubic feet of dry earth rising lazily on the summer air. Rock slides, they guessed; certainly no fire. The Forestry Service had other worries at the moment, and filed the report.

But after a week had gone by, the town of Edison, a good twenty miles away from the slides, was still complaining of the dust. Springs were going dry, too, apparently from underground disturbances. Not even in the Rockies could anyone remember a series of rock slides as bad as this.

Newspapers in the mountain states gave it a few inches on the front page; anything is news in late August. And the geologists became interested. Seismologists were reporting unusual activity in the area, tremors too severe to be rock slides. Volcanic activity? Specifically, a dust volcano? Unusual, they knew, but right on the Kiowa Fault—could be.

Labour Day crowds read the scientific conjectures with late summer lassitude. Sunday supplements ran four-colour artists' conceptions of the possible volcano. "Only Active Volcano in U.S.?" demanded the headlines, and some papers even left off the question mark.

It may seem odd that the simplest explanation was practically not mentioned. Only Joseph Schwartzberg, head geographer of the Department of the Interior, wondered if the disturbance might not be a settling of the Kiowa Fault. His suggestion was mentioned on page nine or ten of the Monday newspapers (page 27 of the New York *Times*). The idea was not nearly so exciting as a volcano, even a lava-less one, and you couldn't draw a very dramatic picture of it.

To excuse the other geologists, it must be said that the Kiowa Fault had never acted up before. It never sidestepped, never jiggled, never, never produced the regular shows of its little sister out in California, which almost daily bounced San Francisco or Los Angeles, or some place in between. The dust volcano was on the face of it a more plausible theory.

Still, it was only a theory. It had to be proved. As the tremors grew bigger, along with the affected area, as several towns including Edison were shaken to pieces by incredible earthquakes, whole bus- and plane-loads of geologists set out for Colorado, without even waiting for their university and government departments to approve budgets.

170

They found, of course, that Schwartzberg had been perfectly correct.

They found themselves on the scene of what was fast becoming the most violent and widespread earthquake North America—probably the world—has ever seen in historic times. To describe it in the simplest terms, land east of the Fault was settling, and at a precipitous rate.

Rock scraped rock with a whining roar. Shuddery as a squeaky piece of chalk raked across a blackboard, the noise was deafening. The surfaces of the land east and west of the Fault seemed no longer to have any relation to each other. To the west, tortured rock reared into cliffs. East, where sharp reports and muffled wheezes told of continued buckling and dropping, the earth trembled downwards. Atop the new cliffs, which seemed to grow by sudden inches from heaving rubble, dry earth fissured and trembled, sliding acres at a time to fall, smoking, into the bucking, heaving bottom of the depression.

There the devastation was even more thorough, if less spectacular. Dry earth churned like mud, and rock shards weighing tons bumped and rolled about like pebbles as they shivered and cracked into pebbles themselves. "It looks like sand dancing in a child's sieve," said the normally impassive Schwartzberg in a nationwide broadcast from the scene of disaster. "No one here has ever seen anything like it." And the landslip was growing, north and south along the Fault.

"Get out while you can," Schwartzberg urged the population of the affected area. "When it's over you can come back and pick up the pieces." But the band of scientists who had rallied to his leadership privately wondered if there would be any pieces.

The Arkansas River, at Avondale and North Avondale, was sluggishly backing north into the deepening trough. At the rate things were going, there might be a new lake the entire length of El Paso and Pueblo Counties. And, warned Schwartzberg, this might only be the beginning.

By September 16 the landslip had crept down the Huerfano River past Cedarwood. Avondale, North Avondale and Boone had totally disappeared. Land west of the Fault was holding firm, though Denver had recorded several minor tremors; everywhere east of the Fault, to almost twenty miles away, the now-familiar lurch and steady fall had already sent several thousand Coloradans scurrying for safety.

All mountain climbing was prohibited on the Eastern Slope

because of the danger of rock slides from minor quakes. The geologists went home to wait.

There wasn't much to wait for. The news got worse and worse. The Platte River, now, was creating a vast mud puddle where the town of Orchard had been. Just below Masters, Colorado, the river leaped seventy-foot cliffs to add to the heaving chaos below. And the cliffs were higher every day as the land beneath them groaned downwards in mile-square gulps.

As the Fault moved north and south, new areas quivered into unwelcome life. Fields and whole mountainsides moved with deceptive sloth down, down. They danced "like sand in a sieve"; dry, they boiled into rubble. Telephone lines, railroad tracks, roads snapped and simply disappeared. Virtually all east-west land communication was suspended, and the President declared a national emergency.

By September 23 the Fault was active well into Wyoming on the north, and rapidly approaching the border of New Mexico to the south. Trinchera and Branson were totally evacuated, but even so the overall death toll had risen above one thousand.

Away to the east the situation was quiet but even more ominous. Tremendous fissures opened up perpendicular to the Fault, and a general subsidence of the land was noticeable well into Kansas and Nebraska. The western borders of these states, and soon of the Dakotas and Oklahoma as well, were slowly sinking.

On the actual scene of the disaster (or the *scenes*; it is impossible to speak of anything this size in the singular) there was a horrifying confusion. Prairie and hill cracked open under intolerable strains as the land shuddered downwards in gasps and leaps. Springs burst to the surface in hot geysers and explosions of steam.

The downtown section of North Platte, Nebraska, dropped eight feet, just like that, on the afternoon of October 4. "We must remain calm," declared the Governor of Nebraska. "We must sit this thing out. Be assured that everything possible is being done." But what could be done, with his state dropping straight down at a mean rate of a foot a day?

The Fault nicked off the south-east corner of Montana. It worked its way north along the Little Missouri. South, it ripped past Roswell, New Mexico, and tore down the Pecos towards Texas. All the upper reaches of the Missouri were standing puddles by now, and the Red River west of Paris, Texas, had begun to run backwards.

172

Soon the Missouri began slowly slipping away westwards over the slowly churning land. Abandoning its bed, the river spread uncertainly across farmland and prairie, becoming a sea of mud beneath the sharp new cliffs which rose in rending line, ever taller as the land continued to sink, almost from Canada to the Mexican border. There were virtually no floods, in the usual sense. The water moved too slowly, spread itself with no real direction or force. But the vast sheets of sluggish water and jellylike mud formed death-traps for the countless refugees now streaming east.

Perhaps the North Platte disaster had been more than anyone could take. One hundred and ninety-three people had died in that one cave-in. Certainly by October 7 it had to be officially admitted that there was an exodus of epic proportion. Nearly two million people were on the move, and the U.S. was faced with a gigantic wave of refugees. Rails, roads and air-lanes were jammed with terrified hordes who had left everything behind to crowd eastwards.

All through October, hollow-eyed motorists flocked into Tulsa, Topeka, Omaha, Sioux Falls and Fargo. St. Louis was made distributing centre for emergency squads which flew everywhere with milk for babies and dog food for evacuating pets. Gasoline trucks boomed west to meet the demand for gas, but once inside the "zone of terror," as the newspapers now called it, they found their route blocked by east-bound cars on the wrong side of the road. Shops left by their fleeing owners were looted by refugees from further west; an American Airlines plane was wrecked by a mob of would-be passengers in Bismarck, North Dakota. Federal and State troops were called out, but moving two million people was not to be done in an orderly way.

And still the landslip grew larger. The new cliffs gleamed in the autumn sunshine, growing higher as the land beneath them continued its inexorable descent.

On October 21, at Lubbock, Texas, there was a noise variously described as a hollow roar, a shriek and a deep musical vibration like a church bell. It was simply the tortured rock of the substrata giving way. The second phase of the national disaster was beginning.

The noise travelled due east at better than eighty-five miles per hour. In its wake the earth to the north "just seemed to collapse on itself like a punctured balloon," read one newspaper report. "Like a cake that's failed," said a Texarkana housewife

173

who fortunately lived a block *south* of Thayer Street, where the fissure raced through. There was a sigh and a great cloud of dust, and Oklahoma subsided at the astounding rate of about six feet per hour.

At Biloxi, on the Gulf, there had been uneasy shufflings under foot all day. "Not tremors, exactly," said the captain of a fishing boat which was somehow to ride out the coming flood, "but like as if the land wanted to be somewhere else."

Everyone in doomed Biloxi would have done well to have been somewhere else that evening. At approximately 8:30 p.m. the town shuddered, seemed to rise a little like the edge of a hall carpet caught in a draught, and sank. So did the entire Mississippi and Alabama coast, at about the same moment. The tidal wave which was to gouge the centre from the U.S. marched on the land.

From the north shore of Lake Ponchartrain to the Appalachicola River in Florida, the Gulf coast simply disappeared. Gulfport, Biloxi, Mobile, Pensacola, Panama City: two hundred miles of shoreline vanished, with over two and a half million people. An hour later a wall of water had swept over every town from Dothan, Alabama, to Bogalusa on the Louisiana-Mississippi border.

"We must keep panic from our minds," said the Governor of Alabama in a radio message delivered from a hastily arranged all-station hook-up. "We of the gallant southland have faced and withstood invasion before." Then, as ominous creakings and groanings of the earth announced the approach of the tidal wave, he flew out of Montgomery half an hour before the town disappeared for ever.

One head of the wave plunged north, eventually to spend itself in the hills south of Birmingham. The main sweep followed the lowest land. Reaching west, it swallowed Vicksburg and nicked the corner of Louisiana. The whole of East Carroll Parish was scoured from the map.

The Mississippi River now ended at about Eudora, Arkansas, and minute by minute the advancing flood bit away miles of river bed, swelling north. Chicot, Jennie, Lake Village, Arkansas City, Snow Lake, Elaine, Helena and Memphis felt the tremors. The tormented city shuddered through the night. The earth continued its descent, eventually tipping two and a half degrees down to the west. The "Memphis Tilt" is today one of the unique and charming characteristics of the gracious Old Town, but during the night of panic Memphis residents were sure they were doomed.

174

South and west the waters carved deeply into Arkansas and Oklahoma. By morning it was plain that all of Arkansas was going under. Waves advanced on Little Rock at almost one hundred miles an hour, new crests forming, overtopping the wave's leading edge as towns, hills and the thirst of the soil temporarily broke the furious charge.

Washington announced the official hope that the Ozarks would stop the wild gallop of the unleashed Gulf, for in northwest Arkansas the land rose to over two thousand feet. But nothing could save Oklahoma. By noon the water reached clutching fingers around Mt. Scott and Elk Mountain, deluging Hobart and almost all of Greer County.

Despite hopeful announcements that the wave was slowing, had virtually stopped after inundating Oklahoma City, was being swallowed up in the desert near Amarillo, the wall of water continued its advance. For the land was still sinking, and the floods were constantly replenished from the Gulf. Schwartzberg and his geologists advised the utmost haste in evacuating the entire area between Colorado and Missouri, from Texas to North Dakota.

Lubbock, Texas, went under. On a curling reflex the tidal wave blotted out Sweetwater and Big Spring. The Texas panhandle disappeared in one great swirl.

Whirlpools opened. A great welter of smashed wood and human debris was sucked under, vomited up and pounded to pieces. Gulf-water crashed on the cliffs of New Mexico and fell back on itself in foam. Would-be rescuers on the cliffs along what had been the west bank of the Pecos River afterwards recalled the hiss and scream like tearing silk as the water broke furiously on the newly exposed rock. It was the most terrible sound they had ever heard.

"We couldn't hear any shouts, of course, not that far away and with all that noise," said Dan Weaver, Mayor of Carlsbad. "But we knew there were people down there. When the water hit the cliffs, it was like a collision between two solid bodies. We couldn't see for over an hour, because of the spray."

Salt spray. The ocean had come to New Mexico.

The cliffs proved to be the only effective barrier against the westward march of the water, which turned north, gouging out lumps of rock and tumbling down blocks of earth on to its own back. In places scoops of granite came out like ice cream. The present fishing town of Rockport, Colorado, is built on a harbour created in such a way.

175

The water had found its farthest westering. But still it poured north along the line of the original Fault. Irresistible fingers closed on Sterling, Colorado, on Sidney, Nebraska, on Hot Springs, South Dakota. The entire tier of states settled, from south to north, down to its eventual place of stability one thousand feet below the level of the new sea.

Memphis was by now a seaport. The Ozarks, islands in a mad sea, formed precarious havens for half-drowned humanity. Waves bit off a corner of Missouri, flung themselves to Wichita. Topeka, Lawrence and Belleville were the last Kansas towns to disappear. The Governor of Kansas went down with his State.

Daniel Bernd of Lincoln, Nebraska, was washed up half-drowned in a cove of the Wyoming cliffs, having been sucked from one end of vanished Nebraska to the other. Similar hair-breadth escapes were recounted on radio and television.

Virtually the only people saved out of the entire population of Pierre, South Dakota were the six members of the Creeth family. Plucky Timothy Creeth carried and dragged his aged parents to the loft of their barn on the outskirts of town. His brother Geoffrey brought along the younger children and what provisions they could find—"Mostly a ham and about half a ton of vanilla cookies," he explained to his eventual rescuers. The barn, luckily collapsing in the vibrations as the waves bore down on them, became an ark in which they rode out the disaster.

"We must of played cards for four days straight," recalled genial Mrs. Creeth when she afterwards appeared on a popular television spectacular. Her rural good-humour undamaged by an ordeal few women can ever have been called on to face, she added, "We sure wondered why flushes never came out right. Jimanettly, we'd left the king of hearts behind, in the rush!"

But such lightheartedness and such happy endings were by no means typical. The world could only watch aghast as the water raced north under the shadow of the cliffs which occasionally crumbled, roaring, into the roaring waves. Day by day the relentless rush swallowed what had been dusty farmland, cities and towns.

Some people were saved by the helicopters which flew mercy missions just ahead of the advancing waters. Some found safety in the peaks of western Nebraska and the Dakotas. But when the waters came to rest along what is roughly the present shoreline of our inland sea, it was estimated that over fourteen million people had lost their lives.

No one could even estimate the damage to property; almost

the entirety of eight states, and portions of twelve others, had simply vanished from the heart of the North American continent for ever.

It was in such a catacylsmic birth that the now-peaceful Nebraska Sea came to America.

Today, nearly one hundred years after the unprecedented —and happily unrepeated—disaster, it is hard to remember the terror and despair of those weeks in October and November, 1973. It is inconceivable to think of the United States without its beautiful and economically essential curve of interior ocean. Two-thirds as long as the Mediterranean, it graduates from the warm waters of the Gulf of Mexico through the equally blue waves of the Mississippi Bight, becoming cooler and greener north and west of the pleasant fishing isles of the Ozark Archipelago, finally shading into the grey-green chop of the Gulf of Dakota.

What would the United States have become without the 5,600-mile coastline of our inland sea? It is only within the last twenty years that any but the topmost layer of water has cleared sufficiently to permit a really extensive fishing industry. Mud still held in suspension by the restless waves will not precipitate fully even in our lifetimes. Even so, the commercial fisheries of Missouri and Wyoming contribute no small part to the nation's economy.

Who can imagine what the middle west must have been like before the amelioration of climate brought about by the proximity of a warm sea? The now-temperate state of Minnesota (to say nothing of the submerged Dakotas) must have been Siberian. From contemporary accounts Missouri, our second California, was unbelievably muggy, almost uninhabitable during the summer months. Our climate today, from Ohio and North Carolina to the rich fields of New Mexico and the orchards of Montana, is directly ameliorated by the marine heart of the continent.

Who today could imagine the United States without the majestic sea-cliffs in stately parade from New Mexico to Montana? The beaches of Wyoming, the American Riviera, where fruit trees grow almost to the water's edge? Or incredible Colorado, where the morning skier is the afternoon bather, thanks to the monorail connecting the highest peaks with the glistening white beaches?

Of course there have been losses to balance slightly these strong gains. The Mississippi was, before 1973, one of the great

177

rivers of the world. Taken together with it main tributary, the Missouri, it vied favourably with such giant systems as the Amazon and the Ganges. Now, ending as it does at Memphis and drawing its water chiefly from the Appalachian Mountains, it is only a slight remnant of what it was. And though the Nebraska Sea today carries many times the tonnage of shipping in its ceaseless traffic, we have lost the old romance of river shipping. We may only guess what it was like when we look upon the Ohio and the truncated Mississippi.

And transcontinental shipping is somewhat more difficult, with trucks and the freight-railroads obliged to take the sea-ferries across the Nebraska Sea. We shall never know what the United States was like with its numerous coast-to-coast highways busy with trucks and private cars. Still, the ferry ride is certainly a welcome break after days of driving, and for those who wish a glimpse of what it must have been like, there is always the Cross-Canada Throughway and the magnificent U.S. Highway 73 looping north through Minnesota and passing through the giant port of Alexis, North Dakota, shipping centre for the wheat of Manitoba and crossroad of a nation.

The political situation has long been a thorny problem. Only tattered remnants of the eight submerged states remained after the flood, but none of them wanted to surrender its autonomy. The tiny fringe of Kansas seemed, for a time, ready to merge with contiguous Missouri, but following the lead of the Arkansas Forever faction, the remaining population decided to retain political integrity. This has resulted in the continuing anomaly of the seven "fringe States" represented in Congress by the usual two Senators each, though the largest of them is barely the size of Connecticut and all are economically indistinguishable from their neighbouring states.

Fortunately it was decided some years ago that Oklahoma, only one of the eight to have completely disappeared, could not in any sense be considered to have a continuing political existence. So, though there are still families who proudly call themselves Oklahomans, and the Oklahoma Oil Company continues to pump oil from its submerged real estate, the state has in fact disappeared from the American political scene.

But this is by now no more than a petty annoyance, to raise a smile when the talk gets around to the question of State's Rights. Not even the tremendous price the country paid for its new sea—fourteen million dead, untold property destroyed—really offsets the asset we enjoy today. The heart of

178

the continent, now open to the shipping of the world, was once dry and land-locked, cut off from the bustle of trade and the ferment of world culture.

It would indeed seem odd to an American of the 'fifties or 'sixties of the last century to imagine sailors from the merchant fleets of every nation walking the streets of Denver, fresh ashore at Newport, only fifteen miles away. Or to imagine Lincoln, Fargo, Kansas City and Dallas as world ports and great manufacturing centres. Utterly beyond their ken would be Roswell, New Mexico; Benton, Wyoming; Westport, Missouri; and the other new ports of over a million inhabitants each, which have developed on the new harbours of the inland sea.

Unimaginable too would have been the general growth of population in the states surrounding the new sea. As the water tables rose and manufacturing and trade moved in to take advantage of the just-created axis of world communication, a population explosion was touched off of which we are only now seeing the diminuation. This new westering is to be ranked with the first surge of pioneers which created the American west. But what a difference! Vacation paradises bloom, a new fishing industry thrives; her water road is America's main artery of trade, and fleets of all the world sail . . . where once the prairie schooner made its laborious and dusty way west!

COMPASSION CIRCUIT

by *John Wyndham*

By the time Janet had been five days in the hospital she had become converted to the idea of a domestic robot. It had taken her two days to discover that Nurse James *was* a robot, one day to get over the surprise, and two more to realise what a comfort an attendant robot could be.

The conversion was a relief. Practically every house she visited had a domestic robot; it was the family's second or third most valuable possession—the women tended to rate it slightly higher than the car; the men, slightly lower. Janet had been perfectly well aware for some time that her friends regarded her as a nitwit or worse for wearing herself out with looking after a

179

house which a robot would be able to keep spick and span with a few hours' work a day. She had also known that it irritated George to come home each evening to a wife who had tired herself out by unnecessary work. But the prejudice had been firmly set. It was not the diehard attitude of people who refused to be served by robot waiters, or driven by robot drivers (who, incidentally, were much safer), led by robot shop-guides, or see dresses modelled by robot mannequins. It was simply an uneasiness about them, and being left alone with one—and a disinclination to feel such an uneasiness in her own home.

She herself attributed the feeling largely to the conservatism of her own home which had used no house-robots. Other people, who had been brought up in homes run by robots, even the primitive types available a generation before, never seemed to have such a feeling at all. It irritated her to know that her husband thought she was *afraid* of them in a childish way. That, she had explained to George a number of times, was not so, and was not the point, either: what she did dislike was the idea of one intruding upon her personal, domestic life, which was what a house-robot was bound to do.

The robot who was called Nurse James was, then, the first with which she had ever been in close personal contact and she, or it, came as a revelation.

Janet told the doctor of her enlightenment, and he looked relieved. She also told George when he looked in in the afternoon: he was delighted. The two of them conferred before he left the hospital. "Excellent," said the doctor. "To tell you the truth I was afraid we were up against a real neurosis there—and very inconveniently, too. Your wife can never have been strong, and in the last few years she's worn herself out running the house."

"I know," George agreed. "I tried hard to persuade her during the first two years we were married, but it only led to trouble so I had to drop it. This is really a culmination—she was rather shaken when she found that the reason she'd have to come here was partly because there was no robot at home to look after her."

"Well, there's one thing certain, she can't go on as she has been doing. If she tries to she'll be back here inside a couple of months," the doctor told him.

"She won't now. She's really changed her mind," George assured him. "Part of the trouble is that she's never come across a really modern one, except in a superficial way. The newest

180

that any of our friends has is ten years old at least, and most of them are older than that. She'd never contemplated the idea of anything as advanced as Nurse James. The question now is what pattern?"

The doctor thought a moment.

"Frankly, Mr. Shand, your wife is going to need a lot of rest and looking after, I'm afraid. What I'd really recommend for her is the type they have here. It's something pretty new, this Nurse James model. A specially developed high-sensibility job with a quite novel contra-balanced compassion-protection circuit—a very tricky bit of work that. Any direct order which a normal robot would obey at once is evaluated by the circuit, it is weighed against the benefit or harm to the patient and, unless it is beneficial, or at least harmless, to the patient, it is not obeyed. They've proved to be wonderful for nursing and looking after children—but there is a big demand for them, and I'm afraid they're pretty expensive."

"How much?" asked George.

The doctor's round-figure price made him frown for a moment. Then he said: "It'll make a hole, but, after all, it's mostly Janet's economies and simple-living that's built up the savings. Where do I get one?"

"You don't. Not just like that," the doctor told him. "I shall have to throw a bit of weight about for a priority, but in the circumstances I shall get it, all right. Now, you go and fix up the details of appearance and so on with your wife. Let me know how she wants it, and I'll get busy."

"A proper one," said Janet. "One that'll look right in a house, I mean. I couldn't do with one of those levers-and-plastic box things that stare at you with lenses. As it's got to look after the house, let's have it looking like a housemaid."

"Or a houseman, if you like?"

She shook her head. "No. It's going to have to look after me, too, so I think I'd rather it was a housemaid. It can have a black silk dress and a frilly white apron and a cap. And I'd like it blonde—a sort of darkish blonde—and about five feet ten, and nice to look at, but not *too* beautiful. I don't want to be jealous of it. . . ."

The doctor kept Janet ten days more in the hospital while the matter was settled. There had been luck in coming in for a cancelled order, but inevitably some delay while it was adapted

181

to Janet's specification—also it had required the addition of standard domestic pseudo-memory patterns to suit it for housework.

It was delivered the day after she got back. Two severely functional robots carried the case up the front path, and inquired whether they should unpack it. Janet thought not, and told them to leave it in the outhouse.

When George got back he wanted to open it at once, but Janet shook her head.

"Supper first," she decided. "A robot doesn't mind waiting."

Nevertheless it was a brief meal. When it was over, George carried the dishes out and stacked them in the sink.

"No more washing-up," he said, with satisfaction.

He went out to borrow the next-door robot to help him carry the case in. Then he found his end of it more than he could lift, and had to borrow the robot from the house opposite, too. Presently the pair of them carried it in and laid it on the kitchen floor as if it were a featherweight, and went away again.

George got out the screwdriver and drew the six large screws that held the lid down. Inside there was a mass of shavings. He shoved them out, on to the floor. Janet protested.

"What's the matter? *We* shan't have to clear up," he said, happily.

There was an inner case of wood pulp, with a snowy layer of wadding under its lid. George rolled it up and pushed it out of the way, and there, ready dressed in black frock and white apron, lay the robot.

They regarded it for some seconds without speaking.

It was remarkably lifelike. For some reason it made Janet feel a little queer to realise that it was *her* robot—a trifle nervous, and, obscurely, a trifle guilty. . . .

"Sleeping beauty," remarked George, reaching for the instruction book on its chest.

In point of fact the robot was not a beauty. Janet's preference had been observed. It was pleasant and nice-looking without being striking, but the details were good. The deep gold hair was quite enviable—although one knew that it was probably threads of plastic with waves that would never come out. The skin—another kind of plastic covering the carefully built-up contours—was distinguishable from real skin only by its perfection.

Janet knelt down beside the box, and ventured a forefinger to touch the flawless complexion. It was quite, quite cold.

She sat back on her heels, looking at it. Just a big doll, she told herself; a contraption, a very wonderful contraption of metal, plastics, and electronic circuits, but still a contraption, and made to look as it did simply because people, including herself, would find it harsh or grotesque if it should look any other way. . . . And yet to have it looking as it did was a bit disturbing, too. For one thing, you couldn't go on thinking of it as "it" any more; whether you liked it or not, your mind thought of it as "her". As "her" it would have to have a name; and, with a name, it would become still more of a person.

"'A battery-driven model,'" George read out, "'will normally require to be fitted with a new battery every four days. Other models, however, are designed to conduct their own regeneration from the mains as and when necessary'. Let's have her out."

He put his hands under the robot's shoulders, and tried to lift it.

"Phew!" he said. "Must be about three times my weight." He had another try. "Hell," he said, and referred to the book again.

"'The control switches are situated at the back, slightly above the waistline'. All right, maybe we can roll her over."

With an effort he succeeded in getting the figure on to its side and began to undo the buttons at the back of her dress. Janet suddenly felt that to be an indelicacy. "I'll do it," she said.

Her husband glanced at her.

"All right. It's yours," he told her.

"She can't be just 'it'. I'm going to call her Hester."

"All right, again," he agreed.

Janet undid the buttons and fumbled about inside the dress.

"I can't find a knob, or anything," she said.

"Apparently there's a small panel that opens," he told her.

"Oh, no!" she said, in a slightly shocked tone.

He regarded her again.

"Darling, she's just a robot; a mechanism."

"I know," said Janet, shortly. She felt about again, discovered the panel, and opened it.

"You give the upper knob a half-turn to the right and then close the panel to complete the circuit," instructed George, from the book.

Janet did so, and then sat swiftly back on her heels again, watching.

The robot stirred and turned. It sat up, then it got to its feet. It stood before them, looking the very pattern of a stage parlourmaid. "Good day, madam," it said. "Good day, sir. I shall be happy to serve you."

"Thank you, Hester," Janet said, as she leaned back against the cushion placed behind her. Not that it was necessary to thank a robot, but she had a theory that if you did not practise politeness with robots you soon forgot it with other people.

And, anyway, Hester was no ordinary robot. She was not even dressed as a parlourmaid any more. In four months she had become a friend, a tireless, attentive friend. From the first Janet had found it difficult to believe that she was only a mechanism, and as the days passed she had become more and more of a person. The fact that she consumed electricity instead of food came to seem little more than a foible. The time she couldn't stop walking in a circle, and the other time when something went wrong with her vision so that she did everything a foot to the right of where she ought to have been doing it, these things were just indispositions such as anyone might have, and the robot-mechanic who came to adjust her paid his call much like any other doctor. Hester was not only a person; she was preferable company to many.

"I suppose," said Janet, settling back in her chair, "that you must think me a poor, weak thing?"

What one must not expect from Hester was euphemism.

"Yes," she said, directly. But then she added: "I think all humans are poor, weak things. It is the way they are made. One must be sorry for them."

Janet had long ago given up thinking things like: "That'll be the compassion-circuit speaking," or trying to imagine the computing, selecting, associating, and shunting that must be going on to produce such a remark. She took it as she might from—well, say, a foreigner. She said:

"Compared with robots we must seem so, I suppose. You are so strong and untiring, Hester. If you knew how I envy you that. . . ."

Hester said, matter of factly: "We were designed: you were just accidental. It is your misfortune, not your fault."

"You'd rather be you than me?" asked Janet.

"Certainly," Hester told her. "We are stronger. We don't have to have frequent sleep to recuperate. We don't have to carry an unreliable chemical factory inside us. We don't have to grow old and deteriorate. Human beings are so clumsy and fragile and so often unwell because something is not working properly. If anything goes wrong with us, or is broken, it doesn't hurt and is easily replaced. And you have all kinds of words like pain, and suffering, and unhappiness, and weariness that we have to be taught to understand, and they don't seem to us to be

184

useful things to have. I feel very sorry that you must have these things and be so uncertain and so fragile. It disturbs my compassion-circuit."

"Uncertain and fragile," Janet repeated. "Yes, that's how I feel."

"Humans have to live so precariously," Hester went on. "If my arm or leg should be crushed I can have a new one in a few minutes, but a human would have agony for a long time, and not even a new limb at the end of it—just a faulty one, if he is lucky. That isn't as bad as it used to be because in designing us you learned how to make good arms and legs, much stronger and better than the old ones. People would be much more sensible to have a weak arm or leg replaced at once, but they don't seem to want to if they can possibly keep the old ones."

"You mean they can be grafted on? I didn't know that," Janet said. "I wish it were only arms or legs that's wrong with me. I don't think I would hesitate. . . ." She sighed. "The doctor wasn't encouraging this morning, Hester. You heard what he said? I've been losing ground: must rest more. I don't believe he does expect me to get any stronger. He was just trying to cheer me up before. . . . He had a funny sort of look after he'd examined me. . . . But all he said was rest. What's the good of being alive if it's only rest—rest—rest. . .? And there's poor George. What sort of a life is it for him, and he's so patient with me, so sweet. . . . I'd rather anything than go on feebly like this. I'd sooner die. . . ."

Janet went on talking, more to herself than to the patient Hester standing by. She talked herself into tears. Then, presently, she looked up.

"Oh, Hester, if you were human I couldn't bear it; I think I'd hate you for being so strong and so well—but I don't, Hester. You're so kind and so patient when I'm silly, like this. I believe you'd cry with me to keep me company if you could."

"I would if I could," the robot agreed. "My compassion-circuit—"

"Oh, no!" Janet protested. "It can't be just that. You've a heart somewhere, Hester. You must have."

"I expect it is more reliable than a heart," said Hester.

She stepped a little closer, stooped down, and lifted Janet up as if she weighed nothing at all.

"You've tired yourself out, Janet, dear," she told her. "I'll take you upstairs; you'll be able to sleep a little before he gets back."

Janet could feel the robot's arms cold through her dress, but

185

the coldness did not trouble her any more, she was aware only that they were strong, protecting arms around her. She said:

"Oh, Hester, you are such a comfort, you *know* what I ought to do." She paused, then she added miserably: "I know what he thinks—the doctor, I mean. I could see it. He just thinks I'm going to go on getting weaker and weaker until one day I'll fade away and die. . . . I said I'd sooner . . . but I wouldn't, Hester. I don't want to die. . . ."

The robot rocked her a little, as if she were a child.

"There, there, dear. It's not as bad as that—nothing like," she told her. "You mustn't think about dying. And you mustn't cry any more, it's not good for you, you know. Besides, you don't want him to see you've been crying."

"I'll try not to," agreed Janet obediently, as Hester carried her out of the room and up the stairs.

The hospital reception-robot looked up from the desk.

"My wife," George said, "I rang you up about an hour ago."

The robot's face took on an impeccable expression of professional sympathy.

"Yes, Mr. Shand. I'm afraid it has been a shock for you, but as I told you, your house-robot did quite the right thing to send her here at once."

"I've tried to get on to her own doctor, but he's away," George told her.

"You don't need to worry about that, Mr. Shand. She has been examined, and we have had all her records sent over from the hospital she was in before. The operation has been provisionally fixed for tomorrow, but of course we shall need your consent."

George hesitated. "May I see the doctor in charge of her?"

"He isn't in the hospital at the moment, I'm afraid."

"Is it—absolutely necessary?" George asked after a pause.

The robot looked at him steadily, and nodded.

"She must have been growing steadily weaker for some months now," she said. George nodded.

"The only alternative is that she will grow weaker still, and have more pain before the end," she told him.

George stared at the wall blankly for some seconds.

"I see," he said bleakly.

He picked up a pen in a shaky hand and signed the form that she put before him. He gazed at it a while without seeing it.

"She'll—she'll have—a good chance?" he asked.

"Yes," the robot told him. "There is never complete absence
186

of risk, of course, but she has a better than seventy-per-cent likelihood of complete success."

George sighed, and nodded. "I'd like to see her," he said.

The robot pressed a bell-push.

"You may *see* her," she said. "But I must ask you not to disturb her. She's asleep now, and it's better for her not to be woken."

George had to be satisfied with that, but he left the hospital feeling a little better for the sight of the quiet smile on Janet's lips as she slept.

The hospital called him at the office the following afternoon. They were reassuring. The operation appeared to have been a complete success. Everyone was quite confident of the outcome. There was no need to worry. The doctors were perfectly satisfied. No, it would not be wise to allow any visitors for a few days yet. But there was nothing to worry about. Nothing at all.

George rang up each day just before he left, in the hope that he would be allowed a visit. The hospital was kindly and heartening, but adamant about visits. And then, on the fifth day, they suddenly told him she had left on her way home. George was staggered: he had been prepared to find it a matter of weeks. He dashed out, bought a bunch of roses, and left half a dozen traffic regulations in fragments behind him. "Where is she?" he demanded of Hester as she opened the door.

"She's in bed. I thought it might be better if—" Hester began, but he lost the rest of the sentence as he bounded up the stairs.

Janet was lying in the bed. Only her head was visible, cut off by the line of the sheet and a bandage round her neck. George put the flowers down on the bedside table. He stooped over Janet and kissed her gently. She looked up at him from anxious eyes.

"Oh, George dear. Has she told you?"

"Has who told me what?" he asked, sitting down on the side of the bed.

"Hester. She said she would. Oh, George, I didn't mean it, at least I don't think I meant it. . . . She sent me, George. I was so weak and wretched. I wanted to be strong. I don't think I really understood. Hester said—"

"Take it easy, darling. Take it easy," George suggested with a smile. "What on earth's all this about?"

He felt under the bedclothes and found her hand.

"But, George—" she began. He interrupted her.

187

"I say, darling, your hand's dreadfully cold. It's almost like—" His fingers slid further up her arm. His eyes widened at her, incredulously. He jumped up suddenly from the bed and flung back the covers. He put his hand on the thin nightdress, over her heart—and then snatched it away as if he had been stung. "God—*NO!*—" he said, staring at her.

"But George. George, darling—" said Janet's head on the pillows.

"NO—*NO!*" cried George, almost in a shriek.

He turned and ran blindly from the room.

In the darkness on the landing he missed the top step of the stairs, and went headlong down the whole flight.

Hester found him lying in a huddle in the hall. She bent down and gently explored the damage. The extent of it, and the fragility of the frame that had suffered it disturbed her compassion-circuit very greatly. She did not try to move him, but went to the telephone and dialled.

"Emergency?" she asked, and gave the name and address. "Yes, at once," she told them. "There may not be a lot of time. Several compound fractures, and I think his back is broken, poor man. No. There appears to be no damage to his head. Yes, much better. He'd be crippled for life, even if he did get over it. . . . Yes, better send the form of consent with the ambulance so that it can be signed at once. . . . Oh, yes, that'll be quite all right. His wife will sign it."

A PLANET NAMED SHAYOL

by *Cordwainer Smith*

I

There was a tremendous difference between the liner and the ferry in Mercer's treatment. On the liner, the attendants made gibes when they brought him his food.

"Scream good and loud," said one rat-faced steward, "and then we'll know it's you when they broadcast the sounds of punishment on the Emperor's birthday."

The other, fat steward ran the tip of his wet red tongue over his thick purple-red lips one time and said, "Stands to reason, man. If you hurt all the time, the whole lot of you would die. Something pretty good must happen, along with the—what-chamacallit. Maybe you turn into a woman. Maybe you turn into two people. Listen, cousin, if it's real crazy fun, let me know. . . ." Mercer said nothing. Mercer had enough troubles of his own not to wonder about the daydreams of nasty men.

At the ferry it was different. The biopharmaceutical staff was deft, impersonal, quick in removing his shackles. They took off all his prison clothes and left them on the liner. When he boarded the ferry, naked, they looked him over as if he were a rare plant or a body on the operating table. They were almost kind in the clinical deftness of their touch. They did not treat him as a criminal, but as a specimen.

Men and women, clad in their medical smocks, they looked at him as though he were already dead.

He tried to speak. A man, older and more authoritative than the others, said firmly and clearly, "Do not worry about talking. I will talk to you myself in a very little time. What we are having now are the preliminaries, to determine your physical condition. Turn around, please."

Mercer turned around. An orderly rubbed his back with a very strong antiseptic.

"This is going to sting," said one of the technicians, "but it is nothing serious or painful. We are determining the toughness of the different layers of your skin."

Mercer, annoyed by this impersonal approach, spoke up just as a sharp little sting burned him above the sixth lumbar vertebra. "Don't you know who I am?"

"Of course we know who you are," said a woman's voice. "We have it all in a file in the corner. The chief doctor will talk about your crime later, if you want to talk about it. Keep quiet now. We are making a skin test, and you will feel much better if you do not make us prolong it."

Honesty forced her to add another sentence: "And we will get better results as well."

They had lost no time at all in getting to work.

He peered at them sideways to look at them. There was nothing about them to indicate that they were human devils in the ante-chambers of hell itself. Nothing was there to indicate that this was the satellite of Shayol, the final and uttermost place of chastisement and shame. They looked like medical people from his life before he committed the crime without a name.

They changed from one routine to another. A woman, wearing a surgical mask, waved her hand at a white table.

"Climb up on that, please."

No one had said "please" to Mercer since the guards had seized him at the edge of the palace. He started to obey her and then he saw there were padded handcuffs at the head of the table. He stopped.

"Get along, please," she demanded. Two or three of the others turned around to look at both of them.

The second "please" shook him. He had to speak. These were people, and he was a person again. He felt his voice rising, almost cracking into shrillness as he asked her, "Please, ma'am, is the punishment going to begin?"

"There's no punishment here," said the woman. "This is the satellite. Get on the table. We're going to give you your first skin-toughening before you talk to the head doctor. Then you can tell him all about your crime—"

"You know my crime?" he said, greeting it almost like a neighbour.

"Of course not," said she, "but all the people who come through here are believed to have committed crimes. Somebody thinks so or they wouldn't be here. Most of them want to talk about their personal crimes. But don't slow me down. I'm a skin technician, and down on the surface of Shayol you're going to need the very best work that any of us can do for you. Now get on that table. And when you are ready to talk to the chief you'll have something to talk about beside your crime."

He complied.

Another masked person, probably a girl, took his hands in cool, gentle fingers and fitted them to the padded cuffs in a way he had never sensed before. By now he thought he knew every interrogation machine in the whole empire, but this was nothing like any of them.

The orderly stepped back. "All clear, sir and doctor."

"What do you prefer?" said the skin technician. "A great deal of pain or a couple of hours' unconsciousness?"

"Why should I want pain?" said Mercer.

"Some specimens do," said the technician, "by the time they arrive here. I suppose it depends on what people have done to them before they got here. I take it you did not get any of the dream-punishments."

"No," said Mercer. "I missed those." He thought to himself, I didn't know that I missed anything at all.

He remembered his last trial, himself wired and plugged in to the witness stand. The room had been high and dark. Bright blue light shone on the panel of judges, their judicial caps a fantastic parody of the episcopal mitres of long, long ago. The judges were talking, but he could not hear them. Momentarily the insulation slipped and he heard one of them say, "Look at that white, devilish face. A man like that is guilty of everything. I vote for Pain Terminal." "Not Planet Shayol?" said a second voice. "The dromozoa place," said a third voice. "That should suit him," said the first voice. One of the judicial engineers must then have noticed that the prisoner was listening illegally. He was cut off. Mercer then thought that he had gone through everything which the cruelty and intelligence of mankind could devise.

But this woman said he had missed the dream-punishments. Could there be people in the universe even worse off than himself? There must be a lot of people down on Shayol. They never came back.

He was going to be one of them; would they boast to him of what they had done, before they were made to come to this place?

"You asked for it," said the woman technician. "It is just an ordinary anaesthetic. Don't panic when you awaken. Your skin is going to be thickened and strengthened chemically and biologically."

"Does it hurt?"

"Of course," said she. "But get this out of your head. We're not punishing you. The pain here is just ordinary medical pain. Anybody might get it if they needed a lot of surgery. The punishment, if that's what you want to call it, is down on Shayol. Our only job is to make sure that you are fit to survive after you are landed. In a way, we are saving your life ahead of time. You can be grateful for that if you want to be. Meanwhile, you will save yourself a lot of trouble if you realise that your nerve endings will all respond to the change in the skin. You had better expect to be very uncomfortable when you recover. But then, we can help that, too." She brought down an enormous lever and Mercer blacked out.

When he came to, he was in an ordinary hospital room, but he did not notice it. He seemed bedded in fire. He lifted his hand to see if there were flames on it. It looked the way it always had, except that it was a little red and a little swollen. He tried to turn in the bed. The fire became a scorching blast which stopped him in mid-turn. Uncontrollably, he moaned.

A voice spoke, "You are ready for some pain-killer."

It was a girl nurse. "Hold your head still," she said, "and I will give you half an amp of pleasure. Your skin won't bother you then."

She slipped a soft cap on his head. It looked like metal but it felt like silk.

He had to dig his fingernails into his palms to keep from threshing about on the bed.

"Scream if you want to," she said. "A lot of them do. It will just be a minute or two before the cap finds the right lobe in your brain."

She stepped to the corner and did something which he could not see.

There was a flick of a switch.

The fire did not vanish from his skin. He still felt it; but suddenly it did not matter. His mind was full of delicious pleasure which throbbed outwards from his head and seemed to pulse down through his nerves. He had visited the pleasure palaces, but he had never felt anything like this before.

He wanted to thank the girl, and he twisted around in the bed to see her. He could feel his whole body flash with pain as he did so, but the pain was far away. And the pulsating pleasure which coursed out of his head, down his spinal cord and into his nerves was so intense that the pain got through only as a remote, unimportant signal.

She was standing very still in the corner.

"Thank you, nurse," said he.

She said nothing.

He looked more closely, though it was hard to look while enormous pleasure pulsed through his body like a symphony written in nerve-messages. He focused his eyes on her and saw that she too wore a soft metallic cap.

He pointed at it.

She blushed all the way down to her throat.

She spoke dreamily, "You looked like a nice man to me. I didn't think you'd tell on me . . ."

He gave her what he thought was a friendly smile, but with the pain in his skin and the pleasure bursting out of his head, he really had no idea of what his actual expression might be.

"It's against the law," he said. "It's terribly against the law. But it is nice."

"How do you think *we* stand it here?" said the nurse. "You

192

specimens come in here talking like ordinary people and then you go down to Shayol. Terrible things happen to you on Shayol. Then the surface station sends up parts of you, over and over again. I may see your head ten times, quick-frozen and ready for cutting up, before my two years are up. You prisoners ought to know how we suffer," she crooned, the pleasure-charge still keeping her relaxed and happy, "you ought to die as soon as you get down there and not pester us with your torments. We can hear you screaming, you know. You keep on sounding like people even after Shayol begins to work on you. Why do you do it, Mr. Specimen?" She giggled sillily. "You hurt our feelings so. No wonder a girl like me has to have a little jolt now and then. It's real, real dreamy and I don't mind getting you ready to go down on Shayol." She staggered over to his bed. "Pull this cap off me, will you? I haven't got enough will power left to raise my hands."

Mercer saw his hand tremble as he reached for the cap.

His fingers touched the girl's soft hair through the cap. As he tried to get his thumb under the edge of the cap, in order to pull it off, he realised that this was the loveliest girl he had ever touched. He felt that he had always loved her, that he always would. The cap came off. She stood erect, staggering a little before she found a chair to hold on to. She closed her eyes and breathed deeply.

"Just a minute," she said in her normal voice. "I'll be with you in just a minute. The only time I can get a jolt of this is when one of you visitors gets a dose to get over the skin trouble."

She turned to the room mirror to adjust her hair. Speaking with her back to him, she said, "I hope I didn't say anything about downstairs."

Mercer still had the cap on. He loved this beautiful girl who had put it on him. He was ready to weep at the thought that she had had the same kind of pleasure which he still enjoyed. Not for the world would he say anything which could hurt her feelings. He was sure she wanted to be told that she had not said anything about "downstairs"—probably shop talk for the surface of Shayol—so he assured her warmly, "You said nothing. Nothing at all."

She came over to the bed, leaned, kissed him on the lips. The kiss was as far away as the pain; he felt nothing; the Niagara of throbbing pleasure which poured through his head left no room for more sensation. But he liked the friendliness of it. A grim,

193

sane corner of his mind whispered to him that this was probably the last time he would ever kiss a woman, but it did not seem to matter.

With skilled fingers she adjusted the cap on his head. "There, now. You're a sweet guy. I'm going to pretend-forget and leave the cap on you till the doctor comes."

With a bright smile she squeezed his shoulder.

She hastened out of the room.

The white of her skirt flashed prettily as she went out of the door. He saw that she had very shapely legs indeed.

She was nice, but the cap . . . ah, it was the cap that mattered! He closed his eyes and let the cap go on stimulating the pleasure centres of his brain. The pain in his skin was still there, but it did not matter any more than did the chair standing in the corner. The pain was just something that happened to be in the room.

A firm touch on his arm made him open his eyes.

The older, authoritative-looking man was standing beside the bed, looking down at him with a quizzical smile.

"She did it again," said the old man.

Mercer shook his head, trying to indicate that the young nurse had done nothing wrong.

"I'm Doctor Vomact," said the older man, "and I am going to take this cap off you. You will then experience the pain again, but I think it will not be so bad. You can have the cap several more times before you leave here."

With a swift, firm gesture he snatched the cap off Mercer's head.

Mercer promptly doubled up with the inrush of fire from his skin. He started to scream and then saw that Doctor Vomact was watching him calmly.

Mercer gasped, "It is—easier now."

"I knew it would be," said the doctor. "I had to take the cap off to talk to you. You have a few choices to make."

"Yes, doctor," gasped Mercer.

"You have committed a serious crime and you are going down to the surface of Shayol."

"Yes," said Mercer.

"Do you want to tell me your crime?"

Mercer thought of the white palace walls in perpetual sunlight, and the soft mewing of the little things when he reached them. He tightened his arms, legs, back and jaw. "No," he said, "I don't want to talk about it. It's the crime without a name. Against the Imperial family . . ."

194

"Fine," said the doctor, "that's a healthy attitude. The crime is past. Your future is ahead. Now, I can destroy your mind before you go down—if you want me to."

"That's against the law," said Mercer.

Doctor Vomact smiled warmly and confidently. "Of course it is. A lot of things are against human law. But there are laws of science, too. Your body, down on Shayol, is going to serve science. It doesn't matter to me whether that body has Mercer's mind or the mind of a low-grade shell-fish. I have to leave enough mind in you to keep the body going, but I can wipe out the historic you and give your body a better chance of being happy. It's your choice, Mercer. Do you want to be you or not?"

Mercer shook his head back and forth, "I don't know."

"I'm taking a chance," said Doctor Vomact, "in giving you this much leeway. I'd have it done if I were in your position. It's pretty bad down there."

Mercer looked at the full, broad face. He did not trust the comfortable smile. Perhaps this was a trick to increase his punishment. The cruelty of the Emperor was proverbial. Look at what he had done to the widow of his predecessor, the Dowager Lady Da. She was younger than the Emperor himself, and he had sent her to a place worse than death. If he had been sentenced to Shayol, why was this doctor trying to interfere with the rules? Maybe the doctor himself had been conditioned, and did not know what he was offering.

Doctor Vomact read Mercer's face. "All right. You refuse. You want to take your mind down with you. It's all right with me. I don't have you on my conscience. I suppose you'll refuse the next offer too. Do you want me to take your eyes out before you go down? You'll be much more comfortable without vision. I *know* that, from the voices that we record for the warning broadcasts. I can sear the optic nerves so that there will be no chance of your getting vision again."

Mercer rocked back and forth. The fiery pain had become a universal itch, but the soreness of his spirit was greater than the discomfort of his skin.

"You refuse that, too?" said the doctor.

"I suppose so," said Mercer.

"Then all I have to do is to get ready. You can have the cap for a while, if you want."

Mercer said, "Before I put the cap on, can you tell me what happens down there?"

"Some of it," said the doctor. "There is an attendant. He is a man, but not a human being. He is a homunculus fashioned out of cattle material. He is intelligent and very conscientious. You specimens are turned loose on the surface of Shayol. The dromozoa are a special life-form there. When they settle in your body, B'dikkat—that's the attendant—carves them out with an anaesthetic and sends them up here. We freeze the tissue cultures, and they are compatible with almost any kind of oxygen-based life. Half the surgical repair you see in the whole universe comes out of buds that we ship from here. Shayol is a very healthy place, so far as survival is concerned. You won't die."

"You mean," said Mercer, "that I am getting perpetual punishment."

"I didn't say that," said Doctor Vomact. "Or if I did, I was wrong. You won't die soon. I don't know how long you will live down there. Remember, no matter how uncomfortable you get, the samples which B'dikkat sends up will help thousands of people in all the inhabited worlds. Now take the cap."

"I'd rather talk," said Mercer. "It may be my last chance."

The doctor looked at him strangely. "If you can stand that pain, go ahead and talk."

"Can I commit suicide down there?"

"I don't know," said the doctor. "It's never happened. And to judge by the voices, you'd think they wanted to."

"Has anybody ever come back from Shayol?"

"Not since it was put off limits about four hundred years ago."

"Can I talk to other people down there?"

"Yes," said the doctor.

"Who punishes me down there?"

"Nobody does, you fool," cried Doctor Vomact. "It's not punishment. People don't like it down on Shayol, and it's better, I guess, to get convicts instead of volunteers. But there isn't anybody *against* you at all."

"No jailers?" asked Mercer, with a whine in his voice.

"No jailers, no rules, no prohibitions. Just Shayol, and B'dikkat to take care of you. Do you still want your mind and your eyes?"

"I'll keep them," said Mercer. "I've gone this far and I might as well go the rest of the way."

"Then let me put the cap on you for your second dose," said Doctor Vomact.

196

The doctor adjusted the cap just as lightly and delicately as had the nurse; he was quicker about it. There was no sign of his picking out another cap for himself.

The inrush of pleasure was like a wild intoxication. His burning skin receded into the distance. The doctor was near in space, but even the doctor did not matter. Mercer was not afraid of Shayol. The pulsation of happiness out of his brain was too great to leave room for fear or pain.

Doctor Vomact was holding out his hand.

Mercer wondered why, and then realised that the wonderful, kindly cap-giving man was offering to shake hands. He lifted his own. It was heavy, but his arm was happy, too.

They shook hands. It was curious, thought Mercer, to feel the handshake beyond the double level of cerebral pleasure and dermal pain.

"Goodbye, Mr. Mercer," said the doctor. "Goodbye and a good, good night. . . ."

II

The ferry satellite was a hospitable place. The hundreds of hours that followed were like a long, weird dream.

Twice again the young nurse sneaked into his bedroom with him when he was being given the cap and had a cap with him. There were baths which calloused his whole body. Under strong local anaesthetics, his teeth were taken out and stainless steel took their place. There were irradiations under blazing lights which took away the pain of his skin. There were special treatments for his fingernails and toenails. Gradually they changed into formidable claws; he found himself stropping them on the aluminum bed one night and saw that they left deep marks.

His mind never became completely clear.

Sometimes he thought that he was home with his mother, that he was little again, and in pain. Other times, under the cap, he laughed in his bed to think that people were sent to this place for punishment when it was all so terribly much fun. There were no trials, no questions, no judges. Food was good, but he did not think about it much; the cap was better. Even when he was awake, he was drowsy.

At last, with the cap on him, they put him into an adiabatic pod—a one-body missile which could be dropped from the ferry to the planet below. He was all closed in, except for his face.

197

Doctor Vomact seemed to swim into the room. "You are strong, Mercer," the doctor shouted, "you are very strong! Can you hear me?"

Mercer nodded.

"We wish you well, Mercer. No matter what happens, remember you are helping other people up here."

"Can I take the cap with me?" said Mercer.

For an answer, Doctor Vomact removed the cap himself. Two men closed the lid of the pod, leaving Mercer in total darkness. His mind started to clear, and he panicked against his wrappings.

There was the roar of thunder and the taste of blood.

The next thing that Mercer knew, he was in a cool, cool room, much chillier than the bedrooms and operating rooms of the satellite. Someone was lifting him gently on to a table.

He opened his eyes.

An enormous face, four times the size of any human face Mercer had ever seen, was looking down at him. Huge brown eyes, cowlike in their gentle inoffensiveness, moved back and forth as the big face examined Mercer's wrappings. The face was that of a handsome man of middle years, clean-shaven, hair chestnut-brown, with sensual full lips and gigantic but healthy yellow teeth exposed in a half smile. The face saw Mercer's eyes open, and spoke with a deep friendly roar.

"I'm your best friend. My name is B'dikkat, but you don't have to use that here. Just call me Friend, and I will always help you."

"I hurt," said Mercer.

"Of course you do. You hurt all over. That's a big drop," said B'dikkat.

"Can I have a cap, please," begged Mercer. It was not a question; it was a demand; Mercer felt that his private inward eternity depended on it.

B'dikkat laughed. "I haven't any caps down here. I might use them myself. Or so they think. I have other things, much better. No fear, fellow, I'll fix you up."

Mercer looked doubtful. If the cap had brought him happiness on the ferry, it would take at least electrical stimulation of the brain to undo whatever torments the surface of Shayol had to offer.

B'dikkat's laughter filled the room like a bursting pillow.

"Have you ever heard of condamine?"

"No," said Mercer.

"It's a narcotic so powerful that the pharmacopeias are not allowed to mention it."

"You have that?" said Mercer hopefully.

"Something better. I have super-condamine. It's named after the New French town where they developed it. The chemists hooked in one more hydrogen molecule. That gave it a real jolt. If you took it in your present shape, you'd be dead in three minutes, but those three minutes would seem like ten thousand years of happiness to the inside of your mind." B'dikkat rolled his brown cow eyes expressively and smacked his rich red lips with a tongue of enormous extent.

"What's the use of it, then?"

"*You* can take it," said B'dikkat. "You can take it after you have been exposed to the dromozoa outside this cabin. You get all the good effects and none of the bad. You want to see something?"

What answer is there except *yes*, thought Mercer grimly; does he think I have an urgent invitation to a tea party?

"Look out of the window," said B'dikkat, "and tell me what you see."

The atmosphere was clear. The surface was like a desert, ginger-yellow with streaks of green where lichen and low shrubs grew, obviously stunted and tormented by high, dry winds. The landscape was monotonous. Two or three hundred yards away there was a herd of bright pink objects which seemed alive, but Mercer could not see them well enough to describe them clearly. Further away, on the extreme right of his frame of vision, there was the statue of an enormous human foot, the height of a six-storey building. Mercer could not see what the foot was connected to. "I see a big foot," said he, "but—"

"But what?" said B'dikkat, like an enormous child hiding the denouement of a hugely private joke. Large as he was, he would have been dwarfed by any one of the toes on that tremendous foot.

"But it can't be a real foot," said Mercer.

"It is," said B'dikkat. "That's Go-Captain Alvarez, the man who found this planet. After six hundred years he's still in fine shape. Of course, he's mostly dromozootic by now, but I think there is some human consciousness inside him. You know what I do?"

"What?" said Mercer.

"I give him six cubic centimetres of super-condamine and he snorts for me. Real happy little snorts. A stranger might think it was a volcano. That's what super-condamine can do. And you're going to get plenty of it. You're a lucky, lucky man, Mercer. You have me for a friend, and you have my needle for a treat. I do all the work and you get all the fun. Isn't that a nice surprise?"

Mercer thought, You're lying! Lying! Where do the screams come from that we have all heard broadcast as a warning on Punishment Day? Why did the doctor offer to cancel my brain or to take out my eyes?

The cow-man watched him sadly, a hurt expression on his face. "You don't believe me," he said, very sadly.

"It's not quite that," said Mercer, with an attempt at heartiness, "but I think you're leaving something out."

"Nothing much," said B'dikkat. "You jump when the dromozoa hit you. You'll be upset when you start growing new parts—heads, kidneys, hands. I had one fellow in here who grew thirty-eight hands in a single session outside. I took them all off, froze them and sent them upstairs. I take good care of everybody. You'll probably yell for a while. But remember, just call me Friend, and I have the nicest treat in the universe waiting for you. Now, would you like some fried eggs? I don't eat eggs myself, but most true men like them."

"Eggs?" said Mercer. "What have eggs got to do with it?"

"Nothing much. It's just a treat for you people. Get something in your stomach before you go outside. You'll get through the first day better."

Mercer, unbelieving, watched as the big man took two precious eggs from a cold chest, expertly broke them into a little pan and put the pan in the heat-field at the centre of the table Mercer had awakened on.

"Friend, eh?" B'dikkat grinned. "You'll see I'm a good friend. When you go outside, remember that."

An hour later, Mercer did go outside.

Strangely at peace with himself, he stood at the door. B'dikkat pushed him in a brotherly way, giving him a shove which was gentle enough to be an encouragement.

"Don't make me put on my lead suit, fellow." Mercer had seen a suit, fully the size of an ordinary spaceship cabin, hanging on the wall of an adjacent room. "When I close this door, the outer one will open. Just walk on out."

"But what will happen?" said Mercer, the fear turning around in his stomach and making little grabs at his throat from the inside.

"Don't start that again," said B'dikkat. For an hour he had

fended off Mercer's questions about the outside. A map? B'dik-kat had laughed at the thought. Food? He said not to worry. Other people? They'd be there. Weapons? What for? B'dikkat had replied. Over and over again, B'dikkat had insisted that he was Mercer's friend. What would happen to Mercer? The same that happened to everybody else.

Mercer stepped out.

Nothing happened. The day was cool. The wind moved gently against his toughened skin.

Mercer looked around apprehensively.

The mountainous body of Captain Alvarez occupied a good part of the landscape to the right. Mercer had no wish to get mixed up with that. He glanced back at the cabin. B'dikkat was not looking out of the window.

Mercer walked slowly, straight ahead.

There was a flash on the ground, no brighter than the glitter of sunlight on a fragment of glass. Mercer felt a sting on the thigh, as though a sharp instrument had touched him lightly. He brushed the place with his hand.

It was as though the sky fell in.

A pain—it was more than a pain: it was a living throb—ran from his hip to his foot on the right side. The throb reached up to his chest, robbing him of breath. He fell, and the ground hurt him. Nothing in the hospital-satellite had been like this. He lay in the open air, trying not to breathe, but he did breathe anyhow. Each time he breathed, the throb moved with his thorax. He lay on his back, looking at the sun. At last he noticed that the sun was violet-white.

It was no use even thinking of calling. He had no voice. Tendrils of discomfort twisted within him. Since he could not stop breathing, he concentrated on taking air in the way that hurt him least. Gasps were too much work. Little tiny sips of air hurt him least.

The desert around him was empty. He could not turn his head to look at the cabin. Is this it? he thought. Is an eternity of this the punishment of Shayol?

There were voices near him.

Two faces, grotesquely pink, looked down at him. They might have been human. The man looked normal enough, except for having two noses side by side. The woman was a caricature beyond belief. She had grown a breast on each cheek and a cluster of naked baby-like fingers hung limp from her forehead.

"It's a beauty," said the woman, "a new one."

"Come along," said the man.

They lifted him to his feet. He did not have strength enough to resist. When he tried to speak to them a harsh cawing sound, like the cry of an ugly bird, came from his mouth.

They moved with him efficiently. He saw that he was being dragged to the herd of pink things.

As they approached, he saw that they were people. Better, he saw that they had once been people. A man with the beak of a flamingo was picking at his own body. A woman lay on the ground; she had a single head, but beside what seemed to be her original body, she had a boy's naked body growing sideways from her neck. The boy-body, clean, new, paralytically helpless, made no movement other than shallow breathing. Mercer looked around. The only one of the group who was wearing clothing was a man with his overcoat on sideways. Mercer stared at him, finally realising that the man had two—or was it three?—stomachs growing on the outside of his abdomen. The coat held them in place. The transparent peritoneal wall looked fragile.

"New one," said his female captor. She and the two-nosed man put him down.

The group lay scattered on the ground.

Mercer lay in a state of stupor among them.

An old man's voice said, "I'm afraid they're going to feed us pretty soon."

"Oh, no!" "It's too early!" "Not again!" Protests echoed from the group.

The old man's voice went on, "Look, near the big toe of the mountain!"

The desolate murmur in the group attested their confirmation of what he had seen.

Mercer tried to ask what it was all about, but produced only a caw.

A woman—was it a woman?—crawled over to him on her hands and knees. Beside her ordinary hands, she was covered with hands all over her trunk and halfway down her thighs. Some of the hands looked old and withered. Others were as fresh and pink as the baby-fingers on his captress's face. The woman shouted at him, though it was not necessary to shout.

"The dromozoa are coming. This time it hurts. When you get used to the place, you can dig in—"

She waved at a group of mounds which surrounded the herd of people.

"They're dug in," she said.

Mercer cawed again.

"Don't you worry," said the hand-covered woman, and gasped as a flash of light touched her.

The lights reached Mercer too. The pain was like the first contact but more probing. Mercer felt his eyes widen as odd sensations within his body led to an inescapable conclusion: these lights, these things, these whatever-they-were, were feeding him and building him up.

Their intelligence, if they had it, was not human, but their motives were clear. In between the stabs of pain he felt them fill his stomach, put water in his blood, draw water from his kidneys and bladder, massage his heart, move his lungs for him.

Every single thing they did was well meant and beneficent in intent.

And every single action hurt.

Abruptly, like the lifting of a cloud of insects, they were gone. Mercer was aware of a noise somewhere outside—a brainless, bawling cascade of ugly noise. He started to look around. And the noise stopped.

It had been himself, screaming. Screaming the ugly screams of a psychotic, a terrified drunk, an animal driven out of understanding or reason.

When he stopped, he found he had his speaking voice again.

A man came to him, naked like the others. There was a spike sticking through his head. The skin had healed around it on both sides. "Hello, fellow," said the man with the spike.

"Hello," said Mercer. It was a foolishly commonplace thing to say in a place like this.

"You can't kill yourself," said the man with the spike through his head.

"Yes, you can," said the woman, covered with hands.

Mercer found that his first pain had disappeared. "What's happening to me?"

"You got a part," said the man with the spike. "They're always putting parts on us. After a while B'dikkat comes and cuts most of them off, except for the ones that ought to grow a little more. Like her," he added, nodding at the woman who lay with the boy-body growing from her neck.

"And that's all?" said Mercer. "The stabs for the new parts and the stinging for the feeding."

"No," said the man. "Sometimes they think we're too cold and they fill our insides with fire. Or they think we're too hot and they freeze us, nerve by nerve."

The woman with the boy-body called over, "And sometimes they think we're unhappy, so they try to force us to be happy. *I* think that's the worst of all."

Mercer stammered, "Are you people—I mean—are you the only herd?"

The man with the spike coughed instead of laughing. "Herd! That's funny. The land is full of people. Most of them dig in. We're the ones who can still talk; we stay together for company. We get more turns with B'dikkat that way."

Mercer started to ask another question, but he felt the strength run out of him. The day had been too much.

The ground rocked like a ship on water. The sky turned black. He felt someone catch him as he fell. He felt himself being stretched out on the ground. And then, mercifully and magically, he slept.

III

Within a week, he came to know the group well. They were an absent-minded bunch of people. Not one of them ever knew when a dromozoon might flash by and add another part. Mercer was not stung again, but the incision he had obtained just outside the cabin was hardening. Spike-head looked at it when Mercer modestly undid his belt and lowered the edge of his trouser-top so they could see the wound.

"You've got a head," he said. "A whole baby head. They'll be glad to get that one upstairs when B'dikkat cuts it off you."

The group even tried to arrange his social life. They introduced him to the girl of the herd. She had grown one body after another, pelvis turning into shoulders and the pelvis below that turning into shoulders again until she was five people long. Her face was unmarred. She tried to be friendly to Mercer.

He was so shocked by her that he dug himself into the soft, dry crumbly earth and stayed there for what seemed like a hundred years. He found later that it was less than a full day. When he came out, the long, many-bodied girl was waiting for him.

"You didn't have to come out just for me," said she.

Mercer shook the dirt off himself.

He looked around. The violet sun was going down, and the sky was streaked with blues, deeper blues and trails of orange sunset.

He looked back at her. "I didn't get up for you. It's no use lying there, waiting for the next time."

"I want to show you something," she said. She pointed to a low hummock. "Dig that up."

Mercer looked at her. She seemed friendly. He shrugged and attacked the soil with his powerful claws. With tough skin and heavy digging-nails on the ends of his fingers, he found it was easy to dig like a dog. The earth cascaded beneath his busy hands. Something pink appeared down in the hole he had dug. He proceeded more carefully.

He knew what it would be.

It was. It was a man, sleeping. Extra arms grew down one side of his body in an orderly series. The other side looked normal.

Mercer turned back to the many-bodied girl, who had writhed closer.

"That's what I think it is, isn't it?"

"Yes," she said. "Doctor Vomact burned his brain out for him. And took his eyes out, too."

Mercer sat back on the ground and looked at the girl. "You told me to do it. Now tell me what for."

"To let you see. To let you know. To let you think."

"That's all?" said Mercer.

The girl twisted with startling suddenness. All the way down her series of bodies, her chests heaved. Mercer wondered how air got into all of them. He did not feel sorry for her; he did not feel sorry for anyone except himself. When the spasm passed the girl smiled at him apologetically.

"They just gave me a new plant."

Mercer nodded grimly.

"What now, a hand? It seems you have enough."

"Oh, those," she said, looking back at her many torsos. "I promised B'dikkat that I'd let them grow. He's *good*. But that man, stranger. Look at that man you dug up. Who's better off, he or we?"

Mercer stared at her. "Is that what you had me dig him up for?"

"Yes," said the girl.

"Do you expect me to answer?"

"No," said the girl, "not now."

"Who are you?" said Mercer.

"We never ask that here. It doesn't matter. But since you're new, I'll tell you. I used to be the Lady Da—the Emperor's stepmother."

"You!" he exclaimed.

She smiled, ruefully. "You're still so fresh you think it mat-

205

ters! But I have something more important to tell you." She stopped and bit her lip.

"What?" he urged. "Better tell me before I get another bite. I won't be able to think or talk then, not for a long time. Tell me now."

She brought her face close to his. It was still a lovely face, even in the dying orange of this violet-sunned sunset. "People never live for ever."

"Yes," said Mercer. "I knew that."

"*Believe* it," ordered the Lady Da.

Lights flashed across the dark plain, still in the distance. Said she, "Dig in, dig in for the night. They may miss you."

Mercer started digging. He glanced over at the man he had dug up. The brainless body, with motions as soft as those of a starfish under water, was pushing its way back into the earth.

Five or seven days later, there was a shouting through the herd.

Mercer had come to know a half-man, the lower part of whose body was gone and whose viscera were kept in place with what resembled a translucent plastic bandage. The half-man had shown him how to lie still when the dromozoa came with their inescapable errands of doing good.

Said the half-man, "You can't fight them. They made Alvarez as big as a mountain, so that he never stirs. Now they're trying to make us happy. They feed us and clean us and sweeten us up. Lie still. Don't worry about screaming. We all do."

"When do we get the drug?" said Mercer.

"When B'dikkat comes."

B'dikkat came that day, pushing a sort of wheeled sled ahead of him. The runners carried it over the hillocks; the wheels worked on the surface.

Even before he arrived, the herd sprang into furious action. Everywhere, people were digging up the sleepers. By the time B'dikkat reached their waiting place, the herd must have uncovered twice their own number of sleeping pink bodies —men and women, young and old. The sleepers looked no better and no worse than the waking ones.

"Hurry!" said the Lady Da. "He never gives any of us a shot until we're all ready."

B'dikkat wore his heavy lead suit.

He lifted an arm in friendly greeting, like a father returning home with treats for his children. The herd clustered around him but did not crowd him.

206

He reached into the sled. There was a harnessed bottle which he threw over his shoulders. He snapped the locks on the straps. From the bottle there hung a tube. Midway down the tube there was a small pressure-pump. At the end of the tube there was a glistening hypodermic needle.

When ready, B'dikkat gestured for them to come closer. They approached him with radiant happiness. He stepped through their ranks and past them, to the girl who had the boy growing from her neck. His mechanical voice boomed through the loudspeaker set in the top of his suit.

"Good girl. Good, good girl. You get a big, big present." He thrust the hypodermic into her so long that Mercer could see an air bubble travel from the pump up to the bottle.

Then he moved back to the others, booming a word now and then, moving with improbable grace and speed amid the people. His needle flashed as he gave them hypodermics under pressure. The people dropped to sitting position or lay down on the ground as though half asleep.

He knew Mercer. "Hello, fellow. Now you can have the fun. It would have killed you in the cabin. Do you have anything for me?"

Hercer stammered, not knowing what B'dikkat meant, and the two-nosed man answered for him, "I think he has a nice baby head, but it isn't big enough for you to take yet."

Mercer never noticed the needle touch his arm.

B'dikkat had turned to the next knot of people when the super-condamine hit Mercer.

He tried to run after B'dikkat, to hug the lead space suit, to tell B'dikkat that he loved him. He stumbled and fell, but it did not hurt.

The many-bodied girl lay near him. Mercer spoke to her.

"Isn't it wonderful? You're beautiful, beautiful, beautiful. I'm so happy to be here."

The woman covered with growing hands came and sat beside them. She radiated warmth and good fellowship. Mercer thought that she looked very distinguished and charming. He struggled out of his clothes. It was foolish and snobbish to wear clothing when none of these nice people did.

The two women babbled and crooned at him.

With one corner of his mind he knew that they were saying nothing, just expressing the euphoria of a drug so powerful that the known universe had forbidden it. With most of his mind he was happy. He wondered how anyone could have the good luck to visit a planet as nice as this. He tried to tell the Lady Da, but the words weren't quite straight.

A painful stab hit him in the abdomen. The drug went after the pain and swallowed it. It was like the cap in the hospital, only a thousand times better. The pain was gone, though it had been crippling the first time.

He forced himself to be deliberate. He rammed his mind into focus and said to the two ladies who lay pinkly nude beside him in the desert, "That was a good bite. Maybe I will grow another head. That would make B'dikkat happy!"

The Lady Da forced the foremost of her bodies in an upright position. Said she, "I'm strong, too. I can talk. Remember, man, remember. People never live for ever. We can die too, we can die like real people. I do so believe in death!"

Mercer smiled at her through his happiness.

"Of course you can. But isn't this nice . . ."

With this he felt his lips thicken and his mind go slack. He was wide awake, but he did not feel like doing anything. In that beautiful place, among all those companionable and attractive people, he sat and smiled.

B'dikkat was sterilising his knives.

Mercer wondered how long the super-condamine had lasted him. He endured the ministrations of the dromozoa without screams or movement. The agonies of nerves and itching of skin were phenomena which happened somewhere near him, but meant nothing. He watched his own body with remote, casual interest. The Lady Da and the hand-covered woman stayed near him. After a long time the half-man dragged himself over to the group with his powerful arms. Having arrived he blinked sleepily and friendly at them, and lapsed back into the restful stupor from which he had emerged. Mercer saw the sun rise on occasion, closed his eyes briefly, and opened them to see stars shining. Time had no meaning. The dromozoa fed him in their mysterious way; the drug cancelled out his needs for cycles of the body.

At last he noticed a return of the inwardness of pain.

The pains themselves had not changed; he had.

He knew all the events which could take place on Shayol. He remembered them well from his happy period. Formerly he had noticed them—now he felt them.

He tried to ask the Lady Da how long they had had the drug,

208

and how much longer they would have to wait before they had it again. She smiled at him with benign, remote happiness; apparently her many torsos, stretched out along the ground, had a greater capacity for retaining the drug than did his body. She meant him well, but was in no condition for articulate speech.

The half-man lay on the ground, arteries pulsating prettily behind the half-transparent film which protected his abdominal cavity.

Mercer squeezed the man's shoulder.

The half-man woke, recognised Mercer and gave him a healthily sleepy grin.

"'A good morrow to you, my boy.' That's out of a play. Did you ever see a play?"

"You mean a game with cards?"

"No," said the half-man, "a sort of eye-machine with real people doing the figures."

"I never saw that," said Mercer, "but I—"

"But you want to ask me when B'dikkat is going to come back with the needle."

"Yes," said Mercer, a little ashamed of his obviousness.

"Soon," said the half-man. "That's why I think of plays. We all know what is going to happen. We all know when it is going to happen. We all know what the dummies will do—" he gestured at the hummocks in which the decorticated men were cradled—"and we all know what the new people will ask. But we never know how long a scene is going to take."

"What's a 'scene'?" asked Mercer. "Is that the name for the needle?"

The half-man laughed with something close to real humour. "No, no, no. You've got the lovelies on the brain. A scene is just a part of a play. I mean we know the order in which things happen, but we have no clocks and nobody cares enough to count days or to make calendars and there's not much climate here, so none of us know how long anything takes. The pain seems short and the pleasure seems long. I'm inclined to think that they are about two Earth-weeks each."

Mercer did not know what an "Earth-week" was, since he had not been a well-read man before his conviction, but he got nothing more from the half-man at that time. The half-man received a dromozootic implant, turned red in the face, shouted senselessly at Mercer, "Take it out, you fool! Take it out of me!"

When Mercer looked on helplessly, the half-man twisted over

on his side, his pink dusty back turned to Mercer, and wept hoarsely and quietly to himself.

Mercer himself could not tell how long it was before B'dikkat came back. It might have been several days. It might have been several months.

Once again B'dikkat moved among them like a father; once again they clustered like children. This time B'dikkat smiled pleasantly at the little head which had grown out of Mercer's thigh—a sleeping child's head, covered with light hair on top and with dainty eyebrows over the resting eyes. Mercer got the blissful needle.

When B'dikkat cut the head from Mercer's thigh, he felt the knife grinding against the cartilage which held the head to his own body. He saw the child-face grimace as the head was cut; he felt the far, cool flash of unimportant pain, as B'dikkat dabbed the wound with a corrosive antiseptic which stopped all bleeding immediately.

The next time it was two legs growing from his chest.

Then there had been another head beside his own.

Or was that after the torso and legs, waist to toe-tips, of the little girl which had grown from his side?

He forgot the order.

He did not count time.

Lady Da smiled at him often, but there was no love in this place. She had lost the extra torsos. In between teratologies, she was a pretty and shapely woman; but the nicest thing about their relationship was her whisper to him, repeated some thousands of times, repeated with smiles and hope, "People never live for ever."

She found this immensely comforting, even though Mercer did not make much sense out of it.

Thus events occurred, and victims changed in appearance, and new ones arrived. Sometimes B'dikkat took the new ones, resting in the everlasting sleep of their burned-out brains, in a ground-truck to be added to other herds. The bodies in the truck threshed and bawled without human speech when the dromozoa struck them.

Finally, Mercer did manage to follow B'dikkat to the door of the cabin. He had to fight the bliss of super-condamine to do it. Only the memory of previous hurt, bewilderment and perplexity made him sure that if he did not ask B'dikkat when he, Mercer, was happy, the answer would no longer be available when he needed it. Fighting pleasure itself, he begged B'dikkat to check the records and to tell him how long he had been there.

B'dikkat grudgingly agreed, but he did not come out of the doorway. He spoke through the public address box built into the cabin, and his gigantic voice roared out over the empty plain, so that the pink herd of talking people stirred gently in their happiness and wondered what their friend B'dikkat might be wanting to tell them. When he said it, they thought it exceedingly profound, though none of them understood it, since it was simply the amount of time that Mercer had been on Shayol:

"Standard years—eighty-four years, seven months, three days, two hours, eleven and one half minutes. Good luck, fellow."

Mercer turned away.

The secret little corner of his mind, which stayed sane through happiness and pain, made him wonder about B'dikkat. What persuaded the cow-man to remain on Shayol? What kept him happy without super-condamine? Was B'dikkat a crazy slave to his own duty or was he a man who had hopes of going back to his own planet some day, surrounded by a family of little cow-people resembling himself? Mercer, despite his happiness, wept a little at the strange fate of B'dikkat. His own fate he accepted.

He remembered the last time he had eaten—actual eggs from an actual pan. The dromozoa kept him alive, but he did not know how they did it.

He staggered back to the group. The Lady Da, naked in the dusty plain, waved a hospitable hand and showed that there was a place for him to sit beside her. There were unclaimed square miles of seating space around them, but he appreciated the kindliness of her gesture none the less.

IV

The years, if they were years, went by. The land of Shayol did not change.

Sometimes the bubbling sound of geysers came faintly across the plain to the herd of men; those who could talk declared it to be the breathing of Captain Alvarez. There was night and day, but no setting of crops, no change of season, no generations of men. Time stood still for these people, and their load of pleasure

211

was so commingled with the shocks and pains of the dromozoa that the words of the Lady Da took on very remote meaning.

"People never live for ever."

Her statement was a hope, not a truth in which they could believe. They did not have the wit to follow the stars in their courses, to exchange names with each other, to harvest the experience of each for the wisdom of all. There was no dream of escape for these people. Though they saw the old-style chemical rockets lift up from the field beyond B'dikkat's cabin, they did not make plans to hide among the frozen crop of transmuted flesh.

Far long ago, some other prisoner than one of these had tried to write a letter. His handwriting was on a rock. Mercer read it, and so had a few of the others, but they could not tell which man had done it. Nor did they care.

The letter, scraped on stone, had been a message home. They could still read the opening: "Once, I was like you, stepping out of my window at the end of day, and letting the winds blow me gently towards the place I live in. Once, like you, I had one head, two hands, ten fingers on my hands. The front part of my head was called a face, and I could talk with it. Now I can only write, and that only when I get out of pain. Once, like you, I ate foods, drank liquid, had a name. I cannot remember the name I had. You can stand up, you who get this letter. I cannot even stand up. I just wait for the lights to put my food in me molecule by molecule, and to take it out again. Don't think that I am punished any more. This place is not a punishment. It is something else."

Among the pink herd, none of them ever decided what was "something else".

Curiosity had died among them long ago.

Then came the day of the little people.

It was a time—not an hour, not a year: a duration somewhere between them—when the Lady Da and Mercer sat wordless with happiness and filled with the joy of super-condamine. They had nothing to say to one another; the drug said all things for them.

A disagreeable roar from B'dikkat's cabin made them stir mildly.

Those two, and one or two others, looked towards the speaker of the public address system.

The Lady Da brought herself to speak, though the matter was

unimportant beyond words. "I do believe," said she, "that we used to call that the War Alarm."

They drowsed back into their happiness.

A man with two rudimentary heads growing beside his own crawled over to them. All three heads looked very happy, and Mercer thought it delightful of him to appear in such a whimsical shape. Under the pulsing glow of super-condamine, Mercer regretted that he had not used times when his mind was clear to ask him who he had once been. He answered it for them. Forcing his eyelids open by sheer will power, he gave the Lady Da and Mercer the lazy ghost of a military salute and said, "Suzdal, ma'am and sir, former cruiser commander. They are sounding the alert. Wish to report that I am . . . I am . . . I am not quite ready for battle."

He dropped off to sleep.

The gentle peremptories of the Lady Da brought his eyes open again.

"Commander, why are they sounding it here? Why did you come to us?"

"You, ma'am, and the gentleman with the ears seem to think best of our group. I thought you might have orders."

Mercer looked around for the gentleman with the ears. It was himself. In that time his face was almost wholly obscured with a crop of fresh little ears, but he paid no attention to them, other than expecting that B'dikkat would cut them all off in due course and that the dromozoa would give him something else.

The noise from the cabin rose to a higher, ear-splitting intensity.

Among the herd, many people stirred.

Some opened their eyes, looked around, murmured, "It's a noise," and went back to the happy drowsing with super-condamine.

The cabin door opened.

B'dikkat rushed out, *without his suit.* They had never seen him on the outside without his protective metal suit.

He rushed up to them, looked wildly around, recognised the Lady Da and Mercer, picked them up, one under each arm, and raced with them back to the cabin. He flung them into the double door. They landed with bone-splitting crashes, and found it amusing to hit the ground so hard. The floor tilted them into the room. Moments later, B'dikkat followed.

He roared at them, "You're people, or you were. You

understand people; I only obey them. But this I will not obey. Look at that!"

Four beautiful human children lay on the floor. The two smallest seemed to be twins, about two years of age. There was a girl of five and a boy of seven or so. All of them had slack eyelids. All of them had thin red lines around their temples, and their hair, shaved away, showed how their brains had been removed.

B'dikkat, heedless of danger from dromozoa, stood beside the Lady Da and Mercer, shouting.

"You're real people. I'm just a cow. I do my duty. My duty does not include this. These are *children*."

The wise, surviving recess of Mercer's mind registered shock and disbelief. It was hard to sustain the emotion, because the super-condamine washed at his consciousness like a great tide, making everything seem lovely. The forefront of his mind, rich with the drug, told him, "Won't it be nice to have some children with us!" But the undestroyed interior of his mind, keeping the honour he knew before he came to Shayol, whispered, "This is a crime worse than any crime we have committed! *And the Empire has done it*."

"What have you done?" said the Lady Da. "What can we do?"

"I tried to call the satellite. When they knew what I was talking about, they cut me off. After all, I'm not people. The head doctor told me to do my work."

"Was it Doctor Vomact?" Mercer asked.

"Vomact?" said B'dikkat. "He died a hundred years ago, of old age. No, a new doctor cut me off. I don't have people-feeling, but I am Earth-born, of Earth blood. I have emotions myself. Pure cattle emotions! *This* I cannot permit."

"What have you done?"

B'dikkat lifted his eyes to the window. His face was illuminated by a determination which, even beyond the edges of the drug which made them love him, made him seem like the father of this world—responsible, honourable, unselfish.

He smiled. "They will kill me for it, I think. But I have put in the Galactic Alert—*all ships here*."

The Lady Da, sitting back on the floor, declared, "But that's only for new invaders! It is a false alarm." She pulled herself together and rose to her feet. "Can you cut these things off me, right now, in case people come? And get me a dress. And do

214

you have anything which will counteract the effects of the super-condamine?"

"That's what I wanted!" cried B'dikkat. "I will not take these children. You give me leadership."

There and then, on the floor of the cabin, he trimmed her down to the normal proportions of mankind.

The corrosive antiseptic rose like smoke in the air of the cabin. Mercer thought it all very dramatic and pleasant, and dropped off in catnaps part of the time. Then he felt B'dikkat trimming him too. B'dikkat opened a long, long drawer and put the specimens in; from the cold in the room it must have been a refrigerated locker.

He sat them both up against the wall.

"I've been thinking," he said. "There is no antidote for super-condamine. Who would want one? But I can give you the hypos from my rescue boat. They are supposed to bring a person back, no matter what has happened to that person out in space."

There was a whining over the cabin roof. B'dikkat knocked a window out with his fist, stuck his head out of the window and looked up.

"Come on in," he shouted.

There was the thud of a landing craft touching ground quickly. Doors whirred. Mercer wondered, mildly, why people dared to land on Shayol. When they came in he saw that they were not people; they were Customs robots, who could travel at velocities which people could never match. One wore the insignia of an inspector.

"Where are the invaders?"

"There are no—" began B'dikkat.

The Lady Da, imperial in her posture though she was completely nude, said in a voice of complete clarity, "I am a former Empress, the Lady Da. Do you know me?"

"No, ma'am," said the robot inspector. He looked as uncomfortable as a robot could look. The drug made Mercer think that it would be nice to have robots for company, out on the surface of Shayol.

"I declare this Top Emergency, in the ancient words. Do you understand? Connect me with the Instrumentality."

"We can't—" said the inspector.

"You can ask," said the Lady Da.

The inspector complied.

The Lady Da turned to B'dikkat. "Give Mercer and me those

215

shots now. Then put us outside the door so the dromozoa can repair these scars. Bring us in as soon as a connection is made. Wrap us in cloth if you do not have clothes for us. Mercer can stand the pain."

"Yes," said B'dikkat, keeping his eyes away from the four soft children and their collapsed eyes.

The injection burned like no fire ever had. It must have been capable of fighting the super-condamine, because B'dikkat put them through the open window, so as to save time going through the door. The dromozoa, sensing that they needed repair, flashed upon them. This time the super-condamine had something else fighting it.

Mercer did not scream but he lay against the wall and wept for ten thousand years; in objective time, it must have been several hours.

The Customs robots were taking pictures. The dromozoa were flashing against them too, sometimes in whole swarms, but nothing happened.

Mercer heard the voice of the communicator inside the cabin calling loudly for B'dikkat. "Surgery Satellite calling Shayol. B'dikkat, get on the line!"

He obviously was not replying.

There were soft cries coming from the other communicator, the one which the customs officials had brought into the room. Mercer was sure that the eye-machine was on and that people in other worlds were looking at Shayol for the first time.

B'dikkat came through the door. He had torn navigation charts out of his lifeboat. With these he cloaked them.

Mercer noted that the Lady Da changed the arrangement of the cloak in a few minor ways and suddenly looked like a person of great importance.

They re-entered the cabin door.

B'dikkat whispered, as if filled with awe. "The Instrumentality has been reached, and a Lord of the Instrumentality is about to talk to you."

There was nothing for Mercer to do, so he sat back in a corner of the room and watched. The Lady Da, her skin healed, stood pale and nervous in the middle of the floor.

The room filled with an odourless intangible smoke. The smoke clouded. The full communicator was on.

A human figure appeared.

A woman, dressed in a uniform of radically conservative cut, faced the Lady Da.

"This is Shayol. You are the Lady Da. You called me."

The Lady Da pointed to the children on the floor. "This must not happen," she said. "This is a place of punishments, agreed upon between the Instrumentality and the Empire. No one said anything about children."

The woman on the screen looked down at the children.

"This is the work of insane people!" she cried.

She looked accusingly at the Lady Da, "Are you imperial?"

"I was an Empress, madam," said the Lady Da.

"And you permit this!"

"Permit it?" cried the Lady Da. "I had nothing to do with it." Her eyes widened. "I am a prisoner here myself. Don't you understand?"

The image-woman snapped, "No, I don't."

"I," said the Lady Da, "am a specimen. Look at the herd out there. I came from them a few hours ago."

"Adjust me," said the image-woman to B'dikkat. "Let me see that herd."

Her body, standing upright, soared through the wall in a flashing arc and was placed in the very centre of the herd.

The Lady Da and Mercer watched her. They saw even the image lose its stiffness and dignity. The image-woman waved an arm to show that she should be brought back into the cabin. B'dikkat tuned her back into the room.

"I owe you an apology," said the image. "I am the Lady Johanna Gnade, one of the Lords of the Instrumentality."

Mercer bowed, lost his balance and had to scramble up from the floor. The Lady Da acknowledged the introduction with a royal nod.

The two women looked at each other.

"You will investigate," said the Lady Da, "and when you have investigated, please put us all to death. You know about the drug?"

"Don't mention it," said B'dikkat, "don't even say the name into a communicator. It is a secret of the Instrumentality!"

"I am the Instrumentality," said the Lady Johanna. "Are you in pain? I did not think that any of you were alive. I had heard of the surgery banks on your off-limits planet, but I thought that robots tended parts of people and sent up the new grafts by rocket. Are there any people with you? Who is in charge? Who did this to the children?"

B'dikkat stepped in front of the image. He did not bow. "I'm in charge."

"You're under people!" cried the Lady Johanna. "You're a cow!"

"A bull, ma'am. My family is frozen back on earth itself, and with a thousand years' service I am earning their freedom and my own. Your other questions, ma'am. I do all the work. The dromozoa do not affect me much, though I have to cut a part off myself now and then. I throw those away. They don't go into the bank. Do you know the secret rules of this place?"

The Lady Johanna talked to someone behind her on another world. Then she looked at B'dikkat and commanded, "Just don't name the drug or talk too much about it. Tell me the rest."

"We have," said B'dikkat very formally, "thirteen hundred and twenty-one people here who can still be counted on to supply parts when the dromozoa implant them. There are about seven hundred more, including Go-Captain Alverez, who have been so thoroughly absorbed by the planet that it is no use trimming them. The Empire set up this place as a point of uttermost punishment. But the Instrumentality gave secret orders for *medicine*"—he accented the word strangely, meaning super-condamine—"to be issued so that the punishment would be counteracted. The Empire supplies our convicts. The Instrumentality distributes the surgical material."

The Lady Johanna lifted her right hand in a gesture of silence and compassion. She looked around the room. Her eyes came back to the Lady Da. Perhaps she guessed what effort the Lady Da had made in order to remain standing erect while the two drugs, the super-condamine and the lifeboat drug, fought within her veins.

"You people can rest. I will tell you now that all things possible will be done for you. The Empire is finished. The Fundamental Agreement, by which the Instrumentality surrendered to the Empire a thousand years ago, has been set aside. We did not know that you people existed. We would have found out in time, but I am sorry we did not find out sooner. Is there anything we can do for you right away?"

"Time is what we all have," said the Lady Da. "Perhaps we cannot ever leave Shayol, because of the dromozoa and the *medicine*. The one could be dangerous. The other must never be permitted to be known."

The Lady Johanna Gnade looked around the room. When her glance reached him, B'dikkat fell to his knees and lifted his enormous hands in complete supplication.

"What do you want?" said she.

"These," said B'dikkat, pointing to the mutilated children. "Order a stop on children. Stop it now!" He commanded her with the last cry, and she accepted his command. "And lady—" He stopped, as if shy.

"Yes? Go on."

"Lady, I am unable to kill. It is not in my nature. To work, to help, but not to kill. What do I do with these?" He gestured at the four motionless children on the floor.

"Keep them," she said. "Just keep them."

"I can't," he said. "There's no way to get off this planet alive. I do not have food for them in the cabin. They will die in a few hours. And governments," he added wisely, "take a long, long time to do things."

"Can you give them the *medicine*?"

"No, it would kill them if I give them that stuff first before the dromozoa have fortified their bodily processes."

The Lady Johanna Gnade filled the room with tinkling laughter that was very close to weeping. "Fools, poor fools, and the more fool I! If super-condamine works only *after* the dromozoa, what is the purpose of the secret?"

B'dikkat rose to his feet, offended. He frowned, but he could not get the words with which to defend himself.

The Lady Da, ex-empress of a fallen empire, addressed the other lady with ceremony and force: "Put them outside, so they will be touched. They will hurt. Have B'dikkat give them the drug as soon as he thinks it safe. I beg your leave, my lady . . ."

Mercer had to catch her before she fell.

"You've all had enough," said the Lady Johanna. "A storm ship with heavily armed troops is on its way to your ferry satellite. They will seize the medical personnel and find out who committed this crime against children."

Mercer started to speak. "Will you punish the guilty doctor?"

"*You* speak of punishment," she cried. "You!"

"It's fair. I was punished for doing wrong. Why shouldn't he be?"

"Punish—punish?" she said to him. "We will cure that doctor. And we will cure you too, if we can."

Mercer began to weep. He thought of the oceans of happiness which super-condamine had brought him, forgetting the hideous pain and the deformities on Shayol. Would there be no next needle? He could not guess what life would be like off

219

Shayol. Was there to be no more tender, fatherly B'dikkat coming with his knives?

He lifted his tear-stained face to the Lady Johanna Gnade and choked out the words, "Lady, we are all insane in this place. I do not think we want to leave."

She turned her face away, moved by enormous compassion. Her next words were to B'dikkat. "You are wise and good, even if you are not a human being. Give them all of the drug they can take. The Instrumentality will decide what to do with all of you. I will survey your planet with robot soldiers. Will the robots be safe, cow-man?"

B'dikkat did not like the thoughtless name she called him, but he held no offence. "The robots will be all right, ma'am, but the dromozoa will be excited if they cannot feed them and heal them. Send as few as you can. We do not know how the dromozoa live or die."

"As few as I can," she murmured. She lifted her hand in command to some technician unimaginable distances away. The odourless smoke rose about her and the image was gone.

A shrill, cheerful voice spoke up. "I fixed your window," said the Customs robot. B'dikkat thanked him absentmindedly. He helped Mercer and the Lady Da into the doorway. When they got outside, they were promptly stung by the dromozoa. It did not matter.

B'dikkat himself emerged, carrying the four children in his two gigantic, tender hands. He laid the slack bodies on the ground near the cabin. He watched as the bodies went into spasm with the onset of the dromozoa. Mercer and the Lady Da saw that his brown cow eyes were rimmed with red and that his huge cheeks were dampened by tears.

Hours or centuries.

Who could tell them apart?

The herd went back to its usual life, except that the intervals between needles were much shorter. The once-commander, Suzdal, refused the needle when he heard the news. Whenever he could walk, he followed the Customs robots around as they photographed, took soil samples, and made a count of the bodies. They were particularly interested in the mountain of the Go-Captain Alvarez and professed themselves uncertain as to whether there was organic life there or not. The mountain did appear to react to super-condamine, but they could find no blood, no heart-beat. Moisture, moved by the dromozoa, seemed to have replaced the once-human bodily process.

V

And then, early one morning, the sky opened.

Ship after ship landed. People emerged, wearing clothes.

The dromozoa ignored the newcomers. Mercer, who was in a state of bliss, confusedly tried to think this through until he realised that the ships were loaded to their skins with communications machines; the "people" were either robots or images of persons in other places.

The robots swiftly gathered together the herd. Using wheelbarrows, they brought the hundreds of mindless people to the landing area.

Mercer heard a voice he knew. It was the Lady Johanna Gnade. "Set me high," she commanded.

Her form rose until she seemed one-fourth the size of Alvarez. Her voice took on more volume.

"Wake them all," she commanded.

Robots moved among them, spraying them with a gas which was both sickening and sweet. Mercer felt his mind go clear. The super-condamine still operated in his nerves and veins, but his cortical area was free of it. He thought clearly.

"I bring you," cried the compassionate feminine voice of the gigantic Lady Johanna, "the judgment of the Instrumentality on the planet Shayol.

"Item: the surgical supplies will be maintained and the dromozoa will not be molested. Portions of human bodies will be left here to grow, and the grafts will be collected by robots. Neither man nor homunculus will live here again.

"Item: the underman B'dikkat, of cattle extraction, will be rewarded by an immediate return to earth. He will be paid twice his expected thousand years of earnings."

The voice of B'dikkat, without amplification, was almost as loud as hers through the amplifier. He shouted his protest, "Lady, Lady!"

She looked down at him, his enormous body reaching to ankle height on her swirling gown, and said in a very informal tone, "What do you want?"

"Let me finish my work first," he cried, so that all could hear. "Let me finish taking care of these people."

The specimens who had minds all listened attentively. The brainless ones were trying to dig themselves back into the soft

221

earth of Shayol, using their powerful claws for the purpose. Whenever one began to disappear, a robot seized him by a limb and pulled him out again.

"Item: cephalectomies will be performed on all persons with irrecoverable minds. Their bodies will be left here. Their heads will be taken away and killed as pleasantly as we can manage, probably by an overdosage of super-condamine."

"The last big jolt," murmured Commander Suzdal, who stood near Mercer. "That's fair enough."

"Item: the children have been found to be the last heirs of the Empire. An over-zealous official sent them here to prevent their committing treason when they grew up. The doctor obeyed orders without questioning them. Both the official and the doctor have been cured and their memories of this have been erased, so that they need have no shame or grief for what they have done."

"It's unfair," cried the half-man. "They should be punished as we were!"

The Lady Johanna Gnade looked down at him. "Punishment is ended. We will give you anything you wish, but not the pain of another. I shall continue.

"Item: since none of you wish to resume the lives which you led previously, we are moving you to another planet nearby. It is similar to Shayol, but much more beautiful. There are no dromozoa."

At this an uproar seized the herd. They shouted, wept, cursed, appealed. They all wanted the needle, and if they had to stay on Shayol to get it, they would stay.

"Item," said the gigantic image of the lady, overriding their babble with her great but feminine voice, "you will not have super-condamine on the new planet, since without dromozoa it would kill you. But there will be caps. *Remember the caps.* We will try to cure you and to make people of you again. But if you give up, we will not force you. Caps are very powerful; with medical help you can live under them many years."

A hush fell on the group. In their various ways, they were trying to compare the electrical caps which had stimulated their pleasure-lobes with the drug which had drowned them a thousand times in pleasure. Their murmur sounded like assent.

"Do you have any questions?" said the Lady Johanna.

"When do we get the caps?" said several. They were human enough that they laughed at their own impatience.

"Soon," said she reassuringly, "very soon."

"Very soon," echoed B'dikkat, reassuring his charges even though he was no longer in control.

"Question," cried the Lady Da.

"My Lady . . . ?" said the Lady Johanna, giving the ex-empress her due courtesy.

"Will we be permitted marriage?"

The Lady Johanna looked astonished. "I don't know." She smiled. "I don't know any reason why not—"

"I claim this man Mercer," said the Lady Da. "When the drugs were deepest, and the pain was greatest, he was the one who always tried to think. May I have him?"

Mercer thought the procedure arbitrary but he was so happy that he said nothing. The Lady Johanna scrutinised him and then she nodded. She lifted her arms in a gesture of blessing and farewell.

The robots began to gather the pink herd into two groups. One group was to whisper in a ship over to a new world, new problems and new lives. The other group, no matter how much its members tried to scuttle into the dirt, was gathered for the last honour which humanity could pay their manhood.

B'dikkat, leaving everyone else, jogged with his bottle across the plain to give the mountain-man Alvarez an especially large gift of delight.

INTO THE SHOP

by *Ron Goulart*

The waitress screamed, that was the trouble with live help, and made a flapping motion with her extended arm. Stu Clemens swung sideways in the booth and looked out through the green-tinted window at the parking lot. A dark-haired man in his early thirties was slumping to his knees, his hands flickering at his sides. Silently the lawagon spun back out of its parking place and rolled nearer to the fallen man. "There's nobody in that car," said the waitress, dropping a cup of coffee.

She must be new to this planet, from one of the sticks systems maybe. "It's my car," said Clemens, flipping the napkin toggle on the table and then tossing her one when it popped up. "Here, wipe your uniform off. That's a lawagon and it knows what it's doing."

The waitress put the napkin up to her face and turned away.

Out in the lot the lawagon had the man trussed up. It stunned him again for safety and then it flipped him into the back seat for interrogation and identification. "It never makes a mistake," said Clemens to the waitress's back. "I've been marshal in Territory 23 for a year now and that lawagon has never made a mistake. They build them that way."

The car had apparently given the suspect an injection and he had fallen over out of sight. Three more napkins popped up out of the table unasked. "Damn it," said Clemens and pounded the outlet with his fist once, sharply.

"It does that sometimes," said the waitress, looking again at Clemens, but no further. She handed him his check card.

Clemens touched the waitress's arm as he got up. "Don't worry now. The law is always fair on Barnum. I'm sorry you had to see a criminal up close like that."

"He just had the businessman's lunch," the waitress said.

"Well, even criminals have to eat." Clemens paid the cash register and it let him out of the drive-in oasis.

The cars that had been parked near the lawagon were gone now. When people were in trouble they welcomed the law but other times they stayed clear. Clemens grimaced, glancing at the dry yellow country beyond the oasis restaurant. He had just cleaned up an investigation and was heading back to his office in Hub 23. He still had an hour to travel. Lighting a cigarette he started for the lawagon. He was curious to see whom his car had apprehended.

"This is a public service announcement," announced the lawagon from its roof speakers. "Sheldon Kloog, wanted murderer, has just been captured by Lawagon A10. Trial has been held, a verdict of guilty brought in, death sentenced and the sentence carried out as prescribed by law. This has been a public service announcement from the Barnum Law Bureau."

Clemens ran to the car. This was a break. Sheldon Kloog was being hunted across eleven territories for murdering his wife and dismantling all their household androids. At the driver's door the marshall took his ID cards out of his grey trouser pocket and at the same time gave the day's passwords to the lawagon. He next gave the countersigns and the oath of fealty and the car let him in.

Behind the wheel Clemens said, "Congratulations. How'd you spot him?"

The lawagon's dash speaker answered, "Made a positive identification five seconds after Kloog stepped out of the place. Surprised you didn't spot him. Was undisguised and had all the telltale marks of a homicide prone."

"He wasn't sitting in my part of the restaurant. Sorry." Clemens cocked his head and looked into the empty back seat. The lawagons had the option of holding murderers for full cybernetic trial in one of the territorial hubs or, if the murderer checked out strongly guilty and seemed dangerous, executing them on the spot. "Where is he?"

The glove compartment fell open and an opaque white jar rolled out. Clemens caught it. *Earthly Remains of Sheldon Kloog*, read the label. The disintegrator didn't leave much.

Putting the jar back, Clemens said, "Did you send photos, prints, retinal patterns and the rest on to my office."

"Of course," said the car. "Plus a full transcript of the trial. Everything in quadruplicate."

"Good," said Clemens. "I'm glad we got Kloog and he's out of the way." He lit a fresh cigarette and put his hands on the wheel. The car could drive on automatic or manual. Clemens preferred to steer himself. "Start up and head for the hub. And get me my junior marshal on the line."

"Yes, sir," said the car.

"Your voice has a little too much treble," said Clemens, turning the lawagon on to the smooth black six-lane roadway that pointed flat and straight towards Hub 23.

"Sorry. I'll fix it. This is a public announcement. This is a public announcement. Better?"

"Fine. Now get me Kepling."

"Check, sir."

Clemens watched a flock of dot-sized birds circle far out over the desert. He moistened his lips and leaned back slightly.

"Jr. Marshal Kepling here," came a voice from the dash.

"Kepling," said Clemens, "a packet of assorted ID material should have come out of the teleport slot a few minutes ago. Keep a copy for our files and send the rest on to Law Bureau Central in Hub 1.

"Right, sir."

"We just got that murderer, Sheldon Kloog."

"Good work. Shall I pencil him in for a trial at Cybernetics Hall?"

"We already had the trial," said Clemens. "Anything else new?"

"Looks like trouble out near Townten. Might be a sex crime."

225

"What exactly?"

"I'm not sure, sir," said Kepling. "The report is rather vague. You know how the android patrols out in the towns are. I dispatched a mechanical deputy about an hour ago and he should reach there by mid-afternoon. If there's a real case I can drive our lawagon over after you get back here."

Clemens frowned. "What's the victim's name?"

"Just a minute. Yeah, here it is. Marmon, Dianne. Age twenty-five, height five feet six inches, weight . . ."

Clemens had twisted the wheel violently to the right. "Stop," he said to the lawagon as it shimmied off the roading. "Dianne Marmon, Kepling."

"That's right. Do you know her?"

"What are the details you have on the crime?"

"The girl is employed at Statistics Warehouse in Townten. She didn't appear at work this morning and a routine check by a personnel andy found evidence of a struggle in her apartment. The patrol says there are no signs of theft. So kidnapping for some purpose seems likely. You may remember that last week's report from Crime Trends said there might be an upswing of sex crimes in the outlying areas like Townten this season. That's why I said it might be a sex crime. Do you know the girl?"

Clemens had known her five years ago, when they had both been at the Junior Campus of Hub 23 State College together. Dianne was a pretty blonde girl. Clemens had dated her fairly often but lost track of her when he'd transferred to the Police Academy for his final year. "I'll handle this case myself," he said. "Should take me a little over two hours to get to Townten. I'll check with you en route. Let me know at once if anything important comes in before that."

"Yes, sir. You do know her then?"

"I know her," said Clemens. To the lawagon he said, "Turn around and get us to Townten fast."

"Yes, sir," said the car.

Beyond Townseven, climbing the wide road that curved between the flat fields of yellow grain, the call from Jr. Marshal Kepling came. "Sir," said Kepling. "The patrol androids have been checking out witnesses. No one saw the girl after eleven last night. That was when she came home to her apartment. She was wearing a green coat, orange dress, green accessories. There was some noise heard in the apartment but no one thought much of it. That was a little after eleven. Seems like someone jimmied the alarm system for her place and got in. That's all so far. No prints or anything."

"Damn it," said Clemens. "It must be a real kidnapping then. And I'm an hour from Townten. Well the lawagon will catch the guy. There has to be time."

"One other thing," said Kepling.

"About Dianne Marmon?"

"No, about Sheldon Kloog."

"What?"

"Central has a report that Sheldon Kloog turned himself in at a public surrender booth in a park over in Territory 20 this morning. All the ID material matches. Whereas the stuff we sent shows a complete negative."

"What are they talking about? We caught Kloog."

"Not according to Central."

"It's impossible. The car doesn't make mistakes, Kepling."

"Central is going to make a full check-up as soon as you get back from this kidnapping case."

"They're wrong," said Clemens. "Okay. So keep me filled in on Dianne Marmon."

"Right, sir," said the Jr. Marshal, signing off.

To his lawagon Clemens said, "What do you think is going on? You couldn't have made a mistake about Sheldon Kloog. Could you?"

The car became absolutely silent and coasted off the road, brushing the invisible shield around the grain fields. Everything had stopped functioning.

"I didn't order you to pull off," said Clemens.

The car did not respond.

Lawagons weren't supposed to break down. And if they did, which rarely happened, they were supposed to repair themselves. Clemens couldn't get Lawagon A10 to do anything. It was completely dead. There was no way even to signal for help.

"For God's sake," said Clemens. There was an hour between him and Dianne. More than an hour now. He tried to make himself not think of her, of what might be happening. Of what might have already happened.

Clemens got out of the lawagon, stood back a few feet from it. "One more time," he said, "will you start?"

Nothing.

He turned and started jogging back towards Townseven. The heat of the day seemed to take all the moisture out of him, to

227

make him dry and brittle. This shouldn't have happened. Not when someone he cared for was in danger. Not now.

Emergency Central couldn't promise him a repairman until the swing shift came on in a quarter of an hour. Clemens requested assistance, a couple of lawagons at least from the surrounding territories. Territory 20 had had a reactor accident and couldn't spare theirs. Territory 21 promised to send a lawagon and a Jr. Marshal over to Townten to pick up the trail of Dianne Marmon's kidnapper as soon as the lawagon was free. Territory 22 promised the same, although they didn't think their car would be available until after nightfall. Clemens finally ordered his own Jr. Marshal to fly over to Townten and do the best he could until a lawagon arrived. A live Jr. Marshal sure as hell couldn't do much, though. Not what a lawagon could.

The little Townseven café he was calling from was fully automatic and Clemens sat down at a coffee table to wait for the repairman to arrive. The round light-blue room was empty except for a hunched old man who was sitting at a breakfast table, ordering side orders of hash browns one after another. When he'd filled the surface of the table he started a second layer. He didn't seem to be eating any of the food.

Clemens drank the cup of coffee that came up out of his table and ignored the old man. It was probably a case for a Psych Wagon but Clemens didn't feel up to going through the trouble of turning the man in. He finished his coffee. A car stopped outside and Clemens jumped up. It was just a customer.

"How can I do that?" said the repairman as he and Clemens went down the ramp of the automatic café. "Look." He pointed across the parking area at his small one man scooter.

Clemens shook his head. "It's nearly sundown. A girl's life is in danger. Damn, if I have to wait here until you fix the lawagon and bring it back I'll lose that much more time."

"I'm sorry," said the small sun-worn man. "I can't take you out to where the car is. The bureau says these scooters are not to carry passengers. So if I put more than two hundred pounds on it it just turns off and won't go at all."

"Okay, okay." There were no cars in the parking lot, no one to commandeer.

"You told me where your lawagon is. I can find it if it's right on the highway. You wait."

"How long?"

The repairman shrugged. "Those babies don't break down

much. But when they do . . . Could be a while. Overnight maybe."

"Overnight?" Clemens grabbed the man's arm. "You're kidding."

"Don't break my damn arm or it'll take that much longer."

"I'm sorry. I'll wait here. You'll drive the lawagon back?"

"Yeah. I got a special set of ID cards and passwords so I can get its hood up and drive it. Go inside and have a cup of coffee."

"Sure," said Clemens. "Thanks."

"Do my best."

"Do you know anything about the dinner-for-two tables?" the thin loose-suited young man asked Clemens.

Clemens had taken the table nearest the door and was looking out at the twilight roadway. "Beg pardon?"

"We put money in for a candle and nothing happened, except that when the asparagus arrived its ends were lit. This is my first date with this girl, marshal, and I want to make a good impression."

"Hit the outlet with your fist," said Clemens, turning away.

"Thank you, sir."

Clemens got up and went in to call the Law Bureau answering service in Townten. The automatic voice told him that Jr. Marshal Kepling had just arrived and reported in. He was on his way to the victim's apartment. No other news.

"She's not a victim," said Clemens and cut off.

"Arrest those two," said the old man, reaching for Clemens as he came out of the phone alcove.

"Why?"

"They shot a candle at my table and scattered my potatoes to here and gone."

The young man ran up. "I hit the table like you said and the candle came out. Only it went sailing all the way across the room."

"Young people," said the old man.

"Here," said Clemens. He gave both of them some cash. "Start all over again."

"That's not—" started the old man.

Clemens saw something coming down the dark road. He pushed free and ran outside.

As he reached the roadway the lawagon slowed and stopped. There was no one inside.

"Welcome aboard," said the car.

Clemens went through the identification ritual, looking off

229

along the roadway, and got in. "Where's the repairman? Did he send you on in alone."

"I saw through him, sir," said the lawagon. "Shall we proceed to Townten?"

"Yes. Step on it," said Clemens. "But what do you mean you saw through him?"

The glove compartment dropped open. There were two white jars in it now. "Sheldon Kloog won't bother us any more, sir. I have just apprehended and tried him. He was disguised as a repairman and made an attempt to dismantle an official Law Bureau vehicle. That offence, plus his murder record, made only one course of action possible."

Clemens swallowed, making himself not even tighten his grip on the wheel. If he said anything the car might stop again. There was something wrong. As soon as Dianne was safe Lawagon A10 would have to go into the shop for a thorough check-up. Right now Clemens needed the car badly, needed what it could do. They had to track down whoever had kidnapped Dianne. "Good work," he said evenly.

The headlights hit the cliffs that bordered the narrow road and long ragged shadows crept up the hillside ahead of them.

"I think we're closing in," said Clemens. He was talking to Jr. Marshal Kepling whom he'd left back at the Law Bureau answering service in Townten. He had cautioned Kepling to make no mention of the Kloog business while the car could hear them.

"Central verifies the ID on the kidnapper from the prints we found," said Kepling. Surprisingly Kepling had found fingerprints in Dianne's apartment that the andy patrol and the mechanical deputy had missed. "It is Jim Otterson. Up to now he's only done short sentence stuff."

"Good," said Clemens. That meant that Otterson might not harm Dianne. Unless this was the time he'd picked to cross over. "The lawagon," said Clemens, "is holding on to his trail. We should get him now any time. He's on foot now and the girl is definitely still with him the car says. We're closing in."

"Good luck," said Kepling.

"Thanks." Clemens signed off.

Things had speeded up once he and the lawagon had reached Townten. Clemens had known that. The lawagon had had no trouble picking up the scent. Now, late at night, they were some twenty-five miles out of Townten. They'd found Otterson's car seven miles back with its clutch burned out. The auto had been there, off the unpaved back road, for about four hours. Otterson had driven around in great zigzags. Apparently he had spent the whole of the night after the kidnapping in a deserted storehouse about fifty miles from Townten. He had left there, according to the lawagon, about noon and headed towards Towneleven. Then he had doubled back again, swinging in near Townten. Clemens and the lawagon had spent hours circling around on Otterson's trail. With no more car Otterson and the girl couldn't have come much further than where Clemens and the lawagon were now.

The lawagon turned off the road and bumped across a rocky plateau. It swung around and stopped. Up above was a high flat cliffside, dotted with caves. "Up there, I'd say," said the lawagon. It had silenced its engine.

"Okay," said Clemens. There wasn't much chance of sneaking up on Otterson if he was up in one of those caves. Clemens would have to risk trying to talk to him. "Shoot the lights up there and turn on the speakers."

Two spotlights hit the cliff and a hand mike came up out of the dash. Taking it, Clemens climbed out of the lawagon. "Otterson, this is Marshal Clemens. I'm asking you to surrender. If you don't I'll have to use stun gas on you. We know you're in one of those caves, we can check each one off if we have to. Give up."

Clemens waited. Then half way up the cliffside something green flashed and then came hurtling down. It pinwheeled down the mountain and fell past the plateau.

"What the hell." Clemens ran forward. There was a gully between the cliff and the plateau, narrow and about thirty feet deep. At its bottom now was something. It might be Dianne, arms tangled over interlaced brush.

"Get me a handlight and a line," he called to the lawagon.

Without moving the car lobbed a handbeam to him and sent a thin cord snaking over the ground. "Check."

"Cover the caves. I'm going down to see what that was that fell."

"Ready?"

Clemens hooked the light on his belt and gripped the line. He backed over the plateau edge. "Okay, ready."

The line was slowly let out and Clemens started down. Near the brush he caught a rock and let go of the line. He unhitched the light and swung it. He exhaled sharply. What had fallen was

231

only an empty coat. Otterson was trying to decoy them. "Watch out," Clemens shouted to his car. "It's not the girl. He may try to make a break now."

He steadied himself and reached for the rope. Its end snapped out at him and before he could catch it it whirred up and out of sight. "Hey, the rope. Send it back."

"Emergency," announced the lawagon, its engine coming on.

Up above a blaster sizzled and rock clattered. Clemens yanked out his pistol and looked up. Down the hillside a man was coming, carrying a bound up girl in his arms. His big hands showed and they held pistols. Dianne was gagged but seemed to be alive. Otterson zigzagged down, using the girl for a shield. He was firing not at Clemens but at the lawagon. He jumped across the gully to a plateau about twenty yards from where Clemens had started over.

Holstering his gun Clemens started to climb. He was half way up when he heard Otterson cry out. Then there was no sound at all.

Clemens tried to climb faster but could not. The gully side was jagged and hard to hold on to. Finally he swung himself up on the plateau.

"This is a public service announcement." said the lawagon. "Sheldon Kloog and his female accomplice have been captured, tried, sentenced and executed. This message comes to you from the Law Bureau. Thank you."

Clemens roared. He grabbed up a rock in each hand and went charging at the car. "You've killed Dianne," he shouted. "You crazy damn machine."

The lawagon turned and started rolling towards him. "No you don't, Kloog," it said.

THE SECRET SONGS

by *Fritz Leiber*

Promptly after supper, before Gwen had cleared away the dishes, Donnie began the Sleep Ritual. He got a can of beer from the refrigerator, selected a science-fiction magazine, and shut off the TV sound.

"The picture too?" he asked. "Might as well."

Gwen smiled at him as she shook her head. With the gesture of one who eats peanuts she threw her right hand to her mouth, swallowed, then dropped her hand with the tiny bottle it held back to the pocket of her smock.

Donnie sighed, shrugged his shoulders, settled himself in the easy chair, opened his magazine, and began to read and sip rapidly.

Gwen, who had been ignoring the TV, now began to study the screen. A kindly old rancher and a tall young cowpoke, father and son, were gazing out across broad acres framed by distant mountains. Gwen tuned her ears and after a bit she could faintly hear what they were saying.

THE OLD RANCHER : *Aim to plant her to hemp and opium poppy, Son, with benzedrine bushes between the rows.*

THE YOUNG COWPOKE : *Yeah, but what legal crop you fixin' to raise, Dad?*

THE OLD RANCHER (smiling like God) : *Gonna raise babies, Son.*

Gwen looked away quickly from the screen. It never paid to try to hear too much too soon.

Donnie was studying her with a teasing grin.

"I bet you imagine all sorts of crazy things while you watch it," he said. "Those terrible bennies get your mind all roiled up."

Gwen shrugged. "You won't allow any noise while you're putting yourself to sleep. I have to have something," she said reasonably. "Besides," she added, "you're having orgies out in space with those girls in fluorescent bikinis."

"That shows how little you know about science fiction," Donnie said. "They dropped the sex angle years ago. Now it's all philosophy and stuff. See this old guy?"

He held up the magazine, keeping his place with his forefinger. On the cover was a nicely drawn picture of a smiling intelligent-looking young man in a form-fitting futuristic uniform and standing beside him, topping him by a long head, a lean green-scaled monster with a large silver purse slung over his crested shoulder. The monster had a tentacle resting in comradely fashion across the young man's back and curling lightly past his feather epaulet.

"You mean that walking crocodile?" Gwen asked.

Donnie sniffed. "That walking crocodile," he said, "happens to be a very wise old member of a civilisation that's advanced far beyond man's." He lifted his other hand with two fingers pressed together. "Him and me are like that. He tells me all sorts of things. He even tells me things about you."

"Science fiction doesn't interest me," Gwen said lightly, looking back to the TV. There was a commercial on now, first a white-on-black diagram of the human body with explosions of bubbles occurring in sequence at various points, then a beautiful princess in a vast bathroom, then a handsome policeman. Gwen expertly retuned her ears.

VOICE OF MEDICAL EXPERT : *Benzedrine strikes at hidden sleepiness! Tones muscles! Strengthens the heart! Activates sluggish wake centres . . . One . . . Two . . . Three!*

THE BEAUTIFUL PRINCESS (looking depressed) : *Yesterday I was overweight, listless, intensely unhappy. Mother called me The Ugly Dumpling. Now* (becoming radiant) *I build beauty with benzedrine!*

THE HANDSOME POLICEMAN (flashing badge with huge "N" for Narcotic Squad) : *You're all under arrest! Grrr . . . aarrarrgghhh!*

Gwen quickly looked away. It was the only thing you could do when you got static or the wrong voice channel. She began to carry the supper dishes to the sink.

Donnie winced violently without putting down his beer can or looking up from his page. "Don't clank them," he said. Gwen removed her shoes and began to do the dishes as if she were a diver in the silent world under the surface of the sea, ghosting between table, sink and cupboard.

She was still lost in this rather fascinating operation and even beginning to embroider it with little arabesques when Donnie continued the Sleep Ritual by opening his second can of beer, this time a warm one by choice. Before taking the first sip he swallowed a blue capsule of amytal. At the *kerzing!* of the opener Gwen stopped to watch him. She carefully dried the suds off her right hand, popped on to her tongue another benzedrine tablet from the bottle in her smock pocket, and still watching him thoughtfully, rinsed a glass, ran an inch of water into it and drank it.

If Donnie had his Sleep Ritual, she told herself in not exactly those words, she had her Vigil.

Donnie stood shaking his head at her.

"I suppose now you'll be wandering around all night," he said, "making all sorts of noise and disturbing me."

"I don't make any more noise than a snowflake," Gwen countered. "Not one-tenth as much as the autos and streetcars and planes. Almost every night the people next door have their TV on high."

"Yes, but those noises are outside," Donnie said. "It's your

234

noises that bother me—the inside noises." He looked at Gwen speculatively. "Why don't you try a sleeping pill just for once?" he said with insidious appeal.

"No," Gwen answered instantly.

"A three-grain amytal," Donnie persisted, "would cancel those bennies and still have enough left over to make you nice and dozy. We'd go to sleep together and I wouldn't worry about noises."

"You don't want to go to sleep until you know everyone else is asleep," Gwen said. "Just like my mother. If I took one of your pills, you'd watch me sleep and you'd gloat."

"Well, isn't that what you do to me?"

"No, I do other things. By myself."

Donnie shrugged resignedly and went back to his chair and magazine.

Gwen wiped the itchy suds off her left hand, and leaving the rest of the dishes soaking, sat down opposite the TV. A curly haired disc jockey was looking out thoughtfully across a record he was holding:

THE DISC JOCKEY : *Some might think it strange that with such divergent tastes in drugs Donnie and Gwen Martin should seek happiness together and in their fashion find it . . . but life holds many mysteries, my friends. I could mention Jack Sprat and wife. We'll all hope the Hubbard . . . oops! . . . Martin medicine cupboard is never bare. And now we will hear, by the joint request of Mr. and Mrs. Martin—are you out there, Don and Gwennie?—that popular old favourite* (glancing down at record) *The Insane Asylum Blues!*

The music was real gone.

Donnie leaned back from his magazine and looked up at the ceiling. Gwen wondered if he were watching one of the glittering stars he'd named and pointed out to her on one of the rare Saturday nights they got outdoors. But after a while he said, "Benzedrine is an utterly evil drug, worse than coffee. Other drugs soothe and heal, but benzedrine only creates tension and confusion. I'll bet if I ask the Wise Old Crocodile he'll tell me the Devil invented it."

Gwen said, "If we ever went out nights and did anything, maybe I wouldn't need so much benzedrine. Besides, you have your sleeping pills and things."

"You don't need less benzedrine when you go out, you need more," Donnie asserted unalterably. "And if I ever went out on week nights, I'd get excited and start to drink and you know what would happen. How often do I have to tell you, Woman,

235

that the only reason I take my barbiturates and 'things', as you call them, is to keep calm and get enough sleep. If I didn't get enough sleep, I wouldn't be able to stand my job. If I couldn't stand my job, I'd start to drink. And if I started to drink, I'd be back in the Booby Hatch. And since the only reason you're outside is that I'm outside, holding a job, why you'd be back in the Booby Hatch too and they'd put you on tranquillisers and you wouldn't like it at all. So don't criticise my sleeping medicines, Woman. They're a matter of pure necessity whatever the doctors and psychologists say. Whereas your bennies and dexies—"

"We've been through all this before," Gwen interrupted without rancour.

Donnie nodded owlishly. "Show we half," he agreed, his words blurring for the first time.

"Besides," Gwen said, "you're behind schedule."

Donnie squinted at the clock and snapped his fingers. The sound was dull but there was no unsteadiness in his walk as he went to the refrigerator and poured himself two fingers of grapejuice. Then he reached down from the top shelf of the cupboard the bottle of paraldehyde and poured himself a glistening tablespoonful. Swift, almost as though the intense odour, midway between gasoline and banana oil, leaped to the corners of the half-merged living-room and kitchen. Gwen momentarily wrinkled her nose.

Donnie mixed the paraldehyde with the grapejuice and licked the spoon. "Here's to the druggists and the one understanding doctor in ten," he said and took a sip.

Gwen nodded solemnly and swallowed another benzedrine tablet.

Donnie transported his cocktail back to the armchair with great care and did not take his eye off the purple drink until he felt himself firmly anchored. He found his place in the science-fiction lead novelette, but the print began to slip sideways and so, as he sipped his stinging drink, he began to imagine the secrets the Wise Old Crock might tell him if he were the young man on the cover.

THE WISE OLD CROCK : *Got a hot trip shaping for tonight, Son. Three new novas flaring in the next galaxy southeast-by-up and dust cloud billowing out of Andromeda like black lace underwear.* (Dips in his purse.) *Drop this silver sphere in your pocket, Son. It's a universal TV pickup on the old crystal-ball principle. It lets you tune in on any scene in the universe. Use it wisely, Son, for character building as well as delight. Don't use it to spy on your wife.* (Dips again.) *Now I want to give you this small black cylinder. Keep it always on your person. It's a psychic whistle by which you can summon me at all times. All you have to do is concentrate on me, Son. Concentrate . . .*

There was a courtroom scene on the TV screen. A lawyer with friendly eyes but a serious brow was talking quietly to the jury, resting his hand on the rail of the box. Gwen had her ears fine-tuned by now and his voice synchronised perfectly with the movements of his lips.

THE FRIENDLY LAWYER : *I have no wish to conceal the circumstance that my client met her husband-to-be while they were both patients in a mental hospital. Believe me, folks, some of life's sweetest romances begin in the nut house. Gwen's affection inspired Don to win his release, obtain employment as a precision machinist, offer my client marriage upon her release, and shower her with love and the yellow health-tablets, so necessary to her existence, which you have watched her consume during these weary days in court. Needless to remark, this was before Don Martin began travelling in space, where he came under the influence of* (suddenly scowls) *a certain green crocodile, who shall be referred to as hereinafter as Exhibit A. Enter it, clerk.*

Donnie rose up slowly from the armchair. His drink was finished. He was glaring at the TV.

"The Old Crock wouldn't be seen dead looking at junk like that," he cried thickly. "He's wired for real-life experience."

Donnie was half of a mind to kick in the picture tube when he looked towards the bedroom doorway and saw the Wise Old Crocodile standing in it, stooping low, his silver purse swinging as it dangled from his crested shoulder. Donnie knew it wasn't a hallucination, only a friendly faint green film on the darkness.

Fixing his huge kindly eyes on Donnie, the Wise Old Crock impatiently uncurled a long tentacle towards the darkness beyond him, as if to say, "Away! Away!" and then faded into it. Donnie followed him in a slow motion like Gwen's underwater ballet, shedding his shoes and shirt on the way. He was pulling his belt from the trouser loops with the air of drawing a sword as he closed the door behind him.

Gwen gave a sigh of pure joy and for a moment even closed her eyes. This was the loveliest time of all the night, the time of the Safe Freedom, the time of the Vigil. She started to roam.

First she thought she'd brush the bread crumbs from the supper table, but she got to studying their pattern and ended by picking them up one by one—she thought of it as a problem in subtraction. The pattern of the crumbs had been like that of the stars Donnie had showed her, she decided afterwards, and she was rather sorry she'd disturbed them. She carried them tenderly to the sink and delicately dusted them on to the cold grey dishwater, around which a few suds still lifted stubbornly, like old foam on an ocean beach. She saw the water glass and it reminded her to take another benzedrine tablet.

Four bright spoons caught her eye. She lifted them one by one, turning them over slowly to find all the highlights. Then she looked through the calendar on the wall, studying the months ahead and all the numbers of the days.

Every least thing was enormously fascinating! She could lose herself in one object for minutes or let her interest dart about and effortlessly follow it.

And it was easy to think good thoughts. She could think of every person she knew and wish them each well and do all kinds of wonderful things for them in her mind. A kind of girl Jesus, that's what I am, she told herself with a smile.

She drifted back into the living-room. On the TV a bright blonde housewife was leading a dull brunette housewife over to a long couch. Gwen gave a small cry of pleasure and sat down on the floor. This show was always good.

THE BRIGHT BLONDE : *What do you feed your husband when he comes home miserable?*

THE DULL BRUNETTE : *Poison*

THE BRIGHT BLONDE : *What do you feed yourself?*

THE DULL BRUNETTE : *Sorrow.*

THE BRIGHT BLONDE : *I keep my spirits high with benzedrine. Oh happy junior high!*

THE DULL BRUNETTE : *What was happy about it? I had acne.*

THE BRIGHT BLONDE (bouncing as they sit on the couch) : *You mean to say I never told you how I got started on benzedrine? I was in junior high and unhappy. My mother sent me to the doctor because I was fat and at the foot of my class. He gave me some cute little pills and zowie!—I was getting slim, smart and giddy. But pretty soon they found I was going back for an extra refill between refills. They cut me off. I struck. Uh-huh, little old me called a lie-down strike. No more school, I said, unless I had my pills. If the doctor wouldn't give them to me, I'd forage for them—and I did. Two years later my mother had me committed. If I hadn't become a TV star I'd still be in the Loony Bin.*

THE DULL BRUNETTE : *Did they give you electroshock?*

THE BRIGHT BLONDE : *Think happy thoughts. What do you do for kicks? Are you on bennies too?*

THE DULL BRUNETTE : *No.* (Her face grows slack and subtly ugly.) *I practise witchcraft.*

Gwen switched off her ears and looked away from the screen. She did not like the thought that had come to her: that she had somehow planted that idea about witchcraft in the brunette's mind. It was months since Gwen had let herself think about witchcraft, either white or black.

There came a long low groan from the bedroom, adding to Gwen's troubled feeling because it seemed too much of a coincidence that it should have come just after the word witchcraft had been spoken.

DONNIE was twisting on the bed, going through hell in his dreams. The Wise Old Crock had abandoned him in a cluster of dead stars and cosmic dust on the far side of the Andromeda Galaxy, first blindfolding him, turning him around three times, and giving him a mighty shove that had sent him out of sight of whatever asteroid they had been standing on. Floating in space, Donnie went through his pockets and found only a Scout knife and a small silver sphere and black cylinder, the purpose of which he had forgotten. A cameo-small image of Gwen's face smiled at him from the sphere. He looked up. Worms twenty feet long and glowing dull red were undulating towards him through the dusty dark. He had an intense sensation of the vast distance of the Earth. He made swimming movements only to discover that a cold paralysis was creeping through his limbs. Eternities passed.

GWEN had got out her glue and glitter and sequins and had spread newspapers on the table and was making a design on a soup plate that she hoped would catch something of the remembered pattern of the bread crumbs. The idea was to paint with glue the design for one colour of glitter and then sprinkle the glitter on it, knocking off the excess by tapping the edge of the plate on the table. Sprinkling the glitter was fun, but the design was not developing quite the way she wanted it to. Besides she had just discovered that she didn't have any red or gold glitter, though there were three bottles of green. Some of the green glitter stuck to the back of her finger where she had got glue on it.

She stole a look over her shoulder at the TV. The two women had been replaced by a large map of the United States and a rugged young man wearing glasses and holding a pointer. The first word she heard told her she wasn't going to like it, but she hitched her chair around just the same, deciding that in the long run it would be best to know the worst.

THE THINGS FORECASTER : *A witchcraft high is moving down from Western Canada. Werewolf warnings have been posted in three states. Government planes are battling in the black front with white radio rays, but they're being forced back. Old folks who ought to know say it's the end of the world.* (Scans sheet handed him by page girl.) *Flash from outer space! Don Martin, famed astronaut, is facing nameless perils in the Lesser Magellanic Cloud!*

DONNIE had just blown the psychic whistle, having remembered its use only as the red worms began to spiral in around him, and the Wise Old Crock had appeared at once, putting the worms to flight with a shower of green sparks flicked from the tip of his right-hand tentacle.

THE WISE OLD CROCK : *You passed the test, Son, but don't pride yourself on it. Some night we're going to give it to you without paraldehyde. Now it's time you returned to Terra. Think of your home planet, Son, think of the Earth. Concentrate. . . .* (They are suddenly in orbit a thousand miles above North America. The larger cities gleam dully, the moon is reflected in the Great Lakes. Donnie has become a green-scaled being a head shorter than the Wise Old Crock, who weaves a tentacle majestically downwards.) *Observe the cities of men, my Son. Think of the millions sleeping and dreaming there, lonely as death in their apartment dwellings and all hating their jobs. The outward appearance of these men-beings may horrify you a little at first, but you have my word that they're not fiends, only creatures like you and me, trying to control themselves with drugs, dreads, incantations, ideals, self hypnosis and surrender, so that they may lead happy lives and show forth beauty.*

GWEN was looking intently in the living-room mirror, painting evenly-spaced bands of glue on her face. The bands curved under her eyes and outward, following the line of her jaw. She painted another band down the middle of her forehead and continued it straight down her nose. Then she closed her eyes, held her breath, lifted her face and shook green glitter on it for a long time. At last she lowered her face with a jerk, shook it from side to side, puffed out through her nostrils what breath she had left, and inhaled very slowly. Then she looked at herself again in the mirror and smiled. The green glitter clung to her face just as it had to her finger.

A feeling of deadly fatigue struck her then, the first of the night, and the room momentarily swam. When it came to rest she was looking at a flashing-eyed priest in a gorgeous cloak who was weaving across the TV screen.

THE GORGEOUS PRIEST : *The psychology of Donnie and Gwen must be clear to you by now. Each wants the other to sleep so that he may stand guard over her, or she over him, while yet adventuring alone. They have found a formula for this. But what of the future? What of their souls? Drugs are no permanent solution, I can assure them. What if the bars of the Safe Freedom should blow away? What if one night one of them should go out and never come in?*

DONNIE and the Wise Old Crock were hovering just outside the bedroom window three stories up. Friendly trees shaded them from the street lights below.

THE WISE OLD CROCK : *Goodbye, my Son, for another night. Use your Earthly tenement well. Do not abuse your powers. And go easy on the barbiturates.*

DONNIE : *I will, Father, believe me.*

THE WISE OLD CROCK : *Hold. There is one further secret of great consequence that I must impart to you tonight. It concerns your wife.*

DONNIE : *Yes, Father?*

THE WISE OLD CROCK : *She is one of us!*

DONNIE flowed through the four-inch gap at the bottom of the bedroom window. He saw his body lying on its back on the bed and he surged towards it through the air, paddling gently with his tentacle tips. His body opened from the crotch to chin like a purse and he flowed inside and the lips of the purse closed over his back with a soft *click*. Then he squirmed around gently, as if in a sleeping bag, and looked through the two holes in the front of his head and thrust his tentacles down into his arms and lifted his hands above his eyes and wriggled his fingers. It felt very strange to have fingertipped arms with bones in them instead of tentacles. Just then he heard laughter from the living-room.

Gwen was laughing admiringly at the reflection of her breasts. She had taken off her smock and brassière and painted circles of glue around the nipples and sprinkled on more glitter.

Although her ears were switched off, she thought she heard the priest call from behind her, "Gwen Martin, you ought to be ashamed of yourself!" And she called back to the TV, "You shouldn't peek, Father!" and she turned around, haughtily shielding her breasts with a forearm held crosswise.

241

The bedroom door was open and Donnie was standing in it, swaying and staring. Gwen felt another surge of deadly fatigue but she steadied herself and stared back at her husband.

Woman, the Cave Keeper, the Weaver of Words, faced Man, the Bread Winner, the Far Ranger.

They moved together slowly, dragging their feet. until they were leaning against each other. Then more slowly, still, as if they were supporting each other through quicksands, they moved towards the bedroom.

"Do you like me, Donnie?" Gwen asked.

Donnie's gaze brushed across her glittering green-striped face and breasts. His hand tightened on her shoulder and he nodded.

"You're one of us," he said.

STRANGER STATION

by *Damon Knight*

The clang of metal echoed hollowly down through the Station's many vaulted corridors and rooms. Paul Wesson stood listening for a moment as the rolling echoes died away. The maintenance rocket was gone, heading back to Home; they had left him alone in Stranger Station.

Stranger Station! The name itself quickened his imagination. Wesson knew that both orbital stations had been named a century ago by the then British administration of the satellite service; "Home" because the larger, inner station handled the traffic of Earth and its colonies; "Stranger" because the outer station was designed specifically for dealings with foreigners ... beings from outside the solar system. But even that could not diminish the wonder of Stranger Station, whirling out here alone in the dark—waiting for its once-in-two-decades visitor.

. . .

One man, out of all Sol's billions, had the task and privilege of enduring the alien's presence when it came. The two races, according to Wesson's understanding of the subject, were so fundamentally different that it was painful for them to meet.

Well, he had volunteered for the job, and he thought he could handle it—the rewards were big enough.

He had gone through all the tests, and against his own expectations he had been chosen. The maintenance crew had brought him up as dead weight, drugged in a survival hamper; they had kept him the same way while they did their work, and then had brought him back to consciousness. Now they were gone. He was alone.

. . . But not quite.

"Welcome to Stranger Station, Sergeant Wesson," said a pleasant voice. "This is your alpha network speaking. I'm here to protect and serve you in every way. If there's anything you want, just ask me." It was a neutral voice, with a kind of professional friendliness in it, like that of a good schoolteacher or rec supervisor.

Wesson had been warned, but he was still shocked at the human quality of it. The alpha networks were the last word in robot brains—computers, safety devices, personal servants, libraries, all wrapped up in one, with something so close to "personality" and "free will" that experts were still arguing the question. They were rare and fantastically expensive; Wesson had never met one before.

"Thanks," he said now, to the empty air. "Uh—what do I call you, by the way? I can't keep saying, 'Hey, alpha network.' "

"One of your recent predecessors called me Aunt Nettie," was the response.

Wesson grimaced. Alpha network—Aunt Nettie. He hated puns; that wouldn't do. "The aunt part is all right," he said. "Suppose I call you Aunt Jane. That was my mother's sister; you sound like her, a little bit."

"I am honoured," said the invisible mechanism politely. "Can I serve you any refreshments now? Sandwiches? A drink?"

"Not just yet," said Wesson. "I think I'll look the place over first."

He turned away. That seemed to end the conversation as far as the network was concerned. A good thing; it was all right to have it for company, speaking when spoken to, but if it got talkative. . . .

The human part of the Station was in four segments: bedroom, living room, dining room, bath. The living room was comfortably large and pleasantly furnished in greens and tans: the only mechanical note in it was the big instrument console in one corner. The other rooms, arranged in a ring around the

243

living room, were tiny; just space enough for Wesson, a narrow encircling corridor, and the mechanisms that would serve him. The whole place was spotlessly clean, gleaming and efficient in spite of its twenty-year layoff.

This is the gravy part of the run, Wesson told himself. The month before the alien came—good food, no work, and an alpha network for conversation. "Aunt Jane, I'll have a small steak now," he said to the network. "Medium rare, with hashed brown potatoes, onions and mushrooms, and a glass of lager. Call me when it's ready."

"Right," said the voice pleasantly. Out in the dining room, the autochef began to hum and cluck self-importantly. Wesson wandered over and inspected the instrument console. Airlocks were sealed and tight, said the dials; the air was cycling. The Station was in orbit, and rotating on its axis with a force at the perimeter, where Wesson was, of one *g*. The internal temperature of this part of the Station was an even 73°.

The other side of the board told a different story; all the dials were dark and dead. Sector Two, occupying a volume some eighty-eight thousand times as great as this one, was not yet functioning.

Wesson had a vivid mental image of the Station, from photographs and diagrams—a five-hundred-foot duralumin sphere, on to which the shallow thirty-foot disc of the human section had been stuck apparently as an afterthought. The whole cavity of the sphere, very nearly—except for a honeycomb of supply and maintenance rooms, and the all-important, recently enlarged vats—was one cramped chamber for the alien. . . .

"Steak's ready!" said Aunt Jane.

The steak was good, bubbling crisp outside the way he liked it, tender and pink inside. "Aunt Jane," he said with his mouth full, "this is pretty soft, isn't it?"

"The steak," asked the voice, with a faintly anxious note.

Wesson grinned. "Never mind," he said. "Listen, Aunt Jane, you've been through this routine—how many times? Were you installed with the Station, or what?"

"I was not installed with the Station," said Aunt Jane primly. "I have assisted at three contacts."

"Um. Cigarette," said Wesson, slapping his pockets. The autochef hummed for a moment, and popped a pack of G.I.s out of a vent. Wesson lit up. "All right," he said, "you've been through this three times. There are a lot of things you can tell me, right?"

244

"Oh, yes, certainly. What would you like to know?"

Wesson smoked, leaning back reflectively, green eyes narrowed. "First," he said, "read me the Pigeon report—you know, from the *Brief History*. I want to see if I remember it right."

"Chapter Two," said the voice promptly. "First contact with a non-Solar intelligence was made by Commander Ralph C. Pigeon on July 1, 1987, during an emergency landing on Titan. The following is an excerpt from his official report:

"'While searching for a possible cause for our mental disturbance, we discovered what appeared to be a gigantic construction of metal on the far side of the ridge. Our distress grew stronger with the approach to this construction, which was polyhedral and approximately five times the length of the *Cologne*.

"'Some of those present expressed a wish to retire, but Lt. Acuff and myself had a strong sense of being called or summoned in some indefinable way. Although our uneasiness was not lessened, we therefore agreed to go forward and keep radio contact with the rest of the party while they returned to the ship.

"'We gained access to the alien construction by way of a large, irregular opening. . . . The internal temperature was minus seventy-five degrees Farenheit; the atmosphere appeared to consist of methane and ammonia. . . . Inside the second chamber, an alien creature was waiting for us. We felt the distress which I have tried to describe, to a much greater degree than before, and also the sense of summoning or pleading. . . . We observed that the creature was exuding a thick yellowish fluid from certain joints or pores in its surface. Though disgusted, I managed to collect a sample of this exudate, and it was later forwarded for analysis. . . .'

"The second contact was made ten years later by Commodore Crawford's famous Titan Expedition—"

"No, that's enough," said Wesson. "I just wanted the Pigeon quote." He smoked, brooding. "It seems kind of chopped off, doesn't it? Have you got a longer version in your memory banks anywhere?"

There was a pause. "No," said Aunt Jane.

"There was more to it when I was a kid," Wesson complained nervously. "I read that book when I was twelve, and I remember a long description of the alien . . . that is, I remember its being there." He swung around. "Listen, Aunt Jane—you're a sort of universal watchdog, that right? You've got cameras and mikes all over the Station?"

245

"Yes," said the network, sounding—was it Wesson's imagination?—faintly injured.

"Well, what about Sector Two—you must have cameras up there, too, isn't that so?"

"Yes."

"All right, then you can tell me. What do the aliens look like?"

There was a definite pause. "I'm sorry, I can't tell you that," said Aunt Jane.

"No," said Wesson, "I didn't think you could. You've got orders not to, I guess, for the same reason those history books have been cut since I was a kid. Now, what would the reason be? Have you got any idea, Aunt Jane?"

There was another pause. "Yes," the voice admitted.

"Well?"

"I'm sorry, I can't—"

"—tell you that," Wesson repeated along with it. "All right. At least we know where we stand."

"Yes, Sergeant. Would you like some dessert?"

"No dessert. One other thing. *What happens to Station watchmen, like me, after their tour of duty?*"

"They are upgraded to Class Seven, students with unlimited leisure, and receive outright gifts of seven thousand stellors, plus free Class One housing. . . ."

"Yeah, I know all that," said Wesson, licking his dry lips. "But here's what I'm asking you. The ones you know—what kind of shape were they in when they left here?"

"The usual human shape," said the voice brightly. "Why do you ask, Sergeant?"

Wesson made a discontented gesture. "Something I remember from a bull session at the Academy. I can't get it out of my head; I know it had something to do with the Station. Just a part of a sentence—'blind as a bat, and white bristles all over.' Now, would that be a description of the alien . . . or the watchman when they came to take him away?"

Aunt Jane went into one of her heavy pauses. "All right, I'll save you the trouble," said Wesson. "You're sorry, you can't tell me that."

"I *am* sorry," said the robot, sincerely.

As the slow days passed into weeks, Wesson grew aware of the Station almost as a living thing. He could feel its resilient metal ribs enclosing him, lightly bearing his weight with its own as it swung. He could feel the waiting emptiness "up there" and he sensed the alert electronic network that spread around him everywhere, watching and probing, trying to anticipate his needs.

Aunt Jane was a model companion. She had a record library of thousands of hours of music; she had films to show him, and micro-printed books that he could read on the scanner in the living room; or if he preferred, she would read to him. She controlled the Station's three telescopes, and on request would give him a view of Earth, or the Moon, or Home. . . .

But there was no news. Aunt Jane would obligingly turn on the radio receiver if he asked her, but nothing except static came out. That was the thing that weighed most heavily on Wesson, as time passed: the knowledge that radio silence was being imposed on all ships in transit, on the orbital stations, and on the planet-to-space transmitters. It was an enormous, almost a crippling handicap. Some information could be transmitted over relatively short distances by photophone, but ordinarily the whole complex traffic of the spacelanes depended on radio.

But this coming alien contact was so delicate a thing that even a radio voice, out here where the Earth was only a tiny disc twice the size of the Moon, might upset it. It was so precarious a thing, Wesson thought, that only one man could be allowed in the Station while the alien was there, and to give that man the company that would keep him sane, they had to install an alpha network. . . .

"Aunt Jane?"

The voice answered promptly, "Yes, Paul."

"This distress that the books talk about—you wouldn't know what it is, would you?"

"No, Paul."

"Because robot brains don't feel it, right?"

"Right, Paul."

"So tell me this—why do they need a man here at all? Why can't they get along with just you?"

A pause. "I don't know, Paul." The voice sounded faintly wistful. Were those gradations of tone really in it, Wesson wondered, or was his imagination supplying them?

He got up from the living room couch and paced restlessly back and forth. "Let's have a look at Earth," he said. Obediently, the viewing screen on the console glowed into life: there was the blue Earth, swimming deep below him, in its first quarter, jewel bright. "Switch it off," Wesson said.

"A little music?" suggested the voice, and immediately began to play something soothing, full of woodwinds.

247

"No," said Wesson. The music stopped.

Wesson's hands were trembling; he had a caged and frustrated feeling.

The fitted suit was in its locker beside the air lock. Wesson had been topside in it once or twice; there was nothing to see up there, just darkness and cold. But he had to get out of this squirrel cage. He took the suit down and began to get into it.

"Paul," said Aunt Jane anxiously, "are you feeling nervous?"

"Yes," he snarled.

"Then don't go into Sector Two," said Aunt Jane.

"Don't tell me what to do, you hunk of tin!" said Wesson with sudden anger. He zipped up the front of his suit with a vicious motion.

Aunt Jane was silent.

Seething, Wesson finished his check-off and opened the lock door.

The air lock, an upright tube barely large enough for one man, was the only passage between Sector One and Sector Two. It was also the only exit from Sector One; to get here in the first place, Wesson had had to enter the big lock at the "south" pole of the sphere, and travel all the way down inside, by drop hole and catwalk. He had been drugged unconscious at the time, of course. When the time came, he would go out the same way; neither the maintenance rocket nor the tanker had any space, or time, to spare.

At the "north" pole, opposite, there was a third air lock, this one so huge it could easily have held an interplanet freighter. But that was nobody's business—no human being's.

In the beam of Wesson's helmet lamp, the enormous central cavity of the Station was an inky gulf that sent back only remote, mocking glimmers of light. The near walls sparkled with hoar-frost. Sector Two was not yet pressurised; there was only a diffuse vapour that had leaked through the airseal and had long since frozen into the powdery deposit that lined the walls. The metal rang cold under his shod feet; the vast emptiness of the chamber was the more depressing because it was airless, unwarmed and unlit. *Alone,* said his footsteps; *alone. . .*

He was thirty yards up the catwalk when his anxiety suddenly grew stronger. Wesson stopped in spite of himself, and turned clumsily, putting his back to the wall. The support of the solid wall was not enough. The catwalk seemed threatening to tilt underfoot, dropping him into the lightless gulf.

Wesson recognised this drained feeling, this metallic taste at the back of his tongue. It was fear.

The thought ticked through his head. *They want me to be afraid*. But why? Why now? Of what?

Equally suddenly, he knew. The nameless pressure tightened, like a great fist closing, and Wesson had the appalling sense of something so huge that it had no limits at all, descending, with a terrible endless swift slowness. . . .

It was time.

His first month was up.

The alien was coming.

As Wesson turned, gasping, the whole huge structure of the Station around him seemed to dwindle to the size of an ordinary room . . . and Wesson with it, so that he seemed to himself like a tiny insect, frantically scuttling down the walls towards safety.

Behind him as he ran, the Station *boomed*.

In the silent rooms, all the lights were burning dimly. Wesson lay still, looking at the ceiling. Up there his imagination formed a shifting, changing image of the alien—huge, shadowy, formlessly menacing.

Sweat had gathered in globules on his brow. He stared, unable to look away.

"That was why you didn't want me to go topside, huh, Aunt Jane?" he said hoarsely.

"Yes. The nervousness is the first sign. But you gave me a direct order, Paul."

"I know it," he said vaguely, still staring fixedly at the ceiling. "A funny thing. . . . Aunt Jane?"

"Yes, Paul?"

"You won't tell me what it looks like, right?"

"*No*, Paul."

"I don't want to know. Lord, I don't *want* to know. . . . Funny thing, Aunt Jane, part of me is just pure funk. I'm so scared I'm nothing but a jelly—"

"I know," said the voice gently.

"—and part is real cool and calm, as if it didn't matter. Crazy, the things you think about. You know?"

"What things, Paul?"

He tried to laugh. "I'm remembering a kids' party I went to twenty . . . twenty-five years ago. I was, let's see, I was nine. I remember, because that was the same year my father died.

"We were living in Dallas then, in a rented mobilehouse, and
249

there was a family in the next tract with a bunch of red-headed kids. They were always throwing parties; nobody liked them much, but everybody always went."

"Tell me about the party, Paul."

He shifted on the couch. "This one, this one was a Hallowe'en party. I remember the girls had on black and orange dresses, and the boys mostly wore spirit costumes. I was about the youngest kid there, and I felt kind of out of place. Then all of a sudden one of the redheads jumps up in a skull mask, hollering, 'C'mon, everybody get ready for hidenseek.' And he grabs *me,* and says, *'You* be it,' and before I can even move, he shoves me into a dark closet. And I hear that door lock behind me."

He moistened his lips. "And then—you know, in the darkness—I feel something hit my *face.* You know, cold and clammy, like, I don't know, something dead. . . ."

"I just hunched up on the floor of that closet, waiting for that thing to touch me again. You know? That thing, cold and kind of gritty, hanging up there. You know what it was? A cloth glove, full of ice and bran cereal. A joke. Boy, that was one joke I never forgot. . . . Aunt Jane?"

"Yes, Paul."

"Hey, I'll bet you alpha networks make great psychs, huh? I could lie here and tell you anything, because you're just a machine—right?"

"Right, Paul," said the network sorrowfully.

"Aunt Jane, Aune Jane. . . . It's no use kidding myself along. I can *feel* that thing up there, just a couple of yards away."

"I know you can, Paul."

"I can't stand it, Aunt Jane."

"You can if you think you can, Paul."

He writhed on the couch. "It's—it's dirty, it's clammy. My God, is it going to be like that for *five months*? I can't, it'll kill me, Aunt Jane."

There was another thunderous boom, echoing down through the structural members of the Station. "What's that?" Wesson gasped. "The other ship—casting off?"

"Yes. Now he's alone, just as you are."

"Not like me. He can't be feeling what I'm feeling. Aunt Jane, you don't know. . . ."

Up there, separated from him only by a few yards of metal, the alien's enormous, monstrous body hung. It was that poised weight, as real as if he could touch it, that weighed down his chest.

Wesson had been a space dweller for most of his adult life, and knew even in his bones that if an orbital station ever collapsed the "under" part would not be crushed but would be hurled away by its own angular momentum. This was not the oppressiveness of planetside buildings, where the looming mass above you seemed always threatening to fall: this was something else, completely distinct, and impossible to argue away.

It was the scent of danger, hanging unseen up there in the dark, waiting, cold and heavy. It was the recurrent nightmare of Wesson's childhood—the bloated unreal shape. no-colour, no-size, that kept on hideously falling towards his face. . . . It was the dead puppy he had pulled out of the creek, that summer in Dakota . . . wet fur, limp head, cold, cold, *cold.* . . .

With an effort, Wesson rolled over on the couch and lifted himself to one elbow. The pressure was an insistent chill weight on his skull; the room seemed to dip and swing around him in slow, dizzy circles.

Wesson felt his jaw muscles contorting with the strain as he knelt, then stood erect. His back and legs tightened; his mouth hung painfully open. He took one step, then another, timing them to hit the floor as it came upright.

The right side of the console, the one that had been dark, was lighted. Pressure in Sector Two, according to the indicator, was about one and a third atmospheres. The air-lock indicator showed a slightly higher pressure of oxygen and argon; that was to keep any of the alien atmosphere from contaminating Sector One, but it also meant that the lock would no longer open from either side. Wesson found that irrationally comforting.

"Lemme see Earth," he gasped.

The screen lighted up as he stared into it. "It's a long way down," he said. A long, long way down to the bottom of that well. . . . He had spent ten featureless years as a servo tech in Home Station. Before that, he'd wanted to be a pilot, but had washed out the first year—couldn't take the maths. But he had never once thought of going back to Earth.

Now, suddenly, after all these years, that tiny blue disc seemed infinitely desirable.

"Aunt Jane, Aunt Jane, it's beautiful," he mumbled.

Down there, he knew, it was spring; and in certain places, where the edge of darkness retreated it was morning: a watery blue morning like the sea light caught in an agate, a morning with smoke and mist in it; a morning of stillness and promise. Down there, lost years and miles away, some tiny dot of a woman was opening her microscopic door to listen to an atom's song. Lost, lost, and packed away in cotton wool, like a specimen slide: one spring morning on Earth.

Black miles above, so far that sixty Earths could have been piled one on another to make a pole for his perch, Wesson swung in his endless circle within a circle. Yet, vast as the gulf beneath him was, all this—Earth, Moon, orbital stations, ships; yes, the Sun and all the rest of his planets, too—was the merest sniff of space, to be pinched up between thumb and finger.

Beyond—there was the true gulf. In that deep night, galaxies lay sprawled aglitter, piercing a distance that could only be named in a meaningless number, a cry of dismay: O, O, O. . . .

Crawling and fighting, blasting with energies too big for them, men had come as far as Jupiter. But if a man had been tall enough to lie with his boots toasting in the Sun and his head freezing at Pluto, still he would have been too small for that overwhelming emptiness. Here, not at Pluto, was the outermost limit of man's empire: here the Outside funnelled down to meet it, like the pinched waist of an hour-glass: here, and only here, the two worlds came near enough to touch. Ours—and Theirs.

Down at the bottom of the board, now, the golden dials were faintly alight, the needles trembling ever so little on their pins.

Deep in the vats, the vats, the golden liquid was trickling down: *"Though disgusted, I took a sample of the exudate and it was forwarded for analysis. . . ."*

Space-cold fluid, trickling down the bitter walls of the tubes, forming little pools in the cups of darkness; goldenly agleam there, half alive. The golden elixir. One drop of the concentrate would arrest ageing for twenty years—keep your arteries soft, tonus good, eyes clear, hair pigmented, brain alert.

That was what the tests of Pigeon's sample had showed. That was the reason for the whole crazy history of the "alien trading post"—first a hut on Titan, then later, when people understood more about the problem, Stranger Station.

Once every twenty years, an alien would come down out of Somewhere, and sit in the tiny cage we had made for him, and make us rich beyond our dreams—rich with life—and still we did not know why.

Above him, Wesson imagined he could see that sensed body a-wallow in the glacial blackness, its bulk passively turning with the Station's spin, bleeding a chill gold into the lips of the tubes: drip, drop.

Wesson held his head. The pressure inside made it hard to

think; it felt as if his skull was about to fly apart. "Aunt Jane," he said.

"Yes, Paul." The kindly, comforting voice: like a nurse. The nurse who stands beside your cot while you have painful, necessary things done to you. Efficient, trained friendliness.

"Aunt Jane," said Wesson, "do you know why they keep coming back?"

"No," said the voice precisely. "It is a mystery."

Wesson nodded. "I had," he said, "an interview with Gower before I left Home. You know Gower? Chief of the Outerworld Bureau. Came up especially to see me."

"Yes?" said Aunt Jane encouragingly.

"Said to me, 'Wesson, you got to find out. Find out if we can count on them to keep up the supply. You know? There's fifty million more of us,' he says, 'than when you were born. We need more of the stuff, and we got to know if we can count on it. Because,' he says, 'you know what would happen if it stopped? Do you know, Aunt Jane?"

"It would be," said the voice, "a catastrophe."

"That's right," Wesson said respectfully. "It would. Like, he says to me, 'What if the people in the Nefud area were cut off from the Jordan Valley Authority? Why, there'd be millions dying of thirst in a week.

"'Or what if the freighters stopped coming to Moon Base. Why,' he says, 'there'd be thousands starving and smothering to death.'

"He says, 'Where the water is, where you can get food and air, people are going to settle, and get married, you know? and have kids.'

"He says, 'If the so-called longevity serum stopped coming. . . .' Says, 'Every twentieth adult in the Sol family is due for his shot this year.' Says. 'Of those, almost twenty per cent are one hundred and fifteen or older.' Says, 'The deaths in that group in the first year would be at least three times what the actuarial tables call for.'" Wesson raised a strained face. "I'm thirty-four, you know?" he said. "That Gower, he made me feel like a baby."

Aunt Jane made a sympathetic noise.

"Drip, drip," said Wesson hysterically. The needles of the tall golden indicators were infinitesimally higher. "Every twenty years we need more of the stuff, so somebody like me has to come out and take it for five lousy months. And one of *them* has to come out and sit here, and *drip. Why*, Aunt Jane? What for? Why should it matter to them whether we live a long time or not? Why do they keep on coming back? What do they take *away* from here?"

But to these questions, Aunt Jane had no reply.

All day and every day, the lights burned cold and steady in the circular grey corridor around the rim of Sector One. The hard grey flooring had been deeply scuffed in that circular path before Wesson ever walked there: the corridor existed for that only, like a treadmill in a squirrel cage; it said "Walk," and Wesson walked. A man would go crazy if he sat still, with that squirming, indescribable pressure on his head; and so Wesson paced off the miles, all day and every day, until he dropped like a dead man in the bed at night.

He talked, too, sometimes to himself, sometimes to the listening alpha network; sometimes it was difficult to tell which. "Moss on a rock," he muttered, pacing. "Told him, wouldn't give twenty mills for any damn shell. . . . Little pebbles down there, all colours." He shuffled on in silence for a while. Abruptly: "I don't see *why* they couldn't have given me a cat."

Aunt Jane said nothing. After a moment Wesson went on, "Nearly everybody at Home has a cat, for God's sake, or a goldfish or something. You're all right, Aunt Jane, but I can't *see* you. My God, I mean if they couldn't send a man a woman for company, what I mean, my God, I never liked *cats*." He swung around the doorway into the bedroom, and absent-mindedly slammed his fist into the bloody place on the wall.

"But a cat would have been *something*," he said.

Aunt Jane was still silent.

"Don't pretend your damn feelings are hurt. I know you, you're only a damn machine," said Wesson. "Listen, Aunt Jane, I remember a cereal package one time that had a horse and a cowboy on the side. There wasn't much room, so about all you saw was their faces. It used to strike me funny how much they looked alike. Two ears on the top with hair in the middle. Two eyes. Nose. Mouth with teeth in it. I was thinking, we're kind of distant cousins, aren't we, us and the horses. But compared to that thing up there—we're *brothers*. You know?"

"Yes," said Aunt Jane quietly.

"So I keep asking myself, why couldn't they have sent a horse, or a cat, *instead* of a man? But I guess the answer is because only a man could take what I'm taking. God, only a man. Right?"

"Right," said Aunt Jane, with deep sorrow.

Wesson stopped at the bedroom doorway again and shuddered, holding on to the frame. "Aunt Jane," he said in a low, clear voice, "you take pictures of *him* up there, don't you?"

"Yes, Paul."

"And you take pictures of me. And then what happens? After it's all over, who looks at the pictures?"

"I don't know," said Aunt Jane humbly.

"You don't know. But whoever looks at 'em, it doesn't do any good. Right? We got to find out why, why, why. . . . And we never do find out, do we?"

"No," said Aunt Jane.

"But don't they figure that if the man who's going through it could see him, he might be able to tell something? That other people couldn't? Doesn't that make sense?"

"That's out of my hands, Paul."

He sniggered. "That's funny. Oh, that's funny." He chortled in his throat, reeling around the circuit.

"Yes, that's funny," said Aunt Jane.

"Aunt Jane, tell me what happens to the watchmen."

". . . I can't tell you that, Paul."

He lurched into the living room, sat down before the console, beat on its smooth, cold metal with his fists. "What are you, some kind of monster? Isn't there any blood in your veins, damn it, or oil or *anything*?"

"Please, Paul—"

"Don't you see, all I want to know, can they talk? Can they tell anything after their tour is over?"

"No, Paul."

He stood upright, clutching the console for balance, "They can't? No, I figured. And you know why?"

"No."

"Up there," said Wesson obscurely. "Moss on the rock."

"Paul, what?"

"We get changed," said Wesson, stumbling out of the room again. "We get changed. Like a piece of iron next to a magnet. Can't help it. You—non-magnetic, I guess. Goes right through you, huh, Aunt Jane? You don't get changed. You stay here, wait for the next one."

". . . Yes," said Aunt Jane.

"You know," said Wesson, pacing, "I can tell how he's lying up there. Head *that* way, tail the other. Am I right?"

"Yes," said Aunt Jane.

Wesson stopped. "Yes," he said intently. "So you *can* tell me what you see up there, can't you, Aunt Jane?"

"No. Yes. It isn't allowed."

255

"Listen, Aunt Jane, *we'll die* unless we can find out what makes those aliens tick! Remember that." Wesson leaned against the corridor wall, gazing up. "He's turning now—around this way. Right?"

"Well, what else is he doing? Come on, Aunt Jane, tell me!"

A pause. "He is twitching his—"

"What?"

"I don't know the words."

"My God, my God," said Wesson, clutching his head, "of course there aren't any words." He ran into the living room, clutched the console and stared at the black screen. He pounded the metal with his fist. "You've got to show me, Aunt Jane, come on and show me, show me!"

"It isn't allowed," Aunt Jane protested.

"You've got to do it just the same, or we'll *die*, Aunt Jane—millions of us, billions, and it'll be your fault, get it, *your fault*, Aunt Jane!"

"*Please,*" said the voice. There was a pause. The screen flickered to life, for an instant only. Wesson had a glimpse of something massive and dark, but half transparent, like a magnified insect—a tangle of nameless limbs, whiplike filaments, claws, wings. . . .

He clutched the edge of the console.

"Was that all right?" Aunt Jane asked.

"Of course! What do you think, it'll kill me to look at it? Put it back, Aunt Jane, put it back!"

Reluctantly, the screen lighted again. Wesson stared, and went on staring. He mumbled something.

"What?" said Aunt Jane.

"*Life of my love, I loathe thee,*" said Wesson, staring. He roused himself after a moment and turned away. The image of the alien stayed with him as he went reeling into the corridor again; he was not surprised to find that it reminded him of all the loathesome, crawling, creeping things the Earth was full of. That explained why he was not supposed to see the alien, or even know what it looked like—because that fed his hate. And it was all right for him to be afraid of the alien, but he was not supposed to hate it. . . . Why not? Why not?

His fingers were shaking. He felt drained, steamed, dried up and withered. The one daily shower Aunt Jane allowed him was no longer enough. Twenty minutes after bathing the acid sweat dripped again from his armpits, the cold sweat was beaded on his forehead, the hot sweat was in his palms. Wesson felt as if there were a furnace inside him, out of control, all the dampers

256

drawn. He knew that under stress, something of the kind did happen to a man: the body's chemistry was altered—more adrenalin, more glycogen in the muscles; eyes brighter, digestion retarded. That was the trouble—he was burning himself up, unable to fight the thing that tormented him, or run from it.

After another circuit, Wesson's steps faltered. He hesitated, and went into the living room. He leaned over the console, staring. From the screen, the alien stared blindly up into space. Down in the dark side, the golden indicators had climbed: the vats were more than two-thirds filled.

To *fight*, or *run*. . . .

Slowly Wesson sank down in front of the console. He sat hunched, head bent, hands squeezed tight between his knees, trying to hold on to the thought that had come to him.

If the alien felt a pain as great as Wesson's—or greater—

Stress might alter the alien's body chemistry, too.

Life of my love, I loathe thee.

Wesson pushed the irrelevant thought aside. He stared at the screen, trying to envisage the alien, up there, wincing in pain and distress—sweating a golden sweat of horror. . . .

After a long time, he stood up and walked into the kitchen. He caught the table edge to keep his legs from carrying him on around the circuit. He sat down.

Humming fondly, the autochef slid out a tray of small glasses—water, orange juice, milk. Wesson put the water glass to his stiff lips; the water was cool and hurt his throat. Then the juice, but he could drink only a little of it; then he sipped the milk. Aunt Jane hummed approvingly.

Dehydrated—how long had it been since he had eaten, or drunk? He looked at his hands. They were thin bundles of sticks, ropy-veined, with hard yellow claws. He could see the bones of his forearms under the skin, and his heart's beating stirred the cloth at his chest. The pale hairs on his arms and thighs—were they blond or white?

The blurred reflections in the metal trim of the dining room gave him no answers—only pale faceless smears of grey. Wesson felt light-headed and very weak, as if he had just ended a bout of fever. He fumbled over his ribs and shoulderbones. He was thin.

He sat in front of the autochef for a few minutes more, but no food came out. Evidently Aunt Jane did not think he was ready for it, and perhaps she was right. *Worse for them than for us,* he thought dizzily. *That's why the Station's so far out; why radio silence, and only one man aboard. They couldn't stand it at all, otherwise. . . .* Suddenly he could think of nothing but sleep—the bottomless pit, layer after layer of smothering velvet, numbing and soft. . . . His leg muscles quivered and twitched when he tried to walk, but he managed to get to the bedroom and fall on the mattress. The resilient block seemed to dissolve under him. His bones were melting.

He woke with a clear head, very weak, thinking cold and clear: *When two alien cultures meet, the stronger must transform the weaker with love or hate.* "Wesson's Law," he said aloud. He looked automatically for pencil and paper, but there was none, and he realised he would have to tell Aunt Jane, and let her remember it.

"I don't understand," she said.

"Never mind, remember it anyway. You're good at that, aren't you?"

"Yes, Paul."

"All right. . . . I want some breakfast."

He thought about Aunt Jane, so nearly human, sitting up here in her metal prison, leading one man after another through the torments of hell . . . nursemaid, protector, torturer. They must have known that something would have to give. . . . But the alphas were comparatively new; nobody understood them very well. Perhaps they really thought that an absolute prohibition could never be broken.

. . . the stronger must transform the weaker. . . .

I'm *the stronger,* he thought. *And that's the way it's going to be.* He stopped at the console, and the screen was blank. He said angrily, "Aunt Jane!" And with a guilty start, the screen flickered into life.

Up there, the alien had rolled again in his pain. Now the great clustered eyes were staring directly into the camera; the coiled limbs threshed in pain: the eyes were staring, asking, pleading.
. . .

"*No,*" said Wesson, feeling his own pain like an iron cap, and he slammed his hand down on the manual control. The screen went dark. He looked up, sweating, and saw the floral picture over the console.

The thick stems were like antennae, the leaves thoraxes, the buds like blind insect eyes. The whole picture moved slightly, endlessly, in a slow waiting rhythm.

Wesson clutched the hard metal of the console and stared at the picture, with sweat cold on his brow, until it turned into a calm, meaningless arrangements of lines again. Then he went into the dining room, shaking, and sat down.

After a moment he said, "Aunt Jane, does it get worse?"

"No. From now on, it gets better."

"How long?" he asked vaguely.

"One month."

A month, getting "better" . . . that was the way it had always been, with the watchman swamped and drowned, his personality submerged. Wesson thought about the men who had gone before him—Class Seven citizenship, with unlimited leisure, and Class One housing, yes, sure—in a sanatorium.

His lips peeled back from his teeth, and his fists clenched hard. *Not me!* he thought.

He spread his hands on the cool metal to steady them. He said, "How much longer do they usually stay able to talk?"

"You are already talking longer than any of them. . . ."

Then there was a blank. Wesson was vaguely aware, in snatches, of the corridor walls moving past, and the console glimpsed, and of a thunderous cloud of ideas that swirled around his head in a beating of wings. The aliens: what did they want? And what happened to the watchmen in Stranger Station?

The haze receded a little and he was in the dining room again, staring vacantly at the table. Something was wrong.

He ate a few spoonsful of the gruel the autochef served him, then pushed it away; the stuff tasted faintly unpleasant. The machine hummed anxiously and thrust a poached egg at him, but Wesson got up from the table.

The Station was all but silent. The resting rhythm of the household machines throbbed in the walls, unheard. The blue-lit living room was spread out before him like an empty stage setting, and Wesson stared as if he had never seen it before.

He lurched to the console and stared down at the pictured alien on the screen: heavy, heavy, a-sprawl with pain in the darkness. The needles of the golden indicators were high, the enlarged vats almost full. *It's too much for him,* Wesson thought with grim satisfaction. The peace that followed the pain had not descended as it was supposed to; no, not this time!

He glanced up at the painting over the console: heavy crustacean limbs that swayed gracefully in the sea. . . .

He shook his head violently. *I won't let it; I won't give in!* He held the back of one hand close to his eyes. He saw the dozens of tiny cuneiform wrinkles stamped into the skin over the knuckles, the pale hairs sprouting, the pink shiny flesh of recent

259

scars. *I'm human*, he thought. But when he let his hand fall on to the console, the bony fingers seemed to crouch like crustaceans' legs, ready to scuttle.

Sweating, Wesson stared into the screen. Pictured there, the alien met his eyes, and it was as if they spoke to each other, mind to mind, an instantaneous communication that needed no words. There was a piercing sweetness to it, a melting, dissolving luxury of change into something that would no longer have any pain. . . . A pull, a calling.

Wesson straightened up slowly, carefully, as if he held some fragile thing in his mind that must not be handled roughly, or it would disintegrate. He said hoarsely, "Aunt Jane!"

She made some responsive noise.

He said, "Aunt Jane, I've got the answer! The whole thing! Listen, now wait—listen!" He paused a moment to collect his thoughts. *"When two alien cultures meet, the stronger must transform the weaker with love or hate.* Remember? You said you didn't understand what that meant. I'll *tell* you what it means. When these—monsters—met Pigeon a hundred years ago on Titan, *they knew* we'd have to meet again. They're spreading out, colonising, and so are we. We haven't got interstellar flight yet, but give us another hundred years, we'll *get* it. *We'll wind up out there, where they are.* And they can't stop us. Because they're not killers, Aunt Jane, it isn't in them. They're *nicer* than us. See, they're like the missionaries, and we're the South Sea Islanders. *They* don't kill their enemies, oh no—perish the thought!"

She was trying to say something, to interrupt him, but he rushed on. "Listen! The longevity serum—that was a lucky accident. But they played it for all it's worth. Slick and smooth—they come and give us the stuff free—they don't ask for a thing in return. Why not? Listen.

"They come here, and the shock of that first contact makes them sweat out that golden gook we need. Then, the last month or so, the pain always eases off. Why? Because the two minds, the human and alien, they stop fighting each other. Something gives way, it goes soft, and there's a mixing together. And that's where you get the human casualties of this operation—the bleary men that come out of here not even able to talk human language any more. Oh, I suppose they're happy—happier than I am!—because they've got something big and wonderful inside 'em. Something that you and I can't even understand. But if you took them and put them together again with the aliens who spent time here, *they could all live together—they're adapted.*

260

"That's what they're aiming for!" He struck the console with his fist. "Not now—but a hundred, two hundred years from now! When we start expanding out to the stars—when we go a-conquering—we'll have already been conquered! Not by weapons, Aunt Jane, not by hate—by love! Yes, love! *Dirty, stinking, low-down, sneaking love!*"

Aunt Jane said something, a long sentence, in a high, anxious voice.

"What?" said Wesson irritably. He couldn't understand a word.

Aunt Jane was silent. "What, what?" Wesson demanded, pounding the console. "Have you got it through your tin head or not? *What?*"

Aunt Jane said something else, tonelessly. Once more, Wesson could not make out a single word.

He stood frozen. Warm tears started suddenly out of his eyes. "Aunt Jane—" he said. He remembered, *You are already talking longer than any of them.* Too late? Too late? He tensed, then whirled and sprang to the closet where the paper books were kept. He opened the first one his hand struck.

The black letters were alien squiggles on the page, little humped shapes, without meaning.

The tears were coming faster, he couldn't stop them: tears of weariness, tears of frustration, tears of hate. *"Aunt Jane!"* he roared.

But it was no good. The curtain of silence had come down over his head. He was one of the vanguard—the conquered men, the ones who would get along with their strange brothers, out among the alien stars.

The console was not working any more; nothing worked when he wanted it. Wesson squatted in the shower stall, naked, with a soup bowl in his hands. Water droplets glistened on his hands and forearms; the pale short hairs were just springing up, drying.

The silvery skin of reflection in the bowl gave him back nothing but a silhouette, a shadow man's outline. He could not see his face.

He dropped the bowl and went across the living room, shuffling the pale drifts of paper underfoot. The black lines on the paper, when his eye happened to light on them, were worm shapes, crawling things, conveying nothing. He rolled slightly in his walk; his eyes were glazed. His head twitched, every now and then, sketching a useless motion to avoid pain.

261

Once the bureau chief, Gower, came to stand in his way. "You fool," he said, his face contorted in anger, "you were supposed to go on to the end, like the rest. Now look what you've done!"

"I found out, didn't I?" Wesson mumbled, and as he brushed the man aside like a cobweb, the pain suddenly grew more intense. Wesson clasped his head in his hands with a grunt, and rocked to and fro a moment, uselessly, before he straightened and went on. The pain was coming in waves now, so tall that at their peak his vision dimmed out, violet, then grey.

It couldn't go on much longer. Something had to burst.

He paused at the bloody place and slapped the metal with his palm, making the sound ring dully up into the frame of the Station: *rroom, rroom.*

Faintly an echo came back: boo-oom.

Wesson kept going, smiling a faint and meaningless smile. He was only marking time now, waiting. Something was about to happen.

The kitchen doorway sprouted a sudden sill and tripped him. He fell heavily, sliding on the floor, and lay without moving beneath the slick gleam of the autochef.

The pressure was too great: the autochef's clucking was swallowed up in the ringing pressure, and the tall grey walls buckled slowly in. . . .

The Station lurched.

Wesson felt it through his chest, palms, knees and elbows: the floor was plucked away for an instant and then swung back.

The pain in his skull relaxed its grip a little. Wesson tried to get to his feet.

There was an electric silence in the Station. On the second try, he got up and leaned his back against a wall. *Cluck,* said the autochef suddenly, hysterically, and the vent popped open, but nothing came out.

He listened, straining to hear. What?

The Station bounced beneath him, making his feet jump like a puppet's; the wall slapped his back hard, shuddered and was still; but far off through the metal cage came a long angry groan of metal, echoing, diminishing, dying. Then silence again.

The Station held its breath. All the myriad clickings and pulses in the walls were suspended; in the empty rooms the lights burned with a yellow glare, and the air hung stagnant and still. The console lights in the living room glowed like witchfires. Water in the dropped bowl, at the bottom of the shower stall, shone like quicksilver, waiting.

The third shock came. Wesson found himself on his hands and knees, the jolt still tingling in the bones of his body, staring at the floor. The sound that filled the room ebbed away slowly and ran down into the silences: a resonant metallic sound, shuddering away now along the girders and hull plates, rattling tinnily into bolts and fittings, diminishing, noiseless, gone. The silence pressed down again.

The floor leaped painfully under his body: one great resonant blow that shook him from head to foot.

A muted echo of that blow came a few seconds later, as if the shock had travelled across the Station and back.

The bed, Wesson thought, and scrambled on hands and knees through the doorway, along a floor curiously tilted, until he reached the rubbery block.

The room burst visibly upwards around him, squeezing the block flat. It dropped back as violently, leaving Wesson bouncing helplessly on the mattress, his limbs flying. It came to rest, in a long reluctant groan of metal.

Wesson rolled up on one elbow, thinking incoherently, *Air, the air lock.* Another blow slammed him down into the mattress, pinched his lungs shut, while the room danced grotesquely over his head. Gasping for breath in the ringing silence, Wesson felt a slow icy chill rolling towards him across the room . . . and there was a pungent smell in the air. *Ammonia!* he thought; and the odourless, smothering methane with it.

His cell was breached. The burst membrane was fatal: the alien's atmosphere would kill him.

Wesson surged to his feet. The next shock caught him off balance, dashed him to the floor. He arose again, dazed and limping; he was still thinking confusedly, *The air lock, get out.*

When he was half way to the door, all the ceiling lights went out at once. The darkness was like a blanket around his head. It was bitter cold now in the room and the pungent smell was sharper. Coughing, Wesson hurried forward. The floor lurched under his feet.

Only the golden indicators burned now: full to the top, the deep vats brimming, golden-lipped, gravid, a month before the time. Wesson shuddered.

Water spurted in the bathroom, hissing steadily on the tiles, rattling in the plastic bowl at the bottom of the shower stall. The lights winked on and off again. In the dining room, he heard the autochef clucking and sighing. The freezing wind blew harder: he was numb with cold to the hips. It seemed to Wesson abruptly that he was not at the top of the sky at all, but down,

263

down at the bottom of the sea . . . trapped in this steel bubble, while the dark poured in.

The pain in his head was gone, as if it had never been there, and he understood what that meant: Up there, the great body was hanging like butcher's carrion in the darkness. Its death struggles were over, the damage done.

Wesson gathered a desperate breath, shouted, "Help me! The alien's dead! He kicked the Station apart—the methane's coming in! Get help, do you hear me? *Do you hear me?*"

Silence. In the smothering blackness, he remembered: *She can't understand me any more. Even if she's alive.*

He turned, making an animal noise in his throat. He groped his way on around the room, past the second doorway. Behind the walls, something was dripping with a slow cold tinkle and splash, a forlorn night sound. Small, hard, floating things rapped against his legs. Then he touched a smooth curve of metal: the air lock.

Eagerly he pushed his feeble weight against the door. It didn't move. Cold air was rushing out around the door frame, a thin knife-cold stream, but the door itself was jammed tight.

The suit! He should have thought of that before. If he just had some pure air to breathe, and a little warmth in his fingers. . . . But the door of the suit locker would not move, either. The ceiling must have buckled.

And that was the end, he thought, bewildered. There were no more ways out. But there *had* to be— He pounded on the door until his arms would not lift any more; it did not move. Leaning against the chill metal, he saw a single light blink overhead.

The room was a wild place of black shadows and swimming shapes—the book leaves, fluttering and darting in the air stream. Schools of them beat wildly at the walls, curling over, baffled, trying again; others were swooping around the outer corridor, around and around: he could see them whirling past the doorways, dreamlike, a white drift of silent paper in the darkness.

The acrid smell was harsher in his nostrils. Wesson choked, groping his way to the console again. He pounded it with his open hand, crying weakly: he wanted to see Earth.

But when the little square of brightness leaped up, it was the dead body of the alien that Wesson saw.

It hung motionless in the cavity of the Station, limbs dangling stiff and still, eyes dull. The last turn of the screw had been too much for it: but Wesson had survived. . . .

For a few minutes.

264

The dead alien face mocked him; a whisper of memory floated into his mind: *We might have been brothers*. . . . All at once Wesson passionately wanted to believe it—wanted to give in, turn back. That passed. Wearily he let himself sag into the bitter *now*, thinking with thin defiance, *It's done—hate wins. You'll have to stop this big giveaway—can't risk this happening again. And we'll hate you for that—and when we get out to the stars—*

The world was swimming numbly away out of reach. He felt the last fit of coughing take his body, as if it were happening to someone else besides him.

The last fluttering leaves of paper came to rest. There was a long silence in the drowned room.

Then:

"Paul" said the voice of the mechanical woman brokenly; "Paul," it said again, with the hopelessness of lost, unknown, impossible love.

HOT PLANET

by *Hal Clement*

I

The wind which had nearly turned the *Albireo*'s landing into a disaster instead of a mathematical exercise was still playing tunes about the fins and landing legs as Schlossberg made his way down to Deck Five.

The noise didn't bother him particularly, though the endless seismic tremors made him dislike the ladders. But just now he was able to ignore both. He was curious—though not hopeful. "Is there anything at all obvious on the last set of tapes, Joe?"

Mardikian, the geophysicist, shrugged. "Just what you'd expect . . . on a planet which has at least one quake in each fifty-mile-square area every five minutes. You know yourself we had a nice seismic programme set up, but when we touched down we found we couldn't carry it out. We've done our best with the natural tremors—incidentally stealing most of the record tapes the other projects would have used. We have a lot of nice information for the computers back home; but it will take all of them to make any sense out of it."

Schlossberg nodded; the words had not been necessary. His astronomical programme had been one of those sabotaged by the transfer of tapes to the seismic survey.

"I just hoped," he said. "We each have an idea why Mercury developed an atmosphere during the last few decades, but I guess the high school kids on Earth will know whether it's right before we do. I'm resigned to living in a chess-type universe —few and simple rules, but infinite combinations of them. But it would be nice to know an answer sometime."

"So it would. As a matter of fact, I need to know a couple right now. From you. How close to finished are the other programmes—or what's left of them?"

"I'm all set," replied Schlossberg. "I have a couple of instruments still monitoring the sun just in case, but everything in the revised programme is on tape."

"Good. Tom, any use asking you?"

The biologist grimaced. "I've been shown two hundred and sixteen different samples of rock and dust. I have examined in detail twelve crystal growths which looked vaguely like vegetation. Nothing was alive or contained living things by any standards I could conscientiously set."

Mardikian's gesture might have meant sympathy.

"Camille?"

"I may as well stop now as any time. I'll never be through. Tape didn't make much difference to me, but I wish I knew what weight of specimens I could take home."

"Eileen?" Mardikian's glance at the stratigrapher took the place of the actual question.

"Cam speaks for me, except that I could have used any more tape you could have spared. What I have is gone."

"All right, that leaves me, the tape-thief. The last spools are in the seismographs now, and will start running out in seventeen hours. The tractors will start out on their last rounds in sixteen, and should be back in roughly a week. Will, does that give you enough to figure the weights we rockhounds can have on the return trip?"

The *Albireo*'s captain nodded. "Close enough. There really hasn't been much question since it became evident we'd find nothing for the mass tanks here. I'll have a really precise check in an hour, but I can tell right now that you have about one and a half metric tons to split up among the three of you.

"Ideal departure time is three hundred and ten hours away, as you all know. We can stay here until then, or go into a parking-and-survey orbit at almost any time before then. You have all the survey you need, I should think, from the other time. But suit yourselves."

"I'd just as soon be space-sick as seasick," remarked Camille Burkett. "I still hate to think that the entire planet is as shivery as the spot we picked."

Willard Rowson smiled. "You researchers told me where to land after ten days in orbit mapping this rockball. I set you just where you asked. If you'd found even five tons of juice we could use in the reaction tanks I could still take you to another one—if you could agree which one. I hate to say 'Don't blame me,' but I can't think of anything else that fits."

"So we sit until the last of the tractors is back with the precious seismo tapes, playing battleship while our back teeth are being shaken out by earthquakes—excuse the word. What a thrill! Glorious adventure!" Zaino, the communications specialist who had been out of a job almost constantly since the landing, spoke sourly. The captain was the only one who saw fit to answer.

"If you want adventure, you made a mistake exploring space. The only space adventures I've heard of are second-hand stories built on guesswork; the people who really had them weren't around to tell about it. Unless Dr. Marini discovers a set of Mercurian monsters at the last minute and they invade the ship or cut off one of the tractors, I'm afraid you'll have to do without adventures." Zaino grimaced.

"That sounds funny coming from a spaceman, Captain. I didn't really mean adventure, though; all I want is something to do besides betting whether the next quake will come in one minute or five. I haven't even had to fix a suit-radio since we touched down. How about my going out with one of the tractors on this last trip, at least?"

"It's all right with me," replied Rowson, "but Dr. Mardikian runs the professional part of this operation. I require that Spurr, Trackman, Hargedon and Aiello go as drivers, since without them even a minor mechanical problem would be more than an adventure. As I recall it, Dr. Harmon, Dr. Schlossberg, Dr. Marini and Dr. Mardikian are scheduled to go; but if any one of them is willing to let you take his or her place, I certainly don't mind."

The radioman looked around hopefully. The geologists and the biologist shook their heads negatively, firmly and unanimously; but the astronomer pondered for a moment. Zaino watched tensely.

"It may be all right," Schlossberg said at last. "What I want to get is a set of wind, gas pressure, gas temperature and gas composition measures around the route. I didn't expect to be more meteorologist than astronomer when we left Earth, and didn't have exactly the right equipment. Hargedon and Aiello helped me improvise some, and this is the first chance to use it on the Darkside. If you can learn what has to be done with it before starting time, though, you are welcome to my place."

The communicator got to his feet fast enough to leave the deck in Mercury's feeble gravity.

"Lead me to it, Doc. I guess I can learn to read a home-made weathervane!"

"Is that merely bragging, or a challenge?" drawled a voice which had not previously joined the discussion. Zaino flushed a bit.

"Sorry, Luigi," he said hastily. "I didn't mean it just that way. But I still think I can run the stuff."

"Likely enough," Aiello replied. "Remember though, it wasn't made just for talking into." Schlossberg, now on his feet, cut in quickly.

"Come on, Arnie. We'll have to suit up to see the equipment; it's outside."

He shepherded the radioman to the hatch at one side of the deck and shooed him down towards the engine and air lock levels. Both were silent for some moments; but, safely out of earshot of Deck Five, the younger man looked up and spoke.

"You needn't push, Doc. I wasn't going to make anything of it. Luigi was right, and I asked for it." The astronomer slowed a bit in his descent.

"I wasn't really worried," he replied, "but we have several months yet before we can get away from each other, and I don't like talk that could set up grudges. Matter of fact, I'm even a little uneasy about having the girls along, though I'm no misogynist."

"Girls? They're not—"

"There goes your foot again. Even Harmon is about ten years older than you, I suppose. But they're girls to me. What's more important, they no doubt think of themselves as girls."

268

"Even Dr. Burkett? That is—I mean—"

"Even Dr. Burkett. Here, get into your suit. And maybe you'd better take out the mike. It'll be enough if you can listen for the next hour or two." Zaino made no answer, suspecting with some justice that anything he said would be wrong.

Each made final checks on the other's suit; then they descended one more level to the air lock. This occupied part of the same deck as the fusion plants, below the wings and reaction mass tanks but above the main engine. Its outer door was just barely big enough to admit a spacesuited person. Even with the low air pressure carried by spaceships, a large door area meant large total force on jamb, hinges and locks. It opened on to a small balcony from which a ladder led to the ground. The two men paused on the balcony to look over the landscape.

This hadn't changed noticeably since the last time either had been out, though there might have been some small difference in the volcanic cones a couple of miles away to the north-east. The furrows down the sides of these, which looked as though they had been cut by water but were actually bone-dry ash slides, were always undergoing alteration as gas from below kept blowing fresh scoria fragments out of the craters.

The spines—steep, jagged fragments of rock which thrust upward from the plain beyond and to both sides of the cones—seemed dead as ever.

The level surface between the *Albireo* and the cones was more interesting. Mardikian and Schlossberg believed it to be a lava sheet dating from early in Mercury's history, when more volatile substances still existed in the surface rocks to cut down their viscosity when molten. They supposed that much—perhaps most—of the surface around the "twilight" belt had been flooded by this very liquid lava, which had cooled to a smoother surface than most Earthly lava flows.

How long it had stayed cool they didn't guess. But both men felt sure that Mercury must have periodic upheavals as heat accumulated inside it—heat coming not from radioactivity but from tidal energy. Mercury's orbit is highly eccentric. At perihelion, tidal force tries to pull it apart along the planet-to-sun line, while at aphelion the tidal force is less and the little world's own gravity tries to bring it back to a spherical shape. The real change in form is not great, but a large force working through even a small amount of distance can mean a good deal of energy.

If the energy can't leak out—and Mercury's rocks conduct heat no better than those of Earth—the temperature must rise.

269

Sooner or later, the men argued, deeply buried rock must fuse to magma. Its liquefaction would let the bulk of the planet give farther under tidal stress, so heat would be generated even faster. Eventually a girdle of magma would have to form far below the crust all around the twilight strip, where the tidal strain would be greatest. Sooner or later this would melt its way to the surface, giving the zone a period of intense volcanic activity and, incidentally, giving the planet a temporary atmosphere.

The idea was reasonable. It had, the astronomer admitted, been suggested long before to account for supposed vulcanism on the moon. It justified the careful examination that Schlossberg and Zaino gave the plain before they descended the ladder; for it made reasonable the occasional changes which were observed to occur in the pattern of cracks weaving over its surface.

No one was certain just how permanent the local surface was—though no one could really justify feeling safer on board the *Albireo* than outside on the lava. If anything really drastic happened, the ship would be no protection.

The sun, hanging just above the horizon slightly to the watcher's right, cast long shadows which made the cracks stand out clearly; as far as either man could see, nothing had changed recently. They descended the ladder carefully—even the best designed spacesuits are somewhat vulnerable—and made their way to the spot where the tractors were parked.

A sheet-metal fence a dozen feet high and four times as long provided shade, which was more than a luxury this close to the sun. The tractors were parked in this shadow, and beside and between them were piles of equipment and specimens. The apparatus Schlossberg had devised was beside the tractor at the north end of the line, just inside the shaded area.

It was still just inside the shade when they finished, four hours later. Hargedon had joined them during the final hour and helped pack the equipment in the tractor he was to drive. Zaino had had no trouble in learning to make the observations Schlossberg wanted, and the youngster was almost unbearably cocky. Schlossberg hoped, as they returned to the *Albireo*, that no one would murder the communications expert in the next twelve hours. There would be nothing to worry about after the trip started; Hargedon was quite able to keep anyone in his place without being nasty about it. If Zaino had been going with

270

Aiello or Harmon—but he wasn't, and it was pointless to dream up trouble.

And no trouble developed all by itself.

II

Zaino was not only still alive but still reasonably popular when the first of the tractors set out, carrying Eileen Harmon and Eric Trackman, the *Albireo*'s nuclear engineer.

It started more than an hour before the others, since the stratigrapher's drilling programme, "done" or not, took extra time. The tractor hummed off to the south, since both Darkside routes required a long detour to pass the chasm to the west. Routes had been worked out from the stereophotos taken during the orbital survey. Even Darkside had been covered fairly well with Uniquantum film under Venus light.

The Harmon-Trackman vehicle was well out of sight when Mardikian and Aiello started out on one of the Brightside routes, and a few minutes later Marini set out on the other with the spacesuit technician, Mary Spurr, driving.

Both vehicles disappeared quickly into a valley to the northeast, between the ash cones and a thousand-foot spine which rose just south of them. All the tractors were in good radio contact; Zaino made sure of that before he abandoned the radio watch to Rowson, suited up and joined Hargedon at the remaining one. They climbed in, and Hargedon set it in motion.

At about the same time, the first tractor came into view again, now travelling north on the farther side of the chasm. Hargedon took this as evidence that the route thus far was unchanged, and kicked in highest speed.

The cabin was pretty cramped, even though some of the equipment had been attached outside. The men could not expect much comfort for the next week.

Hargedon was used to the trips, however. He disapproved on principle of people who complained about minor inconveniences such as having to sleep in spacesuits; fortunately, Zaino's interest and excitement overrode any thought he might have had about discomfort.

This lasted through the time they spent doubling the vast crack in Mercury's crust, driving on a little to the north of the ship on the other side and then turning west towards the dark

271

hemisphere. The route was identical to that of Harmon's machine for some time, though no trace of its passage showed on the hard surface. Then Hargedon angled off towards the southwest. He had driven this run often enough to know it well even without the markers which had been set out with the seismographs. The photographic maps were also aboard. With them, even Zaino had no trouble keeping track of their progress while they remained in sunlight.

However, the sun sank as they travelled west. In two hours its lower rim would have been on the horizon, had they been able to see the horizon; as it was, more of the "sea level" lava plain was in the shadow than not, even near the ship, and their route now lay in semi-darkness.

The light came from peaks projecting into the sunlight, from scattered sky-light which was growing rapidly fainter and from the brighter celestial objects such as Earth. Even with the tractor's lights it was getting harder to spot crevasses and seismometer markers. Zaino quickly found the fun wearing off . . . though his pride made him cover this fact as best he could.

If Hargedon saw this, he said nothing. He set Zaino to picking up every other instrument, as any partner would have, making no allowance for the work the youngster was doing for Schlossberg. This might, of course, have had the purpose of keeping the radioman too busy to think about discomfort. Or it might merely have been Hargedon's idea of normal procedure.

Whatever the cause, Zaino got little chance to use the radio once they had driven into the darkness. He managed only one or two brief talks with those left at the ship.

The talks might have helped his morale, since they certainly must have given the impression that nothing was going on in the ship while at least he had something to do in the tractor. However, this state of affairs did not last. Before the vehicle was four hours out of sight of the *Albireo,* a broadcast by Camille Burkett reached them.

The mineralogist's voice contained at least as much professional enthusiasm as alarm, but everyone listening must have thought promptly of the dubious stability of Mercury's crust. The call was intended for her fellow geologists Mardikian and Harmon. But it interested Zaino at least as much.

"Joe! Eileen! There's a column of what looks like black smoke rising over Northeast Spur. It can't be a real fire, of course; I can't see its point of origin, but if it's the convection current it seems to be the source must be pretty hot. It's the

272

closest thing to a genuine volcano I've seen since we arrived; it's certainly not another of those ash mounds. I should think you'd still be close enough to make it out, Joe. Can you see anything?"

The reply from Mardikian's tractor was inaudible to Zaino and Hargedon, but Burkett's answer made its general tenor plain.

"I hadn't thought of that. Yes, I'd say it was pretty close to the Brightside route. It wouldn't be practical for you to stop your run now to come back to see. You couldn't do much about it anyway. I could go out to have a look and then report to you. If the way back is blocked there'll be plenty of time to work out another." Hargedon and Zaino passed questioning glances at each other during the shorter pause that followed.

"I know there aren't," the voice then went on, responding to the words they could not hear, "but it's only two or three miles, I'd say. Two to the spur and not much farther to where I could see the other side. Enough of the way is in shade so I could make it in a suit easily enough. I can't see calling back either of the Darkside tractors. Their work is just as important as the rest—anyway, Eileen is probably out of range. She hasn't answered yet." Another pause.

"That's true. Still, it would mean sacrificing that set of seismic records—no, wait. We could go out later for those. And Mel could take his own weather measures on the later trip. There's plenty of time!" Pause, longer this time.

"You're right, of course. I just wanted to get an early look at this volcano, if it is one. We'll let the others finish their runs, and when you get back you can check the thing from the other side yourself. If it is blocking your way there's time to find an alternate route. We could be doing that from the maps in the meantime, just in case."

Zaino looked again at his companion.

"Isn't that just my luck!" he exclaimed. "I jump at the first chance to get away from being bored to death. The minute I'm safely away, the only interesting thing of the whole operation happens—back at the ship!"

"Who asked to come on this trip?"

"Oh, I'm not blaming anyone but myself. If I'd stayed back there the volcano would have popped out here somewhere, or else waited until we were gone."

"If it is a volcano. Dr. Burkett didn't seem quite sure."

"No, and I'll bet a nickel she's suiting up right now to go out

273

and see. I hope she comes back with something while we're still near enough to hear about it."

Hargedon shrugged. "I suppose it was also just your luck that sent you on a Darkside trip? You know the radio stuff. You knew we couldn't reach as far this way with the radios. Didn't you think of that in advance?"

"I didn't think of it, any more than you would have. It was bad luck, but I'm not grousing about it. Let's get on with this job." Hargedon nodded with approval, and possibly with some surprise, and the tractor hummed on its way.

The darkness deepened around the patches of lava shown by the driving lights; the sky darkened towards a midnight hue, with stars showing ever brighter through it; and radio reception from the *Albireo* began to get spotty. Gas density at the ion layer was high enough so that recombination of molecules with their radiation-freed electrons was rapid. Only occasional streamers of ionised gas reached far over Darkside. As these thinned out, so did radio reception. Camille Burkett's next broadcast came through very poorly.

There was enough in it, however, to seize the attention of the two men in the tractor.

She was saying: ". . . real all right, and dangerous. It's the . . . thing I ever saw . . . kinds of lava from what looks like . . . same vent. There's high viscosity stuff building a spatter cone to end all spatter cones, and some very thin fluid from somewhere at the bottom. The flow has already blocked the valley used by the Brightside routes and is coming along it. A new return route will have to be found for the tractors that . . . was spreading fast when I saw it. I can't tell how much will come. But unless it stops there's nothing at all to keep the flow away from the ship. It isn't coming fast, but it's coming. I'd advise all tractors to turn back. Captain Rowson reminds me that only one take-off is possible. If we leave this site, we're committed to leaving Mercury. Arnie and Ren, do you hear me?"

Zaino responded at once. "We got most of it, Doctor. Do you really think the ship is in danger?"

"I don't know. I can only say that *if* this flow continues the ship will have to leave, because this area will sooner or later be covered. I can't guess how likely . . . check further to get some sort of estimate. It's different from any Earthly lava source —maybe you heard—should try to get Eileen and Eric back, too. I can't raise them. I suppose they're well out from under the ion layer by now. Maybe you're close enough to them

274

to catch them with diffracted waves. Try, anyway. Whether you can raise them or not you'd better start back yourself."

Hargedon cut in at this point. "What does Dr. Mardikian say about that? We still have most of the seismometers on this route to visit."

"I think Captain Rowson has the deciding word here, but if it helps your decision Dr. Mardikian has already started back. He hasn't finished his route, either. So hop back here, Ren. And Arnie, put that technical skill you haven't had to use yet to work raising Eileen and Erie."

"What I can do, I will," replied Zaino, "but you'd better tape a recall message and keep it going out on. Let's see—band F."

"All right. I'll be ready to check the volcano as soon as you get back. How long?"

"Seven hours—maybe six and a half," replied Hargedon. "We have to be careful."

"Very well. Stay outside when you arrive; I'll want to go right out in the tractor to get a closer look." She cut off.

"And *that* came through clearly enough!" remarked Hargedon as he swung the tractor around. "I've been awake for fourteen hours, driving off and on for ten or twelve; I'm about to drive for another six; and then I'm to stand by for more."

"Would you like me to do some of the driving?" asked Zaino.

"I guess you'll have to, whether I like it or not," was the rather lukewarm reply. "I'll keep on for a while, though—until we're back in better light. You get at your radio job."

III

Zaino tried. Hour after hour he juggled from one band to another. Once he had Hargedon stop while he went out to attach a makeshift antenna which, he hoped, would change his output from broadcast to some sort of beam; after this he kept probing the sky with the "beam", first listening to the *Albireo*'s broadcast in an effort to find projecting wisps of ionosphere and then, whenever he thought he had one, switching on his transmitter and driving his own message at it.

Not once did he complain about lack of equipment or remark how much better he could do once he was back at the ship.

Hargedon's silence began to carry an undercurrent of approval not usual in people who spent much time with Zaino.

275

The technician made no further reference to the suggestion of switching drivers. They came in sight of the *Albireo* and doubled the chasm with Hargedon still at the wheel, Zaino still at his radio and both of them still uncertain whether any of the calls had got through.

Both had to admit, even before they could see the ship, that Burkett had had a right to be impressed.

The smoke column showed starkly against the sky, blowing back over the tractor and blocking the sunlight which would otherwise have glared into the driver's eyes. Fine particles fell from it in a steady shower; looking back, the men could see tracks left by their vehicle in the deposit which had already fallen.

As they approached the ship the dark pillar grew denser and narrower, while the particles raining from it became coarser. In some places the ash was drifting into fairly deep piles, giving Hargedon some anxiety about possible concealed cracks. The last part of the trip, along the edge of the great chasm and around its end, was really dangerous; cracks running from its sides were definitely spreading. The two men reached the *Albireo* later than Hargedon had promised, and found Burkett waiting impatiently with a pile of apparatus beside her.

She didn't wait for them to get out before starting to organise. "There isn't much here. We'll take off just enough of what you're carrying to make room for this. No—wait. I'll have to check some of your equipment; I'm going to need one of Milt Schlossberg's gadgets, I think, so leave that on. We'll take—"

"Excuse me, Doctor," cut in Hargedon. "Our suits need servicing, or at least mine will if you want me to drive you. Perhaps Arnie can help you load for a while, if you don't think it's too important for him to get at the radio—"

"Of course. Excuse me. I should have had someone out here to help me with this. You two go on in. Ren, please get back as soon as you can. I can do the work here; none of this stuff is very heavy."

Zaino hesitated as he swung out of the cab. True, there wasn't too much to be moved, and it wasn't very heavy in Mercury's gravity, and he really should be at the radio; but the thirty-nine-year-old mineralogist was a middle-aged lady by his standards, and shouldn't be allowed to carry heavy packages . . .

"Get along, Arnie!" the middle-aged lady interrupted this train of thought. "Eric and Eileen are getting farther away and harder to reach every second you dawdle!"

He got, though he couldn't help looking north-east as he went rather than where he was going.

The towering menace in that direction would have claimed anyone's attention. The pillar of sable ash was rising straighter, as though the wind were having less effect on it. An equally black cone had risen into sight beyond Northeast Spur—a cone that must have grown to some two thousand feet in roughly ten hours. It had far steeper sides than the cinder mounds near it; it couldn't be made of the same loose ash. Perhaps it consisted of half-melted particles which were fusing together as they fell—that might be what Burkett had meant by "spatter-cone". Still, if that were the case, the material fountaining from the cone's top should be lighting the plain with its incandescence rather than casting an inky shadow for its entire height.

Well, that was a problem for the geologists; Zaino climbed aboard and settled to his task.

The trouble was that he could do very little more here than he could in the tractor. He could have improvised longer-wave transmitting coils whose radiations would have diffracted a little more effectively beyond the horizon, but the receiver on the missing vehicle would not have detected them. He had more power at his disposal, but could only beam it into empty space with his better antennae. He had better equipment for locating any projecting wisps of charged gas which might reflect his waves, but he was already located under a solid roof of the stuff—the *Albireo* was technically on Brightside. Bouncing his beam from this layer still didn't give him the range he needed, as he had found both by calculation and trial.

What he really needed was a relay satellite. The target was simply too far around Mercury's sharp curve by now for anything less.

Zaino's final gesture was to set his transmission beam on the lowest frequency the tractor would pick up, aim it as close to the vehicle's direction as he could calculate from map and itinerary and set the recorded return message going. He told Rowson as much.

"Can't think of anything else?" the captain asked. "Well, neither can I, but of course it's not my field. I'd give a year's pay if I could. How long before they should be back in range?"

"About four days. A hundred hours, give or take a few. They'll be heading back anyway by that time."

"Of course. Well, keep trying."

"I am—or rather, the equipment is. I don't see what else I can

277

do unless a really bright idea should suddenly sprout. Is there anywhere else I could be useful? I'm as likely to have ideas working as just sitting."

"We can keep you busy, all right. But how about taking a transmitter up one of those mountains? That would get your wave farther."

"Not as far as it's going already. I'm bouncing it off the ion layer, which is higher than any mountain we've seen on Mercury even if it's nowhere near as high as Earth's."

"Hmph. All right."

"I could help Ren and Dr. Burkett. I could hang on outside the tractor—"

"They've already gone. You'd better call them, though, and keep a log of what they do."

"All right." Zaino turned back to his board and with no trouble raised the tractor carrying Hargedon and the mineralogist. The latter had been trying to call the *Albireo* and had some acid comments about radio operators who slept on the job.

"There's only one of me, and I've been trying to get the Darkside team," he pointed out. "Have you found anything new about this lava flood?"

"Flow, not flood," corrected the professional automatically. "We're not in sight of it yet. We've just rounded the corner that takes us out of your sight. It's over a mile yet, and a couple of more corners, before we get to the spot where I left it. Of course, it will be closer than that by now. It was spreading at perhaps a hundred yards an hour then. That's one figure we must refine . . . Of course, I'll try to get samples, too. I wish there were some way to get samples of the central cone. The whole thing is the queerest volcano I've ever heard of. Have you got Eileen started back?"

"Not as far as I can tell. As with your cone samples, there are practical difficulties," replied Zaino. "I haven't quit yet, though."

"I should think not. If some of us were paid by the idea we'd be pretty poor, but the perspiration part of genius is open to all of us."

"You mean I should charge a bonus for getting this call through?" retorted the operator.

Whatever Burkett's reply to this might have been was never learned; her attention was diverted at that point.

"We've just come in sight of the flow. It's about five hundred

278

yards ahead. We'll get as close as seems safe, and I'll try to make sure whether it's really lava or just mud."

"Mud? Is that possible? I thought there wasn't—couldn't be—any water on this planet!"

"It is, and there probably isn't. The liquid phase of mud doesn't have to be water, even though it usually is on Earth. Here, for example, it might conceivably be sulphur."

"But if it's just mud, it wouldn't hurt the ship, would it?"

"Probably not."

"Then why all this fuss about getting the tractors back in a hurry?"

The voice which answered reminded him of another lady in his past, who had kept him after school for drawing pictures in maths class.

"Because in my judgment the flow is far more likely to be lava than mud, and if I must be wrong I'd rather my error were one that left us alive. I have no time at the moment to explain the basis of my judgment. I will be reporting our activities quite steadily from now on, and would prefer that you not interrupt unless a serious emergency demands it, or you get a call from Eileen.

"We are about three hundred yards away now. The front is moving about as fast as before, which suggests that the flow is coming only along this valley. It's only three or four feet high, so viscosity is very low or density very high. Probably the former, considering where we are. It's as black as the smoke column."

"Not glowing?" cut in Zaino thoughtlessly.

"*Black*, I said. Temperature will be easier to measure when we get closer. The front is nearly straight across the valley, with just a few lobes projecting ten or twelve yards and one notch where a small spine is being surrounded. By the way, I trust you're taping all this?" Again Zaino was reminded of the afternoon after school.

"Yes, Ma'am," he replied. "On my one and only monitor tape."

"Very well. We're stopping near the middle of the valley one hundred yards from the front. I am getting out, and will walk as close as I can with a sampler and a radiometer. I assume that the radio equipment will continue to relay my suit broadcast back to you." Zaino cringed a little, certain as he was that the tractor's electronic apparatus was in perfect order.

It struck him that Dr. Burkett was being more snappish than

279

usual. It never crossed his mind that the woman might be afraid.

"Ren, don't get any closer with the tractor unless I call. I'll get a set of temperature readings as soon as I'm close enough. Then I'll try to get a sample. Then I'll come back with that to the tractor, leave it and the radiometer and get the markers to set out."

"Couldn't I be putting out the markers while you get the sample, Doctor?"

"You could, but I'd rather you stayed at the wheel." Hargedon made no answer, and Burkett resumed her description for the record.

"I'm walking towards the front, a good deal faster than it's flowing towards me. I am now about twenty yards away, and am going to take a set of radiation-temperature measures." A brief pause. "Readings coming. Nine sixty. Nine eighty. Nine ninety—that's from the bottom edge near the spine that's being surrounded. Nine eighty-five—" The voice droned on until about two dozen readings had been taped. Then, "I'm going closer now. The sampler is just a ladle on a twelve-foot handle we improvised, so I'll have to get that close. The stuff is moving slowly; there should be no trouble. I'm in reach now. The lava is very liquid; there's no trouble getting the sampler in—or out again—it's not very dense, either. I'm heading back towards the tractor now. No, Ren, don't come to meet me."

There was a minute of silence, while Zaino pictured the spacesuited figure, with its awkwardly long burden, walking away from the creeping menace to the relative safety of the tractor. "It's frozen solid already; we needn't worry about spilling. The temperature is about—five eighty. Give me the markers, please."

Another pause, shorter this time. Zaino wondered how much of that could be laid to a faster walk without the ladle and how much to the lessening distance between flow and tractor. "I'm tossing the first marker close to the edge—it's landed less than a foot from the lava. They're all on a light cord at ten-foot intervals; I'm paying out the cord as I go back to the tractor. Now we'll stand by and time the arrival at each marker as well as we can."

"How close are you to the main cone?" asked Zaino.

"Not close enough to see its base, I'm afraid. Or to get a sample of it, which is worse. We—goodness, what was that?"

Zaino had just time to ask, "What was what?" when he found out.

280

For a moment, he thought that the *Albireo* had been flung
bodily into the air. Then he decided that the great metal pillar
had merely fallen over. Finally he realised that the ship was still
erect, but the ground under it had just tried to leave.

Everyone in the group had become so used to the almost
perpetual ground tremors that they had ceased to notice them;
but this one demanded attention. Rowson, using language
which suggested that his career might not have been completely
free of adventure after all, flashed through the communication
level on his way down to the power section. Schlossberg and
Babineau followed, the medic pausing to ask Zaino if he were
all right. The radioman merely nodded affirmatively; his attention was already back at his job. Burkett was speaking
a good deal faster than before.

"Never mind if the sample isn't lashed tight yet—if it falls off
there'll be plenty more. There isn't time! Arnie, get in touch
with Dr. Mardikian and Dr. Marini. Tell them that this volcano
is explosive, that all estimates of what the flow may do are off
until we can make more measures, and in any case the whole
situation is unpredictable. Everyone should get back as soon as
possible. Remember, we decided that those big craters Eileen
checked were not meteor pits. I don't know whether this thing
will let go in the next hour, the next year, or at all. Maybe
what's happening now will act as a safety valve—but let's get
out. Ren, that flow is speeding up and getting higher, and the
ash rain is getting a lot worse. Can you see to drive?"

She fell silent. Zaino, in spite of her orders, left his set long
enough to leap to the nearest port for a look at the volcano.

He never regretted it.

Across the riven plain, whose cracks were now nearly hidden
under the new ash, the black cone towered above the nearer
elevations. It was visibly taller than it had been only a few hours
before. The fountain from its top was thicker, now jetting
straight up as though wind no longer meant a thing to the
fiercely driven column of gas and dust. The darkness was not so
complete; patches of red and yellow incandescence showed
briefly in the pillar, and glowing sparks rather than black
cinders rained back on the steep slopes. Far above, a ring of
smoke rolled and spread about the column, forming an ever-
broadening blanket of opaque cloud above a landscape which

had never before been shaded from the sun. Streamers of lightning leaped between cloud and pillar, pillar and mountain, even cloud and ground. Any thunder there might have been was drowned in the howl of the escaping gas, a roar which seemed to combine every possible note from the shrillest possible whistle to a bass felt by the chest rather than heard by the ears. Rowson's language had become inaudible almost before he had disappeared down the hatch.

For long moments the radioman watched the spreading cloud, and wondered whether the *Albireo* could escape being struck by the flickering, ceaseless lightning. Far above the widening ring of cloud the smoke fountain drove, spreading slowly in the thinning atmosphere and beyond it. Zaino had had enough space experience to tell at a glance whether a smoke or dust cloud was in air or not. This wasn't, at least at the upper extremity . . .

And then, quite calmly, he turned back to his desk, aimed the antenna straight up, and called Eileen Harmon. She answered promptly.

The stratigrapher listened without interruption to his report and the order to return. She conferred briefly with her companion, replied "We'll be back in twelve hours," and signed off. And that was that.

Zaino settled back with a sigh, and wondered whether it would be tactful to remind Rowson of his offer of a year's pay.

All four vehicles were now homeward bound; all one had to worry about was whether any of them would make it. Hargedon and Burkett were fighting their way through an ever-increasing ash rain a scant two miles away—ash which not only cut visibility but threatened to block the way with drifts too deep to negotiate. The wind, now blowing fiercely towards the volcano, blasted the gritty stuff against their front window as though it would erode through; and the lava flow, moving far faster than the gentle ooze they had never quite measured, surged—and glowed—grimly behind.

A hundred miles or more to the east, the tractors containing Mardikian, Marini and their drivers headed south-west along the alternate route their maps had suggested; but Mardikian, some three hours in the lead, reported that he could see four other smoke columns in that general direction.

Mercury seemed to be entering a new phase. The maps might well be out of date.

Harmon and Trackman were having no trouble at the

moment, but they would have to pass the great chasm. This had been shooting out daughter cracks when Zaino and Hargedon passed it hours before. No one could say what it might be like now, and no one was going out to make sure.

"We can see you!" Burkett's voice came through suddenly. "Half a mile to go, and we're way ahead of the flow."

"But it's coming?" Rowson asked tensely. He had returned from the power level at Zaino's phoned report of success.

"It's coming."

"How fast? When will it get here? Do you know whether the ship can stand contact with it?"

"I don't know the speed exactly. There may be two hours, maybe five or six. The ship can't take it. Even the temperature measures I got were above the softening point of the alloys, and it's hotter and much deeper now. Anyway, if the others aren't back before the flow reaches the ship they won't get through. The tractor wheels would char away, and I doubt that the bodies would float. You certainly can't wade through the stuff in a spacesuit, either."

"And you think there can't be more than five or six hours before the flow arrives?"

"I'd say that was a very optimistic guess. I'll stop and get a better speed estimate if you want, but won't swear to it."

Rowson thought for a moment.

"No," he said finally, "don't bother. Get back here as soon as you can. We need the tractor and human muscles more than we need even expert guesses." He turned to the operator.

"Zaino, tell all the tractors there'll be no answer from the ship for a while, because no one will be aboard. Then suit up and come outside." He was gone.

Ten minutes later, six human beings and a tractor were assembled in the flame-lit near-darkness outside the ship. The cloud had spread to the horizon, and the sun was gone. Burkett and Hargedon had arrived, but Rowson wasted no time on congratulations.

"We have work to do. It will be easy enough to keep the lava from the ship, since there seems to be a foot or more of ash on the ground and a touch of main drive would push it into a ringwall around us; but that's not the main problem. We have to keep it from reaching the chasm anywhere south of us, since that's the way the others will be coming. If they're cut off, they're dead. It will be brute work. We'll use the tractor any

283

way we can think of. Unfortunately it has no plough attachment, and I can't think of anything aboard which could be turned into one. You have shovels, such as they are. The ash is light, especially here, but there's a mile and a half of dam to be built. I don't see how it can possibly be done . . . but it's going to be."

"Come on, Arnie! You're young and strong," came the voice of the mineralogist. "You should be able to lift as much of this stuff as I can. I understand you were lucky enough to get hold of Eileen—have you asked for the bonus yet?—but your work isn't done."

"It wasn't luck," Zaino retorted. Burkett, in spite of her voice, seemed much less of a schoolmistress when encased in a spacesuit and carrying a shovel, so he was able to talk back to her. "I was simply alert enough to make use of existing conditions, which I had to observe for myself in spite of all the scientists around. I'm charging the achievement to my regular salary. I saw—"

He stopped suddenly, both with tongue and shovel. Then, "Captain!"

"What is it?"

"The only reason we're starting this wall here is to keep well ahead of the flow so we can work as long as possible, isn't it?"

"Yes, I suppose so. I never thought of trying anywhere else. The valley would mean a much shorter dam, but if the flow isn't through it by now it would be before we could get there—oh! Wait a minute!"

"Yes, sir. You can put the main switch anywhere in a D.C. circuit. Where are the seismology stores we never had to use?"

Four minutes later the tractor set out from the *Albireo*, carrying Rowson and Zaino. Six minutes after that it stopped at the base of the ash cone which formed the north side of the valley from which the lava was coming. They parked a quarter of the way around the cone's base from the emerging flood and started to climb on foot, both carrying burdens.

Forty-seven minutes later they returned empty-handed to the vehicle, to find that it had been engulfed by the spreading liquid.

With noticeable haste they floundered through the loose ash a few yards above the base until they had outdistanced the glowing menace, descended and started back across the plain to where they knew the ship to be, though she was invisible through the falling detritus. Once they had to detour around a crack. Once they encountered one which widened towards the chasm on their right, and they knew a detour would be impossible. Leaping it seemed impossible, too, but they did it. Thirty seconds after this, forty minutes after finding the tractor destroyed, the landscape was bathed in a magnesium-white glare as the two one-and-a-half kiloton charges planted just inside the crater rim let go.

"Should we go back and see if it worked?" asked Zaino.

"What's the use? The only other charges we had were in the tractor. Thank goodness they were nuclear instead of H.E. If it didn't work we'd have more trouble to get back than we're having now."

"If it didn't work, is there any point in going back?"

"Stop quibbling and keep walking. Dr. Burkett, are you listening?"

"Yes, Captain."

"We're fresh out of tractors, but if you want to try it on foot you might start a set of flow measures on the lava. Arnie wants to know whether our landslide slid properly."

However, the two were able to tell for themselves before getting back to the *Albireo*.

The flow didn't stop all at once, of course; but with the valley feeding it blocked off by a pile of volcanic ash four hundred feet high on one side, nearly fifty on the other and more than a quarter of a mile long, its enthusiasm quickly subsided. It was thin, fluid stuff, as Burkett had noted; but as it spread it cooled, and as it cooled it thickened.

Six hours after the blast it had stopped with its nearest lobe almost a mile from the ship, less than two feet thick at the edge.

When Markidian's tractor arrived, Burkett was happily trying to analyse samples of the flow, and less happily speculating on how long it would be before the entire area would be blown off the planet. When Marini's and Harmon's vehicles arrived, almost together, the specimens had been loaded and everything stowed for acceleration. Sixty seconds after the last person was aboard, the *Albireo* left Mercury's surface at two gravities.

The haste, it turned out, wasn't really necessary. She had been in parking orbit nearly forty-five hours before the first of the giant volcanoes reached its climax, and the one beside their former site was not the first. It was the fourth.

"And that seems to be that," said Camille Burkett rather tritely as they drifted a hundred miles above the little world's surface. "Just a belt of white-hot calderas all around the planet. Pretty, if you like symmetry."

"I like being able to see it from this distance," replied Zaino, floating weightless beside her. "By the way, how much bonus should I ask for getting that idea of putting the seismic charges to use after all?"

"I wouldn't mention it. Any one of us might have thought of that. We all knew about them."

"Anyone *might* have. Let's speculate on how long it would have been before anyone *did*."

"It's still not like the other idea, which involved your own specialty. I still don't see what made you suppose that the gas pillar from the volcano would be heavily charged enough to reflect your radio beam. How did that idea strike you?"

Zaino thought back, and smiled a little as the picture of lightning blazing around pillar, cloud and mountain rose before his eyes.

"You're not quite right," he said. "I was worried about it for a while, but it didn't actually strike me."

It fell rather flat; Camille Burkett, Ph.D., had to have it explained to her.

THE CHOICE

by *Wayland Young*

Before Williams went into the future he bought a camera and a tape-recording machine and learned shorthand. That night, when all was ready, we made coffee and put out brandy and glasses against his return.

"Goodbye," I said. "Don't stay too long."

"I won't," he answered.

I watched him carefully, and he hardly flickered. He must have made a perfect landing on the very second he had taken off from. He seemed not a day older; we had expected he might spend several years away.

"Well?"

"Well," said he, "let's have some coffee."

I poured it out, hardly able to contain my impatience. As I gave it to him I said again, "Well?"

"Well, the thing is, I can't remember."

"Can't remember? Not a thing?"

He thought for a moment and answered sadly, "Not a thing."

"But your notes? The camera? The recording-machine?"

The notebook was empty, the indicator of the camera rested at "1" where we had set it, the tape was not even loaded into the recording-machine.

"But good heavens," I protested, "why? How did it happen? Can you remember nothing at all?"

"I can remember only one thing."

"What was that?"

"I was shown everything, and I was given the choice whether I should remember it or not after I got back."

"And you chose not to? But what an extraordinary thing to—"

"Isn't it?" he said. "One can't help wondering why."